What People Are Saying About
An Island Just for Us
and Barbara Hattemer

"Barbara Hattemer's *An Island Just for Us* is a breath of fresh air, grace, and redemption that is dear to my heart. I enjoy reading it over and over. It is that good, compelling, and winsome. I recommend it highly. It will capture your heart, entertain you, and help to transform you and those you love!"

TED BAEHR, Publisher, *Movieguide,* Chairman, Christian Film and Television Commission

"Heartwarming and unforgettable, *An Island Just for Us* is smart fiction that packs a powerful punch. The love story is sweet and Edenic, the family values will finetune yours, and the issue will open your eyes (70 percent of American men view pornography sometime in their life). A stellar must-read.

RAMONA TUCKER, Former Editor, *Today's Christian Woman,* Christianity Today, International

"Barbara Hattemer knows the topic she writes about. As a long-time warrior against the destructive force of pornography on women, children, and the men captivated and driven by its seductive lies, she is well qualified to tell, even in fictional form, of this hidden world and call for its evil to end."

ALAN SEARS, Executive Director of the Attorney General's Commission on Pornography, President, CEO, and General Council, Alliance Defending Freedom

Novels
by Barbara Hattemer

* * *

Field of Daisies

An Island Just for Us

an island just for us

BARBARA HATTEMER

www.oaktara.com

An Island Just for Us

Published in the U.S. by:
OakTara Publishers
www.oaktara.com

Cover design by Yvonne Parks at www.pearcreative.ca
Cover image © Christopher L. Cooley
Author photo © 2012 Jennifer Hattemer, Dove Photography,
www.DovePhotographyFL.com

All Scripture quotations are taken from the King James Version of the Bible. Public domain.

ISBN-13: 978-1-60290-374-6
ISBN-10: 1-60290-374-3

An Island Just for Us is a work of fiction. References to real people, events, establishments, organizations, or locales are intended only to provide a sense of authenticity and are used fictitiously. All other characters, incidents, and dialogue are drawn from the author's imagination.

Printed in the U.S.A.

* * *

To my parents,
who gave me a priceless property
to enjoy with my husband and children
throughout our lifetimes.
It made a perfect setting
for the fictional family of this story.

1

ELENA RICHARDS GASPED AS THE CAR CRESTED CATERPILLAR HILL. The startling beauty of Penobscot Bay—green spruce-covered islands, sky blue water—stretched before her. Cool pine-scented air struck her as she tumbled out of the car. Sunrays dancing on the surface of the bay flooded her with memories of childhood delights. Waves scrubbing the distant shore washed away her melancholy. She dashed to the edge of the lookout, raised her arms overhead, and whirled around. "It's even more beautiful than I remembered!"

Catching sight of her parents, she watched her father slip an arm around her mother and nuzzle his face in her hair. Dressed in flannel shirts and blue jeans for the hard work of opening the cottages, they made a good-looking couple. A wave of envy surprised her. How she longed for a relationship like theirs.

"It's good to be here, Susan," her father said.

"I appreciate it more every year, Harold." Her mother cuddled close to him.

Elena remembered the joy of leaning against Peter's strong shoulder. On the long drive here from Florida, in the back seat of her parents' blue station wagon, she had ruminated over the failure of her first love. Peter's words still haunted her: "You're not my kind of girl any more, Elena. I don't care a thing about deeper thoughts. Stop trying to make me someone I'm not." Her desire for a deeper relationship had succeeded only in making him uncomfortable. His rejection still stung. How could she have been so undiscerning?

"Okay, kids. Back in the car. All the beds have to be made before dinner." Her father gathered his family.

"Yeah, Dad, we know." Doug, her younger brother, shrugged.

Familiar sights passed by as the family approached their cabin, Camp Four Winds, where she had spent two summers learning to wind sail, canoe, and water ski—closed; Milton's Dream, the hillside restaurant where co-ed counselors met for an early supper—boarded up and abandoned. Self-service sheds replaced barefoot children selling freshly picked blueberries along the roadside. She wondered how much else had changed in her five-year absence.

Now twenty-one years old, Elena was returning to the land she had cherished every summer of her childhood. Because of one awful summer when she was fifteen, she had remained home during family vacations for five years in a row.

She searched the bay that reflected the bright blue of the sky. Hundreds of green spruce-covered islands crowded the waters, hiding the white sails of schooners weaving among them. Across the bay the purplish hue of the Camden Hills reminded her of past adventures on these waters—in sun, in fog, in rain. Exquisite memories flashed before her. Why had she been so reluctant to return?

Harold looked at his watch. "Back to the car, kids. There's much to be done."

Elena kept her eyes fastened on the bay until it disappeared behind rolling barrens of low bush blueberries. They would turn bright red soon after her family departed for home in the fall.

Halfway down the hill, the skeleton of an old farmhouse still stood, isolated, bleak in its grayness, slowly deteriorating. It suited her mood when she thought of the crumbling of her dreams for a deeper relationship with Peter. She wondered about the people who had lived there. Had they purposely given up that spectacular view and moved away or had their time simply passed with no offspring to carry on what they had started? Had they been as disappointed as she was at the loss she now suffered?

But her return to the island she loved held a promise of healing. This land had formed her character. The giant boulders and craggy ravines of its ragged coastline had birthed in her a spirit of adventure and filled her with a deep, abiding love of nature. There was so much beauty here to enjoy.

A sharp poke in the ribs interrupted her musings.

"There's the bridge, Sis." Mike, six years younger, made sure she saw every landmark.

"Mike, pointing is enough."

"Doug, get your head back in the car," Dad called from the front seat. Twelve-year-old Doug poked his head out the window and strained to see over the side rail as the car climbed the towering bridge onto Little Deer Isle.

The sea-scent of clam-flats hit Elena as they crossed the causeway to Deer Isle. Pungent in a good sort of way, the odor evoked memories of clamming with her family in their cove.

Mike turned to his mother. "Can we have steamers for lunch tomorrow, Mom?"

"If the tide is right, and you want to dig them."

"Can we have lobsters tonight?" Doug chimed in.

"Not so fast." She laughed. "Let's get there first."

"We'll have dinner at Fisherman's Friend, and each of you can order your favorite seafood, but not until everyone is unpacked and all beds are made."

"Yes, Dad, we know." Doug scowled and folded his arms.

The car sped by the Island Country Club. Elena hoped for tennis players her own age this year.

The boys' excitement as they spotted Twisted Tree Cove jolted Elena into the present. Multiple fishing boats lay peacefully at anchor. She spotted the gnarled and twisted tree that kept a lonely vigil at the edge of the rocks. The encroachment of high tides had exposed its contorted root structure and prevailing winds had wrapped its entwined branches around its trunk. Elena was grateful that those who lived in the area thought the dead tree too artistic to cut down. Now an island landmark, it told her she was almost home.

The car turned onto a small dirt road. "We're here." Doug bounced on his seat. Three children threw open their doors and scrambled toward the shore. Elena ran to Sunset Rock, the twenty-foot vertical stretch of granite in front of the main cabin where, as small children, they had terrified Susan scampering up and down its steep face.

The outgoing tide exposed a freshwater stream that flowed through the middle of the cove. Elena knew that by nighttime waves would be lapping against shore rocks to lull her to sleep. Joy and gratitude welled up in her as she raised her hands skyward. "Thank You for bringing me back."

Susan caught up to Elena and laid a hand on her shoulder. "Every rock is still in place. The tree on the point that's been there since your father was a boy is still standing. Nothing ever changes."

Elena hoped this summer would bring the change she longed for, someone to share the joy of this beautiful place.

*

Todd Langdon and his grandmother climbed Caterpillar Hill in their rented car. In spite of her eighty-two years, Amanda Faraway acted like a petulant child, irritating Todd and causing him to wonder if it had been a mistake to bring her back to Maine. Her white hair perfectly coiffed, clad in a wool walking suit from the fifties, she sat upright with a frown and rigid shoulders.

Since they discovered the car they had reserved was not available, Todd had listened to her nonstop complaints. This car did not suit her. The airline had torn her bag. The drive from Bangor to Deer Isle dragged on. She shivered, already cold. Although she could be charming during social occasions, he knew his grandmother lived in the negative.

"Grandma," Todd pleaded. Her bitter judgments had grown so harsh over the years they choked out the joy they used to share. "An hour and a half isn't long when you've come all the way from Pittsburgh. Why aren't you enjoying the scenery? All my life you've told me how much you love Maine."

"I'm sorry, Todd. You're right." But her moment of humility passed as she caught sight of the bay sparkling in the sunlight. "Todd, stop the car at once."

At her command, Todd pulled into the scenic turnout. "There it is," his grandmother said with unaccustomed reverence.

Todd helped her out of the car. They stood in silence taking in the splendor of the scene. Beautiful spruce-covered islands dotted the bay's sparkling waters. "Now I understand why you wanted so much to return, Grandma. It's spectacular."

He turned to Amanda and took her hand. Tears brimmed in her often fierce eyes and spilled down well-wrinkled cheeks. "Yes," she said, "even more than I remembered."

Todd allowed her time to absorb the view before looking at his watch. "It's getting late. We want to arrive before dark."

As the car started the long descent, Amanda pointed out the bridge that would take them to the island. Setting aside her cares and complaints, she began to relive her childhood, telling Todd about happy times she had shared with her father. She described the thrills of hiking through the woods. As she toddled along the shore, he had delighted in her naming the seagulls "wiggles." In later years he read books about shore birds aloud to her.

Happy that her recitation of woes had ceased, Todd emitted a long sigh and relaxed for the first time. A shock of brown hair fell across his forehead, partly obscuring his handsome profile. He opened the window, stuck his arm outside, and breathed in the spruce-laden air.

"It took a week to drive here from Pittsburgh in those days. Before the bridge connected Little Deer to the mainland, we took a ferry to the island. I used to stand up front, enjoying the wind in my face, feeling a wonderful sense of adventure. That's where it landed, just over there."

"I can't imagine you facing the elements so eagerly."

"I wasn't always an old woman," she replied, breathing in and squaring her shoulders. "After the farmhouse burned, Dad never found the time to rebuild. Thank you for bringing me back, Todd. If I complain about the cold, pay no attention. Just remember how much this means to me."

Todd laughed at the thought of ignoring her regal commands. "It's a privilege to share this with you, Grandma, but ignore what you say? I don't think so." He had been meeting her needs since he was a small boy.

She had taken a special interest in him as long as he could remember. When his mother and father lost themselves in fighting and drunkenness, she removed him from their house. His room at her home became his haven, a place he could escape his parents' constant criticism and capricious demands. In contrast, his grandmother's wishes seemed reasonable, and he enjoyed pleasing her.

The car passed through the town of Deer Isle and onto a causeway surrounded by water at high tide. To the left, an ornate gazebo crowned a tiny peninsula that jutted into a serene pond.

"Look at that, Grandma."

"What a lovely spot to take a girl," she said.

He shook his head. "A girl is the last thing I need to complicate my life."

To the right, a beautiful harbor almost empty of water left boats stranded on the muddy sea bottom. Todd wrinkled his nose at the strong aroma of clam-flats.

"When my father and I went clamming," Amanda continued, "I spotted the biggest holes. He sunk the fork into the ground behind them and scooped out a mixture of black mud and sand. I dug in it with my hands and pulled out the clams."

"Grandma, you don't expect me to believe you willingly placed your hands in black mud."

"But I did, Todd. It was part of the fun."

"My grandmother playing in the mud. Now that's a picture I'd like to see." Todd laughed. "So that's what you do for entertainment up here."

*

Todd found the market at Twisted Tree Cove bustling with activity. As summer tourists filled their shopping carts, three young boys loitered by the magazine rack. The smallest of the three chose a daily newspaper and fell into the long line at the cash register where the clerk concentrated on moving customers as fast as possible. The tallest boy glanced at the clerk, reached up, grabbed a *Playboy Magazine* from the top shelf, and stuffed it into his jacket. The redhead moved close to him, shielding him from the view of the clerk.

Witnessing their stealthy action, Todd wanted to tell them they should stay away from those magazines. Instead he asked for their help. "Say, boys, can either of you tell me how to find the Hadley cottage?"

"That's on the road beyond Doug Richards' cabin." The redhead looked up at the stranger. "You know Doug?"

"No, but we've rented the Hadley cottage. Can you direct me?"

"Ayuh. You're 'most there now." He had a thick Maine accent and dropped his r's at the end of his words.

"What a relief. I was beginning to think we'd never find it."

"We'll show you. C'mon, Eddie." He pulled on the sleeve of his silent friend and ushered them both out the door. "You'll be wanting to go a spell down that road and over a high hill," he said, pointing. "When you see a road sign marked *Hadley,* that's it. Just turn onto that road, and it's the fourth driveway."

"Thanks a million, boys."

As Todd returned to his car and opened the door, he could hear the boys talking behind him.

"Harv, you shouldn't talk to strangers when we was doing that."

"Ah, Eddie, you're jumpy as a jack rabbit tonight. You'd think we never did it before. Here's Joey. Let's go."

"Hi, guys, you got it?"

"Sure, nothing to it," Eddie said with bravado.

Todd shook his head. If he ran into those boys again, he would have a talk with them. He climbed in beside his grandmother and started off in the direction indicated.

2

ELENA STUDIED THE MENU at Fisherman's Friend as Mike and Doug ordered their favorite seafood. The waitress, pencil poised, waited to record her choice. "I think I'll have haddock chowder," she said at last. "That's about as Maine as it gets."

Minutes later, the waitress set a bowl piled high with steamed clams in front of fifteen-year-old Mike. "Now that's what I call a meal," he exclaimed, sniffing the familiar aroma and grinning widely. His full cheeks indicated he loved eating and his shoulder-length hair, so uncharacteristic for his family, hinted that he was trying out a new identity. Aware of his passion for fishing, Elena knew her good-natured brother enjoyed eating his catch as much as hooking it.

Doug, much thinner than his brother, his freckled face crowned with a blond crew cut, had ordered the all-you-can-eat haddock special. As the waitress set his first helping before him, he beamed, displaying a mouth full of braces.

Not wanting to burn her mouth, Elena blew on a spoonful of chowder. "I hope it's as good as it smells." She swallowed the spoonful, savoring the taste.

"How's the chowder, darling?" Susan said.

"Great, Mom, but yours is better. On the first rainy day, I'll help you make it."

"That's what you said five years ago." Susan smiled. "I'm still waiting."

"This year I want to learn how to cook all the Maine specialties. I plan to invite Julie and two other friends up after graduation next summer. We've talked about it for years. I'll have to do most of the cooking."

"I hope you can afford the rent," Harold said. "Don't forget about the taxes." Elena knew her grandfather had bought their land, including the guest cottage, for $600 in the early thirties. Now the annual taxes were over $6,000 and increasing every year.

"Dad, you wouldn't."

"Your mother and I plan to raise the rent another hundred dollars a week next season."

"Now, Harold, the children are always welcome to use the cabins."

"Thanks, Mom." Elena, turning to glare at her father, saw the twinkle in his eyes that meant he was teasing. Looking beyond him, she gasped aloud, "Whoa! Look at the guy who just walked through the door."

All heads turned to watch a young man escorting an elderly woman. Unaware of the five pairs of eyes focused on him, he seated the lady at a table across the room.

"Maybe this will be your year, Sis." Mike grinned. "He's a stud all right. Look at that profile." He showed her his own, tilting his head until his long hair fell below his shoulders.

"At least he cuts his hair like a man. Are you growing yours as long as mine, Mike?"

Mike flashed an uncharacteristic scowl in Elena's direction and fell silent.

"He's tall enough even for me, but he's probably already married." Elena noted his full head of hair neatly brushed back. A wave of it fell across his forehead as he rose to accompany the lady to the salad bar.

"Excuse me. I think I'm still hungry." Elena flicked her long hair behind her, scrambled to her feet, and hurried across the room, arriving at the end of the line just before the woman. After filling her plate, Elena turned to face her. "Have you tried these blueberry muffins? They're a part of the island you won't want to miss."

"Thank you, my dear," the old lady said. "I have fond memories of blueberry muffins from years ago, but I've never tried these."

"Are you visiting the island?" Elena asked as casually as possible.

"Yes, we've rented the Hadley cottage on the road to Blake's Point for a month."

"Oh." Elena could scarcely believe her good fortune. "We're the Richards, and we're in the first two cottages on that road. By the green pump house. Maybe you've seen our sign at the beginning of the road. You must come over for a visit."

"Why, how nice. We'll look forward to that, won't we, Todd?" Turning back to Elena, she said, "I'm Amanda Faraway, and this is my grandson, Todd Langdon."

"How do you do, Mrs. Faraway? I'm Elena Richards. Hi, Todd." Elena greeted him with a smile. "If you'd like to see the shore, stop by in the morning and I'll show you around. We're just beyond the bridge."

"Sounds great," he said.

Elena searched his face, trying to guess what he was thinking.

A man in line behind them cleared his throat. Elena blushed, realizing how bold she had been. "I must be holding up the line. I hope you enjoy your blueberry muffins." She turned and hurried back to her table.

"Well, wonders never cease. What's happened to my shy little girl?" Susan's eyes lit up as she smiled at her daughter.

"It was an opportunity too good to miss. Can you believe it? They're staying in the third cottage beyond ours."

"Is he married?" Doug asked.

"I didn't learn a thing about him except his name, Todd Langdon. It has a nice sound. And Mrs. Faraway is charming. I think you'll like her, Mother."

"I'm sure we'll enjoy getting to know them. How long are they staying?"

"A whole month, just like we are. He must have a girlfriend. That would be my luck. If he doesn't, there's probably something wrong with him. Guys who look like that are usually lacking somewhere."

"If you look hard enough, I'm sure you'll find something," Harold said.

Mike found his voice. "There goes our family vacation. We won't see much of Elena this summer."

"Don't start before I've even met the guy, Mike."

"You've met him all right. You practically threw yourself at him."

She turned to her mother. "Mom, will you stop and say hello and invite Mrs. Faraway over on our way out? I'm sure we'll be finished before they are."

"Of course, dear. I'd be happy to invite them for a meal."

*

After supper, eager to see the stolen magazine, the three boys rendezvoused at Harvey's house. The well-weathered home was little more than a shack with a large front porch that appeared as if it would collapse at any moment. Laundry hung on lines stretched from the house to the nearest trees. Old tires and discarded machinery cluttered the ill-kept yard. The house stood on an island crossroad, far from water, where land was cheap.

As Harvey greeted them, his father staggered off the porch. "Where's that no-good son o' mine?" He carried a liquor bottle in one hand and a worn leather belt, which he held up to Harvey, in the other. "You chopped that wood pile I told ya to?"

"I did, I did it." Harvey cowered. "Don't hit me. I stacked it just where you told me, on the other side of the house."

"Show me, ya good-for-nothing loafer. Ya better do what I tell ya."

Harvey ran to the side of the house as his father reeled unsteadily after him. His father emerged swearing and bellowing, "It's a good thing you done it. Now git out of my sight."

The boys ran behind the house to a well-constructed tree house

9

supported by the limbs of an old maple. In sharp contrast to the house, it looked new and put together with considerable care.

The boys scrambled up the ladder, giggling with anticipation.

"Gosh, Harv, your old man is scary. I sure hope he never comes up here. What if he found the magazines?"

"Yeah, we'd really be in trouble." Joey, the youngest of the three, peered out the tree house door once more. "My dad would kill me if he knew."

"Naw, he wouldn't even try. Pop drinks too much, and Sis is too busy getting supper after she gets home from work. They don't care what I do. They miss my mom, and so do I. She died when I was five. I can hardly remember what she looked like."

Joey became impatient. "Aren't you going to show us the new one?"

Harvey reached toward a stack of newspapers and well-worn magazines, lifted the newspapers, and pulled out a magazine with a pristine, slick cover. "This is the one we got this afternoon." The boys huddled around him, their eyes wide open as he slowly turned the pages.

"Wow."

"Cool."

"Man, look at that."

When they reached the end, Harvey turned back to the *Playboy* Advisor column and read it aloud.

"Boy, I never knew people asked questions like that," Eddie said as Harvey stopped reading.

"Man, that's cool." Joey's heart pounded, and his body experienced unfamiliar sensations. He took the magazine from Harvey for a closer look. A rush of adrenaline overwhelmed him with feelings of pleasure that would bring him back to the magazines again and again.

"Can I take an old magazine home tonight?" Eddie asked.

"No, everything stays here. We can't take any chances."

"Are we gonna show Doug Richards the tree house this year?" Eddie looked hopeful. "Do you think he can keep a secret?"

"What do you think, Harv?" Joey always turned to Harvey for an answer.

"Doug's okay, but he'll have to swear he won't tell first. We have to be careful. Wow, I bet he's never seen anything like this. Old lady Richards would have a cow if she caught him reading one of these."

"We don't have to tell him right away," Eddie said.

Joey and Eddie both stared at Harvey.

"Yeah, let's see how he acts this summer. We'll decide later." Harvey reopened the magazine and slowly turned the pages once more.

3

A RAY OF SUNLIGHT PEEKED AROUND THE SHADE and fell across Elena's face. Two blasts of the foghorn roused her from sleep and announced mealtime. Sitting upright, she glanced around her bedroom, noting its many changes. Reaching out from under her covers, she ran her fingers over the new paint, marveling at its smoothness. It was the only room in either cabin with finished walls.

She knew her father loved the old room. Not for its style but for its many years. Last summer he had redecorated it, hoping Elena would return. He gave it a face lift, covering the drab yellow with a pleasant blue-green, adding a darker tone of the color to the trim and rocking chair.

Elena, reluctant to face the cold air, snuggled under the colonial spread of pink, green, and white, which, together with a pink dust ruffle, dispelled the dullness that had added to her gloom the year she had been confined there. The color scheme, repeated in curtains, scatter rugs, and a painting Harold had bought at the club auction, completed the transformation. Elena felt princess-like as she surveyed her new surroundings.

The foghorn sounded again. This time she threw back the elegant spread, donned a pair of jeans on her slender figure, topped them with a heavy sweatshirt, and scampered down the granite steps outside her door. The steps triggered a not-so-pleasant memory, which she suppressed, relishing her ability to bound over the path to the main cabin. Nothing would spoil the joy of her being back in this beautiful place.

Her mother, still trim in blue jeans, waited at the door. Susan had worn her hair in a pageboy for as long as Elena could remember. Not even the summer sun could revive its blond highlights, but it still bounced as she moved forward to greet Elena.

"Good morning, sleepyhead," Susan called with her usual good cheer. "The boys are already on the Cliff. I hope you don't mind being left behind." She replaced the foghorn on its nail on the wall and walked through the living room to the kitchen. "I'm hoping you'll help plan the menus and shop with me this morning."

"Sure, Mom, if I can take a walk on the shore first. It's way too beautiful to stay inside. Have you eaten already?"

"I fed the men but kept a few blueberry pancakes in the oven for us."

Elena smiled as Susan piled a plate high with blueberry pancakes and set it before her on the kitchen table. "Gosh, I feel like the guest of honor."

Susan sat where she could see the ocean. Elena chose the less dramatic but pleasant view of the brook that ran beside the cottage.

"I've missed you these past summers, Elena. It was hard thinking of you working at home alone while we were enjoying ourselves up here." Susan's brow wrinkled.

"I wasn't alone, Mom. Nonnie was next door, and I made good friends at work. Alone was lying on my bed in Maine while you were all out boating and hiking."

"That was a hard time for you, I know. Did you notice the shell wreath we made together on the living room wall? I still receive compliments on it." Susan's blue eyes sparkled and showed a hint of pride in her handiwork.

"Let's face it, Mom. It was a good try to get me involved, but you made the wreath. I put shells in the wrong place, and you had to change them." Her pleasant expression hardened. In spite of Susan's good intentions, Elena remembered the making of the wreath as a time of conflict.

"Everything I tried seemed to frustrate you further." Susan sighed. "I stayed home to keep you company, thought up all kinds of projects to keep you busy, but you wanted to be alone to wallow in your misery."

"I guess it was all those gray days we spent enveloped in fog. Solitary, brooding moods suited me fine."

"I'm so glad your teen years are behind you. I kept remembering how Stephanie's attitude toward the family changed the first year she went to college. It took you a little longer."

"I always believed you liked her better than me," Elena murmured.

"Elena, how could you think that? You know I've always treasured our relationship."

"Stephanie was vivacious and made friends easily. But I had to work on every friendship I made."

"You were so different. There was no pushing you. You refused to cultivate friends your own age. Like when you went to camp."

"I tried at camp, Mom, but you cropped my hair in that wretched boyish cut and made me wear braces with head gear. All I could think about was how awful I looked. Even after my hair grew acceptably long, I still felt like an awkward Southern girl who could never measure up to the sophisticated young girls from the East. Then, just as I was beginning to feel comfortable with them, I got mono and had to come home."

"I hoped you'd go back as a counselor the next summer."

"By then, they were strangers to me again. As I jumped down the steps outside my room this morning, I remembered what it was like hopping up the granite step with one sprained ankle, only to sprain the other. A second summer confined to my room reading while the rest of you explored the islands. That was enough for me."

"I'm sorry it was so hard for you, Elena."

"It was at the time. If I had had friends nearby, it wouldn't have been so bad. I've loved making new friends at college. Now that I've done it successfully, I know I can do it again."

"You could have then if you'd given them a chance. Most of the other children needed friends as much as you did."

Elena studied Susan's slender nose and high cheekbones and saw her own face reflected. Her smooth skin, taut and fresh, was simply a younger image of Susan, whose attractive face was beginning to show the well-earned character lines of age. Susan's expression had softened from years of giving and caring for others, but Elena realized their resemblance to each other was striking.

"Mom, I made a lot of mistakes. And I feel really bad that I avoided coming back all those years. But you had fun with the boys without me and look how much money I saved for college."

"I don't mean to complain, Elena. I'm glad you're here, and I marvel at how much you've grown up and matured."

"I don't feel any of those negative feelings I had last time I was here. I guess they were just…"

"Elena, someone's in the cove."

Elena welcomed Susan's change of subject.

"I can't see who it is," Susan continued. "The tree's in the way. Take a look out the front window."

Elena hurried to the living room. "Gosh, Mom, it's him!"

"Who, dear?"

"You know, the guy we met last night, Todd Langdon."

"Well, go ahead and be hospitable."

"You won't feel badly if I don't help with the shopping?"

"No, darling, I can't think of anything nicer than your making a friend. Run along now and have a good time."

"Thanks, Mom. You're the greatest." Elena threw her arms around Susan and gave her a quick hug. "Thanks for the pancakes."

She bounded out the door and ran to Sunset Rock. Todd, looking in the direction of the cabin, raised his hand and called out, "Hi. I've come to take you up on your offer."

"Be there in a jiff." She hurried toward him, her heart pounding with anticipation. As she neared the shore, she slowed her pace, making an effort to appear relaxed and confident. She greeted him with a smile.

"I hope I'm not interrupting," he said.

"No, I was finishing breakfast with Mom. You timed it just right."

"Good," he said, bending down to pick up a colorful stone from the beach. He studied it, rolling it over in his hand. After hurling it into the water, he waved his outstretched arm in the direction of the bay. "This sure beats anything we have in Pittsburgh."

She laughed. "When I was a child, I imagined God surveying Penobscot Bay when He looked at all that He had made and saw that it was good."

"Great thought." He nodded approval. "Now, how 'bout showing me the shore? Tell me about your cabins and how you came here."

Elena smiled, relishing the opportunity to talk about the place she loved so much. "We have what is known as an old Maine camp," she began. "My grandparents built what we call the main cabin with their own two hands."

She swept a gesture toward the cabin and then toward the brook beside it. "They hand-picked every rock in the fireplace from the brook, and Grandpa made all the cabinets himself. It's amazing the cabin keeps standing year after year. The wind blows the trees down, hurricanes pound and wear away the shoreline, but the little cabin they lovingly built with their own hands remains. It's something of a miracle."

"What a great story. They must have been young." Todd's eyes followed her every gesture.

"Yes, they bought the land the year before Dad was born and started building when he was three months old. They stayed in tents, one for them and one for Dad's crib. Grandma loved to tell the story of the night a storm came up and blew Dad's tent down. The sides of the crib kept it from smothering him, and Dad slept through the whole thing."

Todd laughed. When his face broke into a smile, he seemed closer to her age. She wondered how old he was. His eyes held a sadness, a seriousness that made him seem years older than the boys she'd dated. She noted with pleasure that he displayed none of the cockiness of many boys as good-looking as he. Realizing she was staring at him, she glanced away and resumed her tale.

"The guest cabin was a general store on the big island over there." She pointed toward Vinalhaven, a large island across the bay. "Someone floated it over here and set it on this spot when it was more than a hundred years old, sometime before Dad was born. Dad thinks it's a national treasure."

14

"I like the way both cabins blend into the woods. They don't stick out like the white cottages along the rest of the shore. What brought your grandfather here?"

"His neighbor in Philadelphia invited him for a vacation. He'd bought the land for next to nothing from a native fisherman who thought it was worthless once it was timbered. Can you imagine that?" She shrugged at such foolishness.

They laughed, and their eyes locked.

"Grandpa bought the lot where he built the main cabin, then the lot on the point. That's where I'd like to build some day. An English couple owned the middle piece with this cabin on it." She pointed to a second cabin up the hill from where they stood. "When they returned to England, they sold it to him, and it all became one. That's the only way I remember it."

As they wandered along the shore of the cove, they came upon a large, smooth rock that sloped gently toward the clam flats. A dark red stain indicated that water covered two-thirds of the rock at high tide.

"This is where we sunbathe," Elena continued. "The sun bakes the rock and warms up the water as the tide covers it."

"You actually swim in this water? I heard it stays around 55 degrees." Todd faked a shiver.

"That's right, but it's a whole lot warmer than it is off the outer islands. The tide will be perfect this afternoon. Would you like to join me?"

"I guess I'll try anything once," he said, looking like it would be anything but a pleasure.

"You'll like it, I promise, but you have to go in slowly. When your feet turn numb, you don't feel the cold. It's an experience you won't want to miss."

When they came to the end of the large rock, Todd jumped to the lower level of granite and reached out to Elena. She took his hand and leaped down beside him. *He's even polite. Can it get much better?*

A sand beach lay before them. Elena pointed to a pile of small rocks at the edge of the sand. "That's where we have our cookouts. We have to time them precisely 'cause at high tide, the water covers them. Do you think your grandmother would enjoy a clambake?"

"You bet. She's reliving her childhood when her parents summered on the other side of the island. It will remind her of her time with them."

"Maybe we could have one this Friday since Mom has already invited you both for dinner."

His face brightened. "I'm all for it."

Elena sat at the edge of a tidal pool. "This is where my grandmother bathed my dad when he was a little boy, before we had water and electricity."

Todd remained standing. He glanced across the cove. Elena followed his gaze to where his grandmother waved to him from the front porch.

"It looks like Grandma needs me," he said. "I'm sorry. I was enjoying your tour."

"The best is yet to come." Elena felt a stab of disappointment.

"It's been great so far. I'll try to come back for that swim this afternoon. Grandma takes a nap after lunch."

"I hope you can. I promise you'll like it."

"You have yet to convince me." He flashed a smile in her direction, turned, and ran across the empty cove, hopping over the stream that flowed through it.

Elena watched him until he disappeared. She had seen good-looking boys toss their heads around and flip their hair like they thought they were something special, but Todd showed no signs of conceit. His good looks had not attracted her as much as his gentleness and the softness in his sad eyes. She suspected there was more to Todd than she had yet seen, something deep, something of substance.

She thought of all the relationships that had excited her at the start. They promised more than they produced and never advanced beyond surface relationships. Like Peter, the boys she dated couldn't talk about themselves or their feelings. When she wanted to talk about the deeper things on her heart, she ended up making them feel uncomfortable. She hoped this relationship would be different.

4

"MOM, I CAN GO WITH YOU NOW." Elena bounded into the living room, breathless from having run up the path from the beach.

"Has he gone already, dear?" Susan asked. "I'd given you up for the day."

"He has a grandmother." Elena sighed. "At her very appearance, he ran. I hope she won't demand his presence the whole month."

"He's very attentive to her needs. She's fortunate to have such a caring grandson."

"He said he'd come back while she rests this afternoon. I invited him to go swimming." Elena slumped into a chair in the kitchen. "Gosh, Mom, did you ever see anyone so handsome? He's a different kind of good-looking than Peter. I think I like brown hair on a boy even better than blond."

"He's about as good-looking as they come," Susan agreed, adding the final items to her shopping list.

"I wonder if he knows how attractive he is. His eyes look like he's used to bearing a great disappointment. How old do you think he is?"

"Probably in his mid to late twenties, much too old for a college co-ed, I imagine."

"You don't suppose he thinks I'm too young to take seriously? I thought I preferred boys my own age, but I like the serious air about him. As a matter of fact, I like him a lot and we've spent less than an hour together. Wow!"

"Wow, indeed, young lady. Are you ready to think about anything as mundane as the week's menus?"

"Sure, you bring your list and I'll start the car."

*

Elena turned into Twisted Tree Cove. Protected from the prevailing winds, it remained calmer than the cove where the Richards lived. Today not a ripple riled the water. Like toy boats resting on glass, vessels anchored in the cove sat motionless on the still sea.

Elena parked in front of a bait shack, one of several small wooden buildings weathered gray by the elements. Three young boys loitered in front of it, their fishing poles leaning against the wall.

"Hi, boys. Anything biting today? Euweee! Get a whiff of that smell." Elena, overpowered by the odor of decaying fish, pinched her nose and looked at Susan. "Where's the wind when you need it?"

"The mackerel ran all last week, but they're gone again," the youngest boy said.

Elena inspected the stringy, blond hair that hung over very red cheeks. His fragile appearance, contrasted with the robust build of his two older companions, each of whom stood a head taller than he, caught her attention.

"Hello, Joey," Susan said.

"Hey, aren't you Mrs. Richards?" the redheaded boy asked, pointing to Susan. "Is Doug back?" His abundant hair, cropped at random, framed a mass of freckles. Overweight at thirteen, he lumbered toward them.

"Yes, Harvey, Doug came back with us. My, you boys have grown up over the winter," Susan said.

Eddie joined the conversation. "Hey, guys, let's go over to the Richards' place and see what Doug's been up to."

Taller and leaner than Harvey, his skin a deep tan, Eddie looked at the world through dark, almost black eyes. Noting his developing muscles and coordinated movements, Elena thought he must far surpass Harvey in athletic ability.

"Doug isn't home right now. He's out in the boat with his brother for the day. He'll be over after we're settled. Come, Elena, we must buy lobsters."

The two of them walked down a long wooden wharf high above the water. A ramp descended to a floating lobster cart piled high with empty wooden crates, a large iron scale, large circles of rope, and numerous long-handled nets. Two lobstermen docked their boat across the front of the cart, jumped out, and started filling wire baskets with lobsters. The wharf owner weighed them on a large scale and poured them into wooden holding crates housed beneath the cart floor.

Elena started down the steep descent, leaning over the wire ropes on the ramp's side to stare into the water. "Look how clear the water is. I see starfish all over the place."

Susan laughed. "Yes, the bay replenished itself since you were children and scooped up all the starfish."

"Welcome back, Susan." A well-tanned young man with smiling eyes reached out a hand as she stepped onto the cart. He wore nothing but a pair of blue jeans. His weathered face and bare, bronzed chest indicated he had spent many days exposed to the sun. Jamie had taken over running the wharf when his father retired. Something of a hero to the local boys who used the wharf as a hangout, he was known for his practical jokes and pranks and admired for his skill in softball.

"Hello, Jamie, it's good to see you again. I hope you had a good year. My, you must think it's the middle of summer." Susan chuckled. "This is like winter for us, and a sweater feels good to me."

"That's 'cause your blood's thinned out from the Florida sun. Heck, we were down there last winter and I near roasted to death."

"You get used to the heat after a while. We have to come here in the summer to enjoy a fire in the fireplace."

"I bet your mouths are watering for some pound and a half hard-shells." Jamie threw aside a section of the cart's floor and pulled up a crate bulging with lobsters. "How many you need this year?"

"There are five of us. You remember my daughter Elena, don't you?"

"Hi, Jamie. Remember the little brat that always hung around when you came to call on Stephanie?"

"Well, I'll be. Where you been all these years? I haven't seen you since you were in grade school." Jamie smiled and extended his hand to Elena, all the while looking her up and down.

"I went to camp a couple years and the last summer I came to the island, five years ago, I sprained both my ankles and never got this far."

"Oh, yeah, I remember the boys telling me 'bout that. They said you were some sullen that year."

"Yes, I wasn't much of a sport that summer, but it sure is good to be back. I can't wait for one of your lobsters. How about that one?" Elena pointed to a big brownish green creature crawling over the tops of somewhat smaller ones.

"That's a tad over a pound and a half, probably a pound and three quarters. You sure have become a seemly young lady. And my, how those legs have stretched. You fair tower over me."

"Yes, and you better watch your step if you get any ideas. I've heard all about your exploits with the girls."

"Oh, I'm a reformed man. Been behaving myself so well, it's downright boring." He flashed another smile her direction as his dark brown eyes took in her form. "You sure have grown up good."

"Why, thank you, Jamie. Now make sure they're all hard-shells, no matter what they cost. I haven't had a Maine lobster in five years."

"Something the matter with Florida restaurants? We ship all over the country."

"We have a pact never to eat lobster anywhere but here. Having them in a restaurant just isn't the same."

"Well, you better start coming back more often." Jamie threw the last lobster into the cardboard box Elena had brought for that purpose. The lobsters clawed the air and snapped their tails in a futile attempt to return to water.

The three of them started up the ramp together. The boys scampered out of the shack where Jamie weighed the lobsters and kept his cash register. As he ran, the redhead tore the paper wrapper off a candy bar and stuffed it into his mouth.

"Darn those kids; they're bad news. That's the third time they've taken candy bars without paying this month."

"Have they ever been in serious trouble, Jamie?" Susan asked.

"Not that I know of, but I wouldn't put anything past them." He threw the lobsters on the large scale that hung from the ceiling of the room he called an office. "There now, right on, except for the quarter-pound extra for the one 'Lena wanted." Elena knew Jamie prided himself on being able to estimate the exact weight of any lobster. "That'll be $54.25. Hard-shells are $7.00 a pound this year."

"I guess we'll have to settle for soft shells after the first night. Why, I can remember when they were 80 cents a pound, not that long ago." Susan took the money from her wallet and paid him without further argument.

"You wouldn't want everyone but us poor fishermen to prosper, would you? We gotta pay taxes like everybody else."

"Yes, I guess no one escapes those these days. Good-bye, Jamie. I'm glad you're having a prosperous year."

Susan and Elena put their precious cargo into the car and started down the road. "Mom, you acted worried about those boys. Are they really friends of Doug's?"

"Yes, they are, Elena. I can't put my finger on it, but something about them worries me. Doug needs friends up here, so I've let him play with them. But I don't like their taking candy from Jamie without paying for it. I wonder what else they're doing."

*

As the girls arrived home, Harold carried the last load of stored clothes from the other cabin. Elena remembered Susan complaining about his buzzing around fixing things while the family waited impatiently to explore the islands, but she sensed a change in her mother's attitude. She seemed to appreciate his careful preservation of the cabins and planned time for it.

"Hello, darling, you're in the nick of time to help with the groceries. Did you get anything accomplished?" Susan greeted him with a hug and a genuine expression of concern.

"Everything's in order," he said. "All the leaks and stuck doors are fixed. I'll be ready for a day on the water tomorrow."

"What would we do without you, dear? You keep the place in such good shape."

"Someone has to. The rest of you would let it fall down around you while you're admiring the surroundings."

Elena started making lunch without being asked. With the woods so close, she never minded working in the kitchen. Her eyes fed on the green forest outside the window, her favorite ground covers, and the lush patches of green ferns that adorned the base of the trees.

A red squirrel climbed up a tall trunk and jumped from one tree to another. When he hit the ground, he raised his head and tail, alert to possible danger. When none materialized, he scampered up the path to the pump house.

"I can't wait for my first taste of crab salad." Elena licked her lips as she sampled the shelled crab claws she had poured into the salad bowl. "The boys are really missing it."

"The boys had only one thing on their minds: taking off in the boat."

"I would have, too, if I hadn't been so tired. But I'm glad they left me. I wouldn't have been here when Todd came over."

"Now, that would have been tragic." Susan smiled at her daughter. "We saw the Beechers at the store, dear," Susan told Harold as he returned from the shed. "They seemed excited to have us back. It sounded like the church has grown this year. Pastor Dar is striking a chord with people on the island. He's attracting more summer people, too."

"I'm glad to hear that," Harold said. "He's an excellent fellow. I hope you're planning on serving lunch outside on the picnic table, Elena."

"On a day like this? You bet." Elena pulled out the big red tray that sat on the floor of the kitchen and piled it high with plates, glasses, silverware, and napkins. "Here I come, Dad, would you open the screen door for me?"

The two of them set the table and called Susan to join them.

"What a glorious day to eat outside." Susan breathed in the spruce-scented air. "I believe I can do without my sweater here in the sun."

The tide, now in, lapped against the big rock a short distance below, reflecting the bright blue sky. Sunrays reached them in spite of encroaching trees. The yard, once the size of a tennis court, became smaller each year as

21

seedlings grew taller and reclaimed it for the woods. No one minded. They enjoyed being close to the water and the woods at the same time.

"My first Maine crabs in five years." Elena smiled at her parents and raised her arms to the sky. "What more could anyone ask?"

5

AFTER SHOPPING AND PREPARING THEIR MEAL, Todd sat across the lunch table from his grandmother. "I didn't expect you to run off before I even dressed this morning. I suppose you plan to return as soon as I take my rest." Amanda had not stopped complaining since he returned from seeing Elena.

"I came back as soon as I saw you standing on the porch, and we had plenty of time to buy supplies."

"I want you to have a good time, Todd, but I didn't expect you to abandon me so soon." She dabbed her forehead with her handkerchief.

"Grandma, I'll be here for you when you need me, I promise. Last night you were pleased I might have a friend."

"I can see it will be a lonely month for me."

"It will be nice for you. Mrs. Richards has already reached out to you. It will be great for both of us to have nice neighbors."

"Where's that book I was reading, Todd? I couldn't find anything while you were gone this morning."

Todd jumped up and took the book from the shelf where they had agreed to place it the night before.

"Thank you," she said, voice cold. "I'm tired and want to lie down."

Rising from the table, she marched to her bedroom and banged the door shut.

Todd winced. "What a start."

*

Elena lay on the warm, flat granite, enjoying the feel of it. The smoothness of the hard rock and the warmth emanating from it brought back poignant memories. All her life the combination of hard rock and sun, the subtle aroma of sun penetrating mineral, instantly transported her to the Maine shore.

Her fingertips caressed the smooth surface beneath her, and her skin soaked in the sun's hot rays as she mentally prepared to brave the cold water. Delicious plant smells wafted down from the woods above and mixed with those of the seawater below. She listened to the wind stirring the leaves of the quaking aspen, the gulls screeching in the distance, and the waters surging to fill the cove. Each incoming wave stretched toward the dark red stain that lined the shore. There the high tide lingered before turning and receding again.

As much as she enjoyed these quiet moments alone, she wanted even more to share them. *Will Todd keep his promise?* She pictured Todd lying on a towel beside her and their braving the water together. *Will he like my new bathing suit?* She had chosen one that brought out the bright blue of her eyes. No longer reticent in starting new friendships, Elena found herself entering this relationship with open throttle. Surprised she could be interested in another man so soon after Peter, she vowed to be patient and follow his lead.

In no hurry to face the cold water alone, she closed her eyes and shielded them from the bright sun. As the tide crept closer, the gentle lapping of the water lulled her to sleep.

*

Soon after his grandmother retired for her nap, Todd spotted Elena from his cottage. He finished washing the dishes in double time, changed into his bathing suit, and ran down the road past the two cottages that separated them. Arriving at the bridge over the brook, he saw that Elena slept. Slowing his pace, he strolled by the cabin and down the path to where she lay.

Careful not to awaken her, he perched on a rock a few feet away and studied her. His heartbeat quickened as he followed the outline of her trim figure. Her long blond hair, natural, not from a bottle like most girls, spread out luxuriously on the rock beneath her. Natural described her best. Her thin nose and high cheekbones gave her a hint of aristocracy, but still, she looked like an all American athlete.

Conscious of his good luck in meeting her so soon, ignoring his resolve to remain detached, he rejoiced that he had brought his grandmother to Maine.

As a basketball star in high school and college, he had dated his share of beautiful girls with perfect figures and pretty faces. He had been so busy in the three years since graduation, trying to pay off college loans and settle into a profession, he had not sought a lasting relationship with any one of them. Several had thrown themselves at him. Some had hidden agendas and plans he could not trust. When they indicated they were ready for marriage, he stopped seeing them. The women who were dedicated to their careers held no interest for him.

But Elena exuded a wholesomeness of character and expression, a transparency that invited him to join in her delights. She did everything with intensity. Her exuberance drew him from his somber world. At the restaurant and in the cove this morning, she had made him feel welcome and accepted. When she greeted him, her whole countenance lit, warming him deep inside and bringing a surge of life to the deadness that sometimes swallowed him. Her vivacious eyes sparkled. The dimple on the left side of her face intrigued him. He'd wanted to reach out and touch it as she paused in her storytelling, but he remained as noncommittal as possible. He could not make a commitment to any girl right now, especially to a girl like Elena.

He thought of her family's smiling faces as they stopped by his table on their way out of the restaurant. They looked so normal and carefree. *How will they react to my family? What will Elena think when she knows the truth about my father?*

Todd had weighty decisions to make. He had volunteered to bring his grandmother to Maine, partly to distance himself from his home situation. Maybe he could think his way through it and find a new perspective in this different world.

*

A gull flying overhead squawked long and loud, startling Elena. She unfolded her arm and opened her eyes.

"I hope I didn't disturb your nap," Todd said.

"No, it was the gull." She struggled to sit up. "It's easier to lie on hard rock than it is to get up from it." She smiled in his direction, and the endearing dimple formed again. "The tide is high, and it's just right to swim. Are you game?"

"Let me sit awhile and contemplate it."

"I'm ready for the big event." Elena's father appeared, holding up his camera. "Hello, Todd. I see you're a braver man than I."

"That remains to be seen. After telling me I'll freeze to death if I don't keep moving and I have to wait until I turn numb to dive in, I'm not sure how I'm going to react."

"I enjoyed swimming here at your age. I don't know exactly when I decided I was too old for it…maybe when Doug was old enough to go in on his own."

"I guess I can't let Elena think I'm too old for it." Todd leaped to his feet. "Come on. Show me how it's done. Why don't you take before and after pictures, Mr. Richards?" He put his arm around Elena's waist and pointed to the camera.

"Got it. I'll take another to prove you went in."

Elena turned and walked toward the water's edge. "Be careful. The rocks are slippery when they're wet."

"I just noticed." Todd's arms flew up to keep him from falling as he slid down the smooth rock. "That would be one way to get me in."

Elena placed half of one foot in the water. "Ohhhhhh!" she squealed.

"You're not encouraging me."

"Okay, I'll be quiet, but that's half the fun." She waded in up to her ankles, an inch or two at a time. "It's really not bad once you get used to it." But, as the water reached her knees, she squealed again.

"I guess I better do the macho thing and join you." Todd grimaced as the icy water hit his foot. "I can't say I wasn't warned."

Elena reached into the water and splashed it on her arms, down her back, and on her face.

"That looks like torture," Todd said. "I think I'll get it over with all at once."

"Suit yourself." She lowered herself into the water and began swimming as fast as she could toward the large rock ahead.

Todd plunged in after her and came up gasping. "Wowee! It will have to get a whole lot better than this for me to try it again."

"I got it," Harold called before disappearing into the cabin.

"You'll get used to it in no time. Let's go over there." Elena pointed to the opposite shore.

They took long strokes as they made their way through the cold water. The warmth of the sun-baked rock on which they landed lessened the chill.

"I see what you mean about turning numb," Todd said. "It feels great when it stops hurting."

"I'll make a convert of you yet." Elena laughed as she slipped back into the water and swam back and forth in front of Todd. "Your skin tingles for hours afterwards, and you feel totally refreshed. It's great to put on warm clothes and savor the tingling sensations."

When she pulled herself out again, she plopped her body closer to him than she intended. Her thigh landed close to his, surprising them both. Neither of them moved until Todd reached out, grabbed her arms with his hands, and pushed her back into the water.

He grinned. "Come on, I'll race you to the other side."

*

Scrambling up the shore, Elena reached for her towel and wrapped it around her. Todd had difficulty climbing up the barnacle-covered rocks.

"You need a pair of water socks like these," Elena pointed to her feet. "They're wonderful protection from barnacles."

"What makes you think I'll ever venture into that water again?" Todd laughed as he draped his beach towel over his back.

"Let's lie down on the rock a few minutes to get warm."

"How many other guys have you put through this torture?"

"Only my brothers. I've never had a friend my own age here."

"We'll fix that this summer," Todd said.

His words warmed Elena in spite of the chill. She smiled and lowered her eyes, feeling a flush on her cheeks.

A lone gull circled above them. "What's he carrying in his beak?" Todd pointed to the gull.

"It's a sea urchin. Watch. He'll drop it somewhere on the rocks to break it open."

They watched as the gull glided in large circles around the cove, searching for the perfect spot to drop his catch, then headed inland.

"Either he isn't hungry, or he doesn't know how to make a decision," Todd said.

"There—see him pause in the air—now watch."

The gull stopped gliding, hovered high over a stretch of smooth hard rock, and dropped straight down like a helicopter. Halfway to the ground he let go of his prize, which crashed on the rocks below. Dropping beside it, the gull pecked at the broken creature, devouring the flesh inside the spiny green circle of needles.

"I understand humans are eating urchins now," Elena said, "especially in Japan. There's a big market for them there, and many of the islanders started catering to it a few years ago. There aren't many sea urchins left on our point. It used to be full of them. As much as I love Maine seafood, I don't think I'm ready for that."

They stood to get a better view of the gull enjoying his catch. "Okay, it's tour time." Elena took off over the rocks and across the sand beach. She turned and watched Todd stride across the ledges. "You'll be great at rock climbing. It's the major sport here." She thrilled at the thought of spending a day alone with him on an island.

Turning to the tidal pool, she said, "This is where we keep our starfish. We collect them from the ledges and rocks at low tide and bring them here. They hide under the rocks in the daytime, but at night, they come out and crawl around. All the other animals move about and feed on each other."

"How do you see them in the dark?"

"We shine flashlights on the pool. The water seems to disappear, and you can see all the creatures gliding about."

"Wow, that's something I'd like to see."

Climbing toward the ledges that jutted into the bay, Elena signaled Todd to follow. She stopped by an upright post wedged between the rocks. A heavy rope in a clove hitch circled the post many times. "This is the mooring for our boat. The boys have it out now. It's only a rowboat, but it gets us to the islands with its ten horsepower motor. We have a ten-to-twelve-foot tide. When the tide goes out and leaves the boat stranded, four of us can pick it up and carry it back to the water."

"A rowboat on that expanse of water?"

"We don't go out when the wind is blowing or when the fog is in or when a storm is brewing."

"On a day like this, it's hard to imagine the bay as threatening."

"I guess I'm old-fashioned. I still like to hand write letters to my friends. This is where I do it." Elena pointed to a V-shaped crevice in the rocks. "The rocks protect me from the wind. I like to smell the sea, listen to the waves breaking over the rocks, and watch the life on the water. I try to describe its beauty in my notes." She waved toward a proud mother escorting her offspring lined up single file behind her. "See the family of ducks? Aren't the babies adorable?"

"How does she get them to stay in a straight line?"

"Instinct, I guess." Elena continued her story. "At low tide we have a huge rock point. The tidal pool in the middle of it was one of my favorite places to play as a child. I still like to hunt for starfish in the crags at the head of the point when the tide is out."

"I guess I'll have to come back at low tide," Todd said.

"Over here is our best sand beach." Elena bounded over the rocks and hopped down. "I come here to read and enjoy the sun. It's much warmer than on the point." Spreading out her towel, she plopped down on it and ran her hands through the soft, warm sand. "Ah, these are my favorite periwinkles." She handed him a small yellow shell that resembled a miniature snail. "They're so bright they stand out like little sunbeams." She held up another to catch the sun's rays.

"They're much prettier than snails," he said.

As Elena ran her fingers through shell deposits from the tide, she lined Todd's hand with one of each color and design: yellow, green, brown and orange stripes, and varied black and white plaids and patterns. "Look at this one. It's orange all over. I don't think I've ever seen one so bright."

"May I take them to Grandma? She'll be thrilled to see them."

"Of course." As she touched his hand, filling it with limpids, whelks, and twisted pieces of driftwood, a current surged through her body.

"That's all I can hold for now." Todd got up.

Elena smiled, trying to assess how interested he was in these things that mattered so much to her. "When we go to the islands and the tide washes up an unexpected treasure, I imagine God has laid a special gift at my feet."

Their eyes met and held each other's gaze. Elena had seldom felt such a rush of excitement so early in a friendship. She sensed that Todd had more interest in such things than Peter ever could. He seemed so much more mature…and a little mysterious. *What is the story behind his somber eyes? What does he think of my delight in the shells?*

Todd gazed at her in silence. Puzzled, she blushed and rushed into a long story. "When I was little, Dad used to come here with me and play school. He wrote math problems in the sand like this." She picked up a piece of driftwood and drew several multiplication and division problems in the wet sand where the tide receded. "I had to finish them before the tide came in and wiped them away. When the sand was wet, he wrote sentences with all kinds of phrases and had me diagram them. He did it with Stephanie, too, but it seemed like school to the boys, so Dad threw Frisbees and softballs in the cove with them."

"You must have had a happy childhood. My father never did any of those things with me."

"Was he always working?"

"No, he had other things on his mind." A scowl replaced his smile. "What are the islands like?"

"Around every corner there's a unique granite design you've never seen. Tidal pools team with sea life. Stretches of sand hidden between the ledges invite you to search for treasures." Elena's enthusiasm rose. "The shores are always changing. Twice every day the tide rolls in and out, burying and exposing clam flats, coves, and wonderful rock formations. There's nothing like them."

"Awesome. I can't wait to see them. What's it like inside the woods in the middle of the islands?"

"Very different from the shore, but as lovely. I'll show you our woods, but I think we should dress for it. I'm getting cold in this wet bathing suit."

"Okay, I'll run these shells home for Grandma. I'll come back if she's not up yet." He turned and ran from her as he had in the morning.

6

ELENA HURRIED TO HER CABIN, grabbed her clothes, and ran to the main cottage. "Hi, Mom, I'm freezing. I need to take a long, hot shower."

"Did you have a good swim, dear?"

"It was great."

"How did Todd like it?"

"He wouldn't say he enjoyed it. He talked more about torture and not wanting to go in again, but I'm sure I can shame him into it. I need a hot shower now. He said he'd try to come back."

"This afternoon?"

"Yes, I haven't shown him the woods yet." Elena shut the bathroom door.

*

Susan smiled as she listened to her daughter singing in the shower. In the kitchen she started scrubbing potatoes for dinner. As she glanced out the window, she saw Todd crossing the bridge on the run. Opening the kitchen door, she greeted him.

"Hello, Todd. Elena is still in the shower, but I'm sure she'll be out in a minute."

"I took mine fast. Grandma was still napping, but I can't stay long."

"I'll tell her you're here." Susan knocked on the bathroom door. "Elena, Todd is back."

"Great, tell him I'll be right out."

*

Todd and Elena sauntered down the path toward the beach, stopping by a large rock at the edge of the woods. "When I was a little girl, this rock was barren. Then mosses began to cover it, and pine needles and dirt collected on top. One year we discovered little plants growing in the accumulation, and soon spruce seedlings took root. At first they were only an inch high, but every year there were a few more plants and the trees grew higher. Look at it now. A replica of the woods has developed on top of it."

"How can they grow in so little soil?"

"Only nature produces a garden in such a little bit of moss and needles. If we tried to plant it, everything would dry up from lack of water."

She began pointing out her favorite ground covers: red bunchberries with leaves like those of a dogwood tree; wild blueberries wherever the sun penetrated; the shiny green leaves and red berries of the rock cranberry. The spidery tendrils of the black crowberry crawled close to the ground, filling in holes, making the forest floor look like a well-planted rock garden.

"All this was once bare ledges, like the rock I showed you. But this forest is mature with fully grown trees."

"I've never seen woods with all pine trees and no leafy trees like at home."

"Actually, we don't have any long-needled pines. These trees are short-needled spruce and fir," Elena said.

She had concentrated on the ground covers at the edge of the woods, but now she looked up the hill at the whole forest and gasped at the felled trees uprooted by a winter ice storm. They lay haphazardly on top of each other like piles of sticks in the child's Pick Up game. Massive root structures fanned upward from the downed tree trunks. Large areas of once beautiful ground covers stood in the air, dead but still clinging to the snarled roots that had been their home. The sight of barren roots jarred her.

Tears misted her eyes. "How tragic."

Elena ran to the crest of the hill and counted. Over forty trees down, even more than her mother had seen last year. She leaned back against a tree at the edge of the destruction and gazed at Todd, who had followed her up the hill.

He reached out and wiped away the tear that rolled down her cheek. "You really do love every shell and rock and tree, don't you?" He regarded her as tenderly as he might have a child.

"Yes," Elena whispered, mind reeling, heart throbbing from his touch. "When I saw the fallen trees for the first time, it was as though something in my heart had been uprooted."

"Let's make it the project of the month to clean it up. Like you've been saying, take away the dead and the fallen so sunlight can come in and God can begin the work of restoration."

"Incredible. But are you sure you want to help? It's hard work when the trees are this big."

"You'll have enough firewood for the rest of your life. Would the boys help and your father? You and your mother could clean up the smaller branches, and we could set Grandma up in a comfortable chair to watch and cheer us on."

"Mom and I talked about cleaning up this section just this morning, even before I knew how bad it was."

"Then it's settled."

"I've dreamed all my life of building here on the point. With the new laws about building back from the shore, our only choice is here on the hill. Look, Todd." She gestured, struck by surprise. "With so many trees down, you can see the water better from here than closer to the shore. God has prepared the perfect site for the new cabin." Her tears and worried frown gone now, she delighted in her discovery. Thrusting her arms skyward, she exclaimed, "Everything does work together for good, doesn't it?"

*

Todd had responded too readily to this girl, so different from those he had dated. He had no business getting involved. It wouldn't be fair to her. His life was not his own. His father needed him when he returned home. His grandmother wanted his company every day of their vacation.

He needed to distance himself from her now, before it was too late. But her enthusiasm intrigued him. He had tried to look away, not be caught in her innocent excitement, but he had smiled back, ignoring his resolve to leave her quickly.

When she asked if his dad was always working, he had changed the subject. He wasn't ready to deal with the story of his father.

Again and again throughout the afternoon, he had resolved to put a stop to this relationship before it started, but he had said nothing. Instead he felt himself being pulled into her world. It was as though a giant vacuum were rolling over him, sucking him in and carrying him to a place he didn't want to go.

"I must leave, Elena. Grandma will be up from her nap and wondering what's happened to me. Thanks for the tour." He turned and sped away from the woods, leaving her behind.

Todd realized he had made a commitment to spend time with her, to become involved in her projects. *Oh, God, why did You set something so good before me when You know I shouldn't pursue it?*

7

THAT EVENING THE RICHARDS GATHERED around the large oak table in the center of their living room for their first lobster dinner of the summer. At every place, Elena had laid out the implements for their yearly ritual: the special lobster fork, a set of nut crackers, a lobster bib, extra napkins, and a saucer of hot, melted butter for each member of the family. Since they were little children, they had approached the eating of lobster as a near art form. Anticipating Harold's customary blessing, they bowed their heads.

"Thank You, Lord, for the joy of coming before You as a family to ask Your blessing on this vacation. We thank You that we have arrived safely and pray this will be a time of special communication between family members. We lift up to You our daughter Stephanie and her family and pray Your blessings on her, Philip, and our grandchild, Kevin. We thank You for this delicious food. May it prove nourishing and strengthening to our bodies as we use them in Your service. Amen."

A chorus of "amens" rose from the assembled group followed by the sound of tearing lobster limbs.

"Just a minute." Harold got up and grabbed his camera. He snapped a picture of his family seated over five bright red lobsters, a green salad, and baked potatoes. Susan smiled happily his direction, her face glowing with anticipation of their evening together. Blond-haired Doug and Elena looked like their mother, while Mike's brown hair matched Harold's in spite of the difference in its length.

"Now dig in," he said as he resumed his seat. The Richards held tenaciously to the conventional family dinner both at home and on vacation. There were no dinners on a tray in front of television and no rushing from the table in four or five different directions at suppertime.

"Mom, I can't believe I deprived myself of this joy for so long. I must have been crazy." Elena dipped a piece of claw meat into her hot butter and popped it into her mouth.

"I second the motion," said Mike. "I've been telling you that for years. Hey, Mom, Dad, do you know what we saw on the Cliff today?"

"Raspberries?" Elena guessed. "I hope you left some. I want Todd to see them."

Doug shook his head.

"A seal off the far side of the island?" Harold ventured.

"No, not today, though we've seen them off the Cliff before. Any ideas, Mom?" Mike turned to his mother. "This is a great lobster. You sure know how to cook them."

"It's hard to spoil lobster fresh from the bay, Mike, but thank you anyway. Was it animal, vegetable, or mineral?" Susan referred to their favorite game for long car trips—twenty questions.

"It was animal." Mike gave them a clue.

"A great blue heron?" Susan said.

"No, keep going." Doug tossed a large claw shell into one of the basins that sat on the floor at the corners of the table and continued to demolish his lobster, separating the tail from the body. After dismembering the tail fins, he pushed the entire tail through the shell with his fork, pulled the "zipper" down the back of the tail, deftly cleaned the elimination tract, and continued eating with gusto. "Golle-ey, the tail is even better than the claws. Keep guessing."

"Let's see. A porpoise or maybe a soaring eagle?" Harold tried again.

"No, they aren't even close, are they, Mike?" Doug enjoyed sharing a secret with his older brother.

"I don't know which Doug is enjoying more, Mom—the lobster or the guessing game." Elena chuckled as Doug noisily sucked meat out of a lobster leg.

"You've got me, boys. Let us in on the secret so we can enjoy it, too."

"Okay, Dad. We saw a mink standing upright on a rock. When we moved closer, he dropped to all fours and bounded down the hillside. You should have been there with your camera, Dad."

"That is a sighting. I've seen them on Barred Island, but never on the Cliff. Good job, boys."

Displaying his full set of braces, Doug beamed under his father's approval. "We got a long look at it, didn't we, Mike?"

"That is exciting," Susan agreed.

"We saw lots of 5-cent bottles washed ashore, Dad, but we left them for you. We wouldn't want to spoil your fun collecting them and paying for your daily paper with the refunds."

"Good, I'll be looking for them starting tomorrow. That was delicious, dear." He turned to Susan as he pushed back his plate. "Bring on the blueberry pie."

"Not the first day we're here. That's not fair."

34

"Now?" Doug whispered to Mike.

"Yes, now," Mike said.

Doug rose from the dinner table and disappeared through the screen door. When he reappeared, he proudly presented Susan with a quart basket of raspberries. "For our dessert, compliments of Mike and me," he said, grinning ear to ear.

"How wonderful, boys. You picked them yourselves? What a lovely surprise."

"Sit still, Mom. You cooked dinner. It's my turn to make a contribution. I'll clear and serve the berries." Elena took the basket from Doug and popped a plump berry into her mouth. "My, they taste good."

"Tell us about your day, Sis," Mike said. "Did the gorgeous hunk show?"

"That doesn't suit him, Mike. He's much too deep to be called a hunk."

"Deep? Then he did come over. Boy, he didn't waste any time." Mike pursued the subject, calling to Elena in the kitchen. Choosing to ignore him, she returned with a tray bearing a pitcher of fresh milk and a bowl full of berries for each of them. "Tell us about him, Elena," Mike persisted.

"He took me up on my invitation to show him the shore. He had to go home when his grandmother called, but he came back for a swim this afternoon."

"You mean you enticed him into that cold water. He must have fallen for you big time."

"Mike, what are you talking about?" Elena protested. "You love to swim up here."

"Yes, but most first-timers don't go near the water without some forceful persuasion." Mike's eyes danced with pleasure as he challenged his sister.

"Elena worked all her wiles on him and coaxed him in an inch at a time." Harold joined the boys in teasing his daughter.

"These raspberries are every bit as good as they look." Susan changed the subject.

"We're glad you appreciate our backbreaking work, Mom." Mike stuffed a heaping spoonful of berries into his mouth. "But let Elena finish her story."

"You're just jealous because you don't have a girlfriend." Elena tipped her nose in the air and puffed up with an air of superiority. But as quickly as she snapped at Mike, she deflated. "You always make me descend to your level." She groaned. "We had a walk around the point and through the woods and…"

"Did you see all the trees down from the ice storm?" Doug interrupted, an overflow of raspberry juice running down his chin.

"Yes, it was a terrible shock, but Todd suggested we make a project of cleaning them up. Would you all be willing to help?" Elena's enthusiasm returned.

"That's a big job, Elena. I think we need professional help to do it," Harold said.

"With all these able-bodied men? You and Todd can saw the trunks, Mike and Doug can stack the logs in neat piles, and Mom and I can cart the branches out on the rocks. When we're all finished, we can have a huge bonfire."

"You seem to have it all planned, Elena." Harold took his last spoonful of raspberries. "My, boys, those were good."

"I realize we're on vacation, but consider how lovely it is to have the woods around the cabin looking so great. Wouldn't it be just as nice to have the woods cleared on the point?"

"Of course, it would," Susan said. "Why don't we spend a day at it and see how it goes? With so much help, it might not be as bad as we expect."

"If we don't want Elena to be lost to us this summer, we better join in her project with Todd. Otherwise, we'll never see her. I thought this was going to be a family vacation, Sis."

"Of course it is, Mike. I'll be going with you on the picnic tomorrow, and we'll be doing all kinds of things together."

"Yeah, showing Todd the raspberries, showing Todd the shore, showing Todd the islands. We better enlist Todd in the work project. At least we'll get something out of it."

"Mike, how could you?" Elena accused.

"Cheer up, Sis, I'm only kidding. I'm glad you've found a friend. Can't you take a joke?" Ever the peacemaker after riling up emotions, Mike put his arm around her. "We missed you. It's great to have you back." His earnest face pleaded for forgiveness.

"Sorry, Mike, I'm still a little sensitive. You'll like having Todd around."

"If you say so."

Doug jumped up. "What a great evening. It's fun having you back, Elena. I'll clear the table." He looked at Mike.

Mike rose to the occasion. "Elena and I will take first turn at the dishes. Mom and Dad, you're excused. The three of us will take over."

*

Harvey sauntered about his yard picking up trash and looking excitedly up and down the street. Soon Eddie and Joey rode by on their bikes. "Hey, guys, come here. I got something for you." They swung off the road and screeched to a halt in Harvey's driveway.

"What's up?" Eddie asked.

"Let's climb into the tree house." Harvey's face was flushed with anticipation. "I got a surprise for you."

"What is it? You been to the store?" He had caught Joey's interest.

"Come on quick, before Dad sees us." Harvey lumbered over to the ladder and scrambled up fast in spite of his excessive weight.

They squatted on the mattress on the floor. "This better be good," Eddie said, his dark eyes fixed on Harvey. "My dad told me to come straight home."

"This is good." Harvey beamed. He brushed aside the top newspapers, along with copies of *Good Housekeeping* and *Better Homes and Gardens.*

"What are you doing with those?" Joey scrunched his normally sweet face in disgust, his disappointment obvious.

"Look what's next." Harvey handed each boy a stack of old, tattered *Playboy Magazines.*

"Where'd you get so many?" Joey, wide-eyed and eager now, looking more like a rosy-cheeked cherubim than a porn reader, reached for his allotment.

"Someone left them at the dump mixed in with a bunch of other magazines. A friend of mine found them, took out the ones he wanted, and gave me these."

"Wow, we could stay up all night lookin' at these," Eddie said. Just then he heard his father calling his name. "He must have seen our bikes in your yard. I better scram, Harv. When can we meet again?"

"Tomorrow when we're through at Jamie's."

"I never thought of finding magazines outside a store. I'll be looking through things left at the dump from now on, Harv. Thanks for sharing with us." Joey scrambled down the ladder and ran after Eddie.

"My friend said you can find them in all kinds of places if you know where to look," Harvey called after them.

8

HAROLD AND SUSAN LEFT THE TABLE and settled on the couch. "That was the best rule you ever made, darling, that the children take turns doing the dishes. I always look forward to relaxing with you after dinner before the fire." Susan patted Harold's arm as she spoke.

"We should have started it sooner. I can still see you trying to keep everyone happy and doing all the clean-up, too."

"It did make a long day. I'll be forever grateful that you stepped in to help, and it's even nicer that the children do the dishes now without a fuss. We're blessed to have such a family."

"Yes, we are." Harold put his arm around Susan. "You know you look as lovely in the firelight as you did when we were here on our honeymoon. I don't know what I've ever done to deserve you, Susan, but I want you to know how much I appreciate you. I can't imagine living without you."

Susan snuggled closer into Harold's arm and took his hand in hers. "Remember when Kathy called me after we had Doug and welcomed us to the world of large families? There were times when the boys were babies when I wasn't sure that was a good move, but it's lovely now. It must be terrible to grow old alone and have no children. I'm so happy those difficult years with Elena have come to an end. In spite of all the teasing, she seems happy to be with us."

"Yes, she seems to have broken out of her cocoon of self-concern. Sometimes she's as lighthearted as a butterfly, flitting from joy to joy."

"She's giving me a great deal of joy," Susan agreed. "She reminds me of the little girl she used to be, always walking on her tippy-toes and flashing an impish grin at every stranger. I wasn't sure I could survive those sullen teenage years when she withdrew inside herself. She was emotionally impenetrable, only wanting to be left alone. No matter what I did, I couldn't reach her. I'm so grateful she's come out of it."

"Hey, you two love birds," Mike called from the kitchen. "We're almost done, and we have an important game of Charades to play tonight. Are the pencils and paper ready?"

Susan sighed as she forced herself to rise from the couch.

"Remember, you love that family," Harold reminded her.

Susan laughed. "You're right. It won't be much longer 'til we can sit by the fire by ourselves all evening."

"Are you ready?" Mike entered, rolling down his sleeves, from the kitchen.

They decided to play the boys against the girls. Susan and Elena retired to the bedroom to pick the hardest titles they could remember. Harold and the boys huddled, laughing, around the kitchen table as they dredged up new titles sure to stump the girls. Elena could hear that Doug was enjoying being treated like a member of the team instead of the baby of the family who was too young to play.

Soon the cabin shook beneath them as the boys frantically guessed what Harold's crazy antics represented. In spite of the keen competition, squeals of laughter dominated the game, and everyone had a good time.

Doug flopped into a chair when he finished his last title.

"Doug, you gave it your all, but Elena and I have won. Congratulations, dear," Susan said, shaking Elena's hand. "I guess the boys will have a hard time keeping up with us this vacation."

"Wait 'til tomorrow night. We'll be thinking up stoppers all day long," Mike warned.

"Mom, did you buy marshmallows? The coals are perfect."

"They're in the cupboard, Doug. You get them, and I'll find the forks." Elena headed toward the kitchen.

Doug had already burned and eaten two before Elena's began to turn color. Like a work of art, she turned it round and round at just the right distance from the coals, until the inside was soft and the crust golden brown. "Ah, now it's ready." Closing her eyes, she savored the familiar taste of a marshmallow cooked to perfection. She wondered how Todd's family spent their evenings. *Did that have something to do with the sadness in his eyes?*

"Dad, may I make you one?" she asked.

"You mean I'm allowed to have one of those unhealthy things?"

"Just one. They're not to be missed."

"I guess you can twist my arm." Harold looked toward Susan, who was absorbed in her own thoughts. Elena could see she was savoring the joy of the evening, having three of her brood together, happy and laughing.

Harold's marshmallow was half done when the phone rang. Elena pulled it from the fire and handed it to Susan. "I'll get it. Mom, will you finish this for Dad?" Without waiting for a reply, she pressed the long fork into Susan's hand and rushed toward the telephone. "Hello."

"Hello, Elena, is that you?"

Her heart raced as she recognized Todd's voice. "Yes, it is. Hi, Todd." She hoped she sounded casual.

"Your tour was great today. I enjoyed it all."

"You mean you even liked the swim? I hope that means you'll be willing to try it again."

"My skin is still tingling."

"Doesn't it feel good?"

"What I enjoyed most was seeing the shore and the woods through your eyes. I wouldn't have seen half as much if I'd done it on my own."

"There's lots more to show you," Elena said, elated. "The boys saw a mink on the Cliff today and picked a quart of the most wonderful raspberries. I'd like you to see them while they're at their height."

"How 'bout tomorrow?"

Elena hesitated. "We have a family boat trip planned, but maybe we could go the next day."

"I promised to take Grandma to Blue Hill to spend the day with an old friend who's summering there. How does Wednesday look?"

"Wednesday would be fine." Elena brightened.

"We're going to Open Tennis Wednesday morning," Harold reminded her.

Elena's smile disappeared, and her shoulders slumped. Would their family duties keep them apart indefinitely? "We play Round Robin Tennis at the Island Country Club in the morning from 9:00 to 12:00, but we could take a lunch to the Cliff when we return."

"It's a date. Can anyone play tennis?"

"As long as you pay the fee. Do you want to come?"

"At the last minute I threw my racquet into my suitcase. Are there any rules for dress?"

"Only the right kind of shoes."

"I can manage that. I'll walk over about 8:30."

"Perfect. But what about your grandmother?"

"I'll be very attentive the next two days. I'll take her to Sunshine tomorrow to see where she stayed as a girl. That will give her lots to think about."

"Great, I'll look forward to seeing you for tennis and an afternoon boat ride. Good night, Todd." Elena, realizing her family was listening to every word, hung up the phone and let out a deep sigh. "What a perfect end to a perfect day."

Mike and Doug looked knowingly at each other.

9

MONDAY MORNING THE FORLORN SOUND OF THE FOGHORN pierced Elena's dreams. She was on an island. Todd struggled in the icy water. Every time she tried to pull him out, his hand went limp. As he slid slowly back into the bay, she reached for him once more, determined to save him, but his hand turned to flimsy rubber that slipped from her grasp. Horror filled her as he sank deeper into the water. She longed to rescue him, but she was powerless to do so. She had never felt so helpless. Overcome with anguish, she watched his body disappear into the depths of the sea.

The foghorn sounded again and roused her from her sleep. She sat upright, her breath coming hard. Her stomach churned. Her heart raced. She flopped back on her pillow. "It was only a dream," she said aloud as if to convince herself it had no significance. But the anguish lingered. What did it mean? Already she knew she wanted this relationship to grow. She was used to seeing what she wanted, making a plan, and going for it. Was the dream a warning that it wouldn't work?

This time she must let Todd lead. She knew by now that men liked to set the pace. She must be careful not to push him. She sighed. Still two long days before she would see him again.

She stretched her arms outside her warm blanket and felt the chill of northern air. This, she reminded herself, was reality, not the dream. She pounded on the wall behind her bed. "Mike. Doug. It's time to get up. We're going out in the boat today."

A groan from the next room satisfied her that she'd penetrated the boys' sleep. She donned layers of clothes: short-sleeved blouse, long sleeves, sweater, a warm jacket. Though cold now, it would warm up by afternoon.

Bounding over the path to the main cabin, she found her mother placing a plate of hot blueberry muffins in the center of the table. Susan hugged Elena. "Sleep well, dear? I'm scrambling eggs. Harold is sure to want toast as well as muffins. Would you toast and butter the bread and set it in a pan in the oven?" She poured the egg mixture into the well-seasoned black iron skillet that had hung on the kitchen wall since the cabin was built. "I hope the boys will be here by the time they're done. If there's one thing I dislike, its cold eggs for breakfast."

"I'll make sure," Elena said as her father emerged freshly shaven from the bathroom. "Morning, Dad, you smell great." She accepted a quick hug before running back to her cabin and pounding on the door of the boys' bedroom.

"Hey, are you up in there?" When there was no response, she opened the door and peeked into the darkness. Raising the front blinds, she bent over to tickle Doug. "Mom's already started the eggs, and you know how she is about serving them cold."

Doug squealed with laughter and rolled around the bed in a vain attempt to escape Elena's tickling fingers. "Have a heart, 'Lane. It's early in the morning."

"I guess you're awake," she said. "Now for Mike."

"Hold it. Hold it. I'm up." He sat upright in his bed. "Hey, look at that." His frown disappeared, and his face brightened as he caught sight of the sparkling blue water. "That's got to be the greatest view to wake up to this side of heaven." He waved his hand in Elena's direction. "Out, out…we'll be there before the plates are on the table."

Elena returned to help Susan serve breakfast. As Harold started the blessing, the boys slipped into their chairs, shirt tails hanging out, and hair disheveled. "That was cutting it mighty close, boys."

"Hi, Mom, Dad," Mike said. "It's a fantastic day for a boat trip."

"Good thing you took Todd for a swim yesterday." Doug rubbed his arms.

"You'll need an extra layer in the boat today, but I'm sure it will warm up by lunch time," Susan said, always optimistic. "Eat heartily. We have a big day ahead."

In a matter of minutes, they had emptied both the muffin plate and the pan full of toast.

By the time Elena and Susan arrived on shore with the lunch, the men had loaded the boat and were poised for takeoff. Mike passed out life jackets and helped the girls board. Doug shoved the boat off shore and deftly jumped in over the bow as the boat slid into the bay.

"Good send off, Doug," Harold complimented his son. Doug beamed. "Mike, it's about time you became the captain and let your old father relax." He let down the motor and pulled the starter cord. Nothing happened.

Noticing that they were drifting rapidly toward shore, Elena grabbed an oar from under the seat.

"I'll get it this time," Harold spoke with confidence. He pulled the cord again. The engine merely sputtered. The tide pushed the boat against the rocks.

"Mike, grab the other oar and help me," Elena called out.

Mike and Elena held the boat off shore, and Harold pulled the cord once more. Susan gave an audible sigh at the familiar roar of the engine.

"It's a trustworthy little engine," Harold said. "It never lets us down."

As he accelerated the throttle, Elena searched for Todd on the shore. *How much nicer it would be to have Todd beside me.*

The little boat bounced along the surface of the water as Harold opened the motor to full throttle. Soon Elena could see the brown and gray masses that were harbor seals on the ledges ahead. While some blended into the rocks, others formed large crescents with their tails and noses raised in the air. As Harold cut the motor, the seals watched, poised to dive into the water. Once one plunged in, the others followed. As the boat drifted closer, heads popped up all around them.

"Oh, I forgot how adorable they are." Elena turned her head in all directions, enjoying the bobbing heads that encircled the boat. Some of the seals, more curious than others, stretched their heads above the water to take a good look. Others, barely visible, kept their heads at water level, their big, soulful eyes searching the intruders.

They reminded Elena of Todd's sad eyes, staring at her as he disappeared into the water. Her heart flip-flopped as she felt again the pain of her failure to save him.

As the boat drifted away from the rocks, several seals heaved their blubbery bodies out of the water back onto the ledge. Much more graceful in the water, they waddled to the top of the rocks and settled down again.

After taking his annual pictures of the seals, Harold headed for the island farthest out in the bay, exciting the boys. The farther out they went, the more likely they were to find treasure washed ashore.

Elena, mesmerized by the sun sparkling on the water, isolated by the roar of the engine, returned to her thoughts. Did the dream portend the end of their relationship before it had even begun? She watched a seagull soaring overhead, cormorants skimming the water top, sailboats gliding effortlessly through the water. *It's even better than I remembered. Why did I stay away so long?*

A stately schooner billowed out of Stonington Thoroughfare in full sail and crossed before them. Wondering what exciting adventures lay before the elegant craft, she clutched the sides of their little boat as it bounced in the schooner's wake. As spray hit her face, tasting salt water and smelling sea air, she felt her own sense of adventure.

After anchoring the boat, they set off in search of treasures, the boys running ahead. Elena, too, bounded off, hopping from rock to rock, pleased that her long legs could still leap across wide crevices. When she caught up to the boys, she ran ahead to join them.

"Look, Sis." Mike seemed excited. "A wooden lobster trap wedged between these rocks. It's in one piece, but I'm not sure we can get it out without breaking it."

"It's a beauty, all right." Elena joined in their excitement. "Mom's always wanted one for a coffee table. Her birthday's in two weeks."

"Doug, crawl down there and push while I pull but don't break anything," Mike ordered. They tugged and pushed, but the trap seemed bigger than the crag into which it had floated.

The space between each wooden slat allowed water to drain in and out. Enticed by dead herring stuffed inside a net pouch, the lobsters crawled in but could not escape. The flat bottom and perfectly rounded top and sides of the traditional lobster trap gave it a unique character. For years it had been vogue to use them as coffee tables in a rustic setting.

"There must be a way," Elena insisted, poking at the side slats. "It made it in here, and the rocks haven't put on weight. What if we push it down to where the opening is bigger and slide it out?"

"Can you push it without breaking the sides?" Mike asked.

"Let's try. It's no good to us this way." Doug dropped to his knees and pushed as hard as he could.

"All the lobstermen are using straight metal traps now," Mike informed them. "They have no character at all. We better get a wooden one while they still exist."

The three of them pushed and poked until bit by bit the trap lowered deeper into the cleft. The distance between the suspended trap and the bottom of the crag grew smaller until, at last, the trap dropped free. With great care the three of them nudged it forward until it cleared the rocks.

"Now that's what I call teamwork," Mike said. "Hey, here come Mom and Dad. We have to get this out of sight, or Mom will see it for sure." They struggled to move the weighted trap into the woods as Susan and Harold approached.

"What are you three up to?" Susan called to them.

"Nothing much. Just seeing what the woods looked like," Doug said.

"Look what we found." Susan held out two perfect rose-colored scallop shells. "Usually they're covered with barnacles or broken on the edges. They'll make good candle holders."

"Great find, Mom. Have you found enough bottles for your paper tomorrow, Dad?" Doug tried to distract them.

"For the next three days." Harold opened his bulging trash bag to display an assorted array of cans and bottles, each worth five cents, which he applied to the cost of his daily newspaper.

Elena ran ahead and picked up a piece of driftwood. "Doesn't this look like a sailfish jumping out of the water?" she called back, holding it up for them to see.

"The top fin does look like a sailfish," Susan said. "It'll be a perfect addition to our collection."

Every year their island expeditions produced trophies to decorate the unfinished cabin walls. The exposed two-by-fours made perfect spots to hang the prized lobster buoys while empty cubicles at the top of the walls framed interesting pieces of driftwood.

*

After a picnic lunch, they reloaded the boat and set off for Lighthouse Island. With no beach to welcome them, Doug jumped out on the slippery seaweed and lost his balance. Not deterred, he and Mike rushed off as soon as the boat was secured to explore the island's more treacherous granite ledges. Harold and Susan begged off, and Elena elected to circle the island with the boys.

Harold's parents had known the family who had lived in the lighthouse years ago. Though now deserted, its eerie foghorn never ceased, and its bright light guided ships toward Stonington Harbor at night. Elena lingered to explore the remains of an old vegetable garden. Only the red-skinned stalks of the rhubarb plant looked edible now.

Elena tried to imagine life isolated from society, particularly in winter. She hoped the couple had been very much in love. She wondered what it would be like to live on an island with Todd.

Catching up with the boys, she found Mike halfway up a forty-foot vertical ledge. While his arms hugged its rough surface, his fingers strained to keep him there. Elena thought he could not possibly make it to the top. Horrified, but afraid she would startle Mike and cause him to lose his grip, she remained silent. Doug, unaware of the seriousness of Mike's predicament, screamed encouragement.

Seeing no footholds, Elena thought he must be holding onto the face of the rock with sheer determination. He was suspended on a vertical cliff of granite as though his hands and feet were glued to it, but the slightest wrong move and gravity would take over.

Filled with anxiety, Elena realized how much she loved her brother in spite of his awful teasing. Oblivious to her misery and excited by the challenge, Mike inched forward, groping for a new place to rest his foot. As he set it down, a piece of rock broke away beneath him. Elena gasped and held her breath. Her mouth dry with fear, she watched his expression change from expectation to tension and uncertainty.

She closed her eyes and prayed, "Father, You love your foolish children. Please forgive Mike for this foolhardiness and show him how to reach the top." It made her feel better, but she dared not look.

"Mike, watch out!" Doug's voice, shrill with fear, told Elena he now realized the danger.

Elena opened her eyes in time to see Mike grimace and inch his hands upward. She watched aghast as he searched for new footholds, finding them where Elena could see none, but as he neared the top of the rock, his progress stopped. There seemed to be no place to go.

Her hands trembling, feeling sick inside, Elena closed her eyes. She couldn't save Mike any more than she could have saved Todd in her dream. Not until she heard Doug's explosion of congratulations did she open her eyes to see a triumphant Mike standing on top of the sheer cliff, his arms raised like a conqueror. He had met the challenge!

Grateful but exhausted from the tension, Elena collapsed on the rocks beneath her. "Boys," she exclaimed to herself. "From now on, every time Mother says she's never lost a child to the rocks, I'll see Mike hanging there." She shuddered. Her mother would be better off not knowing about this one.

Elena suspected they had all learned perseverance from the demands of the rocky coast. Mike had just demonstrated the persistence required to overcome its many obstacles. She watched him descend to the shore rocks and ran ahead to meet him. "Mike, don't ever do that to me again. It was awful, seeing you hanging there with no place to go. I found myself willing to put up with years of teasing just to see you safe again." They walked on, arm in arm.

"I'm glad to know I have your permission to tease you in the future, Sis."

"Well, I didn't exactly mean that, but I'm grateful you made it. Whatever made you think you could?"

"I don't know. It's something I've wanted to do for years, and today seemed to be the day."

"You mean you waited all this time just for me to see it." They laughed, and she tousled his hair as she pushed him away.

"Now that I've done it, I guess I won't have to try it again anytime soon."

"I'll be eternally grateful."

"It's getting rough. The wind has changed, and the waves are beginning to pound," Mike said. "We better beat it around the island. Dad will be furious by the time we get back."

When they arrived back at the boat, they found Harold as agitated as they expected. The afternoon wind had whipped up whitecaps on the water. The waves, breaking over the rocks, had pushed the boat onto a ragged ledge where it stayed as the tide moved out. "Come on, boys, give me a hand at getting this boat back to the water, and let's get out of here."

Tensions mounted as they worked together, and the wind grew stronger still. With his family settled in the boat, Harold pushed the motor to open throttle, spraying them with water each time the boat pounded on a wave. Doug hustled to find ponchos for Susan and Elena. The boys took the spray.

As they entered their cove, Elena spotted Todd on his porch and waved to him. He rushed over to help. Harold had to yell to be heard over the wind. "Doug, throw the bowline to Todd."

Todd caught the line and held the boat as steady as he could as the surging waters dashed it against the rocks and the undertow pulled it out again.

Once they were safely ashore and the boat unloaded, Todd and Elena exchanged news of the day.

"Priscilla and Dean Crowley said they'd be delighted to plan a clam bake for us on Friday, so we're all set." Elena was pleased to share her good news.

"Great. Grandma will love it. I can't wait to tell her," Todd said. "I found her childhood vacation home today right away. Nothing's been built on the spot where her farmhouse stood, so she felt it still belonged to her."

Elena shared the day's adventures—seeing the seals, watching eagles fly overhead, Mike's foolhardy ascent up the granite ledge.

"What a day. I'm anxious to see it all."

Family members arrived at the cottage, their arms loaded with gear. Susan began giving orders. "Elena, clean out the picnic basket. Doug, Mike, take the cushions and life jackets to your cabin."

"Where are the map and compass?" Harold arrived, his usually neat hair disheveled and falling down in his face. As he attempted to restore order, Todd departed as fast as he had arrived.

10

THE NEXT DAY DOUG ENJOYED THE COMRADESHIP of his father and brother as they retrieved the lobster trap from the island and hid it in the woods next door. With the job completed, Harold went back to work on the cabin and Mike left to find his fishing buddy. Elena and Susan were gone.

"Dad, can I walk over to Twisted Tree Cove to say hello to Jamie?"

"Sure, Doug. You've earned a treat. Say 'hi' from me."

"Thanks, Dad," he said as he sprinted toward the road.

As Doug approached the wharf, he found Harvey, Joey, and Eddie. The boys had always enjoyed hanging around the floating lobster cart where Jamie stored his lobsters. They liked joking with the lobstermen when they brought in their catch.

"Hey, guys," Doug said.

"Hey, Doug." Harvey looked glad to see him. "We've been waiting for you. Saw your mom a few days ago."

"She didn't tell me. This is the first chance I've had to come over."

"We're working for Jamie now. We'll be done in half an hour," Harvey said. "Want to come over to my place afterwards? We got something to show you."

"Sure, I'll go down on the cart and talk to Jamie." Doug, pleased the boys accepted him so readily, called from the top of the ramp. "Jamie, how's it going?"

"Well, I'll be. It's Doug Richards, half grown up. Looking for a job this summer? I'm paying those boys a small sum to work off the cost of candy bars they've taken."

"No, just wanted to say hello, Jamie."

"Well, come down here and shake my hand like a man." Jamie flashed his wide smile at Doug.

"That was a great lobster we had the other night. Is it a good year for lobsters?" Doug asked as he shook Jamie's hand.

"Not bad. Can't complain. They're a bit scarce, but that keeps the price up. Never sold you a bad one, have I?"

"No. Mike and I sure would like to go lobstering again this year. Your brother still have his boat?" Doug tried not to seem too eager.

"Sure, I'll tell him you're here. He got a kick out of taking you last year. Hey, Doug, that's some sister of yours. Doesn't seem like the same kid that complained so much last time she was here."

"No, Elena's changed a lot. She loves it here now."

"Thought I might come calling on her some night," Jamie said.

"Sure, Jamie, only she's got a boyfriend. I think they're pretty thick already."

"That so? Oh, well, she's a mite tall for me."

"Okay if I watch you work? I'd like to be a lobsterman when I'm old enough."

"Would you, now? Why would you want to do that?"

"It's a great job, and I'd love to live here for a time. I suppose I'll have to go to college someday, but I'd sure like to start as a lobsterman."

"Takes a lot of money to buy a lobster boat," Jamie said as he filled another crate with crabs.

"I'd have to start out in the stern on someone else's boat. Do you think they'd take a guy from away, Jamie?"

"I guess your summers here on the island count for something," Jamie said as he filled more crates.

"Hey, Doug, we're ready to go," Harvey called to him. "We marked our hours on the sheet, Jamie. Marked off another candy bar, too. See ya tomorrow."

"Okay, Harv," Jamie called back without looking up.

*

Doug sat on the back of Harvey's bike as the boys peddled over to Harvey's. When they arrived, he jumped off and ran to the bottom of the tree house. "Hey, guys, this is great. When did you build it?"

"This spring. It took a whole year to get Harv's dad to give his okay. We went down to the lumber yard and asked if we could have any old boards or scrap lumber. Lots of people had a few pieces of wood left over in their garages. We collected them and my dad came over and helped us pound them together," Joey said. "Girls can't come up. Guys can't either unless they belong to our club."

"Oh. It looks like a great tree house," Doug said.

"Would you like to go up?" Eddie asked.

"I thought you had to belong to the club."

"Yeah, but we could vote you in," Harvey said. "But you have to swear you'll keep a secret first."

"Keep what a secret? Anybody can see the tree house."

"It's what we do up there."

"What do you do?"

"We'll let you in on it. Nobody's been up here but us three. You would make four. But you got to promise you won't tell."

"Tell what?" Doug looked from one to the other.

"You got to promise first," Eddie said, his dark eyes fixed on Doug. "It was my idea to ask you, Doug. I know you won't tell anybody."

"I don't know what you're talking about, but I won't tell, I promise."

"That's good enough for me. I vote yes," Eddie said.

"Me, too," Joey echoed. "What about you, Harv?"

"Yeah. Go on up. We'll follow you." Harvey punched Doug in the shoulder.

"Thanks, guys." Doug started up the ladder, happy to be included.

Harvey followed.

Doug surveyed the snug five-by-six room. No room to stand inside, but ample room for an old mattress and some boat cushions on the floor. A two-drawer painted chest stood along one wall.

"This here's our food supply," Harvey said. "We stocked it, knowing you'd be coming." Bags of chips, pretzels, and soda cans filled the bottom shelf. The top shelf held a bag of apples and individual boxes of raisins.

"We don't have ice," Harvey apologized, "but it still tastes good."

"It's great. You have everything you need. What else do you do up here?" Doug asked as his eyes fell on the pile of old newspapers.

Joey and Eddie giggled and jostled each other. Harvey ignored them. Opening a can of soda, he shoved it into Doug's hand.

"Those papers are our reading material." Harvey's eyes gleamed.

"The good stuff is under them," Eddie said.

"We got a kind of magazine club." Harvey pulled some newspapers and beat-up magazines off the top of the pile. Underneath was a stack of glossy magazines with pictures of scantily clad, pretty girls on the covers.

"Oh," Doug said. "I've seen those in racks behind counters."

"Yeah, only some stores have them where you can get them. Have you ever seen one, Doug?" Harvey kept his eyes on Doug, as if trying to gauge his reaction.

"No, I haven't."

"You're gonna like this." Harvey carefully took the top magazine and, opening it to the centerfold, placed it on Doug's lap. All three boys stared as

50

Doug looked at a picture of a naked girl in a sexy pose.

"What do you think, Doug?" Harvey forced the question.

Doug swallowed hard. His first reaction was to run. He knew his parents wouldn't approve, but the guys would never ask him to play again if he turned them down. He didn't want to be dropped from the club. When he said, "I won't tell," he had no idea what he was promising.

"Great, isn't it?" Harvey said, encouraging him. "Take a good look."

Doug looked at the picture, which was a blur at first, but as his eyes focused, pleasure pulsed through his body. He closed his eyes.

"What do you think, Doug?"

He opened his eyes and looked at the picture a second time. "Wow," he said and meant it as that tingling sensation hit him again. *It's just a beautiful woman. I bet a magazine like this could teach me a lot of things I want to know.* Aware the boys expected an answer, he hesitated only moments. "Yeah, guys, I'm with you. I won't tell."

11

TODD ARRIVED AT THE RICHARDS' CABIN at 8:30 Wednesday morning. Harold waited in the car supping his second cup of coffee and reading yesterday's newspaper.

The boys appeared carrying golf clubs. Susan brought midmorning snacks. Elena rushed out the kitchen door pulling on her warm-up jacket. "Hi, Todd, you're here."

"He's been here since 8:30 as scheduled," Harold said. "If we're too late to sign up for Open Tennis, it won't be his fault."

"Did your grandmother mind being left alone?" Elena felt a shiver of excitement as Todd's shoulder pressed against hers as she settled into her seat.

"She complained some, but she was tired after two days of long car rides and wanted to stay in bed this morning. She'll mull over all we experienced the last two days and enjoy her memories."

"Tell us about them, Todd," Susan encouraged him.

Todd entertained them with tales of their excursions into the past all the way to the courts. "If I had been able to arrange the perfect experience for Grandma's return, I couldn't have planned it better. She'll never forget it," he concluded as Harold pulled into the Island Country Club and began giving orders. "Elena, run over and sign us all in for tennis. I'll pay our dues for the summer. Todd, come with me and we'll register you to play. Mike and Doug, you're on your own. We'll see you at 12:00."

Running up to sign them in, Elena breathed a sigh of relief as they took four of the last five places. The mixer attracted most of the regular players, from young adults to old-timers in their eighties, a popular event every Wednesday morning and Sunday afternoon.

Sitting out the first round, Elena and Todd settled on a bench to watch from the sidelines.

"How are plans coming for the beach party?" Todd asked.

"Great. Mom and I will shop tomorrow, and Dean and Priscilla will come in time to help with the cooking. I'm praying the weather holds."

"Grandma loved the idea. It brought up a rush of memories, just like I expected. Is it okay with your mom and dad?"

"Yes, Mom liked the fact that we'll be doing most of the cooking."

The whistle blew, and everyone came in from the courts. The leader assigned Elena and Todd to the same court but on opposite sides of the net. Elena's partner, a friend of her father, looked like a consistent player, but not a strong one. Todd had one of the best women players in the club.

"This will be quite a match," Elena whispered to Todd as they moved toward the court.

Elena's side won the serve, and her partner indicated she should serve first. Elena, too, played a solid game, hitting the ball with style and grace but not with force. Excellent at placement, she won her serve as did Todd's partner. The score was one-one when Elena's partner started to serve. He served well, displaying the strength of a man, and Todd responded in kind. Elena saw that Todd had been holding back out of consideration for the women. Though her partner served well, he gave Todd too many opportunities to rush the net and put the ball away. The score was five-two in Todd's favor when the whistle announced the end of the half hour. They shook hands and left the court.

"You were a great sport, Elena," Todd said as soon as they moved out of hearing range of the others. "It was a lopsided match, but you made us feel you enjoyed it."

"I did. You have a terrific game, Todd. I could see you were holding back. If you had opened up, you'd have smeared us."

"There's a sign-up sheet in the clubhouse for a mixed doubles tournament at the end of the month," he said. "Would you like to enter as partners?"

"I'd much rather have you for a partner than opponent. I'd love to."

"Great, let's go in and sign up now."

They disappeared into the clubhouse as the next foursomes assembled.

*

When it was their turn to play again, Elena and Todd were on different courts, but side by side. Todd noticed that Elena often looked over to watch him play. He did his best to make good put-a-way shots and ace some of his serves. He enjoyed her smiles of approval when their eyes met. *I better not get used to this,* he thought, still concerned he was allowing their relationship to progress too fast.

As the final tennis set came to a conclusion, Elena spotted Mike and Doug coming up the hill from the ninth hole accompanied by the three boys she and her mom had seen at the lobster pound. The redhead whispered something into Doug's ear, and they both laughed.

She rushed over to her mother. "Mom, did you see Doug and those boys together?"

"Yes, I did." Just then Harvey gave Doug a playful poke in the stomach and scampered toward the clubhouse. He called back in a loud voice that everyone could hear, "I'll be over after lunch, Doug. See ya."

"I don't want Doug playing with those boys this summer, Harold."

"I understand Harvey has a very bad family situation. Maybe we should try to help him—invite him to attend church with us, give him something to hold on to in his difficult world."

"He's the one that worries me most. I don't know what it is. I just have a feeling he isn't good for Doug."

"We can't protect Doug from the world forever," Harold said. "Guess Harvey could use some help, too."

Todd, remembering how the boys had stolen the magazine, agreed they could use some help, and decided to look for an opportunity to talk to them.

*

"I'm back, Grandma. How was your morning? Our tennis was great."

"I enjoyed being lazy this morning, Todd, but I'll miss having lunch with you. I hope you won't make this a practice."

"It's the first time I've spent any time with Elena since our first day here. I thought you'd be tired of me after two long days together."

"No, Todd. I never tire of your company. You're the only pleasure I have."

"Don't make me feel guilty for leaving you today, Grandma. It's too beautiful to be unhappy. I'll set up your lunch on the porch so you can watch our boat as we head for the Cliff."

"That would be nice, but please don't stay long. I don't want to be left alone all afternoon."

Todd ignored his grandmother's forlorn expression and busied himself setting up her lunch on the deck. *Why am I fighting so hard to be with Elena when I know I should take it easy? But this is an afternoon too good to miss.* For the past two days he had done everything he knew to make his grandmother happy, and he wanted this time with Elena on the island.

He set a pair of binoculars beside her plate. "There, Grandma, you can watch everything we do on the island with these." He turned to her, flashed a handsome smile her direction, and bounded out the cottage door before she could protest further.

54

12

TODD, EXCITED AND FULL OF ANTICIPATION, followed Elena down the path through the woods toward the shore. Sunbeams broke through the tall spruce to dance on bits of mica in the granite chips along the path. He carried the oars and gas tank while Elena carried a picnic basket, chart, and compass in one hand and life jackets and seat cushions in the other.

When they reached the shore, Todd followed her directions on pulling the boat in and starting the motor. It started on his second try.

"Good job. We're on our way. You don't have to rev it up," she said. "I like going at a slow pace." Elena smiled in Todd's direction. "We can enjoy just being on the water."

Their eyes met and held each other's gaze.

As they headed for the island, cormorants, hovering close to the bay as if too heavy to rise above the water, flew by them. Herring gulls, in contrast, circled overhead, gliding high in the sky.

"If I had a choice," Elena said, "I'd choose to be a seagull rather than a cormorant. The gulls look like they have much more fun."

"Their grace suits you," Todd said. "I think I'd like to be a porpoise rolling through the waves and diving to the ocean floor."

Halfway to the island, Elena reached over and put her hand in the water. "It's even colder out here than it is in our cove. I jumped in once and swam from here to the Cliff."

"What made you do a thing like that?" Todd looked at her astonished.

"I was arguing with my family and wanted to be sure they knew I disapproved of their attitudes. It was a little dramatic, I admit, but I was at that stage in life." Elena shrugged. "Fourteen, I think. I made it to the island, but I was grounded for a week. My parents were furious and frightened at the same time. Mom never forgot that the mother of one of her friends had a heart attack after a sailing accident and died in these waters. I enjoyed all the commotion I caused at the time, but I've never been tempted to do it again."

"I can't imagine your being that obstinate." Todd wondered if he really knew this girl. So far he had seen a completely different Elena, but the memory of his own dark moods in his growing-up years helped him identify with her dramatic protest. "We're almost there." He changed the subject.

"Land on the sand beach. I'll get up in the bow to look for rocks. Push the throttle back and take her in slowly."

Elena guided him between the rocks by pointing in the direction she wanted him to go. "Cut the motor now," she called. "Let her glide in." The boat hit ground just short of the shore. Elena climbed into the bow, took the bowline, and jumped ashore missing the water by two inches. "It's almost slack tide, so it won't change much for a while. We can leave the boat and tour the island. I can't wait to show it to you. Let's eat later."

"Suits me."

They unloaded the boat and stuck the anchor deep in the sand at the top of the beach. "Here are our boxes for berry picking." Elena handed Todd three quart boxes made of green cardboard, took three for herself, and scampered up the steep rise to the raspberry fields. "Look," she said, pointing to the green bushes dotted with red. "There they are. The whole island is covered with them." She picked a handful of the plump, ripe berries and gave them to Todd. "Taste these. Have you ever eaten anything so good?"

Todd tasted and licked his lips. "They're even better than advertised."

"We'll pick for Mom and your grandmother after lunch. Come, I want you to see the whole island."

Elena dropped the boxes in the middle of the field and began running up the hillside. She ran through the bushes to the base of the rocks in the center of the island and started climbing to the top, pointing out blueberries nearly ready for harvest and blackberry plants covered with green berries not yet ripe. Climbing to the highest point, she raised her arms to the sky and exclaimed, "Isn't it wonderful?"

Todd slowly turned, marveling at the view in every direction: Goose Cove Lodge and its cluster of cottages, the graceful mounds of the Camden Hills, the large islands of Vinalhaven and North Haven, the scattered islands of the bay, and the concentration of islands off the coast of Stonington. "Everywhere you look, it's incredible. You haven't exaggerated at all."

A cool breeze on top of the island lifted Elena's hair like a slow-motion shampoo commercial. Todd thought she was more beautiful than the models in the ads. She was freshness itself. His heart beat faster as he watched this long-legged beauty bound from rock to rock on the heights of a beautiful island in Maine. Todd surprised himself by sharing her exuberance. The experience felt as exhilarating as the cold Maine water, without any of the discomfort of their swim.

As Todd watched her, Elena descended the summit and headed toward the bold edge of the island where tall granite cliffs caught breaking waves. She sat on the edge of the rocks and dangled her legs over their steep sides. Todd followed and dropped beside her. They watched the lobster buoys rise and fall with the waves, like decoys of ducks floating endlessly up and down but never coming to life. Every seventh wave sent spray flying in the air as it crashed into tall vertical ledges.

"Look," they called out in unison, pointing to two porpoises rolling in the surf.

"Aren't they fun to watch? They're smaller and browner than our Florida porpoises, but just as fascinating. They'll surface again. There they are." Elena pointed again several feet to the right. "That's our first sighting. They're the first I've seen this summer."

"And I bet they're not even cold. That's the way to enjoy the water."

They walked along the edge of the boulders and down a steep path to a sand beach close to their anchored boat. Wandering along the sandy shore holding Elena's hand, Todd ignored his reluctance to encourage their relationship, focusing instead on the beauty of the day and the wonder of their happy moments together.

"Tennis and rock climbing have given me a ravenous appetite," he said. "I'm starving."

"I'm ready for lunch. Where shall we have it?"

"Let's try up there." Todd pointed to the highest spot of the island where they had surveyed the view in every direction.

Elena nodded, picked up the water jug and cushions, and gave Todd the cooler.

When they reached the top, she sat down and handed Todd a sandwich. "Would you like to ask a blessing?"

"Sure." Todd reached for her hand and held it in both of his. "Thank You, Lord, for this incredible day, for creating such a perfect island and for providing a great lunch for us. Thank You for guiding me here. I ask You to help Grandma find You as her Lord before the month is over." He squeezed Elena's hand. "I hope you'll join me in that prayer until it happens. Grandma needs to know Jesus before she dies."

"Of course I will, Todd," she said, smiling at him.

Todd felt comforted that she would be praying with him.

She reached into the cooler and brought out cut carrots, pieces of celery, and dill pickles.

Todd bit into his sandwich. "Hey, this hits the spot."

"I didn't know what you liked, but almost everyone eats turkey sandwiches. Do you like dark bread? My family won't eat anything else."

"The sandwiches are great. I'm easy to please." Todd laughed. "I've been trying to give Grandma nutritional tips, but she says she's too old to change. She cooks the way she always has. She likes white bread and rolls and persists in putting sauces on her vegetables and gravies on her meats. When I give her a hand at cooking, it's plain, steamed vegetables and broiled fish or other meat. She seems to like them, but when she cooks, she wears herself out. You can't tell her anything. It's her way or else."

"You're very close to your grandmother, aren't you, Todd?"

"Yes, I never had a family like yours, Elena. I'm grateful to her for all she's done for me. I stayed with her for weeks at a time. She paid for much of my college education. I owe her a lot." A hint of melancholy returned to Todd's voice.

Elena handed him a second sandwich. "Do you have brothers and sisters, Todd? I've never heard you speak of them."

"I had a brother three years younger, but he overdosed on drugs. I always thought he committed suicide. He didn't know how to handle the harshness of our lives." His sadness deepened.

"The memories must be painful," Elena said.

"Yes, it was the two of us against the world. We agreed that as long as we had each other, we'd be okay, but Bobby started taking marijuana to help him forget what was going on at home. He hid it a long time, knowing I wouldn't approve, but once he tried cocaine, he became hopelessly hooked. I did everything I knew to help him, but I think he'd given up and didn't even want to try. When Dad went to prison, Bobby figured he was made of the same mold and he'd end up the same way."

"Oh, Todd." She clasped her chest with one hand and reached toward him with the other.

Todd stared at his half-eaten sandwich as Elena patted his arm, remembering the sad picture of his broken father, his shoulders hunched, his face dour and lifeless as the prison guard brought him to the visitor's booth.

"I left a good job in Baltimore to move back to Pittsburgh so I could be there when he's released in two months. I wanted to help him establish a new life. I visited him in prison just a week before we left for Maine and tried to get him to make plans, where we might live, what kind of work he would look for, but all he said was, "I don't care. You shouldn't have come. You shouldn't see me in this place."

"Didn't he thank you for trying to help him?"

"He didn't have anything nice to say to me. I hadn't seen him for three years."

Elena winced. Todd looked out to sea as he continued his story. "Bobby had little strength of his own, nothing to draw from. He couldn't believe in a God who had given him a home life that was hell. I tried to be his strength, but I didn't succeed. I think he came to see himself as a burden to everyone, including me, and thought the best thing he could do was end it.

"I found a letter Bobby had written to me. It wasn't a suicide note, but I think it was on his mind when he wrote it. He told me I was the only person he loved. He was sorry he hadn't turned out the way I wanted him to, and I shouldn't feel responsible for his failure. He said he knew I would do something worthwhile with my life and break out of the mold for both of us."

He broke away from the grip of his memories and looked back at the sandwich in his hands. "Sorry to bring such gloom into our perfect afternoon, Elena."

Lifting his gaze, he noted with surprise that her eyes brimmed with tears. Two spilled over and ran down her cheeks. "Look at that," he said. "I've made you as sad as I am. Forgive me for spoiling our day."

"It isn't spoiled, Todd. I knew you were troubled. I've seen it in your eyes. I'm grateful you feel comfortable enough to share it with me. It's such a heavy burden to bear alone. Do you ever discuss it with your grandmother?"

"No, I don't like to remind her. She feels guilty enough about the way she spoiled my mother. She was her only child." The mention of his mother made Todd's insides constrict. *Where is she now?*

Turning back to Elena, he searched her glistening and sympathetic eyes, hoping his revelation had not lowered her respect for him. "Have you changed your opinion of me, Elena?"

"Todd, your father's problems are no reflection of who you are. You're strong and compassionate, with more depth than most men. You're not responsible for who your father is, only who you are."

"That's what I like about you, Elena. You don't play guessing games. You let a guy know exactly where he stands." His expression softened. "Thank you for being so understanding. I appreciate that."

The knot in his stomach relaxed. *Maybe my luck is changing.*

She smiled at him. "I wish I could give you happy memories to replace the sad ones that haunt you." She handed him an oatmeal chocolate chip cookie.

He took a large bite. "Ummm. These are great. Did you make them?"

"No, I bought them at Twisted Tree. We hardly ever eat sweets at home anymore, but up here we allow some of our old favorites. What's a summer in Maine without chocolate chip cookies, s'mores, and raspberry and blueberry pie?" She got up and started gathering the remains of their lunch. "Speaking of raspberry pies, let's do some berry picking before we leave."

"Leave?" Todd questioned. "Could any other island be any better? Why not spend the whole afternoon here?"

"If you want to. My brothers are always restless once they've gone around the shore of an island and want to move on to find new treasures."

"My treasure is with me here. I don't have to move on to find her." Todd was smiling now. Having successfully passed through the ordeal of telling Elena his father was in prison, he would enter into her fun. The reason his father was there could wait for another time.

*

They descended the hill and checked on the boat. "It's time for some serious berry picking," Elena announced as she bolted toward the berry fields. "The last one to find our boxes is a rotten egg."

Elena mystified Todd when she broke out of her usual mold and became spontaneous and child-like. Startled by it at first, Todd decided he liked her spontaneity. It was infectious and helped to break his more somber moods.

"There they are," she called again, pointing to the middle of the field.

Todd saw where she pointed and raced her to the spot. They arrived at the same time. Todd dove as if sliding into home plate and catching a grounder all at once. He picked up the stack of boxes, rolled over, and held them up in the air.

"You're the rotten egg," he cried out.

"Todd, that wasn't fair. I saw them first."

Elena descended on him and tickled him like she did her brothers when she tried to wake them in the morning. Laughing, Todd struggled to get away from her tickling fingers and rolled into a clump of raspberry bushes.

"Help, truce, truce. Okay, you won. Oh help, I'm wounded," he complained, still laughing even though he felt blood oozing from the scratches on his cheeks.

"Oh, Todd, you're hurt. Forgive me."

"It's okay. Don't look so serious. I'll live. I haven't laughed this hard in years."

"Talk about acting like a couple of children. The last time I was here, I sulked most of the time."

"How could you in a place like this?" Todd found that hard to believe.

"When you have two sprained ankles, no place is fun."

"True enough, but it could happen in worse places. Shall we tackle the berries now?" He picked up a quart box and swiped the blood from his face. "Does someone cultivate these for their own use?"

"No one has planted them and no one cultivates them. The seeds are dropped by the birds. Plants come up year after year and multiply until they cover the open spaces."

Todd watched Elena shed her long-sleeved outer shirt. "It's like the Garden of Eden must have been. No man worked the soil. God provided everything man needed."

"It's a great thought, Elena." Todd pondered what she had said. *Had the Lord indeed created places to remind them of the life He had planned for them to live?*

They picked in silence, moving in opposite directions, each enjoying their private thoughts. Todd had never experienced anything like this before. His parents' lives centered on parties and city activities. He could remember only a few walks in the park before life with his parents became so chaotic. He felt he was experiencing the joys of the childhood he had never known. Savoring a berry for himself now and then, he thought he had never tasted anything so good. He might not have any answers yet on how to rehabilitate his father, but at this moment he felt more optimistic than he could remember.

"Come over here, Todd," Elena called to him. "They're absolutely huge and more than you can imagine."

They picked on, helping themselves to a plump, ripe berry in between, until Elena declared, "That's enough." She sat in a grassy spot and lined up the boxes.

Todd lay back in the grass.

"I hope to start coming every year again," Elena said. "I thought I might bring a group from college after graduation next year."

"Sounds like an ideal graduation trip to me. An ideal place for a honeymoon, too," he added.

"You're right." Elena sank into the grass beside him. "Stephanie and her husband honeymooned in our cabin two years ago. We often rent it to honeymooners in June. I guess the rest of us expect to honeymoon here, but it depends on our spouses. People either love it or hate it."

"I can't imagine anyone hating it."

"Sometimes that happens when it rains for two weeks the first time people come. It's hard to erase the dreary memory. But you've had a perfect introduction," Elena said, turning her head to look at Todd.

"Couldn't get any better than this." He smiled at her and reached for her hand. She looked away from him and studied the sky.

"What do you see up there in the clouds?"

"A little dog barking and jumping at the heels of his master. And over there, a lion crouching. I see a profile of an old woman and up there is a beautiful young woman with long flowing hair like yours, Elena."

"My professor said intelligent people see action like animals moving. It's even better to see human figures. You pass the test, Todd."

"Glad to hear that." Todd pretended to be relieved. "And I'm glad I didn't know I was taking a test." It hadn't felt like one. More relaxed than he had been in years, he could sense tensions draining from his body.

"Did you ever lie back like this and watch the clouds when you were growing up?"

"No, we lived in the city and I never had access to open fields like this."

"You missed something good."

"I missed a lot of things."

"There's so much I want to show you." Her intensity startled him.

He jumped up. "Do you think we should be checking on the boat?"

"Yes, that's a good idea," she said, "though I hate to leave. I feel I could be lazy and enjoy this forever."

"It does have a timeless quality, but you've taught me to keep the boat out of trouble and we want to keep it in good order so we can do this again."

He reached out his hand and pulled her up. "It was a perfect afternoon, Elena. Thank you." He gave her a long hug, trying to express his appreciation for the laughter, her understanding, her empathy, and the joy of the day.

13

THE NEXT MORNING ELENA LAY IN BED reliving the joys of yesterday. She had been thrilled when Todd asked her to partner with him in the Club Championships. Not only would the tournament be fun, he had made a second commitment to spend time with her. She liked his being the stronger player. Her steadiness and his strength would make a great combination.

She had anticipated sharing the joys of the Cliff with Todd since the day they met. Not only had the day lived up to her expectations, it far surpassed them. She remembered how strong he looked steering the motor, his thick brown hair blowing in the wind, a perfect picture of young masculinity.

She wanted to know more about this man who seemed so composed at first meeting but who had secrets to hide. She suspected he had much more to tell her. She remembered the feel of his hand, soft and strong and hard and tender all at once. He had called her his treasure. She had wanted to tell him that he passed every test she could think of. It had been so good she would not entertain thoughts of it not lasting.

*

Friday morning arrived with the good weather unbroken. Still savoring waffles with Maine maple syrup, the Richards children pulled on high rubber boots. Mike and Doug collected the clam rollers and forks, Elena phoned Todd, and the three set off to dig their dinner.

Susan watched them go, happy to see the children working on a project together. Surveying the dirty dishes, she decided to tidy the kitchen before attacking the raspberry pies.

Harold set out for the wharf to buy lobsters.

*

First to arrive on the floor of the emptied cove, Doug located a large hole, placed his fork carefully behind it, pushed the prongs straight down, and lifted a fork full of gritty mud. Plunging his hand into the midst of it, he pulled out a large clam. "You're going to be mine, all mine tonight," he declared ecstatically to the clam. Heaving it into the empty clam roller, he announced with great pride, "I got the first one."

"You've got the first," Mike said, "but I'll dig more."

"Hey, guys, we have only two forks. Why don't you two work together with one, and Todd and I will use the other?" The two boys eyed her without moving. "Okay, Doug, let me have yours. You can share Mike's."

"I wish we had one for each of us." Doug handed his to Elena.

"You can always dig deeper with your hands. That way you won't break as many," she said, ignoring Doug's disappointment. "In a few minutes we'll all be glad to take turns."

*

Seeing Todd stride toward her, anticipation written all over his handsome face, she burst into a radiant smile and greeted him with customary enthusiasm. "Hi, Todd. It's just the kind of day we hoped for."

He grinned back at her. The fact that they had conspired together to pull off an authentic Maine clam bake made its accomplishment an intimate affair of enormous significance.

"Hey, you two, quit gawking at each other and get to work. The tide won't stay out forever," Doug called to them.

Todd followed Elena's instructions on the proper way to harvest clams. "I've got the picture now," Todd said.

"You found a good hole," she encouraged him as they both reached in and fished around for more.

Todd clasped one of Elena's fingers and pretended to pull it slowly out of the hole. Hey, I've got a big one. I think it's trying to get away from me."

"You don't believe they dig down. Wait 'til you get a big one. You'll feel it fight as you pull it up," Elena responded, laughing.

Doug hauled over his roller and set it next to theirs. "We've got twice as many as you do, Sis. What's the matter?"

"Todd is just learning, and you two are old hands. You're doing great, Doug. Keep it up, and we'll have dinner in no time."

"Now that you know how, Todd, you better catch up to us, or we'll be here all day." Doug acted superior.

"That wouldn't be so bad," Todd said, not rising to the challenge. "It's a beautiful morning, and this is fun."

"You think anything's fun with Elena around," Doug teased.

"You're not far wrong, Doug."

*

Todd continued to dig one hole after another. Having spent most of his winters and summers in a big city, he enjoyed learning the new skill. Elena's enthusiasm drew forth an optimism he could hardly recognize as his. He glanced at her as he plunged the fork into the sand again and enjoyed the way the sunlight danced on her hair. Such unaccustomed joy flooded him, he felt guilty to be having so much fun when he was supposed to be seeking solutions to his problems.

And what about his resolution to stop this relationship before it began? A momentary cloud passed over his happiness, but he decided to ignore that nagging inner voice once more.

When they had accumulated two rollers full, Mike called out, "Anyone for stopping?"

"Yes, Mike, I am. Oh, my poor back," Elena said as she straightened up, "and my hands are cut to shreds." She inspected her fingers. Her nails were full of sand and her fingertips tender, covered with cuts from hitting rocks while digging in the sand. "Some people wear gloves, but I can't imagine how they feel the clams that way. I have trouble enough telling the clams from the stones when I can't see them."

"Let's show Todd how we clean them," Doug said as he and Mike headed for deeper water. Mike jumped onto a large flat rock surrounded by salt water and started dunking his roller up and down, then rolling it back and forth. A steady flow of dirt and sand floated out through the open slats of the roller.

"That's the way we wash them for starters," Elena said. "I always enjoy this part the most because the hard work is behind us, and it's fun to be out here in the middle of the cove."

When they were done, they put the clams into orange bags with holes big enough to let the water in but small enough to retain the clams. Mike led them to the mooring and pulled in the boat. After they had tied the bags to the bowline and put them overboard, Mike pulled the boat out again.

"Hey, how do you know that will hold? What if we lose them all?" Todd asked.

"We never have," Elena said, "but I guess there's always a first time."

"Just don't let it be this time," Doug pleaded.

*

Friday afternoon Susan busied herself in the kitchen making a large salad. Harold worked under the cabin shoring up insulation pulled out by the squirrels. When Todd returned from having lunch with his grandmother, he found Priscilla and Dean Crowley already supervising the construction of the pit for the clam bake.

They had selected a spot above the high tide mark and dug a large hole in the sand, which they filled with rocks two or three deep. On top of the rocks they built a fire with slow-burning hardwood they had brought with them. The hardwood came from deciduous trees, mostly poplar and birch. The fast-burning spruce and fir worked well in the fireplace, but they burned so fast, they needed constant replacements.

Dean Crowley directed the boys each step of the way. Seeing he had everything under control, Elena felt her time would be better spent straightening up the guest cabin for the party. Leaving the boys following Dean's directions, she returned to her cabin, made her bed, and put everything in its proper place. Elena surveyed her straightened room with satisfaction. *My room looks great. I'll surprise the boys and do the same to theirs.*

Opening the door to the boys' room, she picked up stray clothes from the floor. As she made Doug's bed, she noticed a magazine stuck between the mattress and the springs. She gave it a pull and gasped involuntarily as she saw the title: *Playboy.* After paging through it, she called to Doug on the beach, "Doug, will you please come here?"

When Doug arrived, Elena held out the magazine. "I was making your bed in preparation for the party and found this. Where did you get it, and why have you kept it?"

"A friend gave it to me," he said, looking at his feet.

"What friend?"

"Just a friend. It doesn't matter. Give it to me."

"No, I'm not going to give it to you. I'm going to destroy it. I bet Harvey gave it to you." Elena studied Doug to assess his reaction.

"No, he didn't. Give it to me. I have to give it back." He reached out and tried to take it from her, but she refused to let go.

"I guessed right, didn't I, Doug? It was Harvey or one of his friends, the boys you were with on the golf course Wednesday. They came over in the afternoon, didn't they?"

"There's nothing wrong with it, and it's none of your business." Doug denied everything.

"Doug, it's a wrong concept of sex. It will spoil everything for you, believe me."

"All the guys look at it."

"Does Mike know about it?"

"No, it's mine."

"Did Harvey take it from a store like he took those candy bars from Jamie?" By the look on Doug's face, Elena knew she was close to the truth. "It's yours, but you have to give it back?"

"That's right," he said, sitting on the edge of the bed and hanging his head.

"Doug, I don't want anything but what's best for you. You believe that, don't you?"

"I guess so." He stared at the floor.

"I can't believe this is happening." Elena threw her hands in the air. "I don't know what to do. I don't want to spoil the party for Mom and Dad, but they ought to know."

"Please don't tell them, Sis. They wouldn't understand."

"They probably understand better than you do, Doug. I won't tell Mom and Dad if you promise you'll never look at one again."

"Okay, I promise. Give it to me now so I can return it."

"No, Doug, I won't, and if you persist in wanting it back, I will tell Dad."

"It's no big deal. Just forget it." Doug stormed out the door.

She peered through the window as he ran into the woods, looking over his shoulder to see if Elena was following him. She continued cleaning the room, taking out her frustrations on the furniture.

When her parents walked by the cabin heading for the beach, she watched them through the window. As soon as they reached the beach, she hustled to the main cabin, tore the magazine to shreds, and stuffed it into the fireplace. Hurriedly reaching for the matches, she spilled them all over the floor. "Oh, no. What if Mom and Dad come back now and catch me at this. What will I tell them? I gave Doug my word."

She lit the fire and picked up the fallen matches as the flames ignited. The magazine burned quickly, except where she had left too many pages together. Lighting another match, she addressed the fire. "Come on, flames, hurry and make it disappear." She then cried out to God. "Help me know how to handle this. Help Doug understand how harmful this material is. Don't let it ruin his view of women."

As the fire consumed the last traces of the magazine, she peeked out the window and saw her parents still absorbed in the preparations. "At least it won't spoil their evening," she said, exhaling much of the tension that had mounted inside her.

*

"Hi," Elena said as she rejoined her family and friends on the beach. "How's it coming?" Doug busied himself as far away from Elena as possible.

Mike spoke with rising excitement. "You missed the whole thing, Sis. After the coals got hot, we raked them over the stones and put a layer of rockweed on top, then burlap bags over the seaweed. Dean dumped the raw clams on one side and the lobsters on the other. We helped him spread the clams, add the ears of corn and put another layer of burlap on top, with a whole lot more rockweed to hold in the heat. Dean really knows what he's doing. He said the steam comes up through the food layers and steams and smokes them, giving them a special flavor. I can't wait to taste them."

"I hope you'll think I'm an expert after you've eaten the meal," Dean said. "I haven't done this in a long time, but everything should be done in an hour."

Elena climbed up the rocks and walked toward the point. She still felt shaky and needed time to recapture her composure.

Todd came up behind her. "What's wrong, Elena? Your enthusiasm for the clam bake seems to have vanished."

"Nothing's wrong," she lied. "I'm very interested in how it's done. What happened to the potatoes?" Earlier in the day she and Todd had cut them in half and wrapped them in foil.

"They went on the fire first. They take about ten minutes more time to cook through than the other things. Elena, I've never heard your voice so subdued. You're not your usual cheerful self."

"Sorry, I'll perk up, I promise."

"Want to tell me about it?"

"No," she snapped.

He winced as if she had dealt him a blow. "Then I'm off. I'm going home to bring Grandma over. I'll see you shortly."

"Okay." She turned away from him and faced the sea, enjoying the breeze that blew across the point. She hoped it would clear her muddled head. It was not like her to cover up a problem. She liked things out in the open, liked to meet a situation head on. Hiding it made her uncomfortable. It was too much like lying. *Was it right to deceive her parents?* At any rate, this wasn't the time to tell them. Of that she was certain.

14

"LET ME GIVE YOU A HAND WITH THAT," Elena said as she returned to the party and found her mother beginning to toss the salad. "Mom, you've done enough already. You're not supposed to do any more."

"I can't just watch," Susan said.

"Why don't you and Dad take a walk on the rocks? You always say you never do enough of that."

"You're right. Dear, would you like to accompany me?"

"If it means I can escape all this preparation, of course."

"It would have been nicer if you had said you would love to have the pleasure of my company," Susan said, taking his arm.

"I wouldn't want it to go to your head." He kissed her on the cheek. "Whose company have I ever preferred?"

Elena watched them disappear over the rocks, both clad in jeans, holding hands like young lovers. In an effort to recapture her enthusiasm, she tried to make light conversation. "You should enjoy this meal, Mike. It's all your favorite foods: clams, lobsters, corn on the cob, potatoes, and salad."

"You bet. I thought you planned it just for me. Doug, what's taking you so long by that fire? It's going great. We could use your help over here."

"I'm keeping the fire going for Dad and making sure the butter doesn't burn."

"Get real, Doug. We don't need the butter yet. You trying to get out of work?"

Doug set the pot of butter in the sand and shuffled over to Mike, his eyes still concentrating on the ground.

"What's wrong with you anyway?" Mike prodded. "You look like you lost your best friend. This is a party." Evidently even Mike, who was not overly sensitive, felt the chill in the air.

Doug lifted his eyes and looked toward Elena. She smiled. "It's going to be a great party, Doug, and who knows when we'll do it again? Let's enjoy it." Encouraging Doug to cheer up made her feel better and enabled her to join in the fun. Doug nodded his appreciation and helped his brother add wood to the fire under the clams and lobsters.

Harold and Susan returned in time to see Todd escorting Mrs. Faraway down the path to the beach. "Now that's beginning to smell good." Harold sniffed the air. "Nothing like a good meal after having a stroll along the bay with your sweetheart."

"Looks like I wasn't missed at all." Susan surveyed the preparations.

"You and Dad can join Mrs. Faraway at the table as the guests of honor, and the rest of us will eat on the rocks."

"We're so glad you could come, Mrs. Faraway. Isn't it a perfect evening?"

"Please call me Amanda, and may I call you Susan?" Amanda took Susan's extended hand in both of hers. "I'm so pleased to be included. I've been keeping my fingers crossed all week that the weather would hold. This is lovely."

"The young people have worked hard to give us an authentic Maine clam bake. Come and meet the couple who are supervising the project, Amanda. This is Dean and Priscilla Crowley, young friends from church who offered to show us how to do it. Dean and Priscilla, this is Mrs. Faraway, Todd's grandmother. She summered in Sunshine as a child and has come back to relive some happy memories. Isn't that correct, Amanda?"

"Yes, it's something I've wanted to do for years."

"It's very nice to meet you, Mrs. Faraway," Priscilla said. "May I bring you a glass of cranberry-grape juice, or would you prefer sparkling cider?"

"Cranberry-grape juice sounds perfect, my dear."

Elena helped Priscilla serve beverages to everyone. "Would you like to try these crackers with fresh crabmeat, Mrs. Faraway?" Elena asked. "We think they're special."

"I'm sure they are. I always did like the crab meat up here."

They settled into chairs on the beach marveling at the calm sea and warm air just an hour before sundown.

Dean pulled out a clam and an ear of corn with his tongs and checked to see if they were cooked through. He pulled out a lobster and tugged at its feeler, which came out easily. "Seems like they're ready," he announced as he peeled back the top layer of burlap and rockweed. "Elena, Priscilla, bring on the plates. Doug, now you can pour that butter."

"I'll help, too." Todd jumped up and moved toward Elena. "It's good to see you smiling again. I thought I'd done something terrible."

"It wasn't you, Todd," Elena looked at him in alarm. "It had nothing to do with us." Their eyes met and held each other's as the word *us* hung in the air.

Doug approached with the pan of melted butter.

"I'll tell you sometime when we're alone." She returned to setting out dishes, feeling that their moments of separation had brought them closer together.

Mike tugged a clam from its shell, peeled off the rough covering on its long neck, dipped it into his cup of melted butter, and savored its delicious flavor. "Wow. These do have a special taste. Great job, Dean."

"Glad you like them." Dean smiled and bowed his head. "I go clamming most every day this time of year. I get real tired of seeing clams, but, I agree, these are some good."

Doug popped one into his mouth. "How many bushels can you dig a day, Dean?"

"Most days now, 'bout one and a half," he said. "When things are goin' good, we dig a bushel an hour. But with clams so scarce these days, we do good to get a bushel and a half total. Just a few years ago, we got two to six bushels a day. 'Course, you can only clam the three hours the tide is low."

"What's the most you ever got at one time, Dean?"

"It was a time we were up to Swan's Island. We found a cove that'd never been dug before. They were the biggest clams we ever saw. Me and Priscilla gathered them as fast as our fingers could move and we got fourteen bushels that day. We camped there overnight to get another crack at it. That was our all-time record."

"It was very exciting, and the weather was perfect," Priscilla added.

Dean rose to dish out seconds on clams.

*

When the corn cobs and lobster shells were empty and the guests were refusing everything she passed, Elena sent Doug and Mike to bring down the pies and began clearing the plates. "Bring another flashlight while you're at it," Elena called after them. "And grab some bug spray just in case."

Elena cut the pies and served a good-sized portion to everyone. "Todd helped me pick the raspberries, Mrs. Faraway."

"I know, dear. He's never stopped talking about how wonderful your day on the Cliff was. I can't wait to taste Susan's raspberry pie."

The boys followed Elena with cups of hot tea or coffee. "Here's tea just the way you like it, Mom." Doug handed her a steaming mug.

"I can't get used to being served by the boys. I hope this is starting a precedent."

"We hope you enjoy it tonight, Mom, but don't get any ideas about its being permanent," Mike said.

Harold finished his pie and put down his fork. "Susan, that was even better than Mother used to make." In response to his compliment, Susan's blue eyes lit up like the sky responding to the breakthrough of the sun. "Mom was a great cook. I can still see her standing over the grill cooking a pound of bacon, then frying flounder. We gobbled up the bacon as fast as she took it from the pan. No one worried about fat and cholesterol in those days. Do you remember how easy it was to catch flounder years ago, Amanda?"

"Yes," she said, "any time you wanted fish, they were eager to bite your hook."

"That's right. Mom always liked to tell how she put the iron skillet on the kerosene stove, took the bacon from the ice box, and told Dad to go down to the rocks to catch the fish. He always came back in fifteen or twenty minutes with the fish cleaned and ready for the pan."

"Do you remember when the ice box was a piece of ice in a wooden box, Harold?" Amanda asked.

"Yes, when I was a young boy, Mr. Williams delivered ice every other day, and we kept it in a box behind the cabin with a tarp over it."

"I loved the days of kerosene lamps and carrying buckets of water from the well. It's a way of life these children can't even fathom with all the electrical gadgets we have now." Amanda became philosophical.

Doug broke in. "We're so backward up here, we don't even have a TV."

"We wanted the children to know what it was like to read and entertain themselves," Susan said.

"I never think of watching it here or renting a video. There's so much else to do," Mike agreed.

"Hey, guys, it's time to make s'mores." Elena reached for the chocolate.

"So soon after that wonderful meal?" Susan said.

"Yeah, I'm ready now, and the coals are just right." Doug was all for it.

"I guess I can't disappoint you after all the work you've done, but I can't imagine wanting to eat more now." Susan laughed and hugged her stomach.

Elated, Doug rushed to the fire and loaded his fork. Toasting two marshmallows to a golden brown, he placed them between two pieces of Hershey chocolate, surrounded them with graham crackers and stuffed them into his mouth before the chocolate had a chance to melt.

"That even tops raspberry pie." Total contentment spread over his face. "Can I make one for anyone else?"

He had no takers. "Only a twelve-year-old could be hungry after a meal like that," Mike quipped with feigned superiority.

The young people each took a load of plates and glasses to the cabin. When Susan started to help, they objected.

"Remember, you're queen for a day," Doug said. "Here I'll take those."

"You've made me feel like one, Doug." Susan gave her son a grateful smile.

Satisfied that her encounter with Doug had not spoiled their evening, Elena still wondered if she should tell her parents.

*

The family cleaned up the picnic in time to watch the sun's dramatic descent over Blakely Point. Soft wisps of pink appeared above the setting sun and grew steadily brighter. Soon orange blended with pinks and purples. As it touched the tops of the trees on Blakely Point, the sun became a red ball in the sky. When it slid from sight, the entire peninsula became outlined in brilliant red.

Soon the reflection in the water turned the bay crimson. In between the sky and the water, the trees on Blakely Point turned black. Dark clouds rolled in to clothe the upper sky in blackness, alternating layers of brilliant red and contrasting black. Black sky, red sky, black trees, red water, black shore. Todd thought he had never seen anything so dramatic.

"If I had seen it in a painting, I would have said it was contrived, a figment of a disturbed imagination," Amanda said.

The whole family watched spellbound as if it were a scene from science fiction. When the red glow behind Blakely Point began to fade, they gathered around the fire. Harold added a log to the dying coals and began humming "I've Been Working on the Railroad." They all joined in.

"Row, Row, Row Your Boat" followed, then "The Bear Came Over The Mountain" and "Kookaburra Sits On The Old Gum Tree." When they had exhausted the rounds, they turned to songs from the twenties like "Bye, Bye, Blackbird," "Chinese Honeymoon," "Harbor Lights," and old favorites from the thirties and forties, timeless songs sung across generations.

Most of the songs were foreign to Todd. He had spent little time singing as a child. The few campfires he had experienced at college had ended in rowdy drinking songs. Tonight's simple but happy singing, the sense of belonging to a family whose members enjoyed each other's company, was a new experience for him. This week had been full of tantalizing experiences, bringing new pleasures of participation as well as wrenching recognition of all he had missed.

"I thought no one ever sang those songs anymore. I never hear them on the radio." His grandmother broke into his thoughts.

"They aren't part of the popular culture today, Mrs. Faraway, but they still make great campfire songs. We enjoy them as much as Mom and Dad. You know, I think I could enjoy a s'more now." Elena jumped up. "How 'bout it, boys?"

"We're game," they said together.

"May I make one for you, Mrs. Faraway?"

"Yes, my dear, you may. It's been such a perfect evening I don't want to miss any part of it."

"It *has* been a perfect evening," Todd agreed. "Both Grandma and I want to thank you all for a memory we'll take home and cherish for a long time."

Todd smiled at Elena across the firelight. The evening had been every bit as good as their expectations.

15

ELENA AWOKE MIDMORNING, dressed hurriedly, and ran to the main cabin, where she found Harold painting the porch furniture. Inside Susan had cleared the breakfast dishes and set out writing paper and a stack of mail.

"Hi, Mom. Where are the boys?"

"The mackerel are running. Mike has gone fishing with his friend at the wharf in Stonington. Doug's gone to Jamie's with a fishing pole, hoping to find Harvey. They catch mackerel there, too."

Elena gasped at the news.

"What's wrong?" Susan asked.

"Oh, nothing." Elena still didn't want to alarm her mother.

"Todd has already called. He said Amanda is still raving about how lovely the party was and suggested that the two of you go out in the boat. She wants to stay in bed all morning."

Elena, needing no further encouragement, dialed his number. "Good morning, Todd. I heard your grandmother thinks we should take advantage of the beautiful day."

"Sounds great to me. Be there in ten minutes," he said.

*

"There it is," Elena called to Todd as she sighted Sheep Island. "It's one of my favorites."

The island rose majestically out of the sea, like a great fish hurling itself above the water. Open fields above a coarse sand beach swept upward in both directions like the crescent formed by the raised head and tail of a seal. The unique heights in the center of the island invited exploration.

"I think we can slide in there between those two rocks." Elena pointed to the middle of the beach. Todd cut the motor and the boat glided into shore.

"I'm getting better at that," Todd said.

"You do a great job." Elena jumped over the bow as it scraped the first rock. After Todd secured the boat, she led him up a small hill to the top of a pasture. "This is one spot we often picnic. You can see the view on both sides of the island."

She directed Todd's attention to the picturesque town of Stonington, which hugged a hill overlooking the bay. Houses, stacked one on top of the other, had small yards, but each had a magnificent view of the harbor. Known as the perfect example of a quiet but vibrant fishing village on the Maine coast, its myriad moored schooners, yachts, workboats, and small craft dotted the surface of the water.

"We can leave our lunch here in the shade and go exploring," Elena said as she took off running across the crescent-shaped field.

Halfway up on the other side, Todd caught up with her. As she slowed and extended her hand to him, he swept her into his arms and whirled her around and around. They fell in the tall grass, laughing, their heads reeling, not just from dizziness, but from the intoxication of the moment.

"It's hard to be unhappy in a place like this." He flashed a warm smile in her direction, but he seemed to be looking beyond her, sadness again in his gaze.

"What did you study in college, Todd? Do you have a plan for your life?"

"I haven't planned anything beyond getting my father rehabilitated, and I have no idea how to do that. I think about it every day, but so much depends on what he's willing to do, I can't make any progress. I thought it might become clear to me if I traveled far enough away from it, but nothing brilliant has struck me. I think I'll just have to gut it out."

"What's your father like? Is he anything like you?"

"I hope not." Todd shook his head. "He's a broken man. He used to be the life of the party and a good businessman, but he started making shady deals to cover the debt he'd piled up. He's very hard to talk to now, sullen and silent most of the time, kind of vacant, like he isn't really there. I don't know what he'll do when he's released. I feel his first weeks out are crucial. He acts like he has nothing to live for now, but I'm hoping to interest him in some kind of life."

"Sounds hard. But once you get your father settled, what do you want to do?"

"I always wanted to be an architect, design homes, modern buildings, bridges. I particularly like bridges."

"We'll have to tour the bridges in Acadia National Park some day. They're famous for their structure and beauty. I bet you'd be a good designer."

"It's too late for that now," Todd said, weariness in his voice. "It required too many extra years of college. I took business administration so I could get through as fast as possible. Now I wish I had taken Computer Science. I learned a lot about computers working as a Dean's Research Assistant in college. After I graduated, I had a great job with a computer firm in Baltimore. I had to give it up to go back to Pittsburgh to help Dad. Grandma offered to have me live with her while I get Dad settled, but I think I'll have to find an apartment for the two of us. She couldn't stand having him in her home, and I've saved enough to get us started. I'll look for a job in Pittsburgh as soon as I get home. Grandma talked me into stopping a month early so I could bring her here."

"So I have your father to thank for that. I'm beginning to like him already."

*

Her remark took Todd by surprise. That Elena could like something about his father had never occurred to him. He wondered if she would have made a comment like that if he had told her his father's whole story. He knew she wasn't ready for that.

She stood. "It's time to explore the shore of the island."

"I'm ready." Looking up at her long frame outlined against the clear blue sky, he thought she resembled a Nordic warrior woman anticipating a conquest.

*

"Let's climb the high hill," Elena said when they finished circling the island. "I'm as eager to see it again as I am to show it to you."

They set off, hand in hand. Passing blueberry bushes ripe with fruit and occasional raspberry bushes struggling to produce, they stopped to pick and eat.

As they climbed, they enjoyed the breeze, the hot sun, the freshness in the air. Remembering how sad and broken she had felt only two months ago, Elena marveled at how fast her life had changed. What had she done to deserve such happiness? Nothing, of course. She was enjoying God's unmerited favor. She hoped Todd felt blessed to be here, too.

When they reached the steep and narrow trails leading to the top of the hill, Elena called back to Todd, "The sheep have made these paths. They make climbing easier."

Todd chased Elena up one of the sheep paths, around occasional rocks and beds of fern. When they reached the top, he put his arm around her back, and they turned as one to enjoy the view in every direction. The panorama on the ocean side was breathtaking: beautiful green-colored islands and bright blue water for as far as they could see. The islands were thicker here close to the town, gradually opening to vast stretches of water that led to the bay and out to the Atlantic Ocean.

Elena started clicking her camera. "Todd, would you stand over there so I can get you in the foreground?" She clicked again.

"Let me take a picture of the view with you in it, Elena. It will make a great memory."

As Elena posed on the hillside facing into the breeze, her hair lifted and trailed away from her face. "You'll be happy with this one. For the service of taking it, I'll expect a copy. Something to reminisce over on cold, snowy nights."

Leaving Todd searching the view through the camera lens, she walked to the highest point of the hill, which was covered by woods. "Let's look in the woods for the sheep," she called to him. "We often find them there."

He caught up with her, and together they entered the woodland of tall spruce, granite outcroppings, and inviting paths made by wandering sheep. Perched one on top of the other in casual disarray, large pieces of hewn granite, decorated with patches of bright green mosses, formed a pool where the sheep could drink.

"Can't you see Esther Williams poised on a high rock, about to spring into an elegant swan dive and disappear into a pool of bottomless depth?"

The sun sparkled through the trees, brightening a world totally different from the shore, but equally beautiful.

She stopped and pointed. "Look, over there...one of the sheep."

They stood still as a string of sheep passed right in front of them, following their leader.

Sensing adventure, Elena whispered, "Let's follow them."

The sheep picked up their pace and began trotting as Elena and Todd stalked them. Stampeding down the far side of the hill, they slowed to a trot along the shore path and back up the hill through the woods, breaking into a gallop across a field of tall grasses.

By now Elena and Todd were running at full speed and laughing all the way. As they reached the open meadows on the top of the hill where they had started, the sheep turned sharply and descended the steep hillside toward the beach.

Out of breath and exhausted, Elena collapsed on the grass. "I'd make a terrible mountain goat. I can't even keep up with wool-laden sheep."

"But you make a great tour guide and an even better companion for a fantastic picnic." Todd, having joined in her fun, appeared to have forgotten his problems. His smile matched hers.

*

He gazed into her eyes, feeling more alive than he ever had before. The voice inside him that said he was proceeding too fast dimmed and became easier to ignore.

Todd settled down beside her. They both lay back in the grass and watched billowing white clouds drift and change forms in the blue sky.

"Our day on the Cliff was an experience I'll never forget," Todd said. "It was like the childhood I never had. It's been wonderful to spend this time with you and your family, Elena. Do you have any idea how fortunate you are to have all this and a family who loves you and wants you to be happy? I've noticed that your mother lights up when she sees you having a good time. She seems to receive more pleasure from your happiness than she does her own."

"Mom is always happy. She sings when she's alone. I used to kid her about it, because she sings off key. She just said, 'The Lord appreciates a joyful noise, not one that is perfectly tuned.'" She turned her face toward Todd. "What was your mother like, Todd?"

"Nothing like yours," he said. "Pretty like your mother, but nothing like her. Your mother is natural and down to earth. My mother attended the best schools. Grandma always told her she was something special. She had a heart condition as a child and the doctors said she wouldn't live to adulthood, so my grandparents gave her everything she wanted. She grew up thinking material things would make her happy. She always pushed my father to make more money. Dad was a successful businessman for a time, but their lives were chaotic. They drank far too much." He stopped talking and looked away from her. Then he faced her abruptly, eager to know how she had received his confession.

Elena looked sympathetic and concerned, not as startled as he had imagined. Relieved, he continued, "I spent most of my childhood covering up for them. Their raging fights when they were drunk, their three-day mads when they wouldn't speak to each other, and their threats of separation and divorce kept me in a constant state of turmoil. They always said it would be the last time, but it only grew worse. I remember my childhood as an endless stream of broken promises."

"Todd, how tragic." Elena's eyebrows slanted in sympathy and she lay her hand on his shoulder, stroking his arm as if to wipe away the pain.

"I guess my parents loved me in their selfish ways," Todd continued. "They sometimes said they were proud of me when they were sober. Mother bragged to her friends about my looks, and Dad appreciated my academic achievement. I worked hard in school, because it was the one area of my life I could control.

"We had what we needed materially, but Grandma was my only emotional support. She didn't drink at all and had little compassion for my father. She never approved of him even though he was from 'a good family.'

"Mom and Dad never did anything but disappoint her. She loved me and said I was everything she had hoped for in a child. She did her best to make up for them. Nothing could ever do that, but I appreciated everything she tried to do for me."

Todd averted his eyes, not wanting to see the shock that must be on Elena's face. Lost in his remembrances, he continued. "None of the family ever went to church. It wasn't part of their experience. When I was thirteen, one of my teachers gave me a copy of *The Robe* by Lloyd Douglas. I was fascinated by it. Jesus seemed so alive and real."

"Oh, Todd, I loved that book." Elena broke into his story. "It was important to me, too."

He looked at her now and could see that this, finally, was something with which she could identify. "He walked right out of those pages into my heart," he said. "I wanted to know more about Him, so my teacher took me to her church. My parents didn't seem to mind; they were always getting over a hangover on Sundays. I learned all the Bible stories in Sunday school and attended church with her. The preacher almost always talked about Jesus, how He wanted to be our friend, how we would never be alone if He lived in our hearts, how the Bible was His personal love letter to us. He said the Bible was the best guidebook for how to live a successful life. My parents hadn't taught me anything. I knew I needed direction, so I listened to every word he said.

"One Sunday my teacher took me to lunch after church and asked me if I wanted to commit my life to Jesus. When I said yes, she led me in prayer to make that commitment. After that I had a great hunger for the Bible. I read it almost every day.

He dipped his head and fiddled with a piece of grass. "One day after Dad had beaten me with his belt, I hid in my closet. Cringing in a corner, I heard God speak to me over my sobs: 'Follow me,' He said, 'and I'll be both your father and your mother.' I'll never forget it. As I wept and wept, a lot of the bitterness flowed out of me that day. I felt cleansed and surrounded by love for the first time in my life. Every time things were really bad with my parents, I remembered what He'd said. I learned what life is supposed to be like by studying the Bible and spending time in His presence."

Elena clapped her hands. "Todd, I don't know how anyone as wonderful as you could come from such a messed-up family. I'm so glad your teacher introduced you to Jesus. You encourage me to share Him more often."

"I tried hard to share Him with my brother, but he wouldn't listen. His heart remained hard." He turned to face her. "You're the first girl I've ever told about my parents," he said, searching for her reaction. "It ended with my mother running off with another man and Dad getting worse. That's what my family is like. There's no way you can identify with that, and that's why I'm not good for you." He said what he had been thinking all along.

"Todd, that's why your eyes are so sad. I knew you were carrying more than one heavy burden. But look at you. You've made it through all that. I'm glad you can talk to me about it. It helps to bring such terrible memories out in the open. They have less power over us when they're no longer secrets we have to hide."

"Do you have secrets, Elena?"

"My friends say I'm an open book. You can see exactly what I'm thinking by the expressions on my face."

"How great to have nothing to hide." Todd stood and reached down to help her up. "Thank you, Elena, for another beautiful day." As he pulled her close to him, his lips brushed her cheek. He held her for just a moment, enfolding her in his arms. He resisted the passion that stirred inside him, but his strong embrace told her how much he cared for her.

*

On the boat trip home, Elena wondered how long Todd would remember the happy days they were sharing. She knew she would never forget them. When she had seen Todd's smiling face relaxed from all signs of strain, she had felt nothing was impossible. Surely this was something more than a summer romance that would fade with time. How she wished he would say something about their future. He seemed to worry only about how to help his father.

Keenly aware she must not push him as she had Peter, she resolved to be patient and follow his lead. She studied his face now and remembered all the terrible things he had endured as a child. Accustomed to feeling sorry for herself when frustrated by much lighter matters, she felt ashamed. Her heart ached as she imagined Todd's sufferings.

She had tried hard not to look shocked at Todd's story. His experience was so foreign to everything she had known. Thinking of her own petty trials with her family, she regretted the hard time she had given her parents during her teen years. They had wanted only what was best for her. Todd, without knowing, had convicted her of how wrong she had been. She hoped she'd remember his sad life the next time a member of her family irritated her.

How like her heavenly father to reach down to touch the life of a young man so troubled. She had hoped the man she loved would know God. In spite of the somberness of the occasion, she felt a rush of joy at this part of his story.

She smiled at him as he concentrated on driving the boat through the maze of lobster buoys. When he smiled back, she knew no other smile had so impacted her.

*

That afternoon Doug and his friends had a successful afternoon fishing from Jamie's wharf, each having caught a string of a dozen or so mackerel. While the other three started gathering their gear, Doug cast his line one last time. As his hook sank, the line went taut and the end of his rod doubled into the water. "Hey, I got a good one," he cried.

A large mackerel swam to the surface, then plunged back under the water, taking out additional line.

Elated to see his rod bending in half, Doug called out, "This is like deep-sea fishing."

"Hold it up," Harvey yelled, "or you'll lose him."

The fish pulled so hard, Doug could only hold on to his rod. Finally it swam back toward the float, and he reeled it in as fast as he could.

"This one needs a net," Harvey said. "Give it here, Eddie." Eddie handed the net to Harvey who got down on his knees and followed the end of Doug's line with his eyes. The fish came in sight again. "It's a winner. Bring him over here, Doug. I'll scoop him out."

As the fish surfaced, Doug stepped back to bring the line within Harvey's reach. Harvey plunged the net into the water and scooped up a large mackerel, four times the size of the others. "We got it," Harvey said, taking as much credit as Doug.

Doug beamed. "Gee, thanks, Harv. It's a beaut. We'll have enough for the whole family between that one and the others. He must be the Daddy of them all."

"That's no tinker mackerel. I bet it's an Atlantic King that lost his way." Eddie's imagination worked overtime.

"That's the biggest mackerel I ever saw," Joey said.

"I wouldn't want to have missed that one." Doug, flushed with the thrill of landing the biggest and best catch of the day, expressed his delight.

"I got one like that last year," Harvey bragged.

"Yeah, sure you did, Harv." Eddie looked suspicious.

"C'mon, guys, let's go home. Leave our rods in the bait shack for tomorrow. Want to fish tomorrow mornin', Doug?"

"No. I'll be going to church. I better take mine home."

"Okay, put your fish in my basket and hop on. You'll have to hold your pole in one hand."

Doug did as Harvey instructed and the four of them took off down the road on three bikes. Stopping at the end of the road by the twisted tree, they started skipping stones on top of the water.

"Wish Dad was here with his camera. We could climb into the tree and pose on the branches with our fish," Doug said, still excited about his catch.

"Wait here a minute. I'm goin' up to the store." Harvey took off on his bike.

"Bet you can't beat that one. Twelve skips," Eddie said.

Joey bragged, "I can do that, too." He tossed out a smooth, round stone and counted to eight. At that moment, a large black double-masted schooner appeared on the horizon. "Look, guys! It's the *Black Moriah*."

Eddie appeared awestruck. "The ghost ship. They say she just goes back and forth across the bay lookin' for her lost crew. Isn't she a sight?"

Doug joined in the mystery. "I can imagine her with pirates all over the deck and hanging on the masts. Did they have pirates this far North?"

"Sure, they used to be everywhere." Eddie spoke as if he knew.

As the schooner sailed out of sight, Harvey returned, cheeks flushed.

"You should of seen what we saw." Eddie's eyes gleamed. "The *Black Moriah* sailed by out there." He pointed toward the Camden Hills.

"I got somethin' more exciting than that," Harvey said. "Look at this." He reached inside his T-shirt and extracted a shiny new magazine. "It just came in today." Peering around to make sure they were alone, he sat on a stone and beckoned his buddies to gather around him.

Doug felt uneasy looking at the magazine out in the open where anyone could come upon them, but as Harvey slowly turned the pages, he allowed himself to be drawn in. Soon the magazine had his full attention.

"This one is something else," he said, forgetting everything but the tantalizing images that smiled seductively from the pages of *Penthouse*.

16

"I'M GOING TO CHURCH WITH THE RICHARDS this morning, Grandma. Won't you come with us?"

"The Richards have been good to us, Todd, but not so good that I have to endure their church."

"I thought you might go for my sake, Grandma. You know that would mean a lot to me."

"Anything but that, Todd. You know how I feel."

"If you don't forgive God, you'll only become bitter. I know He loves you and our family."

"Just thinking about God makes me angry. What kind of a God would let my daughter ruin her life by drinking and my grandson take his own life…"

"They made those choices. They chose not to know Him. He loves you, and He wants you to know Him."

"No, thank you. Go ahead if you like, but don't ask me." Holding her head upright with a regal air, she rose from the breakfast table and retreated to her bedroom.

"You don't know what you're missing, Grandma," he called after her. He sighed and buried his head in his arms, realizing he was no closer to his goal now than he had ever been.

*

The small church, a typical New England white frame building with a steeple on top, located in the middle of the island, attracted people from all directions. More came than the small building could seat, but they were so eager to join in the worship, latecomers stood along the sides of the wall. A mixture of summer people and islanders who seemed to know each other well joined in praises to God. Their voices, though not in harmony, were enthusiastic and joyful.

When the young pastor welcomed the Richards to the church at the start of the service, Harold rose to introduce the congregation to Elena and Todd. When he had finished, he asked Todd to tell the congregation something about himself. Todd explained that he came from Pittsburgh and had brought his grandmother back to the island where she had summered as a child. He asked those present to join him in praying that she would come to church before they returned home. A murmur of approval spread through the congregation.

In three short years, the young pastor had revitalized the church. A handsome blond in his mid-thirties with round, ruddy cheeks, Pastor Dar was of Swedish descent. His blue eyes, always smiling, and his enthusiastic voice broadcast his warm, friendly nature. Interested in every detail of his parishioners' lives, he preached with intensity, holding his congregation in rapt attention. He challenged them to rise above their circumstances, to cast off bad habits and addictions, and to become new men and women by accepting God's Son, Jesus, as their personal friend and Savior.

This Sunday morning Pastor Dar assured his little flock that God did not care how they dressed. He looked at their inward parts and cared more about what was in their hearts. Pastor Dar's formula to receive God into their personal lives and to accomplish God's purposes here on the island was simple: humble yourself, turn from past wrongdoing, and spend more time in His presence. Develop a personal relationship with Him. Study His Word. From it, they could learn all they needed to know. After the service, every member of his congregation knew he had been challenged to rise above mediocrity in the week ahead.

As members of the congregation lingered to greet one another, people rushed up to the Richards to hug and welcome them back. Todd enjoyed experiencing the congregation's sincere love and the earnestness with which they honored the Lord's Day.

Pastor Dar had made it clear that he believed the whole Sabbath was the Lord's. Feeling uncomfortable about rushing home from church to grab a sandwich and head for Open Tennis, Todd elected to stay home and spend the rest of the day with his grandmother.

*

The courts were more crowded than usual. A group of young people in their twenties had come, giving Elena an opportunity to meet girls and boys her own age. Where had they been the summer she needed them?

Now more confident in her game and more practiced in her social skills than in previous years, she found herself the center of attention among her age group. The shy, little girl who had kept to herself in the past seemed to be someone she had once known, but not very well. She enjoyed the attention of two young men her age but spent most of the afternoon registering thoughts to share with Todd.

The final set she and her father played together, and her mother partnered with one of the young men.

"Seems like Todd has competition," Harold whispered in her ear.

"Dad, the guy is just happy to see someone their own age. Think how happy that would have made me five years ago."

"You would have been mighty happy about it this year if Todd hadn't won your heart first," Harold replied, offering her the balls to begin serving.

"What can I say?" She grinned.

Harold's strength and consistency overpowered the young man who tried too hard to impress Elena. He hit the ball so hard it went out of bounds a good portion of the time. Long points and moments of good tennis made the match fun for all but the chagrined young man who kept missing the lines.

By 4:30 great black clouds gathered overhead and swallowed up the sun. A brisk breeze blew up from the valley playing havoc with the tennis balls. When the wind began to swirl and rain burst from the clouds, the players scattered to their cars.

*

Without a television set, the family spent rainy days reading and playing games. Although the Richards listened to a radio that reported local weather conditions, when they neglected to buy a daily newspaper, they learned little about what was happening in the rest of the world.

Stephanie called her parents midmorning and asked how they were faring.

"Doug is staring out the window wishing he could drive away the rain by sheer willpower, Mike is spreading a jigsaw puzzle over the dining-room table, and your father is oiling his power saw. I'm mending a curtain that must have been attacked by a field mouse during the winter. How are things with you and little Kevin?" Susan asked.

"Don't you know about the hurricane that's heading toward Maine?" Stephanie asked.

"Why no, dear, your father listened to the local weather report, and it only spoke of continued rain. I'm sure it has nothing to do with a hurricane."

"Is it raining there already?"

"Yes, it started yesterday afternoon. It's just a local condition."

"Haven't you seen pictures of what it did to South Carolina? Mother, you really should stay more in touch with the world. The hurricane is approaching New Jersey now and unless it changes course, they're expecting it to come up the coast of New England. You better get in supplies and be ready to evacuate."

"We've had scares before, Stephanie, but the storms always dissipate before they reach our bay."

"Well, they don't expect this one to. Promise me you'll stay tuned and do just what they tell you. Coastal towns have been evacuating all the way up the coast."

"I promise, dear, but tell me about the baby. How's he doing?"

"He's fine, cooing all the time. Thanks a million for the little suit you sent him, Mom. He looks adorable in it. How's Elena? Is she there?"

"She's in the other cabin reading by herself, but she's very happy this year. There's a young man staying three cabins away on our shore. They've been spending a great deal of time together."

"She must be in seventh heaven. Do you like him, Mom?"

"Very much. He seems like a fine young man. I'm so happy Elena's having a good time. She seems to be back with the family."

"I'm glad to hear it. Please give her my love and tell her to call me when the hurricane is over to let me know you're all right. We'll have the church praying."

"Thanks for alerting us, dear. Bye for now."

Susan hung up the phone, then called, "Harold, did you hear that? We better start listening to the national news on the radio. Why don't you take Doug to the store to get extra candles and bottled water? Do you have everything we need if we have to put on the shutters?"

"I have a list of supplies to stock for hurricanes," Harold replied. "I don't think there's any danger, but I'll get them just in case. Get the keys, Doug, I'll find the list."

"And I was hoping it would stop by lunch time so I could go out this afternoon," Doug grumbled.

"It may. This is only a local condition, nothing to do with whatever's brewing in the South. Mike, turn on the radio and find that good Boston station and keep us informed about what's going on."

"Sure, Dad," Mike said, not looking up from his puzzle.

"I'd like to get the news now, Mike. It's almost ten o'clock," Susan said, returning to her sewing. "I wonder what I should do first. There's plenty of food in the house. Maybe I should cook some things ahead."

"How about a chowder, Mom?"

"That's a good idea, Mike. I have plenty of potatoes, milk and onions, but I should have told Harold to get fish and salt pork. See if you can catch him, dear, and tell him I could use eight to ten pounds of haddock or cod, whatever he can find, and a package of salt pork. Elena promised she'd help me the first rainy day."

"This is it if ever there was one," Mike said, striding out the door with his rain jacket over his head.

*

In the other cabin Elena lay on her bed reading. She remembered how she had felt five years ago when her only choice had been to read alone in her room. Today, with the rain pounding on the ancient windows, she rather liked it. The heater made the room cozy and warm, and as much as she liked her family, she enjoyed reading by herself.

As she reached the end of her book, she stretched and looked at her watch. Already 11:30. Most of the morning had slipped by, and the rain continued to pound on her window. She hadn't seen Todd since yesterday morning at church, and she missed him. She laid aside the book and thought of the strong outline of his profile, the shock of hair that fell down in his face, giving him a boyish look that appealed to her motherly instinct. She sighed, wondering if the rains would keep him from her.

She wandered into the boys' room and decided to make their disheveled beds. Picking up Doug's clothes, which had been flung on the floor, she folded them and put them in the chest of drawers at the foot of his bed. The corner of a brightly colored magazine peeked out from the paper lining the drawer. Elaine reached in and drew it out, feeling she had done this before.

She gasped. "Another one." Flipping through its pages, she saw the voluptuous images of *Penthouse Magazine*. The thought of her little brother learning about sex from a source like this unsettled her. The more she thought about it, the more agitated she became.

Feeling angry and betrayed, she rushed out the door into the rain.

*

Harold and Doug were in the kitchen unpacking. "Everyone seemed to be buying everything in a panic, Susan. This must be more serious than we thought." Harold quickly stuffed the shelves with supplies they had bought.

Elena burst through the door, dripping wet, and rushed through the living room to the kitchen. She thrust the magazine at Doug. "You promised me you would stop, and I believed you. You lied to me, Doug. How could you?"

"Elena, what's wrong?" Susan rushed to the kitchen door.

"Elena, d-don't," Doug stammered.

"Mom, Dad, I tried to spare you. I found the first one under Doug's mattress the night of the beach party. Doug promised if I didn't tell you, he'd never look at another one."

"One what?" Susan asked, bewildered.

"Doug has been reading pornographic magazines and hiding them under his mattress and his clothes." Elena held up the magazine for all to see.

"You've been snooping in my things again," Doug accused her, an ugly scowl marring his face.

"I only wanted to surprise you and clean up your room."

"That's what you said last time." He snatched the magazine from her hand. "I never thought you'd snoop a second time."

"I'll have a look at that, young man." Harold reached for the magazine.

"It's mine." Doug looked horrified that Elena had exposed him in front of his family.

"Doug," Susan said, "give that to your father. If there's no problem, he'll return it to you."

"No." Doug backed into the living room. "You don't want to see it."

"As a matter of fact, young man, I do. What's gotten into you?" Harold pivoted toward Mike, who watched the scene with his mouth hanging open. "Mike, what do you know about this?"

"Nothing, Dad. I haven't seen that magazine."

Harold flipped through a few pages and turned back to Doug. Putting his hand on his shoulder, he said, "Son, it's a mistake to put such pictures in your mind. They'll give you the wrong ideas about women. If you want to know about these things, we should have a talk."

Doug was not ready to listen to advice from his family or to answer their questions. Mortified and humiliated, he looked from one to the other, hoping for understanding or sympathy. Finding none and feeling trapped, he sent cutting darts toward Elena. "I hate you. Why didn't you just stay home?"

He turned to his mother. "All you care about this year is Elena. You act like Mike and me don't even exist." He rushed out the door into the rain, leaving his family staring at each other in disbelief.

Doug spent the rest of the day sulking in his cabin, except when his father summoned him for dinner. He remained silent through the meal and turned down Harold's request to talk. Seeing how disturbed he was, Harold excused him to go to his cabin.

The remaining four played bridge. Had not Doug's plight weighed heavily on their hearts, it would have been a joyous evening. The game, both fun and challenging, required more effort than most of the games they played with Doug.

When the second rubber ended, Mike rose from his chair. "Thanks, Sis. That was a great game. I'd like to go talk to Doug before you come over. Do you mind?"

"Of course not. That's a good idea. I'll read here awhile. Dad, Mom, can we pray for Doug and ask the Lord to give Mike the words to reach him?"

"Yes, Elena, I've been praying for him to myself all evening," Harold said.

Mike hugged them good night and departed.

Reaching his cabin, he walked into his room as casually as possible. "Reading a good book?" he asked.

"Not really."

"Got any plans for tomorrow?" Mike tried to keep it casual.

"Are you kidding? In this rain with a hurricane coming?"

"Yeah, I guess we're in for it. Anything you'd like to talk to me about, Doug?"

"No." Doug returned to his reading.

Mike undressed and brushed his teeth. He turned on the light by his bed, picked up a book, and pretended to read.

"Mike."

"Yeah?"

"Did you ever look at porn magazines?" Doug asked in a voice just above a whisper. He rose on one elbow, so he could look at Mike as he spoke.

"Once," Mike said, sitting up and looking toward Doug.

"Did it turn you on?" Doug asked with more animation.

"Yeah, I guess so."

"But you never looked again?"

"That's right."

"Why?" Doug looked like he found that hard to believe.

"Our youth pastor gave us a talk about it. One of the guys told him we had a magazine."

"Was it *Playboy?*"

"Yeah. He told us all about the *Playboy* philosophy and how it wasn't true. He said if we wanted relationships with nice girls, we should keep our minds clean." Mike set aside his book, walked across the room, and sat on Doug's bed. "That magazine will give you the wrong idea about girls, Doug. There are plenty of loose girls looking for sex, but they're not the kind we want. I want a marriage like Mom and Dad have and a romance like Elena and Todd. If they get married, their sex will be great because they waited for each other. If Dad asks me to wear a promise ring next year, I'm going to take it. I don't want a girl that twenty other guys have slept with. And the girl I want won't want me if I've been fooling around or if I've filled my mind with pictures of other women."

"You sound just like Dad." Doug threw his book on the floor. "Why did I have to get stuck in such a holy family?!"

"Dad knows the score, Doug. You'll only be hurting yourself."

"You all act like I'm a pervert or something. Even my own brother."

"Whatever made you want to look at porn magazines in the first place?"

"The guys asked me to be in their club, and I wanted to have friends here. You're always off with Jim, and Elena with Todd. You leave me here all by myself. I promised I wouldn't tell before I even knew what they were doing."

"Gosh, if you want to go fishing with me and Jim, we'd be happy to take you."

"I wanted friends of my own."

"You didn't really mean what you said about Elena, did you?"

"You're more worried about her than you are about me." Doug sighed and yanked the covers over his head, closing the conversation.

Mike turned out the light. He guessed he hadn't done a very good job.

17

THE NEXT MORNING, LOCAL RAINS CONTINUED UNABATED, but the hurricane still hung off the Jersey coast, far away from Penobscot Bay. The Richards relaxed their vigil and became involved in indoor projects.

When Elena received a luncheon invitation from Mrs. Faraway, she donned her rain slicker and headed down the road toward Todd's cabin. She noted with pleasure that the brook, almost empty during the dry weather, was now full. Once again rushing water raced over the rocks on its way to the shore. The rain had slowed to a light drizzle typical of many of Maine's summer days, but it showed no signs of stopping.

Todd greeted her with a warm smile. "Come on in. Is your family surviving?"

"Pretty well, with one notable exception. I'll tell you about that when we're alone. Mike and I had fun playing bridge with Mom and Dad last evening. Today the three of them are busy repairing things. Doug is keeping to himself in the other cabin, except for meals."

Todd helped her off with her slicker and took the dripping coat into the bathroom to hang over the tub. She found her way to the kitchen, where Mrs. Faraway stirred a large pot on the stove. "Hello, Mrs. Faraway. You're nice to invite me for lunch. I hope you haven't gone to any trouble."

"I thought we could both benefit from your cheerful chatter, my dear. It's rather dull around here with the rain. We've about read ourselves out."

"We have lots of books if you want to borrow any. Some people think we're in for a bad time, though it does seem quiet out there just now."

"It doesn't look like a major storm yet." Mrs. Faraway sounded hopeful.

"The raindrops, continually striking the water, seem to have flattened the waves and calmed the winds," Elena said. "I've enjoyed the coziness of reading by the fire, but I agree it can go on too long."

"Would you like some hot cider? It's always our favorite when the weather turns rainy and damp. It warms the bones."

"Sounds delicious. I'd love some. We seldom think of it in the summer. It's more a Halloween treat in the fall for us."

"It feels like fall when the wind blows like it did yesterday. The muffins need another ten minutes," she said, ladling the cider into two large mugs.

"Why don't the two of you drink your cider by the fire and catch up on the news?"

The fire crackled and spit sparks against the screen. "I love that sound in the fire." Elena settled into the big couch and warmed her hands around the giant mug.

"Let's see. What's the most important thing to tell you?" Todd clasped his chin in his hands. "That I've missed you and constantly wondered what you were doing?"

"I haven't missed you a bit," Elena lied with a twinkle in her eye. "I had so many suitors at tennis, I didn't know which one to choose."

"That will teach me to be a considerate grandson," Todd said. "Next time I'll have to go along to protect you from the wolves."

"Dad does a good job of that. You don't have to worry. One of them was so busy trying to impress me he hit everything out of the court. I decided I'd rather have you for a partner."

"What a relief. I'm glad we signed up for the tournament early."

Elena shared everything she could remember about Open Tennis until Mrs. Faraway announced lunch.

The dining table sat in front of a large picture window overlooking the bay. In spite of the drizzle outside, they could see the Cliff and nearby islands. "What a different view you have. It always amazes me that we all view the same islands but see them from such different perspectives. I love the picture window. I've begged Mom and Dad to put one in our living room, but Dad insists on keeping it the way it's always been, with all those little panes. Mom always agrees with Dad so it will stay that way until it passes to the next generation, which I hope won't be any time soon."

"Your parents seem remarkably young and vital to have four nearly grown children." Mrs. Faraway passed the blueberry muffins to Elena.

Elena noted that Todd omitted a blessing in deference to his grandmother. "I wouldn't say Doug is grown up." She reached into the basket. "These look very good, Mrs. Faraway. You must have thought I was foolish recommending blueberry muffins when you make them so beautifully."

"Not at all, my dear. It's been years since I've made them, but having them at Fisherman's Friend reminded me of how good they are."

"And your chicken salad is delicious. I've eaten so much fish it's nice to have a change."

"Thank you, Elena. Now tell me what your mother and father think of this weather. We've been watching the news. The hurricane in the south has done a great deal of damage. The pictures of South Carolina are frightening."

"I guess that's what sent everyone to the store to buy provisions. Mom and Dad have experienced many such warnings, but the hurricanes usually die out before they reach here."

"They aren't concerned then?"

"They're being watchful, but no, they aren't worried yet. My older sister, Stephanie, called after seeing the pictures on TV. She urged us to plan to evacuate."

"Oh my, I hope it doesn't come to that. Where would we go?"

"To the high school. It's on high ground and away from the water. They would have Red Cross people ready to help those in need."

"Well, I hope it blows out to sea, but let's talk about something more pleasant." Mrs. Faraway offered Elena another muffin.

"Thank you, they're much better than the ones in the restaurant. By the way, do you remember the Inn at Jordan Pond on Mount Desert?"

"I do indeed. We used to go there for lunch when we visited friends in Bar Harbor. I remember playing on the grass at the edge of the lake while the grown-ups drank their coffee. You could see the mountains on the other side of the pond. There were gardens of brightly colored flowers all around."

"I never saw the original Inn. Did you know that it had burned down?" Elena asked.

"No, I didn't. What a pity. Was it destroyed by the great fire of 1947?"

"No, it burned much later, but only the building was lost. The trees and the beautiful carriage houses are still there. Do you remember them?"

"Not really. A young girl has other interests."

"I read an article about how they're being restored," Todd joined the conversation. "In the pictures they look like English Tudor style with red brick designs that make them unique."

"Yes, I read the same article," Elena said. "They restored the Inn, too, not as an Inn but as a restaurant called Jordan Pond House. The family went up for a meal several years ago. Mom and Dad raved about it. They sat on an outside porch overlooking flower gardens and a beautiful lake, just like you remember it. It sounded like a lovely spot to eat, and they said the food was delicious. The restaurant specializes in giant popovers. Every guest is given at least one, even if he orders a sandwich."

"Would you like to go there for lunch, Grandma?"

"That would be lovely, Todd. Perhaps Elena would like to come, too."

Elena, thankful Mrs. Faraway had invited her to join them, appreciated not having to worry about intruding. "I'd like that, Mrs. Faraway. If we go on a clear day, we could drive to the top of Cadillac Mountain. You can see for

94

miles in every direction. The views even on the way up are spectacular. And we could drive the Loop Road, which goes all around Acadia National Park."

"That's the second most popular National Park in the country," Todd said, "and the only one on the East Coast. Wasn't John D. Rockefeller responsible for preserving it?"

"He always gets the credit," Elena said. "Actually Dr. Charles Eliot and George Dorr were the ones who had the original idea. They organized a small group of summer residents in 1901 to acquire the land and hold it for public use. Later Mr. Rockefeller built fifty miles of carriage roads in the areas with the best views and added large areas of shoreline. His will stated that his beautiful mansion was to be torn down after his death because he didn't think anyone could keep it in as good repair as he had, and he didn't want it to mar the natural look of the mountainside. Can you believe that? When I went to camp, we took hiking trips there every year and had to study the history of the park.

"It's truly magnificent. A complex of high mountains, peaceful mountain lakes, and dramatic shorelines. You can see water on all sides from many of the mountain tops. It has the largest sand beach on the bay and marvelous views and vistas from hundreds of trails. I wouldn't want to live there with all the people touring through, but we're lucky to be close enough to enjoy the scenery and use the hiking trails."

"Could we drive through the areas where the big estates were?" Mrs. Faraway asked. "Of course, they called them summer cottages."

"Yes, we could have a lovely day and show you a bit of how it used to be. With your memories and what's still there, you should be able to taste the way it was." Elena became excited about how much Mrs. Faraway would enjoy the day.

"You sound like you like it better than here," Todd said. "Can that be?"

"No, Acadia is majestic and dramatic. Deer Isle is more intimate. How can you compare them? They're different, but they're both wonderful. Everything in the Bay area is beyond comparison."

"Now I feel better," Todd said. "For a minute I thought you were saying somewhere else is better than here."

They all laughed, and Mrs. Faraway looked pleased. "You've been a breath of fresh air for us, Elena. I was getting terribly grumpy and not much fun to be around."

"Laughter is always good for the soul, Mrs. Faraway. May I clear the table for you?"

"Todd will do it. Sit here and tell me more about yourself. What do you hope to do with your life?"

"That's a big question. I'm majoring in English now, and I'm not sure what happens next. I don't want to be a journalist or a teacher, but I do love to write. Someday I'd like to write a novel about this place, but I think I need to experience more of life first. My grandfather wrote many books. All his engineering books were in great demand, but his fiction was never published. The last novel he wrote came the closest. One publisher returned it with a note that he was touched by the section about losing a baby. Grandpa had just experienced the death of his first child. They always say you should write about something you know. That's why I'd like to write stories that take place up here."

"I'm sure you could be successful. You've made Todd appreciate this place by seeing it through your eyes. But what are your other goals, dear?"

"I hope to marry and have children and stay home and raise them myself. I don't believe in turning them over to daycare workers. I want them to know who their mother is. We were fortunate to have a mother at home. I didn't always appreciate it at the time. Sometimes I envied the kids who were more on their own, but many of them got into trouble. Now I realize it wasn't good for them."

"You were fortunate to have such a caring mother. I admire Susan. She has a quiet peace about her and a deep inner strength."

"That comes from her faith in God. He's the source of comfort and strength for all of us. Do you read the Bible, Mrs. Faraway?"

"No, Elena, I do not. I'm afraid I don't believe there's a God who cares about us. My experience is that it's everyone for himself. Todd," she called sharply, "what's holding you up?"

"I have the plates all ready," he said as he appeared at the door. He set a bowl of warm Apple Brown Betty before them and returned to the kitchen for his bowl and a pitcher of cream. "Would either of you like more hot cider?"

"I would," Elena said. "I really enjoyed it. You did go to a lot of trouble, Mrs. Faraway. This is a lovely luncheon."

"It was my pleasure, Elena."

Mrs. Faraway said very little during the rest of the meal. Todd and Elena continued to make plans about things they wanted to do when the rain stopped. When dessert was over, Mrs. Faraway excused herself, saying it was time for her nap. Elena and Todd cleared the table and cleaned up the kitchen. When they had finished, they returned to the fire in the living room. Todd stirred the dying embers and added a fresh log to the remaining flames.

"Do you think you'll be like your mother, Elena?" Todd asked.

"I can't imagine being as selfless as Mom, but she and I are growing closer every year. The older I get, the more I want to be like her. I want to be available to my children when they're young, like she was for us. Take time to play with them, wonder over their discoveries, encourage them to become creative. Mom and Dad insisted we make the Christmas presents we gave to each other and to our teachers. Sometimes we grumbled and complained, but we were more excited about the presents we gave on Christmas Day than the ones we received. We had invested ourselves in them.

"I want to invest myself in my children and help them develop their creative talents. Expose them to good books. Take them to plays and ballet and art shows. I don't want them to be couch potatoes watching TV all the time."

"I can't imagine you as a couch potato. I can hardly keep up with you," Todd said.

"I started out to be one. If it wasn't for Mom, I might still be in front of the TV eating too many crackers. When I started to gain weight, Mom warned me, but I didn't listen.

"Then Mom ruled that there would be no more TV and dragged me to the tennis courts. She planned interesting little trips for us and encouraged me to read good books. Now I'd rather read a book than watch TV any day. And look what a tennis partner I found as a result." She grinned.

"I don't want to be anything like my parents," Todd replied without humor. "I spent hours and hours reading my Bible. I prayed that Jesus would spare me from becoming like them. I studied His character and listed all His attributes. I tried to make Him my role model. When anger erupted inside me, I turned it over to Him."

"You don't seem like an angry person. You've succeeded very well."

"I have a long way to go."

"Don't we all?"

"Of course." He left the fire and sat down beside her. "Now tell me about the 'notable exception.' I've been wondering about it all afternoon."

"Oh, Todd," she said, suddenly as serious as he, "I do need your advice."

"About what?"

"It's Doug, my wonderful little brother. I can't believe what he's doing and what I did. I embarrassed him in front of the whole family. I acted out of impulse, but I still think my parents needed to know."

"Know what?" Todd looked puzzled.

Elena sighed, letting out her pent-up concern. "Doug is reading pornographic magazines."

Todd caught his breath, looked away from her, and stared at the floor. "I guess that's normal, but not good at all. Where is he getting them?"

"He won't say. He says they're his, but he has to give them back to someone. I'm sure that someone is Harvey, the red-headed boy Doug plays golf with at the club, but he denies it."

Todd glanced up, his expression hard. "You've got to stop him. Pornography is evil. It destroys people."

Surprised by his vehemence, Elena studied Todd's dark expression.

He paused, focused back on the floor, then spoke again with considerable passion. "I had a close friend who screwed up his life because of pornography. He started out with soft-core magazines, then found the late shows on cable, and ended up watching hard-core videos. He could take it or leave it at first, but he found it so exciting, he always went back for more. Eventually, it took control of him, and all he thought about was raunchy sex. He started making his dates watch Internet porn with him and then tried to act out the scenes with them. He couldn't understand why all the nice girls dropped him.

"He talked to a minister about it, became a Christian, and seemed to put it behind him. He married a nice girl and became the leader of the youth group at our church. Then boys in his youth group started talking about it and that stirred his interest again. He ended up losing his wife and even his job because he had the wrong kind of sex on his mind all the time. It ruined his life."

"How terrible, Todd."

"Yes, and even more terrible is that many girls marry a seemingly nice guy and find out after they're married that their husband is hooked on pornography and can't really love them."

Elena put out a hand. "Don't tell me anymore. It makes me sick. Doug is so young, and he's always been a good kid, interested in sports and wholesome things. He has great friends at home. I can't understand what attracted him to these boys. I guess it was just the normal desire to have friends his age. It was hard for me to be here without friends my age when I was younger."

"It's normal for boys to start thinking about sex after puberty. They want to know what it's all about."

"Dad must have waited too long to talk to him. I know Mom talked to us girls, and I'm sure Dad talked to Mike."

"He'll talk to him now, Elena."

"Yes, if it isn't too late."

"How can I help? Do you want me to tell him what happened to my friend?"

"Would you, Todd? I'd appreciate it. We have to help him understand the danger."

"Of course, first chance I get. Do you think he'll listen?"

"He'll listen. Whether he believes you or not is another matter."

"Hey, it's three o'clock. Let's see if we can get some news on TV about the hurricane."

The hurricane had turned westward and hit the Jersey shore. Pictures showed beaches washed out, trees across roads, and houses without roofs. One town was hard hit. Whole apartment complexes had collapsed, and pictures of shelters showed crying children and old people in dazed conditions.

"You'd better not let your grandmother see those pictures. We don't want her to worry unnecessarily. I'll go home and tell Dad and Mom. We'll keep in touch. If the phone goes out, Dad will be over to help you with whatever needs to be done."

"Thanks, Elena," Todd said, assisting her with donning her slicker.

"Thank your grandmother for a wonderful lunch and a great afternoon." Elena opened the door and slipped out into the rain. She turned to look at Todd once more. It had been good to sit before the fire confiding in him. She wanted to tell him how much better he had made her feel, how comforting it was to face the problem with his help, but she simply said, "Bye," and turned to dash toward her cabin.

"Be careful, Elena," he shouted after her.

*

Todd closed the door and fell back against it. "Ugh," he said aloud, scrunching his eyes closed. *Can't I ever get away from it? Did she notice how I lost it when she started talking about porn?* He ran his hands through his hair as if trying to clear his brain. *Dad, Dad, what will she think of me when she finds out? And what on earth will she think of you?*

18

HAROLD KNOCKED ON THE DOOR of Doug's room.

"Come in," a sullen voice called from inside.

Harold opened the door and glanced around the room, wincing as he saw unmade beds and clothes scattered about the floor. The pulled shades made it dark inside in spite of the daylight outside. "Not a very cheerful place to meditate," he said.

"It's how I feel. Like the rain that never lets up."

Harold moved across the room, avoiding the pile of clothes in his path, and sat on the bed beside Doug. Placing his hand on Doug's shoulder, he said, "I've given you time to come to me, Doug. But since you haven't, I've come to you. It's time for us to talk about it, son."

"I don't want to talk."

Ignoring the remark, Harold continued, "If you had more questions about sex, I wish you had come to me instead of to those magazines. I thought we had a pretty good talk last winter. You seemed satisfied at the time, and I invited you to come to me any time you had more questions." Feeling the need to establish contact, he patted Doug's back.

Doug moved farther away and turned his face to the wall.

"I know you feel exposed and betrayed, Doug, but Elena was acting out of concern for you and so are the rest of us. You're becoming interested in girls and want to understand how to please them, but you're going about it the wrong way. Falling in love is one of the greatest experiences of a man's life, and having sex with the girl you marry is fantastic. You'll know what to do when the time comes. You don't need porn magazines for that. Your mother and I don't want pornography to form your ideas about sex and marriage."

Doug said nothing.

"Pornography makes you think all women are loose and on the make. It makes men think they can have great sex outside of marriage without any responsibilities or commitments." He inhaled deeply. "But it's a lie. The relationship your mother and I have is much better, much more fulfilling than anything portrayed in those magazines. Pornography focuses on the sex act. But the relationship between a man and a woman is so much more than that. When you fall in love, you'll appreciate it if your girl has a great figure, but you'll want to know everything about her, not just about her body. You'll want to know about her personality. Is she fun to be with? Is she a caring person? Does she have a good mind? Can you share on a spiritual level? A lifetime is a long time, and if you have only a physical relationship, you won't make it over the hard times."

Doug finally broke his silence. "I know that, Dad. But what I don't know is…well, how you do it. And the magazines tell you all about that."

"What I want you to understand, Doug, is that pornography is the wrong place to look. If it's embarrassing for you to ask me questions, I'll get you a book that gives you the right instruction." He paused. "But promise me, you'll leave the magazines alone."

Doug lapsed into silence again.

"It isn't a pleasant subject, Doug, but I want you to understand what you're opening yourself up to. I've had a lot of young men come to me from church at home who had a problem with pornography, and I've learned how it can affect a man. It can gain control of his life without his realizing it. It's like an addiction."

"Come on. It's not like taking drugs." Doug pounded his fist into his pillow.

"Yes, son, it's very much like that. The pleasure sensation from looking at pornography is similar to the chemical rush from taking a drug. The only difference is that your body produces its own drug when you're aroused, and it has the same kind of addictive effect as a drug taken in from the outside. A man will come back to pornography again and again to experience that pleasurable sensation. The trouble is he's not satisfied with the same level of pornography for very long. He becomes bored with it and wants something a little more exciting to produce the same thrill he had when he first looked at it. Soon he's drawn toward harder and harder pornography. Eventually he gets bored with just looking at it and wants to experience it in real life."

"Gosh, Dad, I'm not going to do anything."

"I'm sure you're not, son. I'm telling you what happens to some men who keep looking at it. They go from soft-core to hard-core to wanting to try it out on a real woman. One ex-addict in our group stood and told the other men how easily it takes control. He said, 'You think you can handle it at first, but suddenly it takes over, and you lose control of your life. It controls you, everything you think about, and everything you do.'"

"I don't think about it all the time, only once in a while," Doug protested.

"But if you keep going back for more, you open yourself up to the possibility of its becoming an addiction."

Doug jumped off the bed and faced his father. "You don't believe that, Dad. You're just trying to scare me. You're exaggerating." Doug's voice rose and became more belligerent with each accusation.

"Doug, the first magazine Elena found was a *Playboy.* The second was a *Penthouse.* Have you seen a *Hustler* magazine yet?"

Doug could not deny it. Instead he folded his arms and swiveled away from his father.

"You see, they're getting harder and harder. The classic pattern has started in you already. Stop it before it takes control of you," Harold pleaded with his son. He walked over to Doug, put his hands on his shoulders, and turned him around.

"There's something else I want you to realize," he said, looking directly into Doug's defiant eyes. "It's harder to stop looking at pornography than it is to stop drinking alcohol or taking drugs. Even if you stop buying magazines, once you've filled your mind with those images, you carry them with you. You can't get rid of them. When that chemical is released in your body, those images are indelibly imprinted in your mind, and they come back to arouse you again and again. You're not just playing around with kid stuff now, Doug. Do you understand?" He searched Doug's face for a sign that he was receiving his words.

Doug looked him straight in the eye. "What you're saying doesn't make sense to me. I've looked at a few pictures. So what's the big deal? Guys do it all the time." He threw his hands in the air and rolled his eyes.

"Yes, and some of them can take it or leave it, but many of them can't. It's a multi-billion dollar business precisely because men keep coming back for more. They decide to give it up, but they go back once more for that pleasant feeling that blots out their problems, even if only for a few moments. As they get drawn in deeper and deeper, there's a lot more pain in their lives that they need to blot out. It becomes a vicious circle. Stop now, before you risk letting it control you."

"It can't be as bad as you say. I don't believe you," Doug said with determination, folding his arms again to show he meant what he said.

"Doug, have I ever lied to you?"

Glancing at his father and all about the room, Doug looked like he wanted desperately to come up with a good example. "No," he admitted, flopping down on his bed.

"Have I ever tried to scare you by wild exaggeration?"

"I guess not." He scowled.

"Then think about what I've said, son. When you meet a girl you want to be with more than anyone else in the world, you'll be glad you kept yourself pure for her."

Doug rolled over and stared at the dark shade. 'You don't have a very good opinion of me, do you, Dad? Well, I don't like you either at this moment. I wish you'd just go away and leave me alone." Doug shut his eyes.

"We will talk about this again, Doug. Right now I want you to promise me you won't look at those magazines again. I'm not going to force you to tell me where you got them, but I'm telling you not to look at another one, no matter who gives it to you. Do you understand?"

"Yes."

"Will you make that promise to me, Doug? I'm not leaving until you do."

"I guess so," Doug said to the wall.

"I want you to know that your mother and I are praying every day for you. Elena is, too. None of us are against you, Doug. We all love you and want you to have a great life and a great marriage. But pornography can rob you of all that. Trust me, even if you don't understand it now."

Doug remained silent. Harold sighed, then bent and patted him once more on the shoulder. He knew he had not connected with Doug. *He doesn't believe a word of it,* he said to himself as he moved toward the door. *How can I make him understand how serious a matter this is?* His shoulders slumped as he took one last look at his youngest son and retreated.

19

IT RAINED THROUGHOUT THE NIGHT, a slow, steady drizzle characteristic of the Maine coast. Wondering if they were truly in danger, Susan lay awake for long hours listening to the monotonous pitter-patter on the uninsulated roof. The clouds cried soft and ceaseless tears until the rhythm of tiny drops dancing on the roof lulled her to sleep.

When she awoke in the morning, the winds had increased. Harold struggled out of bed to turn on the local weather forecast, which included news of the hurricane, now expected to reach the Maine coast. He could see foot-high walls of water surging into the cove and crashing against the rocks, the effects of the ten-to-fifteen-foot swells predicted in the outer bay.

"It's a good thing I bought those emergency supplies when Stephanie called," Harold congratulated himself. "I imagine they're sold out by now. It would be good for you and Elena to stock extra canned goods when you go to the store. We don't know what we'll be facing. Better buy extra bottled water, too. The pump won't work if we lose power. We could be without electricity a long while."

Susan dressed quickly. Before the oatmeal was half cooked, she blew the foghorn to call the children to breakfast. "Thank you for coming faster than usual," she said when they arrived on the run.

"Gosh, Mom, we could tell the weather worsened overnight," Mike said.

Doug relinquished his silence. "It's getting exciting out there. Look at those waves pounding the rocks."

During breakfast, Susan and Elena made a list of canned goods to stock. "There's no need for us all to go out in weather like this," Susan said. "We can buy emergency supplies for Mrs. Faraway and Todd. Do we have everything for the chowder, Elena?"

"Yes, Mom, but we'll need a lot of milk. Better get an extra gallon."

"Good idea," Susan said, adding it to the list.

Harold had his back to the window. Suddenly he whirled around, peered out the window, and groaned. "Why didn't I think of it sooner. Boys, put on your slickers. We need to bring in the boat. We're lucky it's high tide, but those swells will make it hard to bring her ashore."

The boat, half full of rain water, looked in imminent danger of sinking.

As it rocked frantically up and down in the angry sea, water spilled over the stern where it was weighed down by the motor. It would have been difficult enough to bring it in empty, but next to impossible filled with water. They would have to bail it first, then bring it into the cove and up into the woods.

Gulping down their last bites of toast, they donned their slickers and boots and rushed toward the beach.

*

Fascinated, the boys watched each wave stretch to the edge of the woods. Spray flew everywhere. Intoxicated with high adventure, Doug called out, "Mike, did you ever see the tide so high? It looks like it could roll right into the woods." The sting of the rain whipping against his cheeks told him he was on the brink of a man-sized mission.

"You better hope it won't," Mike called back. "It would erode the soil and sand that hold the roots of the shore trees in place."

Mike ran to the mooring, untied the rope, and pulled at the mooring line. The weighted boat inched toward shore.

"You're doing a good job, Mike," Harold yelled from the rocks below, his voice carried away with the wind. Climbing closer to Mike, he reached out, grabbed the wet line, and tugged in rhythm with Mike. "Doug, get in the middle and pull with us."

Doug had been bounding over the rocks investigating the unusual height of the tide. Happy to be needed, he joined them. They began counting out loud and pulling together on each count of three.

The wind pelted the rain against them as they worked, blowing back the untied hood of Mike's slicker. Since his hands were occupied with the tugging of the rope, his hood remained off. In minutes the rain plastered his long hair against his face, making it doubly hard to see.

"Steady there, Doug," Harold called out. "We're making progress. You're doing a great job. Be careful not to lose your footing." He continued to encourage the boys between each tug as the boat rocked erratically toward shore.

"You'll be able to reach it now, Dad," Mike called. Harold gave it an extra tug and grabbed the bow line. As waves dashed the boat against the rocks, the boys could see their work was just beginning.

The ebb of the tide sucked the water back into the bay like a giant vacuum cleaner, pulling the boat with it. It took both boys to steady it, but the force of the water was too great to keep the boat in one place and deep water inside the boat kept Harold from climbing aboard. He had to bail from the shore. Each incoming wave rolled over the top of his high rubber boots as he flung the bucket over the side of the boat, filled it again with water, and poured it into the surging sea. Finally the water level lessened, and he was able to climb aboard.

"Boys, pull me out so the boat won't keep banging on the rocks. Doug, take the oar and see if you can hold the boat off shore."

Doug, still intoxicated by the adventure, did as he was told. His eyes widened with excitement while Harold's brow wrinkled with concern. Harold, able to sit on a seat now, scooped up the water and poured it overboard. Mike was able to tie the bow line to the mooring line and together he and Doug pulled the boat off shore where the surges of the swells rocked the boat up and down but where it was safe from the rocks. Harold continued filling his bucket and dumping it overboard.

When the water was down to a few inches, Harold called, "That's good enough. Bring the boat in, untie the line, jump aboard, and push off. Doug, bring the oars and give one to Mike."

From years of experience the boys knew what to do. Mike boarded first and readied his oar to hold the boat off the rocks. Doug pushed the boat off shore with all the strength he could muster and jumped over the bow. He grabbed the other oar and together the boys pushed the boat farther out into the water. Harold lowered the motor and pulled the starter cord. On the second try it started.

"How 'bout that," he exclaimed triumphantly. "Let's head for the cove."

"We did it," Doug cried out, elated, licking the salt from his well-sprayed face.

With the tide still high, there was little danger of running into hidden rocks. Harold knew the exact location of each one and skillfully maneuvered the angle of the boat as it rode the swells. Once in the cove, he turned toward the sand beach and revved up the motor. When he cut it, they glided toward the shore in spite of the winds that labored to push them back. The boys helped with the oars to keep the momentum of the motor going in the right direction.

"Get ready to take the line and jump, Doug. Now," Harold called with authority.

Doug landed close to the shore, the waves stopping just short of his boot tops. As he tugged on the bow line, Mike and Harold scrambled over the sides and helped him pull the boat onto the land.

"Hey, we made it," Doug beamed. "Was that teamwork, or what!"

"Great job, boys," Harold calledd approvingly. "I never could have done it without you." He took off the motor and directed the boys as the three of them moved the boat into the woods well above the tide. As they turned the boat bottom up, the sound of rain striking aluminum heralded their triumph.

"Hey, give me five," Mike said, slapping Harold and Doug's hands in a hearty high-five.

Harold put an arm around each boy, and the three of them walked out of the woods and up the beach like the Three Musketeers. Much of Doug's anger dissipated when he felt his father's arm tighten around him as they walked toward the cabin.

*

With the oars and the motor safely stored in the shed, the men burst into the kitchen full of bravado and still in a self-congratulatory mood.

"What great mates we've developed, Susan," Harold said, removing his dripping glasses. "They've learned to take orders and how to handle a boat in a storm."

"From the glow on your faces, I'd say your mission was successfully accomplished." Susan rejoiced to see their camaraderie. "You can't imagine what ours was like. The lines were terrible and the shelves half empty. If I hadn't heard the report myself, I'd have thought Chester dreamed this up just to improve sales."

"We took a load of groceries to Mrs. Faraway and Todd and invited them to join us for chowder tonight," Elena announced cheerfully. "Let's get started, Mom."

"Well, we wouldn't want to interfere with that, now, would we, boys?" Harold took off his slicker. "Let's make a roaring fire and help Mike with his jigsaw puzzle."

"That's a great idea. How 'bout some hot chocolate to warm our insides?" Mike said.

"Before you put your rain gear away, gentlemen, the wood box is half empty. May I humbly request that you fill it up and bring in an extra load of kindling? We can dry it out by the fire. I'll make your hot chocolate while you bring in the wood." Susan never liked to be without dry firewood and certainly not at a time like this.

"She's absolutely right, boys. We'll take the logs from under the tarp. They should still be fairly dry." Pulling their slickers back on, Harold and the boys left the comfort of the cabin and returned to the wet world outside.

Elena and Susan set to work in the kitchen. Susan prepared hot chocolate for the men. Elena started cutting salt pork, the basic ingredient of all old-fashioned Maine chowders. She cut it into little cubes and sautéed it into tiny golden nuggets in the big iron skillet on top of the stove. Carefully leaving the rendered fat in the skillet, she transferred the nuggets to a large pot and filled it half full of water.

Squinting to keep the tears back, Susan diced six extra-large onions and sautéed them in the skillet. They, too, ended up in the pot, as did the potatoes Elena had diced. After the water had boiled for ten minutes, Susan added the eight pounds of cod that she had cleaned and cut into large chunks.

"I can hardly wait to taste your chowder, Mom."

Susan gently stirred the soup pot until the chowder returned to a boil. Then she turned the fire to low. "It will be done in no time," she said. "I'll add the milk, and we'll let it sit on the back of the stove. The longer it sits, the more the flavors mélange, and the better it tastes. I prefer to make it the day before and keep it in the refrigerator overnight, but this will have to do for today."

"I'm sure it'll be delicious," Elena said, straightening up the kitchen. "Let's join the boys in front of the fire. That's the best place to be on a day like this."

20

THE RAIN CONTINUED THROUGH THE AFTERNOON. The Richards passed the time helping Mike complete his jigsaw puzzle and playing their favorite card games. After the morning's excitement, Doug seemed to feel comfortable with the family again. No one spoke of the magazines.

"It's almost time for Todd and Mrs. Faraway to arrive." Elena looked at her watch. "Mom, I'll set the table if you heat up the chowder."

The lazy day burst into activity. The boys cleared away the cards and hurried through the rain to their cabin to change clothes. After turning on the stove, Susan scurried around the living room straightening up for company. Harold braved the rain, moving the family car so Todd could park close to the cabin, but between the parking area and the cabin, a gigantic puddle had formed. There was no way for Mrs. Faraway to enter without navigating a rushing stream that flowed down the path to the doorstep.

Harold reappeared at the kitchen door. "Susan, I told you we needed a load of shale where we park the car. Amanda will have to cross a lake and ford a stream to get into the house."

"It would spoil the look of our entrance, dear. I like it just like it is."

"Dad, you wouldn't," Elena said. "It would look terrible. Instead of nice, soft spruce needles, we'd walk over a pile of stones."

"It would be a good deal more practical. Our guests won't drown coming to our door, and neither will we," Harold countered.

Elena shook her head to show her displeasure. "Then I'll spend the rest of the vacation sweeping needles over the shale. I love the natural look and the softness we have now."

"Right now we have a small lake and a stream of water. You can't even see the needles. But suit yourself, young lady. If you want to sweep needles, sweep them, but we're going to have a load of shale. The next time we set off for church in the pouring rain, both you and your mother will thank me."

Todd drove up and backed into the parking space Harold had vacated. Grabbing an umbrella, Harold rushed out to help Mrs. Faraway navigate the objectionable bodies of water. Nonetheless, she arrived with wet shoes. "I should have worn boots," she said. "I didn't think I'd need them."

"Never mind, Amanda," Susan said. "You can wear my slippers, and we'll dry your shoes by the fire."

"Thank you, my dear. My, that chowder smells good. It brings back delicious memories."

"Elena's been telling me what a wonderful flavor your chowder has. I've been looking forward to it all day," Todd said.

"Hang up your rain gear over the kitchen chairs, Todd. I'll find slippers for your grandmother. Please go sit by the fire, Amanda, and take off your shoes. Elena is popping popcorn for us."

Elena brought in a large tray of mugs brimming with cider and placed it on the coffee table. "Your cider tasted so good the other day, Mrs. Faraway, I've copied your hospitality."

The popcorn and cider disappeared fast. Susan and Elena excused themselves to serve dinner and soon had seven bowls of steaming chowder placed around the table. Oyster crackers, club crackers, and a bowl of raw cut carrots and fresh string beans completed the meal. When Susan announced supper, everyone gathered around the table. Harold seated Amanda to his left, where she could view the fire rather than the storm.

He reached out his arms. "Hands around the table. Dear Lord, we are indeed grateful for the shelter over our heads and for this good food. May it strengthen our bodies as we use them in Your service. We also ask You at this time to protect us from the coming hurricane. We pray that it may burn itself out before it gets here and that it will turn out to sea and do no further damage. We ask Your help for those towns that have already been struck and for those families in need of special help. We pray for calm tempers and harmony inside as we ride out the storm that is outside and ask for Your wisdom in deciding whether or not we should evacuate. We thank You for Your presence with us. We are indeed grateful that Your angels are watching over us and that we don't have to face situations like this in our own power."

Everyone but Amanda added "amen."

"Now," he said, picking up his spoon, "let's fortify ourselves for whatever the Lord sends our way."

*

Todd glanced around the table. It was like the pictures of happy families gathered around a dinner table on Thanksgiving Day, pictures he had viewed with envy as a child. He noted smiling faces, happy chatter, and a warm fire crackling in the fireplace. The scene fed the deep hunger inside him, though he seldom admitted its existence. Even his grandmother guarded her bitter tongue and joined in the good humor. He forgot the storm that had brought them together and enjoyed the moment.

*

After everyone had tasted the chowder, compliments flowed. "No one makes chowder better than Susan," Harold said. "I'm always disappointed when I order it in a restaurant."

"Half the accolades go to Elena. She did just as much as I did," Susan said. "Weren't we fortunate that we bought fish when it first started to rain? It must be impossible to find now with the hurricane on its way."

"Susan, it's lovely. It surely does bring back fond memories. I always loved the chowder my mother made, but I never learned how to make it. Most of the recipes today call for evaporated milk, but this is made the old-fashioned way with salt pork and regular milk. It's just like I remember it. Will you share your recipe with me?" Amanda asked.

"I don't follow a recipe, Amanda. I used to help Harold's mother make it, and I learned the approximate amounts from watching her. I'll be happy to tell you how we go about it."

"Thank you," Amanda said as she turned to Harold, "Do you think we'll have to evacuate, Harold?" Amanda had not forgotten the pending danger. Filled with anxiety and having no faith in a protective deity, she lacked a source of comfort. The peace that persisted in the Richards' home when such destructive forces were hurling toward them from the South was difficult for her to understand.

"I'm not expecting it, Amanda, but we're listening to the weather radio every few hours. Don't worry unnecessarily. We'll keep you informed." Turning to Susan, he said, "I think everyone could use another bowl of chowder, dear."

Elena got up. "Sit still, Mom. I'll get it."

Todd pushed back his chair. "Let me help, too." He followed Elena into the kitchen.

*

"Grandma has been a wreck all afternoon, fretting and worrying about the storm," Todd said once they were in the kitchen. "I'm grateful you invited us for dinner. Besides, I've missed your cheerful smile. I'm becoming addicted to it."

"How nice." Elena pivoted toward him, her face radiating that smile. "I thought it was a good idea myself—a good deed and a selfish desire all in one."

"I hope that means you missed me, too," Todd said as he began to take the refilled bowls of chowder to the dining table. "Grandma, how about you? After all that praise, surely you want some more."

"Yes, indeed, Todd, but make it half a bowl, please. It truly is delicious, Susan. Such a delicate flavor. And every taste makes you want another one."

"It's even better the second day. I'm sure you remember that from your childhood, too," Susan said.

"Yes. Mother used to make it the day before company came so the taste would be even better."

"I guess you'll just have to come back tomorrow," Mike chimed in.

Back in the kitchen, Todd asked Elena if she had ever experienced a hurricane here.

"No, not that I remember," she said. "Maybe when I was very young, but I had faith that Mom and Dad could handle anything then, and it probably didn't make much of an impression."

"Are you worried about this one, Elena?"

"I'm trying not to think about it, Todd. I'm just praying that it will blow itself out before it gets here."

"Yes," he said, "so am I." He took two more bowls of chowder into the living room.

The conversation for the rest of the meal kept returning to the approaching storm. As they sat at the table after dessert drinking coffee and tea, Harold pushed back his chair and headed for the radio. "Since it's on everyone's mind, why don't we find out what's happening? Maybe it's all over," he said as he reached for the dial.

"The hurricane has gathered speed and is heading directly north. It is expected to hit the Maine coast at five o'clock tomorrow afternoon, right at high tide. All coastal towns must evacuate as far north as Rockland. All towns farther north should remain on alert."

Everyone looked at Harold as the weather report broke the news, but no one spoke. Finally Harold said, "I guess we better take this more seriously, folks."

"Isn't Rockland just fifteen miles south of here by water?" Mike asked.

"Yes, it is." Susan rose to clear the table.

"Men, it's time to make definite preparations, in case. We should put the shutters up first thing in the morning. Todd, we'll come over and help you do yours first. Then perhaps you'll come over and help us prepare our cabins."

"I'd be happy to help, Mr. Richards, and thank you for all you've done for us."

"Now, Amanda, you're not to fret. We'll ride this out together. The cabins have withstood the wind and the surf all the years of my life and I expect them to stand throughout the children's lives as well."

"Elena and I will do the dishes," Todd said. "Grandma, go in and sit by the fire and relax awhile before we go home. Mr. Richards knows what to do, so we're in good hands."

When they returned to the living room, Susan busied herself setting out candles for both cabins. Next she filled the kerosene lamps that sat on the same shelves they had occupied in the years when the family was dependent upon them for light.

Mike took down the red lanterns from the kitchen wall and brought them to her. "We might need these, too, Mom."

"Yes, Mike, we probably will. Thank you."

"If the whole idea weren't so frightening, this would be fun," Amanda said with excitement in her voice. "I used to love the old kerosene lamps. It was my job to clean the black residue from them every few days. They were filthy and unattractive, but after shaking them in hot, soapy water and drying them, they sparkled. The contrast made washing them fun. Of course, we had to heat the water on the kerosene stove first. Harold, do you remember having a kerosene stove?"

"I certainly do, Amanda. I can see it sitting in the kitchen now, where our gas range is today. It was green, and it had a container of kerosene hanging upside down to one side of the stove. It was what some people might call 'very picturesque.'"

"Life was more difficult in some ways," Amanda said, "but it was slower and more basic. We didn't have all the gadgets and entertainment centers that we have today. Entertainment was cleaning the mantles on the kerosene lamps and delighting in their sparkle."

"That's what makes times like these fun, Amanda," Susan said as she finished filling the last lamp. "It gives us a chance to share with the children the way things used to be and reduces life to basics and necessities. It's amazing how well we can get along without all the luxuries of modern living."

Turning to the boys, she said, "Mike, you may carry this kerosene lamp over to your cabin and, Doug, here are candle holders for each room and extra candles to go with them."

"Do you think the waves will climb over Sunset Rock, Mom?" Doug asked.

"I certainly hope not," she said.

"I bet the bay will be a mass of white caps," Mike said with inappropriate enthusiasm.

Amanda started twisting her handkerchief again and a frightened expression returned to her eyes.

"Enough, boys," Susan admonished. "Don't let them upset you, Amanda. I don't believe it will make it this far. They still don't think we need to evacuate."

"It's time for us to go home, Grandma," Todd said.

Susan placed extra candles in a waterproof bag and handed them to Todd. After exchanging "good-byes," Todd and Amanda hurried to their car.

*

As Todd and Amanda drove away, Elena went to the telephone, dialed, and waited for the connection.

"Hi, Joyce," she said into the phone. "Have you heard that the hurricane will hit the Maine coast tomorrow? We're taking every precaution, but we'd appreciate your alerting the intercessors and calling the church. All the coastal towns up to fifteen miles south of us must evacuate. We're praying that it will blow out to sea and wear itself out before it comes here."

"Yes, late afternoon. We would appreciate your prayers. I'll call you tomorrow night if our lines are open."

"Thanks, we will." She hung up the phone and turned to her family. "Shall we have a time of prayer before we leave for our cottage?"

21

As DAYLIGHT BROKE, ELENA LAY IN BED listening to the wailing winds. She noted the absence of crows squawking and seagulls calling to each other. Had they already evacuated the coast?

Ready for adventure, the boys appeared in the main cabin wide-eyed and alert, before the girls had even planned breakfast.

To fortify them for their morning's work, Susan and Elena served the men a hearty breakfast of waffles and bacon. At the end of the meal, Doug pushed back his empty plate. "Let's go, Dad. Shall I get the hammers?"

"You may put my tool box in the car, Doug, but we need screwdrivers more than hammers. The shutters need to be screwed to the walls. Be sure to wear your slickers, boys."

The men bundled up and set out into the howling wind. Susan and Elena cleaned up the kitchen, each lost in her thoughts and anticipations. When she had finished, Elena hung up her dish towel. "Mom, you don't mind if I go over to my cabin to read until the men return, do you? I'll help them put on our shutters."

"No, of course not, dear. Just be careful the wind doesn't carry you away as you go back and forth."

*

Elena returned to find the men drying out in front of the fire and refortifying themselves with coffee and hot chocolate. They had successfully put the shutters on Todd's cottage and left Amanda rocking by the fire.

"Hi, everyone." Elena bounced into the cabin with good cheer. "Have you noticed the rain has diminished to a drizzle?"

Doug looked excited. "Does that mean we're in the eye of the hurricane?"

"It's too early for that, Doug." Harold put his arm around his son. "But this is a good time to put shutters on our cabins. No rest for the weary, boys. Let's get to it while we can."

"I'll help you," Elena offered.

They all donned their slickers and piled onto the porch, still buttoning up against the chilling wind. The plants around the cabin shimmered and shook as the wind stormed into the cove. Harold gave the orders. "We'll do the children's cabin first. Mike, you and Doug do the windows in the back. Todd and Elena, you do the windows on the side, and I'll work on the front."

They found the shutters piled in the woods beside the cabin, and placed them at the appropriate windows. Elena struggled to hold the shutters still as the wind tried to rip them from her hands. Harold, skilled from many years of practice, worked alone holding the shutter against the window with his elbow as he screwed it into the window frame on the outside. Soon the cabin looked as if it had been boarded up for a long winter.

"Anyone needing anything from this cabin had better get it now," Harold called into the wind. "We won't be able to enter it after I put the shutter on the door. We'll wait out the storm in the main cabin together." The three children scurried in and brought out a change of clothing and an assortment of books and games, which they piled into Elena's arms. She carried them to the other cabin as Harold screwed the final shutter onto the door.

"That was great work, boys. Now let's see if we can do the main cabin before the rains start again."

Elena dumped their belongings onto the bed in her parents' bedroom. "It's going very well," she encouraged Susan as she dashed through the living room. "The tide is just beginning to change."

She stepped onto Sunset Rock and watched the tide rush back into the cove. White water waves rolled through the rock openings and crashed against the rocks near its entrance. Large breakers pounding against its floor replaced the usual calm flow of water into the cove and produced bubbles of foam as they spread over the sand at the cove's edge.

As the men set about placing the shutters on the main cabin, she rejoined them. "Dad, it's so beautiful to watch. Do you think we could leave one window in the living room uncovered until the last minute?"

"Yes, Elena, I planned to do that."

With the same good teamwork, they boarded up the main cabin, leaving only the middle front window unprotected. By now the rain had begun again in earnest. Todd excused himself and hurried back to his grandmother. The Richards had invited them to return after her nap, so they could sit out the storm together.

*

As two o'clock approached, Elena wondered if Mrs. Faraway was able to sleep or, at least, rest. Her father snored softly in the next room. Knowing what would be required of him before the night was over, she was glad he could sleep now. Elena imagined Susan lying beside him wide awake.

The boys were ecstatic. Never had they seen the little cove churn with such dramatic intensity. Water spewed everywhere. Hidden in their black slickers, looking like penguins flapping their wings, they scuttled over the rocks. They hopped from one rock to another, wherever the sprays of water seemed highest, experiencing the storm as intimately as possible.

Elena thought of all the years her family had enjoyed the cabins...three generations now and still they stood. There must have been many storms like this. Thank goodness her father had kept the buildings in good repair. Would they still be there for her children to enjoy?

Her thoughts turned to Todd. She longed to tell him how deeply she felt for him. They had spoken of missing each other, but she wanted to hear more than that, much more. She stared out the window at a piece of driftwood bouncing up and down in the water outside their cove. As she watched it rise and fall, a large wave lifted the wood and hurled it against the granite, splintering it into many pieces. The pieces fell back into the churning waters, only to be picked up again and dashed against the rocks by the next wave. Would the hurricane pick up their little cabins with equal ease? She shuddered as she glanced around the room she loved so much.

*

Todd stood by the window of their cabin, watching a piece of driftwood picked up by the waves and shattered against the rock into a dozen pieces. He had been absorbed with thoughts of Elena. He wanted to tell her how much this week had meant to him, that he wouldn't have changed a thing, even if the hurricane swept them away. He had thought of hinting at it as a joke but knew he couldn't say anything remotely close. Better to keep it light, rather than tell her what was in his heart.

Seeing the wood fractured, he realized this was no joking matter. Would he be robbed of even the few weeks they still had together? Would they have to move inland and return to find the shore cottages equally battered? He felt angry, deprived of something he wanted more than anything in his life. It would not be the first time what he wanted most would be denied him.

He glanced at his grandmother, who had given up trying to rest. Dressed in her nightgown, she rocked back and forth, still twisting her handkerchief in her hands. *She must have worn out several by now,* he thought, suddenly ashamed of his selfishness. *I've been thinking only of myself.*

Amanda had complained all day, angry that he had left her alone to help put up the Richards' shutters. She complained that the whine of the wind penetrated the walls and even the shuttered windows. "I'm chilled to the bone, Todd. Put another log on the fire."

"I know this is difficult for you, Grandma, but God will take care of us. You must trust Him."

"Your God has never solved my problems, Todd, and I don't expect Him to begin now."

"I'm sorry you refuse to be comforted, Grandma. Please get dressed. It's time to join the Richards for the final watch."

*

The fire crackled in the fireplace keeping the cabin warm in spite of the driving wind and rain outside. The children had played an endless succession of games. Susan worked on a sweater she had begun to knit for Harold the previous summer. Amanda resumed her rocking and twisting. Tension inside the cabin mounted. Soon the tide would reach its highest. All day the weather report had predicted that the hurricane would hit at high tide, the worst possible time.

The shutter remained off the middle window. Earlier the children had taken turns, watching with fascination the huge waves crashing against the rocks, sending high-flying fountains of spray in all directions. Then a change took place. The rains ceased. The winds calmed. Strange lights shone in the sky—not bright and cheerful, but eerie and foreboding.

The four young people decided to investigate. They grabbed their slickers and ran to the rocks on the point. The winds stilled, and the sun broke through dark clouds, casting a purple hue over their world. Violet rays, emanating from ominous clouds outlined in ghastly yellow-greens, fanned the sky.

"It's strange," Elena said. "I've never seen such weird colors in the sky."

"Are we in the eye of the hurricane now, Elena?" Doug asked, blue eyes luminescent with wonder.

"How should I know? I'm no expert. I've never lived through a hurricane."

"Then why is it so still?" Doug's voice was hushed and mysterious.

"I can't think of any other explanation," Elena said, turning from them and looking toward the sea. They all stared into the distance.

Todd walked up behind Elena and put his hands on her shoulders. She whirled around and fell into his arms. "What does it mean, Todd? What will happen to us?"

He enfolded her and stroked her hair. "It's all right, Elena. Like your father said, storms have come and gone for over half a century and the cabins still stand. God will take care of us."

Elena felt the comfort of his strong arms. For a moment she thought she could face anything life had to offer with his arms firmly encompassed about her. She laid her head on his shoulder. The closeness of his physical presence, the tender intensity with which he stroked her hair, and his reminder that their faith was in God, not the storm, gave her strength. A heavenly peace settled over her and lightened her fears.

Mike peered at his watch. "It's almost 4:30. Let's go back and hear the latest weather update."

Doug ran ahead and bounded up the path to the cabin. Mike followed. Todd and Elena, still clinging to each other, strolled slowly up the path behind them.

When they arrived at the cabin, everyone was listening to the weather station, which blared out the same message again and again. "The hurricane is scheduled to hit the Maine coast by 5:30 this afternoon. Waters are expected to rise ten to fifteen feet."

Doug switched off the radio in disgust. "Nothing new there."

"Why is there no more mention of evacuation?" Amanda demanded an answer.

Before Harold could speak, Doug broke in, "Do they ever get tidal waves up here, Dad?"

"I've never heard of one, but I suppose it all has to do with the winds. We should be all right if the tide doesn't come any higher than expected. Amanda, it means it's too late for anyone to go out in the storm. Whatever happens, we'll ride it out here."

"Why would it hit right at high tide?" Susan expressed Amanda's thoughts aloud. "Do you suppose God is trying to tell us something?"

"Why don't we spend the last hour in prayer together?" Todd said.

"That's a great idea, Todd." Elena peeked out the window, then said to her father, "Do you think we could leave the storm window off a little while longer? It's fascinating to watch the changing colors and reassuring to see that everything is still standing."

"Yes, a little while longer," Harold said, trying to find the local news station on the other radio.

We interrupt this program to tell you that news has just come in. When the hurricane struck Portland, damage was extensive. Coastal roads have been washed out, telephone lines are down. There are reports of broken windows and damaged roofs along the coastline but no estimate has yet been made of the extent of the damage.

Harold turned off the radio. Without further comment, they gathered in a circle and bowed their heads. Amanda continued rocking, saying nothing.

Susan began, "Dear Lord, we ask You to quiet the storm or send it out to sea, before any further damage is done."

Elena elaborated, "Lord, we thank You for the winds that have been blowing so strongly. We ask that you use those winds to blow the storm away from Deer Isle, blow it far from towns where people live. Lord, please send the storm into the Atlantic Ocean and protect all the towns in the Penobscot Bay."

"Lord, we ask You to protect all those who are in the storm's path," Mike pleaded.

"Lord, we pray for all those who have been caught in the storm. We ask You to send them help. We ask You to comfort and heal those who have been hurt," Todd added.

Doug spoke up. "Lord, please don't let there be a tidal wave and keep the waters lower than the top of Sunset Rock."

They kept going around the circle, ending in a period of silence except for the creaking of Amanda's rocking chair. Outside the winds picked up again and howled with increasing intensity. They could hear the snapping of branches as they were severed from trees. Amanda let out an involuntary scream as one struck the porch with a resounding *thump.*

"Lord, we commend ourselves into Your hands and we thank You for protecting us. Amen," Harold said, completing the prayer. He checked the time. "Five minutes before 5:30. It's too late to put the shutter on. Children, I think we should watch this."

They gathered in front of the one unshuttered window and watched with fascination as the sky darkened and the lights went off. The whistle of the wind in the trees grew louder. A pink cast brightened the dark sky over the water. The wind blew straight toward them, penetrating the bullet holes in the walls that were made by hunters years ago. No one spoke. No one moved to light a lamp or a candle.

Outside the waning light revealed everything normal around the cabin, but over the distant whitecaps, a mass of purple, outlined in fading pink, interrupted by jagged streaks of gold, gave the sky an eerie look. "No one would believe this if it were painted on canvas," Elena said.

The wind began to swirl, sending fallen leaves and bits of debris dancing in circles. Trees bending toward the cabin righted themselves, swayed back and forth, then changing directions, bowed low toward the water away from the cabin. The activity in the cove quieted and the waters between the Cliff and the shore calmed as the rains started up again in earnest. Beyond the Cliff, under the strangely colored sky, a mass of whitecaps churned. Trees on the tip of Blakely Point doubled over, pointing away from their cove. Todd and the members of the Richards family watched for nearly an hour, entranced and scarcely moving, their eyes riveted on the spectacular drama being played out before them.

The force of the hurricane blew by without entering their cove. Not a tree fell.

Susan turned from the window and put her arms around Amanda, who still twisted her handkerchief in her hands. "There now, I believe the worst is over. God has been good to us, Amanda. The storm has blown right by us." She smiled reassuringly at the older woman. "You can relax now and help me light the kerosene lamps. It's time to prepare for supper."

"Are you sure it's over, Susan?"

"It blew right across the bay, Grandma. Didn't you see it? It started to come at us, but it turned right around and blew away from us. The Lord answered our prayers."

Amanda said nothing as she looked from Todd to Harold to Susan. Her rigid body slumped forward as she breathed in and let out days of accumulated tension. The lines in her face relaxed. She stared at Susan as she stirred into action, then her eyelids closed. Soon her head dropped forward as at last slumber claimed her.

Susan turned to them with a questioning brow. "Let me see. I have a big salad in the refrigerator that must be eaten. How about roasting hotdogs in the fireplace? We can make brown cows with the ice cream in the freezer in case the power stays off."

"It sounds like a party," Doug said. Root beer with vanilla ice cream was his all-time favorite.

"It is indeed a celebration," Harold said. "The Lord has protected us, just as we prayed."

22

THE RAINS CONTINUED INTO THE NIGHT, but by morning all signs of the storm had vanished. With the air clear, the bay calm, the cloudless sky returned to bright blue and a beautiful day greeted the Richards.

The news detailed extensive damage to the south, but damage to the island had been minimal. Though power was still out, phone lines remained open. Calls from friends in Florida started coming early in the morning. Her voice animated with excitement, Elena explained how the wind had changed and how they had watched the hurricane blow by in the outer bay. Their cove had been spared. She thanked her friends for their vigil and assured them their prayers had been answered.

After breakfast, Todd and Amanda had made their way back to their cabin.

Midmorning, Todd appeared at the back door, his handsome face flushed from his haste in running over to share the news. "We've had calls all morning from Pittsburgh. I told them how we prayed and watched the wind change direction. Grandma listened but didn't say much. I hope it sank in. She's exhausted from the emotional struggle and wants to sleep most of the day."

Elena greeted him with wide smiles, but her smile faded as she lowered her voice. "Todd, all the shutters are down, and Doug is alone in his cabin. This would be a great time to talk to him. Now that the storm is over, we have to deal with his problem."

"Sure, if you think he'll listen."

"It's worth a try," she said, her eyes imploring Todd to do his best. "I'll pray the whole time you're with him."

"I'm so thankful the hurricane didn't spoil the remaining half of our vacation, I'll do anything you ask."

*

Todd knocked on the door of the children's cabin. Doug opened it and looked surprised when he saw Todd. "Hi, Doug, after boarding up the place yesterday, I thought I should see what it looks like. Mind showing me around?"

"Sure. Come in. This is the room Mike and I share. It's kind of a mess right now," he said, as if the mess were the exception rather than the norm. Todd looked beyond the scattered clothes to see three beds along the walls. The fishing gear near one of them told him that bed belonged to Mike.

"We have a table for eating and game playing here with a great view of the cove," Doug said, acting as host, "and a kitchen in the back. It has everything we need. Elena lives in the other room. It's the old part, but it's all fixed up now."

Todd moved to the doorway of the adjacent bedroom and glanced inside. He saw a double bed neatly made and everything in its proper place. Pink hearts dominated the large pillow bolsters that leaned against pale green walls. It was easy to imagine Elena in such feminine surroundings.

"This looks more like a guy's room," he said, glancing around the unfinished walls that housed even more lobster buoys than the main cabin. Sitting down on Doug's bed, he picked up a science fiction book on the table next to it. "Is this any good?" he asked.

"Yeah, it's great—all about life on distant planets. Do you think there's life on other planets, Todd?"

"I haven't given it much thought. What do you believe, Doug?"

"I think there is. I read so much science fiction I begin to think it's real."

"We do tend to believe what we read, Doug. Sometimes that can be a problem. Like with pornography. Do you mind if I tell you a story about a friend of mine that's true?"

Doug scowled. "Elena sent you here."

"She loves you very much, Doug. She wants only what's best for you."

"That's what everyone says. As long as I do things their way," Doug made a pinched face and took a few dainty steps on tiptoe, mimicking his elders. Then he whirled to face Todd angrily. "There's nothing wrong with the magazines. All the guys look at them."

Todd was startled by Doug's unaccustomed anger so close to the surface, but he kept his own tumultuous reactions deep inside. "Let me tell you what happened to my friend. He was a youth leader at our church, had a great wife and a little baby. He had looked at magazines like the ones you're looking at now when he was your age before he committed his life to Christ. He said they really messed up his head about what women want in a relationship. When he became a Christian and started dating girls from the church, he scared them. He came on too fast. Expecting the girls to like his advances, he frightened them away. He talked to the minister about it and finally realized the magazines had given him the wrong idea about sex and what girls wanted and needed. That's what worries your family, Doug."

Doug said nothing. He slouched farther into his bed, folded his arms, and stared down at his pillow.

Todd went on. "The minister got through to my friend Peter. He stopped looking at the magazines. In time he met Sherry, a lovely Christian girl, and married her. They were happy at first and, after a time, he became the youth director at our church. Things were going great for him. They had a beautiful baby girl, and he was popular with the kids at church. Then some of the guys in his group began watching porn videos. They knew enough to know they weren't good for them and talked to Peter about it. He shared with them his own experience and encouraged them to stop."

Todd paused. He could tell Doug was listening, but what came next would be difficult for the boy to swallow. "Then he became curious about what they were seeing and convinced himself that he should know so he could better minister to them. One week, when Sherry went home to visit her mother, Peter rented a bunch of videos and watched them at home alone. Fascinated by them, he started fantasizing about having sex with girls like those in the videos—girls who would do anything he wanted. Before the week was out, he went back to the store and rented some hard-core videos with even more bizarre behavior, all the while telling himself that he needed to see what the guys in his youth group were watching. In very little time, he became hooked again."

"I'm not hooked. Gimme a break," Doug pleaded.

"What I'm trying to show you is how easily it can happen, Doug, even when you know better and don't want to get hooked." When Doug didn't respond, Todd went on with his story.

"At times Peter felt truly remorseful, but the fantasies kept going through his mind, and he wanted his wife to do some of the things he'd seen in the videos. When she recoiled from him, he started renting the videos in secret. He encouraged some of the boys to tell him what they were seeing and experiencing. At first, he was convinced he was doing it to help them. But after a time, he realized he was getting a kick from talking to the guys about porn.

"His wife was getting more and more upset by his strange behavior and was becoming more and more distant. He started bringing magazines and videos home and hiding them. She would find them and be hurt and cry. He would promise never to buy them again, but in a few weeks, she'd find more.

"Eventually, he thought about sex so much, he had trouble reading his Bible and preparing lessons. The change in his behavior frightened Sherry so much she took their baby and moved back to her mother's home. Finally free to indulge his fantasies, he became careless. When his senior pastor caught him, he broke down and admitted he'd lost control of his life and desperately needed help."

Doug had unfolded his arms and now looked earnestly at Todd as he told the story.

"Many of the men at our church tried to help him. He'd stay away from pornography for a while, but he carried in his mind all those pictures of women from the magazines and videos. Even if he didn't look at new ones, those pictures kept coming back to his mind every time he'd see something sexually suggestive on TV. He could never escape the power of those pictures he'd planted in his mind. He ended up losing both his family and his job."

As Todd finished the story, Doug turned and stared out the window.

"Doug, you want a great marriage like your mom and dad have, don't you?"

"Sure, but not every guy who looks at a magazine turns out like your friend. Thousands of guys who've looked at them get married and stay together."

"Yes, but many of them have to fight those pictures in their minds all their lives."

"Haven't you ever looked at a porn magazine?" Doug asked.

"Yes, but I didn't want my picture of sex ruined. I knew they weren't good for me, and I made the decision not to look again. If you make that decision and you meet a beautiful young girl someday, you'll be glad your mind is clean and not cluttered with those pictures. Please believe me," Todd pleaded.

"That's what Mike says."

Todd could almost see the boy's mind seesawing back and forth. "Is there something you would like to ask me, Doug?"

"Aw, you're exaggerating. Everyone's got the wrong idea about me. There's nothing wrong with looking at a few pictures. All the guys do it." He opened the door and bounded down the steps. "Just leave me alone," he called back to Todd and bolted into the woods.

Todd, disappointed, watched the boy disappear into the trees. He sighed. He had tried his best and failed, just as he had with his brother. He wished he could tell Doug about his father. That would get his attention. But he wasn't ready for the Richards to know about that. *Will I ever be?* He imagined that would be the end of his relationship with Elena.

Sad that he had failed to reach Doug, he rose from the bed and left the cabin. While telling his story, he had looked out the window and caught a glimpse of Elena and Mike sauntering down the path to the shore. He set out to find them.

Driftwood and all kinds of debris lined the shoreline. The hurricane had deposited it at the high tide mark. Large hunks of seaweed torn from the rocks lay drying in the sun on the beach. Todd saw that there was little permanent damage, but the tide looked exceptionally low.

He caught up to Elena and Mike on the far side of the point. Gripped by the excitement of discovery, they pointed out newly exposed rocks and patches of sand. "Look at Elephant Rock," Elena exclaimed as she spotted the huge expanse of rock where they found most of their starfish. "I've never seen it so far out of water." As Todd joined them, she grabbed his hand and pulled him after her as she ran toward it.

Climbing onto the great rock, she ran to the edge and peered over the side. "Look at all the starfish we can reach." She leaped down onto an exposed rock beside it, rolled up her sleeves, and reached into the icy water. "Todd, I'll throw them to you," she called as she reached down again and again and removed the clinging creatures from their home. "They're every color of the rainbow. Look at this one," she cried out in near ecstasy, holding up a large, rose red starfish twice the size of her hand. "Have you ever seen such a beauty?"

"Never," Todd said truthfully, piling her treasures one on top of the other in one hand. As Elena kept reaching into the water and prying one after another from the side of the rock and throwing them to Todd, he filled the other hand as well. "Shouldn't you leave some for another time? How many can your pool support at once?"

"I suppose you're right. It's thrilling to find so many, but that's more than enough. They'll be beautiful crawling over the pool at night." Withdrawing her hand from the water, she reached toward Todd. "Can you give me a hand up?"

Todd looked at his hands piled high with tentacled sea life. The starfish, already limp from the sun beating on them, looked like spoonfuls of colored jellies melting into each other. "Just a minute," he said, bending over to put them down.

"Never mind, I can make it," Elena called out, not hesitating to try it on her own.

The side of the rock, still wet and slippery, could not provide a secure foothold. When her feet landed short of the top, she lost her balance and began to fall backward. She clutched at the rock with bare hands, scraping the rough surface all the way down. "Todd," she screamed as her legs slid into the icy water and her back crashed against the rock from which she had come. She lay there groaning, unable to move as the water climbed to her waist.

Todd dumped the starfish in a flash and jumped onto the rock where she lay. "Elena, are you all right? Why didn't you wait for me?"

"Oh, my hands," she cried, watching in horror as they turned red from blood pouring out of multitudes of scratches.

"What about your back?" Todd asked as he scooped her out of the water.

"It hurts, but I think it's only bruised," she whimpered. "Todd, I'm so glad you're here." She laid her head on his shoulder.

Todd stood on the rock with Elena in his arms, surveying the situation. "If you couldn't make it alone, I'm not likely to make it with you in my arms."

Without further hesitation, he forged into the cold water. So concerned was he about Elena, he scarcely felt the chilling shock as it crept up his legs and covered his waist. Holding as much of Elena above the water as he could and stumbling over the uneven floor of the bay, he waded around the great rock to the shore.

"Todd, you're soaked," Elena cried.

"That makes two of us," he said, kissing her forehead.

*

As Todd carried her across the rocks and sandy beaches, she lay back in his strong, warm arms, happy to be carried. In spite of her discomfort, Todd's arms around her felt good. *Is this real, or part of my old daydreams? This is where I belong.* She nestled her head deeper into the curve of his neck, oblivious to her pain.

Mike ran over to help. "Gosh, Sis, I saw you fall. Is there anything I can do?" He gaped at her bloody hands.

"Yes," she replied. "Get the starfish on top of Elephant Rock and put them in the starfish pool, will you?"

Todd burst out laughing. "When this lady starts a project, nothing can deter her. Not even falling into the bay and nearly cracking her back in two."

Mike shook his head. "Sure, Sis, if that's what you want."

"Clearly it is." Todd shifted Elena in his arms and started off toward the cabin.

23

DOUG RUSHED TO OPEN THE DOOR as Todd arrived back at the cabin carrying Elena. "Is something the matter, Sis?" he asked, hoping it had nothing to do with his rejection of Todd's story. Then he spotted her bloody hands. "What happened?"

"I tried to jump onto Elephant Rock from the starfish rock, but I didn't make it. The tide was lower than we've ever seen it. Wait 'til you see the starfish we found. Mike is putting them in our tidal pool."

Todd carried her through the door. "Doug, put a slicker on the couch. She's dripping wet."

Susan appeared from the bedroom and cried out, "Oh, my baby."

"I'm okay, Mom. Just a little beat up."

"Elena, what's happened to your hands?"

"She tried to stop herself by using them as brakes," Todd explained.

Susan looked at Todd. "You're soaking, too. Did you jump in after her?"

"Something like that, Mrs. Richards. I knew I couldn't make the jump with Elena in my arms, so I waded ashore."

"You must be freezing. Doug, turn on the fire under the kettle on the stove. Something hot to drink should warm their insides. Elena, do you want a hot bath?"

"That would be great a little later, Mom. I just want to lie here for now. Would you wash my hands?"

"Of course." Susan rushed for a towel and hot washcloth. Tenderly, with a mother's loving touch, she wiped away the blood, the sand, and the pieces of barnacle still embedded in Elena's hands.

"Ohhh," Elena groaned.

Todd stroked her forehead. "It will be a long time 'til you can grip a tennis racquet."

"They better be healed by the time the tournament starts," Elena said with determination.

"Here comes Pastor Dar," Doug called from the kitchen as he opened the door for him.

"Hello, Doug. I've come to see how you survived the hurricane."

"We survived the hurricane fine, but the low tide caught Elena," he said as he ushered Pastor Dar into the living room.

"Well, young lady, what happened to you?" His eyes surveyed Elena and Todd. "You both look like you've been swimming."

"It's a rather long story," Todd said, "but we're glad you're here. Elena needs prayer for her hands and her back. She took a hard fall on the rocks."

Doug came into the room proudly carrying a tray full of cups of hot chocolate. "Anyone like a hot drink?" He offered one to everyone within reach, happy to have the attention on someone else for a change.

"Doug, how lovely." Susan beamed approvingly at him. "I'm sure Elena and Todd would like one. How about you, Pastor Dar?"

"Sounds great to me," he said, reaching for a cup. His merry eyes sparkled and crinkled at the edges above his round, red cheeks with a smile that exuded warmth and confidence. He was just the comfort they needed.

Before Doug could set the empty tray down, there was a loud knock on the back door. He set the tray in front of Susan and went to answer it.

"Hi, Harv. Hi, Eddie and Joey," Doug said. "Yesterday was a blast, wasn't it?"

The boys trooped into the living room following Doug.

"Ayuh, but it must've been more exciting on the shore than it was for us. We've been down to Twisted Tree, and there's all kind of debris washed up." Eddie was pumped.

"We had a ton o' water and fierce winds. We was afraid the tree house would blow down, but it held good. It was tighter than our house. We had buckets catching water everywhere," Harvey said, grinning from ear to ear.

"Doug, why don't you take the boys down to the shore and show them the starfish Elena found?" Susan suggested.

"Sure, Mom. Come on, guys." Doug grabbed his jacket and led them toward the door. "You should've seen the fountains of water spray in our cove. It was awesome. And the whitecaps beyond the Cliff. Wow! The light out. And you wouldn't believe..."

The door slammed behind them.

*

Susan sighed, relieved that the boys had left and given her an opportunity to talk to her minister without Doug present.

"Doug thought it was quite an adventure," Pastor Dar said. "But you didn't have any damage, Susan?"

"No, Dar, the Lord answered our prayers. The storm blew away from our cove. We had no damage. But, Dar," she added, "we have another problem we must talk to you about. About Doug and those boys."

"Would you like us to leave, so you can talk to Pastor Dar alone, Mom?" Elena offered.

"No, it's a problem the whole family is trying to understand. And, Todd, you're welcome to stay, too."

"What have they been up to, Susan?" Dar asked, giving her full attention.

"Elena has twice found a pornographic magazine in Doug's room. We think he's getting them from Harvey, but he won't admit it."

"Has Harold talked to him?"

"Yes, but Doug was still too upset to respond well. Then the hurricane came, and we gave him a temporary pass to help prepare for it. Doug is adamant that there's nothing wrong with looking at the magazines. He insists that he just wants to know what it's all about and all the boys do it."

"He's probably right about that, Susan. Pornography is as available here as in big cities. I'll be happy to talk to him if you want me to."

"Yes, at the right time, Dar, but tell me if it's as harmful as I think it is. I talked to one of Chester's clerks because the market carries the magazines. He laughed at me. 'It's as normal and American as apple pie and ice cream,' he said, not taking me seriously."

Dar's gaze turned even more serious. "You're right, Susan. It's very harmful, particularly when it's a young person's first knowledge of sex. It completely distorts what God intended for the relationship between a man and a woman. Sex was God's idea. He created it and meant it to be good, but His idea and what the pornographers have done with it are altogether different."

"What *have* they done with it, Dar?"

"It presents a pretty degrading picture of women as nothing but sex objects. Pornography is full of lies about women, like they have insatiable sex appetites and are willing to accept anyone as a sexual partner. So men get the idea they're justified in using women to fulfill their desires. *Playboy*, for example, when it first came out, told men that women marry them only for their money. Over the years it's convinced men they can have even better sex outside of marriage with no commitments or limits to their personal freedom.

"I remember the conclusion of one researcher who's done a lot of research on the effects of sexually explicit media. I think his name was Dr. Dolf Zillmann. He described pornography as 'perfect strangers meeting to perform the sex act, reaching unbelievable euphoria, then parting never to meet again.'" Dar shook his head.

130

"What a terrible thing to teach our young men." Susan frowned, feeling a burden not only for her own son but for the thousands of young men whose minds were being corrupted.

"Yes, it is, and the rape theme in pornography does even more harm," Dar explained bluntly. "It teaches that a woman's 'no' really means 'yes' and that every woman secretly wants to be raped. If a man forces himself on a woman, she'll resist at first, then relax, enjoy it, and actually beg for more. Men get the idea that it's all right to rape a woman because she really wants them to do it."

"Do men really believe such a thing, Dar?"

"Yes, I'm afraid many of them do."

"Poor Doug." Elena groaned. "I've always heard that rape has more to do with power than with sex."

"For hardened men, maybe," Dar said. "But when kids are involved for the first time, they're usually imitating something they've seen and can't handle emotionally."

"Doesn't it go over the heads of very young children? I mean, they don't really know what it's all about, do they?" Susan tried to imagine how it affected children even younger than Doug.

"Its greatest impact is on young boys twelve and under," Dar said. "Almost all sex criminals have been introduced to it at a very young age. One expert said that giving a twelve-year-old, whose hormones are already raging, a pornographic magazine is like lighting a match to a stick of dynamite!

"What happens is that men and boys who regularly read pornography come to distrust women. It teaches that women want to take all they can get from a man—sex, his money, his belongings—then move on to another man. That leads, of course, to a kind of sexual callousness where they overlook the injury to a woman and think only of their own pleasure."

"I've never seen it, but I've heard it's all over the Internet. Is there anything that can be done to stop it, Dar?" Susan asked.

"Unfortunately, liberal groups like the ACLU have been successful in making people think they have a right to see whatever they want to see because of the First Amendment. Personally, I'm convinced that the founding fathers had political speech in mind when they wrote that, not sex acts. Now that they've allowed it on the Internet, I'm afraid there's no going back to their original intent.

"Magazines are only the beginning. Videos are bad enough, but now that they allow it on the computer, it's in almost every home, even in a child's bedroom, if his parents don't take precautions. I've always thought the government lost its collective mind when it allowed unlimited pornography on the Internet."

Susan grimaced. "But doesn't it do real harm to women when men's heads are full of it?"

"Yes, Susan. I believe there's a direct connection between it and domestic violence. I feel strongly about it because I've seen it ruin the lives of many men and women in my church. I've read all the articles I could, searching for something to convince men how harmful it is."

Elena broke in. "When I saw the pictures, I knew they would warp Doug. It's a crime to put such pictures in a young boy's mind. They'll rob him of the fun of romance and wonderful things like holding hands and walking arm-in-arm." Elena reached for Todd's hand. "Those things can be so exciting. Pastor Dar, you must make him understand."

Todd spoke for the first time. "I tried to reach Doug this afternoon. I wish I had heard it expressed so well before I talked to him. I just told him what had happened to my friend. He seemed to be moved at first, but then rejected it. I don't think I changed his mind at all. He kept insisting that my friend was the exception, that all guys look at porn and there's no harm in it. It would be helpful if you would explain it to him, Pastor Dar."

"I will Todd, the first opportunity I have. Now, Susan, don't look so worried. Doug is a good boy, and it must be hard for him to oppose everyone in his family. I'm sure this won't be a lasting problem for him. He's fortunate to have so many people who love him.

"Perhaps it would be a good idea for all of us to go out of our way to befriend Harvey and to invite him to church. He has a very bad home situation. His father is drunk most of the time and beats him often. The child hardly remembers his mother. He would appreciate your taking an interest in him. Perhaps we can change his tastes as well."

"Isn't the Sunday school picnic this weekend?" Elena asked. "We could all plan to come and encourage Doug to invite the three boys. I'm sure they'd enjoy the games and all the good food. If he likes it, we could offer to pick Harvey up and take him to church on Sunday."

"That's a very good idea, Elena. What do you think, Susan?"

"It will be difficult for me. I really don't want Doug to play with those boys, but I'm sure you're right. Harold said something of the sort the first time I expressed anxiety about Harvey playing with Doug. I'm sure he'd agree."

"Good, that settles it. Now I must be going, but first let's pray that the pictures won't be indelibly printed in Doug's mind. That's a real danger, and you must pray that won't happen. Let's pray for Elena's healing first, then for

Doug, that his mind will be protected until he comes to his senses and believes what you're all trying to tell him."

*

"Hey, guys, look at this. It must've been torn loose during the hurricane." Harvey held up a brand-new lobster buoy. "I bet we can find more of 'em if we follow the coast 'round to Blakely Point."

"Ayuh, let's try it," Eddie agreed.

"There's sure to be lots of debris from the storm around the next cove," Doug said. "Let's go."

The boys set out, following the coast close to the water. It was more passable now than it usually was with the tide so low. Eddie tugged at something wedged between the rocks. He pulled out half an oar. "Gee, you don't suppose somebody was out in that storm in a rowboat, do ya?"

"Naw, it's probably an old one that got washed in with the tide," Harvey said.

"Wait 'til you see this," Doug exclaimed triumphantly as he held up an artistically gnarled piece of wood with knots coming out of its sides. The bark was gone and its bumpy surface was worn smooth. The top knot made a perfect handle. "What a great walking stick. I bet Dad will love it."

"Hey, that's a-okay, Doug. I never seen one like it." Harvey admired the stick. "Kin I try it?"

"Sure, but be careful. I want to take it back to Dad just like I found it."

Joey ran ahead for a time. Soon he came running back. "Hey, guys, wait 'til you see what I found, laying right in the middle of the beach in the next cove. C'mon, follow me."

Ahead they could see a whole crab crate sitting at the water's edge. They ran up to it, each one trying to reach it first. "Look," Joey said, as he was the first to arrive. He threw back the top of the crate. "The crabs inside are still alive. We can take them home for supper."

"Sure enough, Joey," Harvey said. "You found yourself a good one. Here," he said, holding out a bag that he drew from inside his jacket. "I always carry a bag after a storm. You can take the crabs home in this, and we can push the crate into the bushes and come back later and git it."

"Good idea, Harv. That'll work fine."

When Joey had finished putting the crabs in the bag, Harvey reached into his jacket again and pulled out a shiny new magazine. "Come on," he said, heading up the beach to a group of rocks. He ducked behind the biggest of the rocks and beckoned the others to follow. Totally out of sight from the road, they huddled around Harvey, who held the magazine out in front of him. "My friend Ned gave it to me. This here's a *Hustler*. You guys ain't seen nothin' like this before." Relishing their anticipation, he slowly opened it and turned the pages one by one. Eddie and Joey looked on with open mouths.

Doug hadn't said anything when his father asked him if he had seen a *Hustler*. It helped him believe his father didn't know what he was talking about, but here it was. He had made a promise to his father. He couldn't remember a time when he deliberately had broken his word before. He knew he should run home, but the boys wouldn't understand.

He glanced down at the magazine. Harvey was right. They hadn't seen anything like it before.

24

ELENA HUNG UP THE PHONE after speaking to Todd and smiled at her father as he came through the door. "Todd and I thought it would be a great day to explore another island. Since the boys are playing golf and you have a painting project going, you wouldn't mind, would you, Dad? Mother invited Mrs. Faraway for a shopping spree and lunch, so Todd has a day off."

"Sounds like a good idea to me, if you feel up to it. How's the back today?" He pulled out a chair from the table and looked fondly at his younger daughter.

"A little sore. I wouldn't want to do any jumping, but I think I can sit in the boat."

"Better wear gloves to protect your hands."

"I will, Dad. That's a good idea."

"Elena, wait. There's something I want to add." Harold motioned for her to sit in the chair next to his.

"Have you said anything to Todd about the promise ring you're wearing?"

"No, Dad, it's never come up."

"Well, don't you think it's about time you mentioned it? Todd has more than a casual interest in you, and he is six years older than you are. Don't you think you should set things straight with him before you find yourself in a compromising situation?"

"Dad, Todd is a perfect gentleman. There's no need to bring up the subject," she said, offended at her dad's hint of impropriety.

"I don't mean to suggest that anything is wrong with your relationship with Todd, Elena. Todd seems to be a fine young man, but any girl as lovely as you is bound to raise the blood pressure of any normal young man. The purpose of the promise ring is to protect you both from temptation. My intentions are solely for your good, Elena, and for Todd's good, too, for that matter. Should I speak to him?"

"No, definitely not, Dad. I'll do it myself,' she said with a touch of anger. But immediately she softened. "I'm sorry. I know you meant no harm. I'll mention it before the day is out."

"Thank you, Elena. Have fun." He gave her a hug and went back to his painting.

Susan handed the menu to Amanda. "This is my favorite restaurant for lunch. The view of Stonington Harbor is lovely."

"I feel like we're *in* the harbor." Amanda glanced down at the water surrounding three sides of the building that hung so far over the shore rocks, it appeared to be floating. "It's like being in a boat," she said with unusual good humor.

Stonington Harbor, always beautiful with its myriad of moored boats, its many spruce-covered islands, sparkled on this sunny day. In the far distance the high island, Isle Au Haut, towered above them all, protecting the harbor from Atlantic winds. The activity in the harbor, boats coming in and going out, seagulls clustering and circling above the fishing boats, typified the picturesque Maine seacoast with its mix of summer sailors and year-round working vessels.

"It truly is magnificent," Amanda said.

"Yes, I never grow tired of it," Susan agreed, enjoying the familiar but beloved scene. Turning to the menu, she smiled at Amanda. "I recommend all of their sandwiches on their home made whole wheat bread. But be sure to leave room for their ice cream. It's heavenly."

"I'll have whichever is your favorite, Susan. What a lovely morning it's been, poking in all the island gift shops. I can't believe there are so many. I think you made the perfect choice for a birthday present for Stephanie. She should love it."

As they visited store after store, Susan had debated between sweatshirts painted with pine trees and shore rocks, pieces of silver jewelry by local artists, and an assortment of Maine crafts. She had settled on a centerpiece for a table that featured two large seagulls with spread wings landing on a beautifully shaped piece of driftwood. The base was adorned with native sea shells and items typical of the Maine shore.

"I think she'll like it. If she doesn't, she can return it to me. I'd love to have it. I always like to give gifts that appeal to me, don't you?"

"Without a large family, I don't buy many gifts, Susan."

"Tell me more about your family, Amanda."

"There isn't much to tell."

"Well," Susan prompted, "tell me about Todd's mother. Was she your only child?"

"Yes." Amanda said nothing more as the waitress served their lunch. She concentrated on cutting her sandwich in quarters before she continued, speaking slowly as if it were painful. "We had a baby boy before we had her, but he lived only two days. He was born prematurely. The doctors couldn't save him. I was inconsolable and didn't want to have any more children. I thought I couldn't stand the pain if anything like that happened a second time." She fell silent again as she took a bite of her sandwich.

"But you did try again," Susan encouraged.

"Yes, eventually I did. I wanted to hold a baby so badly, I think I would have done anything. When Cecilia was born, she had rosy, round cheeks, bright blue eyes, and she was fair from the start. Some babies are born with dark hair, you know, and they lose it and are blond for a time, but she was always blond and her complexion was always pink and creamy. By the time she was a year old, she had beautiful, soft, blond curls. I spent hours twisting them around my fingers and setting them just so." Amanda smiled at the memory. "Those were happy days. We had such high expectations for her." She sighed.

"When she was three, we learned she had a heart condition. The doctors told us she wouldn't live past ten. You can imagine how devastated we were. We doted on her and gave her everything she ever wanted. I'm afraid we spoiled her terribly."

"It's hard to love a child too much." Susan tried to ease Amanda's pain.

"I've read about tough love, the kind that loves enough to do the hard work of disciplining. We did it the easy way. Instead of crossing her when she had a tantrum, we gave in to her every wish. We lived to regret it."

"But she did grow up in spite of the doctor's dire predictions?"

"Yes, of course, or I wouldn't have Todd. She grew up doing everything she wanted to do, not learning to care about what suited other people. She married a man we didn't like. They both drank a great deal of alcohol. Every time we saw them, it ended in a fight. It was dreadful."

"I'm so sorry, Amanda. I can imagine how that broke your heart."

"Yes, she did that many times. But she had Todd and later his brother, Bobby, came along."

"I didn't know Todd had a brother." Susan raised her eyebrows in surprise.

"Yes, he's dead now," Amanda said, offering no details. "Todd was always a handsome child. He reminded me of the baby I lost. Cecilia never had time for him, so I tried my best to make up for her neglect. He became the delight of my life. I can't tell you what a joy he's been to me."

"You don't have to," Susan said. "It's obvious. He's a fine young man and he loves you very much, Amanda. He takes good care of you."

"Yes, he thinks he has a lot to repay me for, but he's given me far more than I ever gave him." Amanda looked out the window, as if watching the boats going by. But Susan could see her struggling to keep her emotions under control.

"Are things better with Cecilia now?"

"No, they aren't," Amanda said, the bitter edge to her voice returning. "My relationship with her couldn't be worse. I'm sure it's beyond your understanding, Susan. Let's talk about something else. Have you been to all those islands out there?"

Susan wanted to comfort her but felt any further questions would be intrusive. She chatted about their experiences on the islands, determined to give Amanda a happy memory of their day together, even if she failed to help her with her relationship with her daughter.

When they had finished their sandwiches, they went to the counter to choose the flavor for their cones. "Oh, they're so big," Amanda exclaimed. "I feel like a school girl again."

"That's wonderful, Amanda. That's just how I want you to feel today."

*

"We're way past Stonington," Todd shouted over the roar of the motor. Where do you want to land today?"

"Look at that little island." Elena pointed to a narrow bit of land on their left. "It's an unnamed oval on the map, but isn't it lovely?" Excitement grew as she studied its attributes. "Its terrain is gentle, much less rocky than most of the islands. It's perfect for me today. It shouldn't tax my back at all. Let's circle and find the best place to land."

As they came around the far side of the island, a larger sand beach with no obstructions offered a perfect landing place. Todd headed the boat toward the shore and cut the motor. Elena, wearing gloves to protect her bruised hands, took hold of the rope and crawled carefully over the bow. Todd anchored the boat and moved their possessions up the beach toward the woods.

Suddenly Elena dropped to her knees and poked in the sand. With unveiled delight, she exclaimed, "Look, Todd, a piece of Neptune shell. This is the one I've been telling you about. Mom and I have been trying to find a whole one for years." Elena continued to explore the sand about her and found several other pieces, even larger than the first. "This beach is covered with pieces of Neptune. I've never, ever found so many at once."

Rising up, her gloved hands full of bits of the treasured shell, she raised her arms above her head and whirled around. Her long, blond hair swirled behind her. "This island is wonderful. Let's christen it *Neptune Island.* I bet there's a whole one here somewhere."

She placed the treasured pieces in her shelling bag. Then, grabbing Todd's hand, she hurried their pace to the other side of the island. Elena selected a spot on the beach where they were surrounded by sea oats bowing in the breeze. The sand was fine, both warm and dry from the sun's full strength.

"Let's eat lunch here, but first I want to see it all." She darted back into the narrow strip of trees that filled the center of the island. There was no underbrush, only soft, green grass underneath tall spruce trees. "It looks like someone has tended this garden. Yet it looks so undiscovered. No name. No signs of man anywhere."

Raising her arms again, she twirled in circles, pointing her face upward toward the warm sun. Intoxicated by the island's charm, she ran back to Todd. Spontaneously, she threw her arms around his slender waist and, smiling up at him, proclaimed, "It's an island just for us. Our very own, unnamed and waiting here to be discovered and loved by us."

*

Todd had never before met anyone like her. Her unexpected burst of emotion nearly overwhelmed him. Her smile radiated confidence, innocence, and exuberant life. *What must it be like to be so free, so unburdened that you could abandon yourself to each moment to such an extent as this?* he asked himself. Todd longed to enter into her joy, but he didn't know how. Threatened by her exuberance, he wanted to retreat deep inside and shield himself from the onslaught of her enthusiasm. He could see that Elena was so happy, so absorbed in her joy, she had no idea how he felt.

They spent the next hour exploring the slim interior and the entire shoreline of the island.

"There's nothing dramatic about it," Elena said, "but every area has its special delight. I like the sea oats on the beach the best, but the shady spots under the trees in the woods are lovely, too. The whole island is intriguing. Oh, Todd," she turned to him again, "it's a perfectly wonderful day. Let's sit here in the sand and lean up against this rock while we eat our lunch and enjoy every moment." She patted the hard granite boulder that rose out of the warm sand and spread their picnic blanket before it.

Elena continued to bubble with conversation throughout their lunch. Todd relaxed and allowed himself to be pulled into her enthusiasm.

Suddenly she changed the subject. "Todd, have you ever noticed this ring on my finger?"

Todd was startled. "It doesn't mean you have a relationship with someone, does it?" His joy disappeared.

"Not a boy, if that's what you mean," she hastened to say. "It's more like a promise to God, to myself, and to the man I'll marry."

Todd frowned, confused.

She hurried on with her tale. "When I was sixteen, my father took me on a date. We went out to dinner, just the two of us, to a special restaurant. After dinner, he presented me with this ring. He asked me to wear it as a promise that I'll wait until marriage to enter into a physical relationship with a man. I promised to give that special gift to my husband untarnished by any former relationship, and to keep myself pure for the man I choose to be my husband. This ring serves as a reminder of my promise to myself and to God, should I ever be tempted to experiment with sex before marriage." She looked away from him as she spoke. When she had finished, she turned and faced him. "How do you feel about that, Todd?"

Todd was startled again.

"I knew there was something special about you, Elena," he said, trying to absorb her full meaning. "You don't think I'd ever ask you to break that promise, do you?" His eyes searched hers intently.

"No, Todd, I don't." She sighed. "But Dad asked me to tell you so we'll both know how things are. He's a little prejudiced and not sure any boy who cares about me can resist temptation."

He jumped up and faced her. "So neither you nor your father trusts me. Why should you? Look at the family I come from. Wait 'til your dad learns about my father. Well, tell him you're safe with me. I'd never rob you of that wonderful sense of value you have. Never," he added with finality.

He stood there for a minute staring at her. Then, leaving his unfinished sandwich on the blanket they shared, he sprinted down the beach, disappearing around the end of the island.

*

She had hurt him. Elena wondered if she had sounded confrontational. She hadn't meant to. She had tried to say it just right.

Is he really like he seems, always composed and in control? Or is this angry young man the real Todd? Has his sad past left scars and deficits that control him? Has he retreated because he's feeling too much or too little? She longed for answers.

When he returned, could they go on as they had before? She had hoped for some indication that he cared enough to want to know her more intimately. Fearful that she had erected a wall between them, she realized his eyes were distant and cold as he turned and ran from her. She felt alone, emotionally stranded on their special island.

25

ON THE MORNING OF THE SUNDAY SCHOOL PICNIC, the long, sandy beach at the north end of the island bubbled with giggling children. Brilliant sun and cool air encouraged them to invest their full energy into the games and races that marked the annual get-together. Elena and Todd refereed a game of softball on the beach. Harold and Susan helped Pastor Dar supervise the activities and made sure no child was left out. Mike had elected to go fishing.

All three of Doug's buddies had accepted his invitation. Doug introduced them to his church friends and encouraged them to join the volleyball game at one end of the beach. Uncomfortable, they hung back, huddling together and talking among themselves. In between points, Doug beckoned in their direction, urging them to join him.

Backing slowly away from the threesome, black-haired Eddie, dressed in cut-off jeans and a polo shirt, was the first to respond. He turned and watched from the sidelines for a time, then entered the game beside Doug. A natural athlete, he soon learned the techniques of handling the ball. Light on his feet and taller than most, he jumped high and spiked the ball across the net, winning points for his side. He beamed as he received comradely pats on the back from his teammates.

Doug insisted that all three of the boys compete in the relay races. Joey's frail frame was much better suited to the races than volleyball, enabling him to make good time for his team. His timidity melted away as his teammates expressed their appreciation. Harvey was awkward but enthusiastic and allowed himself to be drawn from one activity to the next. Eddie gravitated back to the continuous volleyball matches, and Joey played on the sidelines with his new friends.

The children took turns paddling around the cove in two canoes that had been brought in for the occasion. Spotting one of them empty halfway through the morning, Doug rounded up his buddies. The four of them piled into the canoe and raced out on the water. With his paddle Harvey started splashing the two boys in the middle, who were defenseless except for the little water they could scoop up with their hands. As the water fight intensified, the canoe wobbled back and forth until their screams and peals of laughter attracted attention on shore. When his father waved at them, Doug calmed himself and his crew, halted the assaults, and steadied the boat before it overturned.

Harvey then focused his attention on the girls at the picnic, asking Doug about several of them—in particular a pretty little blond with a halo of curls that made her look like an angel.

"That's Rhodora," Doug said. "She lives with her mom and two sisters. They haven't seen her dad in years. Her mom works very hard to support the family."

Rhodora was Doug's age, a year younger than Harvey, and just beginning to blossom into a young woman. Her mother had broken away from the loose life she had lived with her husband and worked at one of the local lodges to take care of her three girls. According to Pastor Dar, she would attend church for a time, then stay away for long periods, struggling with questions about why a good God would allow her life to be so hard. Rhodora attended church every Sunday and often came alone on the church bus.

"She's wicked pretty," Harvey said, using a favorite island expression, and making no attempt to hide his admiration for Rhodora. "I'd like to get to know her."

"She'll be in church tomorrow. Why don't you come with us?"

"Not a bad idea. Kin you pick me up on your way?"

"Sure," Doug replied without hesitation, knowing his parents would be pleased at the chance to introduce Harvey to their church.

"Are there going to be any more races, Doug?" Joey, bored with the conversation about girls, wanted to experience the thrill of excelling again.

"Probably."

"Let's go back in," Eddie said. "I want to play more volleyball."

They turned about and paddled in as fast as they could, rocking the boat from side to side and losing speed in their enthusiasm. As they glided onto the beach, Pastor Dar announced a parent-child volleyball game. Doug dropped his paddle in the boat and ran over to grab his dad by the hand. Susan watched with pleasure as they took their places, enjoying Doug's enthusiasm for entering the game with his father. Looking toward the other boys, she glimpsed the disappointment on Eddie's face and walked over to him.

"Would I do for a substitute parent, Eddie?"

"Gosh, would you? That would be great, Mrs. Richards."

"You may call me 'Mom' for this one game, Eddie."

The long lines of his slender face broadened into a wide smile. "Gee, Mrs. Richards, I mean, Mom, you're the greatest. Let's play on the other side against Doug and Mr. Richards."

Harvey watched the game from the sidelines, cheering both sides on until he spotted Rhodora sitting alone in an abandoned adult chair. Dressed in a loose-hanging summer frock, she swung her bare feet above the ground. Her curly blond hair fell softly around her face to her shoulders. Bright red cheeks burned by the sun gave her the glow of good health. Her wide blue eyes were so bright she reminded Harvey of the rows of dolls in the stores at Christmas time.

Gosh, she's beautiful, just like those girls in the magazines, Harvey thought to himself as he wandered toward her. "Your mother didn't come to the picnic?" he asked.

"No, she has to work."

"My dad didn't come neither," he said, looking at the ground. "My ma, she's dead. I scarcely remember her."

Rhodora responded with compassion, "I'm sorry. I know what that's like. My father left us when I was little and I never see him. I can't even remember what he looks like. He was nice when he wasn't drinking and used to hold me on his lap and tell me I was his angel. But when he drank, we all hid under the bed so he wouldn't beat us."

"Yeah, my dad's like that. I always hope he'll stop, but he never does."

"Why don't you bring him to church? Mom says that's what men need."

"Nah, he wouldn't come."

"Why don't you come? That would be a first step."

"Yeah, well, maybe I will. Thanks for asking." Not knowing what to say next, Harvey retreated. "Guess I better get back to the game."

Rhodora smiled at him. "See you tomorrow at church."

*

The games came to an end when Pastor Dar announced lunch. Todd and Elena had cooked hotdogs and hamburgers on a large open grill and piled them on large platters waiting to be served. Pastor Dar commanded everyone into a large circle. They joined hands as he thanked the Lord for the beautiful day, the good fun, and the nourishing food.

The children lined up as the church women served the burgers and hotdogs. The youngsters, ravenous from the activity, wanted one of each and stacked their plates high with chips, pickles, raw vegetables, and potato salad.

Several of the little ones spilled their plates in the sand. There being many more children than parents, Elena wiped their tears and started them afresh. "It's a good thing we cooked them all and planned so many seconds," she called to Todd. "You'd think they hadn't eaten since last year's picnic."

"They're downing hamburgers and hotdogs like the superstars on a football team," Todd agreed.

The children appreciated the good food and repeatedly expressed their thanks. Finally, the adults went through the line.

Todd and Elena, the last to fill their plates, had focused all morning on their chores with minimal personal exchange. Reacting to the flatness in Todd's voice when he spoke to her, Elena remained polite but distant, turning to others to express her delight in the children's fun. Reacting to her reserve, Todd withdrew even further.

After filling her plate, Elena suggested they join another young couple from church. Todd followed her but remained silent as Elena chatted effortlessly.

*

Pastor Dar settled on a rock near the edge of the woods next to Harold and Susan who had brought chairs. "Doug's friends seem to be enjoying themselves. I was afraid they weren't going to mix at first, but they seem to fit in well."

"Yes, Eddie is thrilled to discover his skill in playing volleyball. His eyes lit up like the Northern lights when I asked him if he'd like to adopt me as a parent. He looked eternally grateful. They really aren't bad kids. They just haven't been given very good role models. I hope we can help them."

"I saw an interesting fact in the most recent material I received from Promise Keepers. You're familiar with that movement, aren't you, Harold?"

"You mean the men who filled football stadiums around the country ten years ago and made commitments to keep their promises to God, to their wives, and to their children? Yes, they're starting up again, and we're forming a group in our church at home. It was one of the most encouraging movements to come into vogue in years. I'm glad they're not letting it die."

"They took a survey of the men attending their conferences. One of the questions they asked was how many men regularly looked at pornographic magazines, hard-core videos, or Internet porn. These men, you understand, are among the most committed to their families in the country, and 33 percent of them admitted to this. Imagine what the percentage must be with the rest of the population."

"It gives the claim that it's as normal and American as apple pie and ice cream some validity," Susan said, her wrinkled forehead registering concern. "But normal or not, it's not good. Since I've become aware of the problem, I've seen articles in several publications about the harm it does. We have to help these children understand that if they keep on, it could rob them of enjoying a normal, healthy sexual relationship as adults."

She pursed her lips thoughtfully. "I look at the relationship Elena and Todd are developing in comparison. It's so innocent, so wholesome, so romantic. It's what I want all my children to experience. If we don't help Doug understand the difference, he'll miss all that."

"We'll make him understand," Harold said. "Doug's a good boy."

"We have to help Harvey and the other boys, too," Pastor Dar said.

"That may be a little harder," Harold replied. "They need to experience more wholesome fun like this. It was an excellent suggestion to invite them to the picnic, Dar."

"Yes, I think we've made a good start."

26

ON SUNDAY MORNING HAROLD WITH HIS FAMILY and Todd drove up to Harvey's house. Doug ran to the door to announce their arrival. As he knocked on the door, Harvey stepped out wearing dress slacks, a sports shirt with a collar, and a dark green sweater, his bright red hair uncharacteristically slicked down instead of flying in all directions.

"Gosh, Harv, I've never seen you so dressed up. You look great."

"When my sister heard I was goin' to church with you guys, she said I couldn't wear jeans and took me to Ellsworth yesterday afternoon to buy these. Are they okay?"

"Perfect," Doug assured him as they walked to the car.

"Why, Harvey, you look positively handsome in that outfit," Susan greeted him.

Harvey straightened his normally slumped shoulders and beamed under her compliment. "Thank ya, Mrs. Richards. I sure had a nice time yesterday. The picnic was a blast," he said as he climbed into the car.

"I can still see old Harv going after that volleyball with all his might." Doug demonstrated how Harvey had lunged for the ball and missed. "Even when it went by him, he was as happy as if he'd spiked it for a point."

"Aw, you've just had more practice. I never played the game before. But it was a great day. And that food was *some* good," he said, rubbing his stomach. "Will Rhodora be at church today?" he asked, changing the subject.

"Most likely. She comes even without her mother now," Susan replied.

"Hey, Harv's got a case on Rhodora," Doug kidded him.

"She's a sweet girl. You have very good taste, Harvey," Susan said.

"Yes, ma'am," Harvey said, grinning self-consciously.

As they pulled into the church parking lot, Harold consulted the time on his watch. "Congratulations, everyone, we're actually early today. How did we manage it?"

"Be sure and introduce Harvey to the children who weren't at the picnic, Doug."

"I will, Mom," Doug said as the boys broke from the car and rushed up to the group gathered on the church steps.

The children who had attended the picnic greeted Harvey with unusual warmth. As they settled in their seats, he intended to enjoy the morning. Glancing around the church, his eyes fell on Rhodora, who was wearing her best Sunday dress with lace socks and patent leather shoes. The soft blue of her dress amplified the blue in her eyes, which sparkled as they met Harvey's.

Gosh, she's even prettier than I remembered.

The church quieted as Pastor Dar stepped behind the pulpit and led a mix of hymns, popular gospel songs, and testimonies by those who had been blessed during the week. In between songs and testimonies, Pastor Dar gave a series of sermonettes based on the week's events. He spoke of the joy of the Sunday school picnic and welcomed Harvey to the service. Harvey, not knowing what was expected of him, blushed, rose to his feet, and bowed toward the congregation behind him and then to Pastor Dar. Greeted with smiles and murmurs of approval from both directions, he fell back in his seat.

After the collection of the offering, Pastor Dar invited the congregation to open their Bibles and follow along as he read. Doug found the passage and held it open for Harvey, but by the time Harvey had found the right place, the reading was over. He had not understood a word of the reading, and though he looked toward Pastor Dar for much of the sermon, he had not the slightest idea what it was about. The others listened attentively.

The time passed with amazing speed as Harvey stole glances of the back of Rhodora's golden head and fantasized about their next meeting. When Pastor Dar concluded his sermon and pronounced a benediction, the congregation began to buzz with conversation.

The members of the Richards family greeted their friends, but Harvey remained in his seat. Doug appeared intent on seeing the boys who attended the picnic. Harvey had come to see Rhodora and now was his chance. He watched Rhodora cluster with her girl friends. They whispered and giggled in little circles.

*

After most of the parishioners had left, Harold moved to the back of the church to speak to Pastor Dar. "That was a mighty fine sermon, Dar, one we need to hear again and again."

"Thank you, Harold. It's too bad once isn't enough," he said, his round cheeks crinkling in a broad smile that belied his stern tone.

"Dar," Harold said, suddenly very serious, "I would appreciate it if you would speak to Doug about the business of the magazines. He wasn't very receptive when I tried. Perhaps you could share some of the experiences you've had with men who have become involved in pornography.

"I plan to do that, Harold, and some of the research I've collected as well," Dar said. "I'd like to give a sermon on it, but I don't want to embarrass the boys. This is an important subject, not just for them, but for the whole congregation. You'd be surprised, Harold, how many of the men still look at pornographic magazines and videos after they start coming to church. The women have been taught it's something they have to put up with, so they say very little to their men. But many of them come to me crying their eyes out, saying it's impossible for them to compete with the beautiful women in the pictures."

"I don't want Doug's future wife to have to deal with that, Dar. The time to stop it is right now."

"Yes, of course. How would later this afternoon be for me to call on Doug?"

"Fine, Dar. We won't be home, but I'll make sure Doug is there and expecting you."

*

On the drive home, everyone was in good spirits until Doug asked, "Can I spend the afternoon with Harvey, Mom?"

"Another time, Doug," Susan said.

"I never get to do anything I want," he complained with a mild sigh.

"As a matter of fact, I asked Pastor Dar to call on you this afternoon," Harold said.

His former good mood now gone, Doug narrowed his eyes and spoke accusingly to the back of his father's head. "You told him about the magazines, didn't you? Otherwise he wouldn't be coming to see me."

He could feel Harvey shift nervously next to him.

"Yes, Doug," Harold said, "we talked to him because we were so worried. He confirmed our worst fears."

"It isn't true. Lots of men look at the magazines and it doesn't change anything in their lives."

"Doug, he wasn't giving us his opinion. He told us about scientific studies that prove that pornography is harmful. You must listen to the facts." Susan tried to set him straight.

Todd joined the conversation. "You know what it did to my friend. I told you how it ruined his life."

"He's just one man who had some kind of weakness."

"We all have moments of weakness, and what we do with them can have far-reaching effects on our lives," Harold said. "We want you to realize that you're placing yourself on a very dangerous path."

"I still think you're exaggerating," Doug said, mortified that he'd been so exposed, and even more so that Harvey was in the car with them and now knew Doug had been caught.

There were a few moments of silence. Susan turned to Harvey, who had said nothing. "Harvey, have you ever looked at pornographic magazines?"

"Yes, ma'am, I seen a few," he said weakly. "This is a free country, and I guess anybody can look at anythin' he wants to."

The car pulled into his driveway. "Looks like this is where I get out," he said. "Thank you, Mr. and Mrs. Richards, for taking me to church. People treated me real nice."

"We hope you'll come again, Harvey."

"Yes, ma'am," he said as he dashed into the house.

*

After the family left for tennis and golf, Doug wandered down to the shore. Feeling both abandoned and disgraced, he kicked at the stones in the sand, expressing the anger that had built up inside him. After releasing some of his tension, he started to look for skipping stones. He made a pile of the thinnest, smoothest, round stones on the beach and sat down next to it to wait for the tide to rise another few inches.

Nothing Pastor Dar can say will change my mind, he groused inwardly. *My family makes too big a deal out of me looking at those mags.* Out loud, he said, "Why do I have to come from such an old-fashioned family anyway?!"

As the tide covered the floor of the cove, he began skimming the stones across the smooth surface of the water. Putting the force of his anger behind each toss, he skipped the stones more times than ever before. As one stone bounced eighteen times before it disappeared into the water, he marveled that he felt so little joy from his accomplishment. Pocketing the remaining stones, he walked with his head down toward his cabin.

Once there, he pulled out the trunk in Elena's room and reached under the excess towels and sheets stored in it. "She'll never find this one," he said as he took out a magazine. Sitting down in Elena's newly painted rocking chair,

150

he flipped through its pages. Pictures of beautiful twins with long, wavy, blond hair falling voluptuously over scantily clad bodies grabbed his attention. He turned the page with great anticipation, but what he saw made him feel slightly sick.

Perhaps it was their hair that reminded him of Elena. Even as he was repulsed by the perversion, he stared at the pictures and felt the now familiar rush. It felt so good, he didn't want it to stop. Giving himself to the action in the pictures, he encouraged the exciting sensations to continue. Something inside him longed to see something even more bizarre, so he could feel even higher. "Wow!" he said aloud as he leaned back and closed his eyes, enjoying another surge through his body. "If this is what it feels like, it must really be great."

Before he had finished flipping through the pages, he heard a car door slam. He returned the magazine to the bottom of the trunk and ran to the other cabin in time to see Pastor Dar arriving at the back door. Doug sauntered through the cabin and opened the kitchen door.

"There you are, Doug. I wasn't sure where I'd find you. Shall we walk down to the shore? Living in the middle of the island, I don't get to see the water as often as you do."

"Sure," Doug said, holding the door open for his pastor and leading him down the path to the shore.

"Let's go out on the point, Doug. You're a lucky young man to have a place like this to inherit. Do you think you'll take as good care of the cabins as your father?"

"I guess between the four of us, we will," Doug replied, wishing they could go on talking about anything but the matter Pastor Dar had come to address.

"You've grown from a little boy to a fine young man in the three years I've been on the island, Doug."

"My family doesn't think so." Doug allowed himself to be drawn into the conversation.

"They've told me what a fine son and brother you are, Doug. They love you very much. You know that when you stop to think about it, don't you?"

"I guess so," Doug admitted.

"Do you know that your mother and father have prayed every day since you were born for a lovely Christian wife for you?"

"No." Doug looked Dar in the eye for the first time. Then, surly again, he stared downward, kicking a loose rock into the water. "The way they've been treating me, it seems like they don't want me to get married at all!"

"Of course they want you to marry someday and to enjoy the best sex there is. You know, Doug, sex was God's idea. He created it, and all He created was good. He meant the relationship between a man and a woman to be a beautiful experience." Dar paused.

Doug said nothing.

"But," Dar continued, "as with all things that are good, Satan presents us with a counterfeit that's not good. That counterfeit is pornography. And, yes, it's been around a long time, since men recorded their history on cave walls. But what we have today is very different from what we've had of pornography throughout history."

"What do you mean?" Doug still avoided Dar's gaze.

"It's far more available and more realistic and graphic than ever before. In big cities whole sections are devoted to sex businesses of one sort or another. You can find pornographic magazines in drugstores, gas stations, and convenience stores in every small town in the country. Now many family video stores carry hard-core videos. And that's only the beginning. There's so much porn on the Internet, it's hard to avoid it."

Doug said nothing as he stared at his pastor, who appeared to be studying a family of ducks passing by the point as he waited for Doug's response.

"No town, however small or rural, is free of it today. They're sold by some of our most respected businesses."

"Is it true that 90 percent of the men in America look at the magazines?" Doug interrupted.

"Where did you hear that, Doug?"

"I read it in one of them."

"They print that to make it sound like everyone does, to give pornography a legitimacy it doesn't have. Men like your father and me never look at it, Doug."

"Did you when you were a kid?" Doug persisted.

"Yes, I saw some in college. I guess most kids today are exposed to it somewhere. Several studies show that a high percentage of kids receive their sex education from pornography, but that doesn't make it good. That's one reason we have so much sexual promiscuity today and so much rape. Did you know that half the sex offenders in the country are under the age of eighteen?"

"That can't be true," Doug said.

"I'm afraid it is. Young children exposed to such stimulation don't understand it and don't know what to do about it. Children learn almost everything by imitation, so that's what they do to try to figure it out. The younger they're exposed to it, the more likely it is to become a problem in their lives." Dar paused. "What's the purpose of pornography, do you think?" he asked.

Doug hesitated. "To teach men how to make love, I guess."

"The purpose of pornography, Doug, is to arouse men to lust after women—not to love them but to lust after them. There's a big difference. And it does a very good job of what it's designed to do. Many young men think pornography will teach them something about sex that will help them, but that isn't the case."

"I've learned some things," Doug shot back, kicking a shell dropped on the rocks by a seagull.

Dar's voice was steady. "Pornography is full of lies about sex. It gives you the wrong ideas about what women want. It isn't about love at all. I've had many men and women come to me whose lives have been messed up by pornography. I became so frustrated trying to help them and seeing them fall back into old habits again, I started studying the research to try to understand it better. I'd like to share some of the things I've learned with you. Will you hear me out?"

"I guess so." Doug spoke to the ground again as he walked a few feet away from Dar. Wishing he could walk away from the conversation altogether, he bent over and picked up a dried sea urchin and hurled it into the air. It sailed high over the point and crashed on the rocks below, breaking in pieces. He watched it a minute before returning to Dar.

"The first thing you should know, Doug, is that pornography has nothing to do with love. It's just about bodies coming together. One of the researchers described it this way: strangers meet to have sex and part never to meet again. There is no tenderness, no romance, no caring, no commitment, and no responsibility.

"So, pornography has nothing to teach you about love. It leaves out everything about romance that's important to a woman. There isn't any love in pornography—only self-gratification. A man who looks at pornography again and again becomes more concerned about the sex act than the woman with whom he has it."

Doug didn't respond.

"Doug, I'm not a prude. I want all the young boys and girls in my congregation to enjoy a loving, long-lasting, satisfying sexual relationship with their future mates. But pornography can rob you of that satisfaction. Research has found that, instead of having better sex, men who look at pornography become less satisfied with their wives. When they see beautiful women in the magazines and videos performing bizarre kinds of sex, they think they're missing something. They begin looking critically at the appearance of their loved ones. Have you ever noticed that no normal woman looks as good as the girls in the magazines?"

Doug grunted and shrugged.

"Often they become angry that the women in their lives won't experiment with the kind of sex portrayed in the magazines. So instead of bringing them greater satisfaction, pornography makes them dissatisfied with what they have at home. Many of the couples who come to me have grown so far apart they end up divorced."

Doug stared across the bay.

"Are you hearing me, Doug?" Pastor Dar asked.

"Yes sir," he said without emotion.

Dar presented more evidence. "Research has shown that even couples who are already committed to each other are profoundly changed by looking at pornography. They come to believe there's far more unfaithfulness in our society than there actually is, and they become willing to accept unfaithfulness for themselves, even their partners. They begin to believe the lie that sexual restraint is unhealthy, so men shouldn't restrain themselves from sex outside of marriage. They begin to think marriage isn't necessary to our culture. Watching pornography even lessens their desire to have children. Children become an inconvenience in a world that thinks only about its own gratification and not about the needs of loved ones."

"That doesn't have anything to do with me, Pastor Dar," Doug protested, hurling another shell into the air. "I only wanted to find out what sex is all about."

"You won't find the truth about sex in pornography. It's full of lies about sex, and it encourages young people to experiment with sex too soon. It teaches them woman only want sex, when what a woman wants most is tenderness. The young girls you'll be dating will be more interested in the romance of candlelight dinners and moonlight walks. Look at Todd and Elena..."

"What do they have to do with it?" Doug interrupted the lecture.

"They enjoy holding hands. Elena looks perfectly happy just having Todd's arm around her. She feels cared for and safe with him. If you think of dating in terms of pornography, you'll scare away the nice girls you want to attract."

"That's what Todd said."

"He was right. You'll want a girlfriend someday who can trust you. If you're all roused up by pornography, she'll be afraid to be alone with you."

"I won't be like that. You don't understand." Doug glared defiantly at Dar as tears of frustration spilled down his cheeks. Embarrassed that his pastor was seeing him cry, he dashed across the beach and up to his cabin. Once there, he threw himself on his bed and sobbed.

Why does everyone think the worst of me? I haven't done anything wrong. I'd never hurt a girl. I only looked at a few pictures. Doug tried to justify his behavior to himself. He wasn't used to defying authority and found no joy in it, but something in him rebelled at being told what he could and could not do. *Why do I have such a bad feeling in the pit of my stomach?* The pictures flashed back into his mind, and his body reacted just as it had when he had looked at them in the magazine.

Was his dad right that the pictures would return again and again to haunt him? He didn't know what to do with all these sensations, and he couldn't talk to anyone about them now. Not his father, not his pastor, and certainly not his mother or sister. For the first time in his life, he could not go to his family with his problems. They wouldn't understand. No one understood, except maybe Harvey and the guys.

Outside he could hear Pastor Dar walking back from the beach. The sound of his footsteps grew stronger. Doug lay perfectly still, scarcely breathing, as they stopped outside his door. Not until they had started up again and faded to nothing did he let out a final sob.

27

THE CHILDREN HAD PLANNED SUSAN'S BIRTHDAY to the last detail. Harold, fully cooperating, invited his wife for a day on the water. Elena made her parents a special picnic lunch and waved them off soon after breakfast.

As they disappeared around the point, Elena ran back to the cabin and picked up the phone. "Good morning, Todd, we're all set. Bring Mrs. Faraway over when you're ready." She hung up the phone and set about cleaning the kitchen and preparing the cabin for the birthday celebration. She hoped Todd would have a sunnier disposition today than he'd had all weekend.

The boys appeared on time for breakfast. Even Doug, who had remained sullen and in a dark mood since Pastor Dar's visit, looked forward to working on his mother's gift.

When Todd arrived, Mrs. Faraway and Elena chatted happily as they cut up vegetables and mixed ingredients for Susan's favorite cake. "Tell me what Todd was like as a boy," Elena said.

"He was a sweet child but rather serious. He always tried to solve everyone's problems and keep peace in the family. I told Susan the other day that he was the delight of my life. No one has given me greater joy than Todd."

"He spent a great deal of time with you when he was growing up, didn't he, Mrs. Faraway?"

"Yes, he did, dear," she said, offering no explanation.

"Did he always have silent moods when he seemed to disappear into himself?" She hastened to add, "I don't mean to pry. I'm just trying to understand him better."

"That's how he coped with the family situation. When he hurt too badly, he put emotional distance between himself and his family. Otherwise, he couldn't have survived. His brother didn't." Mrs. Faraway sighed. "We don't have a family like yours, you know, Elena."

"Yes, I do know, Mrs. Faraway. Todd told me."

"That my only daughter turned out so badly and my beautiful grandsons had to suffer so has made me angry. I thought I would never get over the death of Todd's brother. I almost never talk about him, but the anguish of the whole experience is right beneath the surface, always threatening to erupt."

"I'm so sorry. It must have been terrible for all of you."

"For Todd and me, yes. Cecilia didn't even know about it. We tried to locate her, but she had moved and no one knew where she was. As for Todd's father, I don't know what he felt. I hate him. He brought nothing but pain into my daughter's life. He's responsible for the way she turned out. I understand why she had to get away from him, but how she could abandon her two boys and run off with another man, I will never understand."

*

While the ladies worked in the kitchen, the boys cleaned up the lobster trap. It had been caked with sand and mud and the bait bag still reeked of dead fish. Doug took it out and deposited it in the garbage can.

"That should attract plenty of raccoons tonight. I have a new bait bag in our cabin. I'll contribute it to the project," he said as he ran to find it.

When he returned, the boys inserted the bait bag in its proper place and stood back to admire the spotless trap. Satisfied, they moved it into the sun to dry and broke for lunch.

After lunch, they hammered pieces of wood to the round top of the trap, structuring it to hold the glass top they had ordered in Ellsworth. With the squaring off completed, they stood back and surveyed their finished work.

"Can we try the top on it now?" Doug could hardly wait. "It's in our cabin."

"Let's go get it, Mike," Todd said. "You can hold the doors for us, Doug."

They returned and carefully placed the top on the base. Elena appeared with a bottle of Windex and cleaned it until it sparkled.

"Great." Mike beamed with pride at their creation. "Do you think Mom will like the weathered look better than if we stained it?"

"Mom always likes things natural," Doug said. "Should we put it in front of the couch so she sees it when she comes home, or hide it in the woods and bring it out during the party?"

Todd offered his advice. "I vote for hiding it now and bringing it out during the celebration."

"I guess you're right. She won't have any idea when we start the party," Doug said, more excited than he would have been at his own party.

The boys had just finished hiding the table in the woods and covering it with spruce boughs when Mike spotted their parents returning in the boat. The boys rushed back to the cabin.

"Elena, Mrs. Faraway, they're back. Are you ready?" Doug called in to them.

"We will be by the time they get up to the cabin," Elena said, moving faster to clean up the many pots and pans they had dirtied.

Mike and Doug dashed to the beach to help Susan and Harold land the boat, leaving Todd to clean up the tools. When he finished, he found the ladies in the kitchen. "Does this place ever smell good." He sniffed the air. "I'm glad we've been invited for dinner, Grandma." He sounded more cheerful than he had at any time during the past three days.

"After all the work she did today, she better be invited. Todd, will you help me finish setting the table?" Elena asked, still avoiding looking at him.

"Sure. Hey, that looks great," he said, admiring the arrangement of wild flowers she and Mrs. Faraway had gathered earlier in the day. "You may not be able to arrange shells like your mother, but you can do wonders with roadside weeds."

They laughed together for the first time in days.

*

Todd watched Elena as she bubbled with conversation and fussed over the details of the table, making sure everything would be just right. He could see how happy she was, anticipating how much her mother would appreciate their efforts.

In his mind Todd contrasted these happy activities with what his parents' birthdays had meant to his family—merely another excuse to drink too much. He remembered anticipating their arrival with dread. His mother and father usually brushed aside whatever plans the children made and used the occasion as an excuse to leave them with their grandmother and go out on the town. When it came to his birthday, they often forgot. He tried not to remember the pain that had brought him.

Elena reached over and pretended to rub off the dark scowl that had come over his face. "None of that on this happy occasion," she said in a gentle voice.

"I'm sorry, Elena. You see, I'm not as mature as you think I am. I have a dark side that rears its ugly head at the most inappropriate times."

"I understand, Todd. Your grandmother filled me in about some of the details today while we were cooking."

"She did?" he asked, startled. "She almost never talks about it, not to me anyway."

"She thinks you have problems enough without her complaints. But she's very bitter, Todd. I would describe you as being sad, but she's bitter. She has to forgive her daughter and your father before she'll ever find peace."

"Yes, that's what I'm praying for. I've had to do that, too, but every once in awhile, I let it pull me down into the mire."

"You stay on top of it very well, Todd. I admire you for that."

"You're a wonderful encourager, Elena," he said, thankful that her reserve had broken. "I wish I could take you to Pittsburgh to help me face the situation when my father is released."

"I wish I could help you share this burden, but you'll do just fine. I know you will." She smiled at him.

"There now, we're done. Everything is ready. Mom's already out of the boat so you and Mrs. Faraway should go."

"See you at six o'clock," he said, reluctant to leave her.

*

"Was it a happy day, Mom?" she asked, relieving Susan of the picnic gear.

"Very happy, Elena. Your father was in a playful mood, and we laughed like children most of the day. He took a dozen pictures of me, insisting he was memorializing every part of our day on the islands. We stopped at Sheep Island and climbed to the top of the hill. He said he had wanted to roll down the hill for years like he did when he was a kid, but he thought it would just give you children ideas, so he had refrained all these years, but today he planned to do it and he wanted me to do it with him.

"We rolled and laughed and rolled and laughed and ended up in the tall grass at the foot of the hill. We just lay there and watched the clouds change patterns and felt so young. I can't believe so many years have gone by. I don't feel a day over twenty-five." Susan collapsed on the couch, exhausted from her active day.

"Mom, you have forty-five minutes 'til dinner. Why don't you lie down for half an hour, so you're fresh for the celebration tonight?"

"That's a good idea, darling. I really need it." Susan gave Elena a hug and disappeared into the bedroom as Harold brought the boat gear onto the porch.

"Hi, Dad. I hear you had a frolicking good time."

"That we did, Elena. I haven't felt so young in years, and your mother acted like a young girl. It's wonderful that the mind never ages."

"Mom's lying down. Maybe you should, too, so you can enjoy the party to the fullest."

"Did the boys finish the table?" Harold whispered in her ear.

"Yes, it looks wonderful. Mom should be completely surprised. Be quiet when you go into the bedroom. She may already be asleep."

"Okay, if you're sure you have everything under control."

"Absolutely, Dad. See you in half an hour."

*

Susan sat on the couch with her eyes closed. They had just finished toasting her with sparkling cider, and Doug could wait no longer.

"Close your eyes, Mom," he cried out and summoned Mike and Todd to follow him outside. "Elena, make sure she doesn't open them 'til we tell her."

"Hear that, Mom? I'm sure you don't want to spoil their surprise by looking too soon."

"I wouldn't do that for the world," Susan said.

"Doesn't your mother look wonderful tonight, Elena? I can't believe she's six years past half a century."

"Harold, you make me sound like Methuselah," Susan complained, laughing in spite of her closed eyes.

"You've got many centuries to go before that," Harold said, laughing, too, and bending over to kiss her closed eyelids.

"It sounds like a bear on the porch," Susan said.

"Hey, Dad, hold the door open," Doug called in. "Mom, are you keeping your eyes shut?"

"Yes, I'm waiting ever so patiently, and I can't imagine what you're up to."

Harold motioned to Elena to move the old coffee table into the bedroom. It was lightweight and easy to handle.

Susan heard the screen door creak and the rumble of heavy feet moving slowly into the room. She felt the floor shake as something large hit it with a thud, making her jump involuntarily. "Children, whatever on earth are you doing? I hope you're not tearing the cabin down around me."

"Now, Mom, you can open your eyes." Doug's voice was happy, excited, so different from the tone they'd heard from him lately.

Susan opened her eyes and gasped as she saw the glass-covered lobster trap. "Oh, children," she said, both laughing and with tears spilling over her cheeks. "You know, I've always wanted one for a coffee table. And this one is perfect, weathered but in good condition. And what a wonderful top for it! Where did it come from?"

They all started telling her at once. "Wait, slow down. One at a time," she said. "You actually found it and put it together yourselves?" She strained to make sense of the rush of explanations that hit her all at once.

"Now, Doug, tell me. Where did it come from?"

"I found it on the island the first day we all went out in the boat. Mike and Elena helped me pry it loose and drag it into the woods just as you came around on the rocks. We had to tell Dad so he'd let us go out in the boat the next afternoon to bring it in. Elena took you to call on Pastor Dar's wife to keep you occupied, so you didn't even know we were gone."

Doug took a quick breath and continued. "We hid it next door in the woods and took the measurements to Ellsworth. Remember that day we all went shopping in different directions? We ordered the glass top, and Todd and Elena picked it up when they went to the movies there. We started to work on it as soon as you and Dad went out in the boat this morning. We brought her up from the woods, cleaned her all up, and built the braces to hold up the top. Isn't she perfect?"

"Absolutely perfect. And just the kind of table I've dreamed about for years. And the fact that you found it and made it yourselves makes it doubly special. I will treasure it as long as I live." Susan roughed up Doug's hair and gave him a huge hug. "And every one of you was in on it. What a conspiracy."

She hugged Mike and Elena and Harold. "And I'm sure you had a hand in it, too, Todd." Beaming at him, she hugged him just like she had her own children.

*

The unexpected warmth took Todd by surprise and stirred his longing for a mother who cared. As he dwelt on it, he felt angry at his own mother who had neglected and abandoned him.

He caught himself sinking into the mire again. *I'm sorry, Lord,* he repented. *I remember Your promise to me. You're all I need. I am worthy because I am Your son, and You love me."* Dispelling his anger, he rejoined the party.

"How long have you known about this, Amanda?" Susan turned toward her.

"They didn't tell me until this morning when they brought it up and started working on it. They were afraid I'd spill the beans."

"Mrs. Faraway was here all day, Mom, helping me with the cooking. She outdid herself working on dinner."

"I enjoyed being part of the family fun," she said.

"So I have you to thank for this wonderful celebration, too, Amanda." Susan made her way among the children to Amanda and gave her a big hug. "What a fortunate woman I am to be surrounded by such loving children and friends." Susan wiped away another tear. "To say nothing of a wonderful husband to romp in the fields with." She threw her arms around Harold and started tickling him. He tickled back and whirled her around the room, both of them laughing in total abandon.

"Are you sure they're getting older each year? I'd say they've already reached their second childhood," Mike said.

"Oh, children." Susan grinned from ear to ear. "It's been a wonderful day and the evening's just beginning. I'm sure I'll remember it as the best birthday I've ever had."

"We have another present," Elena said. "Do you have the card, Mike?"

Mike stepped forward and handed Susan a large card of the sentimental variety that expressed all the thoughts a mother likes to hear.

Susan opened it to see a beautiful rendering of perfectly groomed woods signed by all her children and Todd. A hill of tall trees sloped gently toward a shore of sand and rocks. The top of the hill was treeless but covered with low plants that hugged the ground. "It's the point all cleared and looking beautiful again." Susan smiled at each of her children.

"That's your other present, Mom," Elena said. "We'll work until it looks that way. The card is our promise to you."

Todd, grateful to see Elena happy again, overwhelmed with longing for all he had missed growing up, found the happiness this family exuded like a fairy tale. If he had been a stranger, he might have doubted that it was genuine, but having spent three weeks in their midst, he knew it was real. The Richards were not without problems, but they genuinely loved each other and received great joy from doing things for and with one another.

*

The main dishes cleared away, the cake so lovingly decorated by Amanda and Elena served and eaten, they relaxed and chatted over cups of coffee and tea until the phone rang.

"That has to be Stephanie." Elena jumped up and ran to the telephone.

"Hi, Steph. We've had a perfect evening...only you weren't here. Mother is radiant, looking not a year over thirty-five. She can't wait to talk to you." Elena put the phone in Susan's outstretched hand.

"Hello, darling. This does make it a perfect evening. How are you?"

*

Elena grabbed Todd's hand and pulled him toward the porch. He willingly followed her out the door.

"We'll give her a little privacy to talk to Stephanie," Elena said.

"We may be giving her privacy, but everyone else is listening with all ears," Todd replied.

"Well, after all that dinner, it's good to get a breath of fresh air. Wasn't it fun, Todd? I'm so happy it worked out just as we planned."

"Yes, it was, in a painful kind of way."

"You looked as happy as the rest of us." Elena appeared perplexed at his remark.

"I was, and it was wonderful to see you so happy. I've been kind of heavy since our trip to Neptune Island, haven't I? I'm truly sorry, Elena," he said, taking her hand and gazing deep into her eyes, which reflected the porch light. "I took the story of your promise ring personally, as though you were telling me you and your father didn't trust me."

"Oh, no, Todd, I didn't mean that." Her eyebrows slanted in that straight diagonal line that showed her deep concern. "I only brought it up because Dad asked me to. And it wasn't that he distrusted you either. He thought it was only fair of me to tell you. We have been spending a lot of time together alone, and Dad thinks I'm irresistible." She shot him a lighthearted smirk.

"It's okay, 'Lena," he said, squeezing her hands in his. "It's just that I have too many emotions I don't know what to do with. I'm a little messed up. I haven't allowed myself to feel anything for such a long time."

"Todd, I wouldn't hurt you for anything in the world," Elena whispered as she raised her hand to his cheeks and traced the line of his strong chin.

"I know that when I think about it straight," he said, "but when you told me, I felt like I did when Mother ran away. Not good enough to be loved and trusted. I guess I wanted to punish you like I wanted to punish her."

"I felt something like that when I sprained my ankles, and my family left me day after day."

*

As they left the porch and strolled toward Sunset Rock, Elena tried hard to imagine what it would be like to feel so unloved. The moon rose in the night sky, and the tide reached its peak. They listened in silence to the waves gently hitting the rocks below.

"The stars are beginning to come out and brighten the dark sky," Elena murmured.

"You do the same for my dark world, Elena."

Todd faced her and drew her closer to him. He put his hand under her chin and lifted it. He bent down and gently, tenderly brushed her lips with his own. They lingered there for just a moment before he held her close in his arms.

It was like the touch of an angel. Perfectly content, Elena wanted nothing more than to be close to him and feel the softness of his lips against her cheek.

28

ELENA AWOKE TO AN OVERCAST DAY. The sun hid behind a layer of thick clouds that threatened to burst open. The air hung heavy with moisture, but no rain fell.

"It's a perfect day to burn on the point. That's just what I ordered, Lord," she said aloud. "I'll drive to town to get the fire permit and then wake the family."

She found the main cottage silent. Her mother and father must have been exhausted from the excitement of their day on the islands. Not wanting to disturb them, she tiptoed into the kitchen and lifted the car keys from their hook on the wall.

Driving into town, she savored the memories of the evening before: the success of the birthday celebration, the delight on her mother's face as she saw the coffee table the boys had worked on together, the delicious meal she and Mrs. Faraway had prepared, and the magic moments afterward with Todd. Still able to feel the tenderness of his touch, she raised her hand to her cheek. His gentle kiss was even better than her girlhood dreams of romance. Feeling suddenly giddy, she put her head back and laughed. A delightful feeling. How could she be so fortunate to have her summer turn out this way?

As she entered into downtown Stonington, she drove into the garage where the fire chief worked and got out of her car. Finding him busy under a truck, she squatted on the ground and called out, "Morning, Mr. Eaton. It looks like a perfect day for a fire, heavy moisture in the air, and hardly a breath of wind. May I have a permit to burn out on our rocks that are covered by high tide?"

He smiled. "Elena Richardson. It's good to see you this summer." Then he turned to business. "What you want to burn?"

"We need to clean up the trees that fell in that terrible November ice storm a few years ago. There are even more this year, and they're lying in all directions. It looks like a disaster area. We'll cut up the tree trunks for firewood, but we'll have to burn the brush to get rid of it. We'll have someone attending the fire at all times. We've been doing it for years, and we know how to do it gradually so it doesn't get too high and carry sparks into the woods. There's almost no wind today."

"All right," he said, "but be sure you put the fire out with water if a wind comes up. We caught up a lot on the rain during the hurricane, but it was wicked dry before that. Still have to take precautions."

"We'll be careful," she assured him. He scribbled his signature on a small form, dated it, and handed it to her.

"Thank you, Mr. Eaton," she said. "We'll be careful. We want to enjoy those woods the rest of our lives."

*

Elena parked the car and rushed into her parents' cabin waving the permit in the air. "Morning, Mom. I've been to the fire captain for a permit to burn on the point today. With all the moisture in the air, it's a perfect day to start cleaning up the woods."

"My, you didn't waste any time," Susan said. "Ask your father if it fits into his plans."

Elena bounced into the living room and called through the bedroom door, "Hi, Dad, I've been to town for a fire permit. How would you like to start work on the point this morning? It's a perfect day to burn. There's so much moisture in the air, any runaway sparks will be drowned before they reach the woods."

Harold appeared with shaving cream still on one side of his face. "I had the very same thought when I looked out this morning. Sounds like a good idea to me. Think you can rouse the boys?" He leaned over to give his daughter a foamy kiss.

"Thanks, Dad. I'll tell them you made me do it." She rubbed her hands in anticipation and scampered out the door.

*

By eleven o'clock, flickering red flames rose from the rocks next to the bay. A swirl of thick smoke rose above the flames and dissipated into the gray sky. Deep within the woods, the harsh buzz of the chain saws roared unceasingly. Susan and Elena, dragging dead branches behind them, crossed the sand beach and climbed onto the rock ledge. With a hefty heave, they hurled their burdens on top of the flames, causing a fresh burst of crackles and pops.

Elena struggled out of her jacket. "I can't remember ever enjoying this job so much. I used to hate it when Dad made us clean up the woods. I moaned to myself all day about child labor and made myself miserable. Now all I can think about is how each trip brings us closer to the goal of restoring the beauty of the woods."

"It thrills me, too." Susan shielded her forehead from the heat of the fire. "Come sit here with me. It's time for a midmorning break."

Elena picked a smooth place on the rocks and sat beside her mother. "The boys seem to be joining in the spirit of the day. I haven't heard a single complaint from them. I remember all the groans and murmurs in the past, like the children of Israel crossing the desert. Even Doug seems to be happy. Ever since the boys helped your father bring the boat in during the hurricane, they seem to have a special camaraderie about doing man things together. I hope Harvey's coming over won't interfere."

"He seems to be joining in with the same spirit," Elena said. "I hope they've both put their fascination with pornography behind them. Dad said Doug agreed not to look at it again. I hope he meant it."

"It's amazing how many articles I've seen about it lately," Susan said, her brow wrinkling with lines of worry. "There was one in *Reader's Digest* this month that talked about its addictive powers. When men get hooked on it, all their relationships suffer."

"Can you imagine how horrible it would be to be married to someone who looked at pornography all the time?" Elena's body involuntarily trembled as a wave of repulsion hit her. Remembering the brazen pictures she had seen, she turned to Susan. "How can men say they're looking at people making love, when it has nothing to do with love?"

"That was the point this article made," Susan said. "When I get home, I think I'll join the anti-pornography group in town. I was always glad they were trying to keep our environment clean when I read about their meetings in the newspaper, but I never wanted to become involved. It's something you really don't want to think about. I never realized how widespread the problem is and how quickly a person can become addicted to it."

"This will be your newest crusade, Mom," Elena said, getting to her feet. "But enough of this dreadful subject. I want to get back to the woods." As she slid down the side of the rock, Todd emerged from the woods carrying a huge pile of brush.

"Hey, where are our helpers?" he called out, grinning. "The piles are getting so big we don't have room to work. Has the fire gone out?"

Elena turned to look at the smoking fire. The flames had died down, and the larger roots and branches were smoldering. Red coals still glowed amidst piles of gray ashes. "It looks perfect for marshmallows," she called back.

They met halfway across the beach. Elena took the branches that were about to fall from his arms. "Looks like you took on more than you can handle. Just like a man, trying to prove how much more he can carry than a woman."

He smirked. "Just trying to get you lazy bones back to work."

Susan caught up to them. "Do you think your grandmother would like to join us for lunch, Todd? Looks like the rain will hold off."

"Thanks, Mrs. Richards, I'll go up to the cabin and call her, so she doesn't start cooking. What time do you want her?"

"Around 12:30. We'll work another hour before Elena and I carry things down. Everyone has to cook his own hotdogs over the fire. I'm sure you won't mind cooking hers."

"Great, I'll give her a call now and bring her over whenever you're ready." With large strides he started up the path to the cabin.

Donning their work gloves, Susan and Elena headed back to the woods. They found logs scattered on the ground right where they had been lopped off from the tree trunks. As fast as Harold could saw them, Mike stacked the larger logs between the trees still standing. Doug and Harvey filled the wheelbarrow with small logs and took them to the woodpile near the main cabin. Brush lay scattered about in not-so-neat piles, waiting for the girls to gather it and haul it to the fire.

Harold cut the motor of the saw and sat on a fallen trunk. Taking out a large work handkerchief, he wiped the sawdust from his face.

"It wouldn't hurt you, Mike, if you took a load of brush out every now and then," Elena said, challenging him. "It would exercise a different group of muscles, and it looks like Dad could use a rest."

"Can I take a turn at it, Dad?" Mike asked, ignoring Elena's remarks. "I'm old enough to handle it now."

"Wait 'til Todd starts his up again. I'd like to enjoy a few moments of silence. How's the fire, girls?"

"Doing fine, dear," Susan said. "The smaller branches have all been consumed and we have great coals for cooking lunch."

"Lunch is beginning to sound like a good idea."

"Don't get too tired, Harold," Susan cautioned. "Elena and I thought we'd work another hour and then bring things down. We've had a good rest and we're ready to tackle the brush piles. I'll be so happy when they're all gone."

"It's going to look wonderful, Mom," Elena said, picking up a large branch in each hand and starting back toward the beach again.

"Still can't get over the change in Elena," Harold said to Susan, shaking his head. "Last time I asked her to do this, she was ready to take me to court for child abuse."

168

Elena overheard and called back, "Isn't it great that children eventually grow up?" She bounced down the hillside.

*

The bumping of the wheelbarrow over the rough ground and the cracking of twigs beneath its weight announced the arrival of Doug and Harvey.

"Where are your friends today, Harv? Are they afraid of a little work?" Harold asked.

"They think they git enough of that at home, I reckon." Harvey returned a freckled grin. "To tell you the truth, most times I feel the same way, but Doug and me are havin' fun today, aren't we, Doug?"

"Yah, it helps to do it with a friend," Doug said. "When's lunch, Mom?"

"In a little while. Harvey, would you like to have lunch with us? We're cooking hotdogs over the fire."

"Yes, ma'am, I would." Harvey's grin returned.

"See that you two earn your keep. We have a long way to go," Harold said. When Todd reappeared, Harold picked up his saw. "Come on, Mike, I'll show you how it's done."

"Aw, Dad, I know how it's...," Mike started to say.

A harsh buzz cut him off. Harold took the saw in both hands and lifted it to show Mike how to hold it, then cut an eighteen-inch log from the tree trunk he had been sitting on, making it just the right size for their fireplace. He held the saw out to Mike who placed his hands just where Harold had and sliced off a log of equal length. Harold patted Mike on the back, pleased with his performance.

*

Amanda sat at a small table in the middle of the beach eating a hotdog smothered in catsup and relish and salads and coleslaw from the market. She sipped a steaming glass of hot cider with cloves and a cinnamon stick. Susan sat on a nearby rock holding similar fare.

The children sliced their sticks in two and cooked two hotdogs at a time. Too warm near the fire, the cider tasted good at a distance where it was still chilly and damp, a fine day for the task they had chosen. The gray sky thinned now and then to reveal a pale sun trying hard to break through the cloud cover but never quite succeeding.

Todd and Elena picked a spot along the shore where erosion had exposed

169

large stretches of horizontal roots. They settled themselves snugly into the roots and enjoyed resting from their hard work. Doug and Harvey set their plates down by the starfish pond and in between bites poked their sticks at sea anemones, which immediately closed their tendrils inward and turned into hard, smooth globs of a jelly-like substance.

*

Harvey hurled live whelks and periwinkles, which had crawled up the rocks to the top of the water, into the pool. "Hey, Doug," he whispered, looking about as if to make sure no one heard him, "want to come to the tree house after lunch and see the great new magazine I got?"

"Nah, not today. I promised my parents I wouldn't look at them again." Doug remembered he had already broken his promise once when he looked at the *Hustler* magazine after the hurricane. He still felt uncomfortable disobeying his father.

"You chicken or somethin'?"

"No, I just told them I wouldn't."

"Come on, they'll never know. This one's really good. You can see even more of the girls close-up. I mean, wowee, they are some gorgeous babes. There's one that wears a black mask, black arm and leg bracelets, and carries a big black whip."

"You're putting me on," Doug said, a funny tingling of arousal coursing through his twelve-year-old body. "You're just trying to get me interested."

"No, honest, Doug. It's got pictures of her coming down hard with the whip on the backs of men and them smiling, beggin' for more."

"I never saw anything like that at the movies."

"Well, I have. One of the older guys on our street showed me some of his porno videos. Man, he had all kinds of stuff like that. I've never seen anythin' like it. It's kinda hard to describe. I'll get him to invite you sometime."

"Nah," Doug repeated. "Mom and Dad wouldn't like it, and if Elena knew, I'd never hear the end of it. You heard the fuss they made in the car. You oughta know."

Harvey wasn't one to give up easily. "Well, I'm gonna leave 'bout an hour after lunch. You think about comin' with me." His lunch now finished, Harvey backed up, took a running leap, and landed solidly on the other side of the pond.

"I can do that, too," Doug said, repeating the performance, letting out the tension building up inside him.

170

"Yeah, you just follow me, Doug. Isn't anything we can't do." Harvey put his arm around him, and the two boys walked back to the fire arm in arm, ready to toast marshmallows and make s'mores.

*

At six o'clock. Elena, aching all over, glowed with satisfaction at the day's accomplishment. Doug and Harvey had run off together midafternoon, everyone agreeing they had labored longer than expected for lads of that age. "Especially on vacation," Doug had reminded them. The rest of them had worked to the end of the day. When the last of the equipment had been stored in its proper place, Elena and Todd returned to guard the fire until the tide covered it.

Sitting at the top of the hill and looking at the new scene, Elena sighed. "I can't believe we did it in just one day." She reached out and laid her hand on Todd's arm. "Of course, we wouldn't have made such progress without you, Todd."

"Harvey did his fair share, too," Todd said. "Though I found that hard to believe."

"Yes, he surprised me, too. I guess he really appreciates Mom and Dad taking an interest in him. All that's left is pulling up the stumps and splitting the wood. We'll leave the splitting to Victor. He does a little every fall and spring and always keeps us supplied with more firewood than we can use. But those stumps...they're the only thing that detracts from the scene now. We'll have to hire someone with a tractor to pull them out. Of course, I'd rather the trees were still standing, but there's much more light in here now and I imagine next year it will be beautiful with little seedlings and new ground covers."

"I guess I'll have to come back to see it."

"Is that a possibility?"

He lifted a brow. "Would you like that?"

"You know I would. You've made this the best summer of my life."

"I wish I could say yes, Elena, but I have no idea what direction my life will take. It's one big question mark. But I can tell you there's nothing I'd rather do."

"I guess we're done for now," she said, standing. "Before I get carried away thinking about the cabin that might be built here some day, let's end the day right and make sure the fire's out."

They walked silently, hand in hand, out of the woods onto the shore.

Their feet sank into the wet sand where the tide had risen. The path to the rock where the fire lay was now too narrow for both of them. But they ignored the water that was pushed in their way by each new wave and continued on, not wanting to break apart.

They climbed onto the rock. The sun had never broken through, and the evening mist chilled them. The warmth of the smoldering fire was diminished, but it felt good now. They stood looking into the coals, thinking their own thoughts.

Elena broke the silence. "We'll have to wade back if we wait any longer." Let's just push what's left of the fire into the water. The tide will carry it out and come up and clean the rocks before it goes out again."

They worked hurriedly now with rakes left for that purpose and ran back over the tiny strip of sand right before the tide claimed it.

"Wow, just in time," Elena laughed.

"Bathtub, here I come. I think I'll soak at least an hour," T odd said.

When they reached the cabin, Elena turned to him, "Goodnight, Todd. Have a nice evening with your grandmother."

He hugged her hard and started down the road to his cabin.

29

ALERTED BY HIS WHISTLING as Todd walked toward the cottage, his grandmother met him at the door. The porch light revealed a very troubled expression, but whether from anger or fright Todd could not tell.

"What is it, Grandma? You look distressed."

"Todd, I'm so glad you're home. I'm going crazy by myself thinking about what I said and what I should have said."

"You look like you've seen a ghost. Who did you say what to?" he asked with light humor.

"Your mother," she said to his back as he hung his jacket on the hook in the hall.

He whirled and stared at her, all the pleasure of the day draining away.

"You heard correctly. Your mother called my lawyer with a tale about being desperately ill, and he gave her my number."

"Grandma, sit down. I need to make a fire, and you can start by telling me everything she said." He set about breaking the twigs he had gathered in the woods for tinder and slowly, deliberately, placed several small branches over them with three larger logs on top. It gave him time to compose his racing thoughts. *Why, after all these years has she called now with my father soon to be released from prison? Don't I have enough on my mind?* It seemed every time he enjoyed a few days of happiness, catastrophe struck again. It had become a too familiar pattern.

Striking the match across the hearth, he held the flame to the dry kindling. His grandmother rocked back and forth. As tiny flames spread, he replaced the fire screen and sat opposite her, nodding that she had his full attention.

Amanda stopped rocking and leaned forward. "I wasn't a bit nice to her, Todd. Do you think I should have been?"

"How long has it been since you talked to her, Grandma?"

"I can hardly remember," she said. "No, no, that isn't true. I remember it as if it were yesterday. You were fifteen years old. She had been drinking. I could tell she was totally inebriated. Her voice sounded friendly, all full of smiles, like nothing had ever happened, and it was the most natural thing in the world for her to call me."

"You never told me," Todd interrupted her.

"That's right, I did not. You were fifteen, and it was a bad call like this one. She said she missed you and Bobby and wanted you to come to California to spend the summer with her. I asked her if she was married or living alone. She said neither. She had just moved in with a new boyfriend, and they had a beautiful apartment overlooking San Francisco Bay. I could hear him laughing in the background.

"Then she said, 'You'd like him, Mother. He's been all over the world and can talk about everything. He's really cute too, aren't you, honey?' Then I could hear them kiss. I was infuriated and told her to stay out of our lives, that we had forgotten all about her and that we were getting along just fine.

"She started to swear and call me names and threatened to take me to court to get her boys. I told her she was unfit to be a mother and that I wouldn't let her disturb your lives again. She called me more names, which I will not repeat and hung up. She never called again until today."

"And how did she sound?" Todd asked, not sure he wanted to know.

"Rather pathetic. I don't think she's that ill. She's just down on her luck. She's never married again, and no one is taking care of her. She didn't want to see us. She only wanted money."

"Did she ask about me?" Todd said almost in a whisper, dreading to hear the answer.

"She said, 'How are my boys?' It startled me to realize she didn't even know Bobby was dead. I wasn't angry yet, just apprehensive, so I told her about him and that we had tried to call her at the time of the funeral, but she had moved on, and we were unable to find her. The operator didn't have any listing under her name in San Francisco and we couldn't call every city in California. For all we knew she could have left the country with her traveling friend. That made her mad, and she started screaming at me." Amanda twisted her handkerchief in her hands, leaned back in her chair with a sigh, and started rocking again.

"But did she ask about me, Grandma?"

"I didn't give her a chance," she said. "I screamed angrily back at her that if she was such a concerned mother, she would want to know how her living son was and that he was doing wonderfully without her and that she better stay away and not mess up his life any further." She studied the twisted handkerchief.

He rose from his chair, walked over, and patted her hand, "It's all right, Grandma. It doesn't hurt anymore."

"What should I have done, Todd?" she asked with a measure of humility.

"I was afraid to let her back into our lives. We've been so happy these past weeks. Won't your God ever let us be happy?" Her voice rose again in defiance.

"I guess we should think what He would have done, Grandma." He paced the floor and rubbed his forehead. "He said we should forgive seventy times seven, which means as many times as we're asked."

"She didn't ask for forgiveness. She didn't admit she's ever done anything wrong. She just wanted money." Her voice was angry and defensive.

"You don't have to justify what you did, Grandma. I wouldn't have reacted well to her call either. I don't know what I would have done, but I'll have to think about it. I have a feeling that won't be the last time she calls. Do you mind if I spend time alone before dinner? Maybe you'd like to lie down a little while, too. I'm sure you don't have much of an appetite after that."

Without waiting for her answer, Todd went to his room and shut the door. He flopped down on his bed feeling numb, his stomach churning. He wasn't angry. He wasn't as frightened as his grandmother had been. He didn't feel much of anything.

He pictured the Richards gathered around their dining table exchanging jokes and reminiscing about the happy day and all they had accomplished. He thought of Elena, the fragrance of her hair as he held her close to him, the joy in her face when she smiled at him. Elena, who had been loved and protected from the day she was born. The worst thing she had ever experienced was having two sprained ankles for a summer in this beautiful place.

What do I know of family life? Will my past haunt me forever and invade every happy period in my life? Could it spoil my relationship with Elena? Will I have to introduce Elena to my mother some day and to my father? What will she think when she knows about my father?

He groaned and buried his head in his pillow. Pictures, unhappy pictures from his childhood, flickered through his mind, the ghosts of his past, rising to interfere with the present. He lay there a long time remembering. He wouldn't let them hurt him anymore. He would remain numb, dead to those pictures. They would have no more power over him. Having made this declaration, he sighed and relaxed his guard. In spite of his resolve, a burning sensation grew in his eyes and moisture misted them. Spilling slowly over his lashes, lonely tears followed a path down his cheeks and over that strong jaw line.

*

The Richards cleared the dining-room table, and Mike and Doug took their turn doing the evening dishes. Elena wiped the table clean and announced, "This is a perfect evening for Balderdash."

Susan groaned. Elena knew it was not her favorite game. She tried too hard to come up with reasonable definitions to the crazy words presented on the cards.

Harold put another log on the fire. "That's a great idea, Elena. I'm in the mood for that."

A chorus of agreement came from the kitchen.

Susan shook her head. "I guess I'm overruled."

The boys finished the dishes in record time and emerged to help Elena lay out the game.

The phone rang above the peals of laughter.

"I'll get it," Elena said, hoping it was Todd. "Hello....Oh, hi, Harv, we really appreciated your help today. Yes, Doug's here. Just a minute. Doug, it's for you."

*

Doug, upon hearing Harvey's name, rose from his chair and reached for the phone. "Hi, Harvey, what's up?"

"Doug, you got to get away from your family and come over to Ned's house. He's gonna show some of us guys more of those videos I told you about. This is your chance to see them. Tell your old man your friends are going to the movies, and Ned will come over and pick you up in his car."

"That would be swell, Harv, but not tonight. We're playing a family game."

"Aw, come on, we may not git another chance like this. I promise you, you haven't seen anything 'til you see it in real life."

"I'd really like to, Harv, but not tonight. Call me next time, Okay?"

"You're really missin' it, Doug."

"I'm sure you're right, but I can't. Okay?" Doug felt very uncomfortable as he glanced at the four faces turned toward him. "Bye, Harv. And thanks." He put down the receiver and returned to his place at the table as fast as he could.

"What was that about, young man?" Harold asked.

"Some guys are going to the movies and wanted me to go with them. I told them some other time."

"Some other time indeed. It's entirely too late to be starting off at this hour of the night. The last show would have started by the time you arrived at the theater," Harold said, looking at his watch.

"It's a home video," Doug said, offering nothing more.

"You made the right decision, Doug. Go ahead, it's your turn to roll the dice and pick the word," Susan encouraged him.

Carefully acting like nothing unusual had occurred, Doug rolled a dice, picked out the next card, and read the word: *"Doog,* that's *D O O G,* pronounced 'Dewg,'" he said, giving no clue whatever as to its meaning, but emphasizing how it differed from his name.

"I don't believe it," Elena exclaimed. "Where do they find these words?"

They each had been given a small piece of paper on which to write the definition of the word. The pieces of paper were passed to Doug, who had written the correct definition on his. He added his to the pile, shuffled them, and began to read each one as though it were a serious definition, repeating the word before each time.

"Doog: Russian slang for companion, friend. *Doog:* A small pistol used in English duels. *Doog:* A word used by the fifteenth-century English, expressing anger and disappointment. *Doog:* A fly that sucks the blood from camels. *Doog:* An Eskimo dog sled. Okay, Mom, you first."

"You're all getting too good for me." Susan groaned. "They all sound possible, and I haven't the slightest idea." She thought a moment. "A fly that sucks the blood from camels."

"Mom, that's gross." Elena grimaced. "I bet Mike thought that one up. Okay, Doug, I'll try 'A small pistol used in English duels.'"

"I like 'An Eskimo dog sled,' Harold said cheerily.

"Sounds good to me, Dad," Mike agreed. "I'll take that one, too."

"Okay, Doug, read us the definition," Elena said.

"Doog." He pronounced it carefully. "A fly that sucks the blood of camels. Mom complains all the time and then she's the only one to get it right."

"What gave you the clue, Mom?" Mike wanted to know.

"You're all getting too good at thinking things up, but that was so bizarre, it had to be the right answer."

"Well, I caught two of you with my definition. That will be two points for me. I can't believe you fell for an Eskimo dog sled," Elena congratulated herself.

The game continued, each person taking his turn as the leader, the others making up more and more bizarre definitions in an effort to trick the others into thinking theirs was correct. Peals of laughter followed the revealing of the true meaning of each word.

Farther down the shore Todd walked out into the night and instinctively moved toward Elena's cabin. From the bridge he could see into the well lit living room. A fire flamed in the fireplace as the family played a game around the dining-room table. Laughter burst through the cabin walls and broke the silence of the night. Elena smiled as she spoke to her father. Harold leaned toward her, put his arm around her, and gave her an affectionate squeeze. Todd saw warmth in the fire, in the laughter, in the relationships.

He shivered in the night air but remained still, his eyes taking in the scene. Surely this was the way God designed life to be. Why did so many people miss it? The absence of memories like this left him empty inside. His relationship with Jesus had done much to fill his void, but right now he needed human warmth. He wanted to belong to that scene, to be an integral part of it.

He could have knocked on the door. He knew they would welcome him and draw him into their circle of warmth. But tonight he did not feel worthy. The shame of his family put up a wall between him and them. Such warmth seemed beyond his grasp. Yearning to move toward it, instead he backed away and returned to his cottage. His burden had not lightened but had grown heavier still.

Inside the Richards' cabin, the game drew to an end. Susan had held her own until the last few turns, when Harold scored heavily to win for the evening.

"That's as it should be," Harold said pompously. "Any time you'd like a lesson in the finer meaning of unusual words, children, just let me know. Your mother has picked up quite a bit living with me all these years."

"Harold, you're insufferable," Susan said, more pleased with his triumph than if she had won herself.

"I think we better reward ourselves with what's left of the marshmallows and chocolate from the picnic." Mike rose from his chair.

"I second the motion." Doug ran into the kitchen and reached for the necessary supplies. "Mike, you get the marshmallow forks."

A few minutes later, the children were seated around the fire, looking tired but satisfied. "Nothing like a s'more to top off a great day," Harold said, rubbing his protruding stomach. Looking at his watch, he added, "Time to call it a day. Elena, you and Todd have to be on the courts at nine sharp tomorrow. You don't want to default the first rung of the tournament."

"You're right, Dad, I don't. Good thing my back isn't sore anymore, and my hands have healed a lot. Good night," she said, giving him a good hug. She bent over and gave Susan a peck on the cheek, "'Night, Mom, sleep well."

"There can be no doubt of that. Thank you all for your hard work on the point. We'll enjoy it for years to come."

As the children piled out the door, flashlights in hand, Harold sat on the couch beside Susan and put his arm around her. "Happy, sweetheart?" he asked.

"You know I am. I couldn't have ordered a better summer. I can hardly believe how blessed we are." She nuzzled closer against his chest.

They sat a long time gazing into the flickering flames. Harold bent over and kissed her hair as Susan stroked his arm. "We are blessed, Susan. God has been good to us."

30

TODD ARRIVED AT 8:30, looking as handsome as ever in his matching shirt and shorts, heavy tennis sweater draped over his shoulders. Elena anticipated the tournament with great joy, never having had so skilled a partner, nor one she cared for so much.

"Hi, Todd," she greeted him.

"Good morning, Elena." His voice sounded so flat it startled her.

"Have a bad night?"

"Yes, I had trouble sleeping."

"After all those trips across the beach, I slept like a log," she exclaimed with only slightly diminished enthusiasm as she climbed into the car.

He closed the car door behind her and walked around to his side.

"Are you sure you're up to the tournament this morning?"

"I'm sure."

They drove on in silence. "Is there anything you'd like to tell me?"

"I'm not quite myself this morning. Don't let it worry you." He lapsed into silence again.

Elena slipped down a bit into her seat and closed her eyes. She prayed for the day, for success in the tournament, but most of all for Todd, for whatever was bothering him. She decided it would be best just to wait it out and not push him to share with her, but something serious must have happened between the time they parted last night and this morning. She hoped it didn't have anything to do with them.

"It's a much nicer day than yesterday," she said. "We certainly picked the right day to burn. The sun is breaking through already."

"Yes, the sun always breaks through after a cloudy day, doesn't it?" he said with no particular enthusiasm.

"I hope it will for you today," Elena said under her breath.

When they arrived at the club, Elena jumped out of the car and ran ahead of him to the courts. He joined her as she was shaking hands with their opponents, a middle-aged couple who played regularly in Open Tennis—good, solid players who kept the ball in play, but whose skills were not outstanding.

During warm-up, Todd hit the ball much too hard.

At exactly 9:00 o'clock, the tennis chairman blew a whistle. "Time to start," he called out. As Todd served the first game, double-faulting twice in a row, she rejoiced that her family had elected to stay home.

He apologized. "I'll settle down in a minute. Hang with me, Elena."

"Of course. Just relax and you'll be fine."

His serve improved as he concentrated on getting it in the court, but he hit several balls beyond the back line and lost the first game.

As they walked to the other side of the net, Elena said, "We'll get this one." However, their opponents, encouraged by the first game, came on strong, keeping the ball in play until Todd hit it out of the court. It was 2-0 when Elena served. Todd stood at the net and aggressively reached for every return, angling the ball to the sidelines or behind their opponents.

"Way to go, Todd. That's putting them away."

Todd stopped acting like a school boy taking out his frustrations on the ball and settled down to play the solid tennis Elena expected. They won the first set 6-4.

During the second set he seemed his usual self again, controlling the ball well, even making sociable replies to Elena's chatter between games. Elena relaxed and enjoyed meeting the challenge almost as much as she had anticipated. They won the second set 6-1 and moved to the second round.

*

On the way home Todd pulled onto a side road and stopped the car. "It's time for me to tell you about my family, Elena," he said, his tone deadly serious. "It will be hard for you to understand. I haven't wanted to tell you, but now I must."

He searched her eyes. "Remember the day on Neptune Island when you told me about the ring you wear? I felt you and your father didn't trust me because I carry the shame of my family." He looked away from her. "I thought, *Why should they trust me when I come from such an untrustworthy family?*"

"Todd," she said gently, "I've told you before that you're not responsible for who your parents are, only who you are."

"Yes, that's what I like about you, Elena." He frowned. "But I must tell you now. My mother called yesterday for the first time since I was fifteen years old. She has never remarried but has lived with many men. She hasn't cared about us in all these years, but she said now she wants her boys. She didn't even know Bobby was dead. She and Grandma argued on the phone. Grandma told her to stay out of our lives and hung up on her."

Elena reached out to stroke his arm. "How sad."

"Yes, but there's more. You know my father is in prison, but you don't know why. He was convicted of selling child pornography." He looked out the window again and waited for her reaction.

Elena, too shocked to respond, said nothing. Thoughts raced through her head that she didn't want to entertain. *Had Todd been involved? Did his father take pictures of him as a child? Did his father pass on a perverted view of sex to his sons?*

"Oh, Todd," she said at last. She was repulsed by the whole idea, but she had to know more. "Tell me why," she said, hoping for some reasonable explanation that separated Todd from what his father had done, but frightened that Todd had been tainted by his father's actions.

"He did it for money," Todd said. "He and my mother lived beyond their means. Mother always wanted nicer things, bigger trips, larger houses. Dad tried to keep up with her wants, but fell behind financially. During the trial I learned that he looked at pornography himself and understood the size of the market. He started selling it online. When Mother left him, he was deeply in debt. Some of his customers wanted harder material to get greater kicks. When he supplied them with pictures that included children, he made more money. Eventually, a law enforcement officer began buying from him over the Internet. My father was indicted and finally convicted."

"He didn't take the pictures himself?' she asked.

"No, I never knew anything about it. I knew he was working on his computer but thought it was work he hadn't finished at the office. He kept his computer locked with secret codes and often locked his office door when he was online."

Elena sighed. "You never saw any of it, Todd?"

"No, I didn't? Does that make it any easier?"

"Yes, much," she said.

"I'm sorry to have to shatter your image of me, but I didn't think it was fair to hide it any longer."

"Yes, thanks for telling me, but give me some time to get used to it. You understand?" She faced him now, her eyebrows slanted with concern.

"Of course," he said. "I'm sure Grandma needs me the rest of the day. I'll try to go to Bible Study with you tonight. I'm sorry to destroy your good impression of me."

They gazed at each other for a time, then Todd started the car and drove the rest of the way to her cabin.

When they had arrived, she said, "I'm trying to remember you're exactly

the same person you were before you told me, Todd. Just give me some time."
She smiled at him, then swiftly exited the car and raced toward her cabin.

*

Elena spent the afternoon on the shore writing letters to friends at home. She inspected the woods they had cleared the day before and decided she should press her father to have the stumps removed at once. She lay on the sheltered sand beach and thought about everything she had shared with Todd. Now she knew why he had withdrawn from her. It made her sad to think how unhappy he must be.

Could they just go on as though everything were the same? She thought of her brother Doug and how Todd had told her Doug must stop looking at pornography. *Was he telling me the truth that he had never seen any of his father's material?* He had delayed telling her the whole truth, but he had never said anything that wasn't true.

"Oh, Todd." She exhaled. "None of us is perfect." She spoke to the wind that cooled her face, picked up her belongings, and hiked back to her parents' cabin. Susan was alone cooking in the kitchen.

"Mother, I've just learned the most terrible thing about Todd's father, and I have to talk to you."

Susan stopped stirring her bowl and took off her apron. "Come into the living room and tell me."

"He's in prison for selling child pornography!"

"Oh, no," Susan said, taking her daughter into her arms.

"Mom, I feel so deeply for him. I'm so repulsed when I think about it, but it doesn't change how I feel about Todd. He's had such a hard life. I just want to comfort him, to make him forget all about it, make him smile, and experience all the good things he's missed. I can't turn away from him."

"You need to think it through, dear. Do you know how much Todd was involved?"

"He said not at all. No pictures. He didn't even know about it."

"That's a relief," Susan said.

"And his mother. She's had affairs with many men and never married any of them. She hasn't been in touch with Todd for years, and now she wants to see him."

"Poor Todd, he does have problems, Elena. He's right, you know, not to have tried to make any commitment to you."

"Yes, I see that now, but I'd still like to hear him say he cares."

"Be patient, dear. Everything will be clear to both of you in time. If Todd is that special person for you, in spite of all his difficulties, you'll know it when the time is right. Anything that good is worth waiting for."

Elena rose and embraced her mother once more. "Thanks, Mom. I'm glad I can talk to you about it."

*

Todd accompanied the Richards to church that evening. They picked up Harvey, who chattered all the way to church and back. He seemed to be keyed up, but no one thought twice about it. After church they dropped Harvey at his house and went directly home.

Todd said a quick good night and walked to his cabin. Susan set out the remains of the blueberry cake from dinner with three glasses of skim milk. She and Harold enjoyed a cup of herbal tea while the children demolished what was left of the cake.

"It's really too late to build a fire and play a game tonight." Elena stretched and covered a yawn. "Todd and I have to play the second round tomorrow morning at 9:00 sharp, so I think I'll turn in early." She rose from her chair and gave Susan and Harold a quick hug. "It was a nice evening, Mom. Sleep well, Dad."

"You're right, Elena. I'm ready to call it a day. How about it, boys?" Susan said.

"Okay by me." Mike gulped the remainder of his milk and rose at the same time. "Come on, Doug, I challenge you to a game of cribbage. Can we take the cribbage board to our cabin, Mom?" He turned to Susan.

"Of course, but don't stay up late. Tomorrow is your day to go lobstering with Jamie's brother. Your lunches are all packed and in the refrigerator."

"Thanks, Mom," Doug said. "That's one thing I don't have trouble waking up for. We'll be gone long before Elena stirs."

"Have fun, boys, but be quiet in the morning. I need all the strength I can muster to keep up with Todd's game. I'd be so embarrassed if we lost. It would be my fault."

"We'll be there to watch the finals, Sis. I'm sure you'll make it all the way," Mike encouraged her as he followed her out the door.

Doug paused to grab the cribbage board and followed behind him. "Pray for great weather for us, Mom, Dad," he called from the other side of the door.

Susan cleared the table and finished the dishes. "Doug seems like his old self again, doesn't he, dear?"

"Yes. I hope he won't give in to temptation again. Every kid gets exposed to it in this culture," Harold said. As Susan turned out the light and emerged from the kitchen, Harold put his arm around her and escorted her to the bedroom. "You see, it wasn't such a tragedy, after all. The summer is turning out just as you hoped it would…bringing the family together again."

*

The phone broke the silence of the night. Susan woke up with a start. "Who would call us at this hour?"

Harold struggled to come to and fumbled for the light. "I'll get it. Must be important." He found his way into the living room, turned on the light, and lifted the receiver to his ear. "Hello."

"I'm sorry, Harold, I can tell I've awakened you, but I thought you ought to know. It's Pastor Dar. Did Doug go out after church tonight?"

"Know what?" Harold's fuzzy head cleared as he sensed something bad had happened. "Doug came home with us and had a snack. The children all went to bed early. He and Mike were going to play cribbage before they went to sleep. I'm sure he's in bed. The boys are going lobstering before sunrise."

"Good. Let him go without saying anything. We'll know more by the time he gets home."

"Dar, what on earth are you talking about?"

"There's been a very serious problem, Harold. It appears that Harvey has raped Rhodora…."

"Harvey's done what?" Harold raised his voice so loud, Susan leaped out of bed and came running into the room.

"What's happened?" she asked frantically.

He covered the phone with his hand. "Go back to bed, dear, I'll tell you all about it when I make sense of it myself."

Susan returned to their bedroom.

Speaking into the phone again, Harold said, "Now start at the beginning, Dar, and tell me exactly what happened. We took Harvey home after church; he seemed happy as could be. He talked about how great it was to see Rhodora again and what a good lookin' doll she was, but she is. Any guy at any age would agree with that." He raised his voice again.

Dar spilled out the story. "He must have gone back out on his bike. Rhodora takes the church bus home. It goes in and out of roads and takes longer than driving straight home. He must have waited in the bushes for her and enticed her into the woods before she went into her house. Her mother hadn't gone to church and looked anxiously for her out the front window. Finally she heard sobbing outside the back door. She found Rhodora sitting on the back steps, afraid to come in. She wouldn't talk at first. As soon as her mother could get her to say something, she called and told me Rhodora wasn't making any sense. I went over right away."

"That poor child." Harold's happy world shattered.

"Rhodora was hysterical when I got there, talking about how she was dirty and could never get clean again. Neither of us could understand what had happened. I took her in my arms and tried to comfort her. When she calmed down and rested her head against my chest...her little head kept jerking as she let out another sob. She is such a beautiful girl, and to see her in such distress...it was heart-breaking.

"Finally, I asked her, 'Who hurt you, Rhodora?' She didn't say anything for the longest time, just let out another sob every now and then. I told her I couldn't help her unless she told me. Finally she said, 'Harvey.' Nothing more, just 'Harvey' and then finally 'Why would he do it?' 'Do what?' I asked. She just shook her head. 'Did Harvey push you down and make you dirty?' I asked. She shook her head yes. I said, 'You can have a nice bath, and we can wash your dress, and it will be clean again.'

"'No,' she said, jumping off my lap, and looking at me defiantly. 'You don't understand,' she said, her blue eyes blazing. 'Inside! I'm dirty inside. No one will want me now,' and she threw herself on the couch and curled up in a fetal ball and rocked back and forth, letting her sobs out more frequently. When I understood, I felt sick. That beautiful, pure little girl! Only twelve years old! And I felt so guilty, Harold, encouraging you to bring him to church. But don't you and Susan feel guilty. I'm the one who suggested it.

"We were all in it, Dar." Harold closed his eyes and shook his head.

"I think he was alone. Doug wasn't with him. I just thought of the pornography the boys had watched and that made me think of Doug. I thought you should know before you hear it from the grapevine. Rhodora's mother was beside herself and called two of her friends before I got there. Harvey will have to be arrested, and there's no keeping it a secret. Everyone will have to know, and you'll have to deal with Doug. Harold, do you understand?"

"Yes, Dar, I understand. Is there anything I can do for you or Rhodora or her mother?" Harold said slowly as the full impact hit him.

"No, Rhodora is resting now. It would be more trauma for her to be examined tonight. I'll have to take her for a medical exam first thing in the morning before she bathes, and Harvey will have to be booked. It's a messy business. If they were adults, I'd report it to the Sheriff in Ellsworth tonight, but they're so young. I think it can wait 'til morning. You'll have to tell your family, Harold, and deal with Doug. It's going to be very hard on him. He always took care of Rhodora. He's going to have all kinds of guilt. I'd like to help him when he's ready to talk to me."

"Yes, Dar, thanks." Harold relaxed his grip on the phone and placed the receiver back on the hook. His thoughts turned to Susan. His instinct was to spare her, but he knew he must tell Susan tonight and Elena in the morning. Maybe he could wait until she returned from her tennis match, but would tongues be wagging already? News like this traveled fast on the island.

He wouldn't see the boys in the morning. Maybe by late afternoon he would know what to say to them. He thought of the red-cheeked, fair Rhodora with her tousle of blond curls. She looked as much like an angel as any child he had ever seen. Anger against Harvey rose within him. But it was he who had taken Harvey to the Sunday school picnic and to church. He put his head in his hands and groaned.

"Harold, what's wrong? Has something terrible happened?" Susan called from the next room, anxiety lacing every word.

He would have to tell Susan now.

31

HAROLD COMFORTED SUSAN FAR INTO THE NIGHT. Broken-hearted, her dreams of a perfect summer evaporated. Irreparable damage had been done, and her family had had a part in it. They prayed together, asking for forgiveness, entreating their Lord to heal Rhodora's deep wounds and to draw her close to Him. They thanked the Holy Spirit for the comfort they knew He wanted to give her and asked that He prepare her heart to receive it. They prayed for Rhodora's mother, who had already suffered so much, that she, too, would be comforted and would be able to forgive this desecration of her beautiful daughter.

They prayed that Pastor Dar would be guided in his handling of the problem and that he would say just the right words to everyone involved, for strength and wisdom to speak to their own children. They asked the Lord to take this terrible experience and somehow use it for good. They remembered how Joseph's brothers in Scripture had sold him into slavery in Egypt, and how he had forgiven them and said, "You meant it for evil, but God meant it for good." They asked the Lord to redeem the situation and the summer for Rhodora and Harvey and all of them.

As they prayed, their angry feelings toward Harvey lessened. Realizing that he was in some ways as much a victim as Rhodora, they prayed for him with equal compassion. He had had too little love from his parents. He had been overstimulated by the voracious pornography industry, which preyed upon the natural instincts of teenage boys and led them down a path of destruction. Doug, their own son, was a victim, too. Had he really broken free from the enticements of pornography? This was the first question they needed to ask.

Then Susan told Harold the disturbing news about Todd's father. Harold closed his eyes. "What more, Lord?" he said. They prayed on, now for Todd and Elena and Todd's broken family. "Thank You, Lord, that You will show us how to walk through all these problems," Harold concluded.

They were silent a long time, holding each other tightly. Harold relaxed and drifted off first, sleeping fitfully for several hours and waking while it was still dark. He heard the boys leave for their day of lobstering. Surely, the word had not spread to any of the fisherman yet. Dar was not going to alert anyone until he had taken Rhodora to the doctor for an examination.

He dozed off again but was awakened by Elena moving about the kitchen as she fixed her breakfast. She must be wondering why they were still in bed. Susan slept by his side. He suspected she had remained awake most of the night. She needed all the sleep she could get; it would be a difficult day for them both. He lay still until Elena's car pulled out of the driveway and up the dirt road. Relieved that the children were gone, he tiptoed out of the bedroom and shuffled into the kitchen to make a strong cup of coffee. This was one morning he needed a good dose of caffeine.

Taking the coffee into the living room, he sat in his favorite chair and reached for his Bible on the bookshelf. He opened its well-worn pages and began a search for the wisdom he would need for the day's ordeals. Shivering from the morning chill, he set the Bible aside to build a fire in the fireplace and watched the flames as they spread from paper to kindling to logs. Then, turning back to serious prayer for Dar, for Rhodora, her mother, for Harvey, and for each member of his family, he thanked the Lord that he didn't have to face such a problem in his own strength.

Susan awakened and joined Harold in prayer. She knelt beside him on the carpet in front of the fire. He looked into her eyes, puffed and tired from little sleep and many tears. He missed the usual radiance of her face, now drawn and pale, beginning to show the inevitable signs of age, but she had regained her composure. They both closed their eyes and poured out their troubled hearts to the Lord. When the fervent prayer no longer poured forth, she remained at Harold's feet, gazing into the fire while he stroked her tousled hair.

After a time, she said, "I feel better, don't you? It was such an unexpected blow. I felt almost as badly last night as I would have if it had been Doug."

"I'm grateful I knew he was there in the cabin with Mike and Elena," Harold agreed. "What I want to know is how much more of that stuff he's looked at with Harvey. We, unfortunately, have given him many chances."

"But he promised he wouldn't," Susan protested. "We've always trusted our children."

"This stuff has a drawing power beyond anything our kids have experienced, Susan. We've been able to protect them from most worldly enticements until now, but once a boy experiences the pleasure of arousal from pornography, it's hard for him not to go back for more. In counseling young men at home, I've talked to many who wanted desperately to give it up, but after a week of cold turkey, they'd start all over again. It's like a drug. They want to experience the high that blots out all their pain, even if they know it's only for a short time. Pornography is very seducing, Susan. I didn't want to alarm you before, but it can become a very serious problem."

A car pulled into their parking spot and two doors banged shut.

"Elena is home," Susan said.

Quick to protect his wife from the stress, Harold said, "I'll tell her. She'll have to know sooner or later, and maybe she can help us with Doug."

Elena bounced through the kitchen with Todd close behind. "We won," she announced with the thrill of victory still written on her glowing cheeks. "Todd was simply wonderful putting...Mom, Dad, what's wrong? You look so serious. Neither of you is dressed. It's eleven o'clock in the morning."

"Sit down, Elena. You, too, Todd. You might as well hear it now," Harold said.

"Hear what?" Elena's smile faded.

"Last night, after church, something very unfortunate happened," Harold began slowly. "Mike and Doug were with you in the other cabin, weren't they, Elena? I mean, Doug didn't go out after you left here, did he?"

"Of course not. He and Mike played cribbage just like they planned," Elena said. "What's all this about?"

"Thank, God!" Susan whispered, covering her face with her hands and letting her rigid body go limp.

"Dad, what is it?" Elena persisted.

"After we dropped Harvey at his house, instead of going in, he rode his bicycle to Rhodora's house and waited for her to get off the bus. The bus goes through town and comes back by way of her house, so it took her much longer to get home. Harvey greeted her, took her hand, and asked her to take a walk with him. When she said she had to go in, he pulled her into the woods and...and..."

"Yes, Dad, then what?"

"Oh, no." Todd jumped up from his chair and began pacing the floor.

"Yes, I'm afraid so," Harold said, as though it was now clear.

"What did they do? Won't someone tell me?" Elena pleaded.

Susan rose and walked over to Elena. Putting her arms around her and looking straight into Elena's bewildered eyes, she said, "Harvey raped Rhodora."

Elena gasped, looking from one parent to the other. "The pornography?" she said, half as an affirmation and half as a question.

"It is very likely that is what motivated him." Harold shook his head in the affirmative.

"Oh, Mom, we introduced Harvey to Rhodora when we knew what he had been doing!" She put her hand over her mouth, as though the admission of it was too much to bear.

"Yes, we did," Susan said, making no attempt to justify what they had done. "We knew Doug had seen it, too. It never occurred to us to stop him from seeing Rhodora."

"We thought we could help Harvey. We never dreamed of anything like this," Harold said. To escape the wide-eyed look of horror on his daughter's face, Harold rose from his chair and placed another log on the fire.

"Is Rhodora all right?" Elena asked. Then, "No, of course she isn't."

"Pastor Dar stayed with her and her mother last night. He planned to call the Sheriff's Department in Ellsworth first thing in the morning and have her examined by a doctor."

"Does Doug know?" Elena rose and walked around the room.

"No, he and Mike left early this morning."

"Then I'm going to search his room again and see if he kept his word." Elena threw open the door and marched off to the other cabin.

Todd started to follow her.

Harold put up his hand as if to halt him. "Let her go, Todd. It's something we have to find out, and it will be good for her to do something while she sorts out her emotions."

"Mr. Richards, Mrs. Richards," Todd began, obviously searching for the right words. Deep concern registered on his handsome face, making him look years older. "You mustn't blame yourselves. You were trying to help Harvey."

"Yes, we were, Todd, but it backfired, didn't it?" Harold's shoulders bowed as if by a heavy burden.

"The magazines, and especially porn videos, make rape seem like a great thing. The girl might resist at first, but she always gives in and appears to enjoy it. Often, she even asks for more, my friend who got caught in it told me," Todd said. "How's a kid like Harvey going to realize that isn't the way girls are made and it's all lies!" He spoke with rising emotion. "My friend actually believed everything he read in those magazines."

The phone rang. Harold answered, "Hello."

Pastor Dar explained how he had taken Rhodora to the doctor and was now with Harvey and the policeman from Ellsworth. "He would like you to come down to the town office for questioning since you were the last person to see Harvey last night, Harold. Would it be too much trouble?"

"No, I'll be there as soon as I get clothes on, Dar. We've been so upset around here, we're not even dressed."

"I understand, Harold. As soon as you can make it."

"That was Pastor Dar. He wants me to come down for questioning. I'll throw some clothes on and go." Harold looked from Susan to Todd.

"You'll need some breakfast first, dear," Susan said, moving toward the kitchen.

"It's okay. I'm not hungry."

Elena burst back through the front door, holding a magazine in her hand. "He's still reading them," she cried. "Look at this, Dad. It's much worse than the others. Doug really needs help."

Susan moved toward Elena. Harold intercepted her and took the magazine. "Never mind, girls, I'll take care of this." He stuffed it under his arm and left the room without looking at anyone.

*

The police officer, a man of medium build with the typical weather-beaten face of a native of the area, had thick brows that met in the middle of his forehead, making him look fiercer than he actually was. He spoke rapidly with a thick Maine accent. Harold had a hard time following him, but he answered his questions to the best of his ability.

The officer directed his attention back to Harvey, who had been studying the cracks in the linoleum floor while the police officer questioned Harold. "Do you agree with everything Mr. Richards has said, Harvey?"

"Yes sir," Harvey muttered, still concentrating on the floor.

"So you were alone, and this was all your idea?' he questioned further.

"Yes sir."

"Whatever made you do such a thing to such a nice little girl?" He looked at Harvey as if he genuinely wanted to know.

Harvey glanced up into his piercing gaze and winced. His eyes darted from the policeman to Pastor Dar to Harold. "In the videos, the g-girls l-liked it," he stammered. "They got real happy after a while. She looked just like one of 'em. I just wanted to have some fun. I didn't mean to hurt her, honest. I never liked a girl so much." He looked frantically from one to the other, for some expression of sympathy.

Pastor Dar responded first. "We believe you didn't understand the full impact of what you were doing, Harvey, but you must have known it was wrong."

"I guess I wasn't thinkin' much at all," he said, staring at the floor again. He paused, and gazed up, eyes full of fear. "What's gonna happen to me? Are you gonna tell my dad? He'll kill me when he hears."

"I'm going to ask for a court order to put you in my care until the court decides." Pastor Dar spoke up as though he had thought the whole thing through. "Do you think your father would object, Harvey?"

"Naw, one less mouth to feed. Can I go with you right away and not go back home?" Harvey appeared relieved. Avoiding his father's wrath seemed to be the main thing on his mind.

*

Despite the trauma of the previous day, Wednesday morning arrived just like every other morning. Susan moved slowly around the kitchen when Elena, dressed in an attractive blue-green tennis outfit that enhanced her eyes, bounced into the living room and threw her racquet on the couch.

"Hi, Mom, you look tired. I'll get my breakfast. Sure you don't want to come to Open Tennis with Todd and me?"

"Quite sure, dear. Doug is grounded, and I want to be here for him if he wants to talk."

"Of course, you should be." Elena ate a few spoonfuls of cereal, grabbed a bagel, gathered her tennis gear, and started for the door. "Todd's here. I'll see you later." She kissed her mother on the cheek. "I love you, Mom."

"I know, dear, thank you." Susan smiled weakly.

Elena smiled back, willing her mother the strength she would need to face this day. "See you shortly," she said as she bounded out the door.

Todd waited for her in the car. "Hi, going my way?"

"I sure am." She smiled as he opened the door for her.

Taking the driver's seat, he said, "Looks like you weathered the storm pretty well."

"It wasn't fun. Thank heavens, Doug finally understood. When he heard the news, he denied it at first and said it wasn't possible. No one said anything. He kept looking from one of us to the other and finally said, 'He really did do that to Rhodora? Oh, no!' He put his head in his hands and started to cry.

"After a while Dad said, 'Harvey told us that she looked like one of the girls in the videos he had seen. Did you see any of those videos, Doug?" Doug said he hadn't, that Harvey had coaxed him to watch one night at the home of one of the older boys, but Doug had stayed with the family. Dad said, 'I'm glad to hear that, son. Now, Doug, I have to ask you another question, and I expect you to answer me truthfully. Since you gave your word to us that you wouldn't look at any pornographic magazines again, have you kept that word?'

"Doug looked up at all of us, searching our faces as if for a clue. I think he could sense we already knew. You could almost see his thought process, angry at first that we had snooped into his things again, ashamed that he had done wrong, then finally all his defiance broke and he blurted out, 'You found the magazine. You know already. I'm sorry, you're right. I shouldn't have done it, but I thought there was no harm...'

"Dad interrupted him, 'You understand the harm now, Doug, don't you? You understand that we want only what's best for you. The magazines are exciting, but they lead young men to have thoughts they aren't ready emotionally to handle and to do things they'll regret all their lives.'

"Doug jumped up and cried out, 'I understand, I understand, I'm sorry.'"

"I'm glad Doug saw the light right away," Todd said. "That must have been a relief to all of you."

"Yes, it was. No excuse could blot out what Harvey did. He was left without a defense. After that, Doug ran from the room and over to our cabin. He stayed there a long time. Dad went over and had a long talk with him before dinner. They came back arm in arm. Doug was very subdued throughout the evening and conversation was a bit strained, but we managed to get through it and everyone was relieved when it was over.

"Doug is grounded for now. Dad plans to have him work with him making repairs. I think he hopes to talk to Doug about all this as they work side by side. Mom stayed home today in case Doug wants to open up to her. The worst is over for us, but, of course, that doesn't help Rhodora or Harvey. Pastor Dar is trying to be a father figure for them both, but healing will take time, especially for Rhodora." Elena gave a long sigh as she came to the end of her story.

"It must have been hard for Doug, Elena. Sometimes it's worse to have the truth so clearly revealed to you. Some kids would have remained in denial and defiance."

"But Doug isn't a rebellious kid." Elena tried to understand what Doug had experienced. "He just let the testosterone pulsating through his body rule his common sense. I think our whole culture is in denial that pornography is a problem. It encourages kids all over the country to get involved in sex too early."

"The porn industry plays on kids' natural curiosity about sex," Todd said. "Their only concern is making money. They hide behind the First Amendment, but that's only a smoke screen to keep people from dealing with the real issue. Lots of my friends have bought the lie."

"I'm so glad you haven't," Elena said, putting her arm through his and smiling up at him. "Until you told me about your father, I felt so safe with you."

"And now?"

"I don't like to think about it. I know you're still the same person, but it's hard not to wonder if what your father did has affected you."

"Thanks for being honest. Hurting you is the last thing in all the world I'd want to do."

"I believe you," she said.

They pulled into the club and found a large group already congregating for Open Doubles. "Sign us up and I'll park," Todd instructed, reaching over and squeezing her hand.

She leaned over and kissed him on the cheek. "Anything for my favorite partner."

32

FRIDAY MORNING THE ENTIRE RICHARDS FAMILY gathered at the tennis courts to watch the finals of the mixed doubles tournament. Doug received permission to join them, his first activity out since his grounding.

"Go for it, darling." Harold planted a big kiss on Elena's cheek.

"With such a rooting section, we better not lose."

"Don't worry if you do, dear." Susan hugged her. "Just play your best, have fun, and be a good sport. That's what counts."

"How could I forget? You've been telling me that ever since you first put a racquet in my hand. 'Learn to be a good loser, Elena. The real winner is the one who loses well.' I'll never forget it, Mom, I promise." Elena picked up her racquet and headed for the courts to warm up with Todd.

Their opponents hit consistently hard balls. "This isn't going to be easy," Elena said to Todd.

"You're right. This couple knows how to play tennis."

"They were the club champions last year, and I'm sure they expect to win this year," Elena said as a ball went smashing just beyond her racquet.

"We're ready whenever you are," the stocky, redheaded woman across the net called to them. Solidly built with thick ankles, she ran to the net and smashed another ball down the middle past both of them, reminding Elena of a tank pushing forward regardless of what lay in its path.

"I'd like to take a few at the net first if you don't mind," Elena called out as she picked up the ball and came forward to the net position.

"Take your time," Todd encouraged her.

Elena returned every ball the redhead directed to her, hitting them just in front of her. She would save her put away shots until the game.

"I guess I'm ready now, Helen," she said, extending her hand over the net. As Helen came forward to shake it, Elena added, "You're very nice players. I can see you'll be a tough challenge."

Hod, Helen's husband, came forward to shake the hand Todd offered. Sweat already formed on his brow, dampening his curly brown hair. He, too, was of stocky build.

"They look like they belong together. Helen and Hod, two peas in a pod." Elena giggled to herself, releasing some of the pre-game tension.

"May the best man win." Hod's voice was as strong as his arm.

"I'll spin. You call it," Todd said as he spun his racquet on the court.

"Up," Helen called.

"Up it is. You start, and we'll stay on this side. Good luck," Todd said.

Hod took the ball and began pounding practice serves across the net.

"Take a few more. They were just behind the line," Todd called as he hit the balls back.

Hod hit two more practice balls well into the serving court and said in his booming voice, "These will be good."

The watchers stopped talking and settled onto spectator benches or blankets on the grass. More people than usual had come to see the final match, anticipating good tennis from the four finalists.

Hod played an impressive game and held his first serve. As they changed courts, Elena whispered to Todd, "I said it wouldn't be easy."

"They're a challenge, all right, but we'll rise to the occasion. Don't let them scare you."

Elena wished she shared his confidence. "You serve first, Todd. I'm not ready yet."

The score was tied at 40-40, but Todd came through and won his serve. Helen served well, and Hod was all over the net, putting away every ball she and Todd returned. Elena, clearly nervous, served at 1-2, double-faulting twice. She heard Harold's voice calling out, "Settle down, Elena. You can do it." She determined to try harder, but in her eagerness overshot the back line, and they were soon down 1-3.

Todd walked over to her, put his arm around her waist, and turned her toward the back of the court. "It's okay, Elena. Great strategy. They're overconfident now and we'll catch up to them."

"Like I did it on purpose," she said, not a bit encouraged.

Todd was right. Hod sensed victory. Trying to show off his strength, he hit all his first serves out. His second serve landed in the court but was easier to return. Elena and Todd won his game, and Todd served an excellent game to even the score.

Helen won her serve. Elena's first serve skidded off the inside corner and Helen failed to put her racquet on it. Encouraged, Elena served to Hod. He returned the ball within Elena's reach, but as she ran toward it, she looked up and saw Doug walking toward Eddie and Joey on the golf course. She hit the ball late and heard Hod announce triumphantly, "Wide!" She did not regain her composure and lost her serve for the second time, 5-3. They went on to lose the set 6-4.

"What's wrong, Elena?" Todd asked. "You seem to have lost your concentration."

"Doug is talking to Eddie and Joey."

"I see." Todd nodded. "They have to talk about it sometime. They can't get in any trouble out here in the sight of everyone. Your mother and dad can handle that, but I need your attention on the game. We can do a whole lot better than that."

"I'm sorry, Todd. Of course we can. We'll get the next one."

Helen and Hod, more confident now, relaxed their guard. Elena, knowing she was letting Todd down, willed herself to ignore Doug and his friends and to concentrate on the ball. As everything started clicking between them, Todd played the top of his game. They won the second set 6-3. A roar went up from the spectators as they realized these couples were evenly matched, and the third game was sure to be a good one.

The players came off the courts to take a break before the final set. Susan ran up to Elena and threw her arms around her. "That was a wonderful comeback, Elena. You looked like a different person during the second set."

"Thanks, Mom. Do you know that Doug is with Eddie and Joey?"

"Yes, dear, they have to talk about it."

"That's what Todd said."

"We told Doug to make it clear to them that there was a connection between those magazines and the pornographic videos and what Harvey did and to encourage them to stop before they get in trouble themselves."

"Do you think he'll really do that, Mom?"

"Yes, Elena, I do. Your father has spent a good deal of time the past two days explaining things to Doug. He understands the problem and is taking it seriously. I think he can help the others. Harold will talk to them, too, later on. Now, don't think about it anymore. Just get out there and concentrate on your game. You and Todd worked wonderfully together that set. Keep it up."

"Okay, Mom. Win or lose, I'll give it all I've got."

"That's my girl." Harold came over and put his arm around Elena. "We're rooting for you all the way."

"Thanks, Dad." She smiled at them, realizing how fortunate she was to have parents who rooted for their children no matter what they did. Todd had missed all that. She had to be there for him now. It was only a game, but suddenly it was much more than that. She could give Todd the support and encouragement he had never had from his parents. She wouldn't let anything distract her this time.

Hod had become visibly angry during the last set. Elena could see that he intended to win this one. Elena's resolve to do her very best, no, better than her best, was strengthened.

"We can do it," she encouraged Todd.

He tossed her the balls. It was her turn to serve.

Elena sent up a quick prayer as she stepped up to the serving line. "Lord, help me play my very best and to be gracious, no matter what happens." She felt good as she threw the ball high above her head for the first serve.

Her racquet connected with the ball perfectly. Helen hit it back poorly, popping it up in the air close to the net. Elena had no trouble putting it away. Hod was not happy. He returned Elena's next serve with all the force he could muster. Elena ducked out of the way.

"Out," Todd announced as the ball hit well behind the baseline.

Elena gained confidence with each point, winning her first serve with four points in a row. Todd kissed her ear as he whispered, "That's my girl."

Hod was up to serve and gave it all he had. The ball smashed across the net at such a speed Elena had a hard time following it. But he knew enough not to throw the set by being wild. He steadied himself and found his control again.

"Don't worry, I'll get it back," Todd called to Elena.

He served well, and he and Elena rushed the net in perfect synchronization. Neither had the raw strength of Hod, but they were good, very good. They played with graceful strokes and moved forward and backward as if finely tuned to one another. Hod and Helen, in contrast, were beginning to argue after each point they lost. Hod flared at her when Todd put a fastball down the middle between them to win his game.

Helen served next and held her own as did each player in turn, until Elena found herself serving at 4-4. She had learned by now to keep the ball away from Hod at the net and had lobbed over his head so often, she thought it was time for a surprise. She faked a lob and as Helen started to run behind Hod, Elena changed her swing and hit a fastball down the line.

Hod watched it go by and screamed, "Where were you, Helen?"

"Backing you up. Why didn't you cross over when you saw she was going to lob?" she threw back.

"She didn't lob."

"But she started to," Helen argued.

Elena continued her game, concentrating on placing the ball wherever there was a gap. Between every point, Hod told Helen where to stand, and Helen did not take it well. Trying too hard now, she hit the ball at a good angle, but it landed over the line to give the game to Todd and Elena.

They were leading 5-4 when Hod took the serve. He hit the ball with all of his might and sent it beyond the serving line. His second serve hit the net with terrible force. Helen walked over to talk to him. They turned their backs away from Todd and Elena and spoke in muted tones. Helen wiped his brow, which was dripping with sweat, and managed to calm him. They were seasoned players and knew better than to throw the match away in an adolescent display of anger.

Hod took his time preparing for his next serve. Elena's concentration was disturbed by the delay, but Hod's returned to him. His next three serves were among his best. The score was deuce at 40 all. The next serve would be to Elena. He looked fiercely across the net at her.

I will not be distracted by his antics. Keep your eye on the ball, Elena.

Unlike the fastballs Hod had been shooting at her all day, he hit a short, slow ball so full of spin it bounced backward toward the net instead of forward toward Elena. She had been watching closely and sensed his change of pace. Charging toward the net as the ball left his racquet, she saw the ball spin away from her. She stretched out her long arm and lunged forward, scooping the ball up with her racket just before it hit the ground. It hit the top of the net still spinning. All the spectators gasped as they watched to see on which side of the net the ball would fall. Elena struggled to pull her body together and stop before hitting the net. The ball dribbled over the net and fell at Helen's feet. There was no way she could have returned it. A roar of approval went up from the audience, and she heard Doug yell, "Way to go, Sis."

Todd ran up to steady her and keep her on her feet. She fell, laughing, into his arms. "I don't believe it," she exclaimed.

"Never have I seen such an extended arm. But don't get too excited. We have one point to go."

The crowd silenced as Hod stepped up to serve to Todd. The first ball was fast and wide. The second landed squarely in the middle of the serving court but not with exceptional force. Hod was playing it safe. Todd did likewise and returned the ball deep and cross court. Elena and Todd rushed toward the net. Anticipating their move, Hod hit a deep lob over Elena's head. "I've got it. Cross over," Todd instructed Elena.

He ran with all his might behind the ball and returned a high ball to Helen. She slammed it back, but Todd was there for the return. Back and forth it went—the longest play of the entire match—both sides cautious not to throw it away. By now the four of them were at the net, slamming the ball back and forth at each other. Elena saw Hod hit the ball full force directly at her. With no time to think or plan, she raised her racquet in an effort of self-preservation. The ball hit the racquet and bounced high over Hod's head, falling a good foot within the back line.

A roar went up from the crowd. Seldom had any of them seen such a dramatic finish. Elena fell to her knees, partially out of fright and partially from thanksgiving. Todd rushed over to her, pulled her to her feet, and pushed her forward to shake hands with Hod and Helen.

"The gods were with you," Hod said. "You could do no wrong."

"You played a great game." Todd reached out his hand to Hod. "It could have gone either way."

"You're really strong players. Thank you so much." Elena shook hands with Helen, then with Hod.

As the losers turned to walk off the courts, Todd opened his arms wide and scooped Elena off the ground, whirling her around and around. She raised her arms and abandoned herself to the moment. *Winning with Todd, what a delicious feeling!* They had moved together in perfect harmony. They were winners together!

Todd hugged her hard as Doug and Harold rushed up to congratulate them. The four of them walked off the court arm in arm until Mike and Susan intercepted them.

"Hey, guys, you were great," Mike said, high-fiving them both.

"You were wonderful, dear." Susan embraced Elena, her eyes teary. "Truly superb, wasn't she, Todd?"

"Those last two points were too much," he agreed.

"We didn't nickname you 'Stretch' for nothing," Doug chimed in.

"Hey, don't forget Todd. I wouldn't have even been there if Todd hadn't carried us all the way."

"You played a magnificent game, Todd. We expected it of you, but remembering how Elena complained when she was taking lessons, it's a joy to see them pay off."

"I understand, Mrs. Richards. I thought she was great, too."

*

Todd and Mrs. Faraway joined the luncheon celebration. Several families from the Country Club invited themselves at the last minute, stopping at Twisted Tree Cove to bring extra drinks and food from the deli. Susan loaded the picnic table with food and set out paper plates. With the tide out, children grabbed handfuls of potato chips and ran up and down Sunset Rock. Doug escorted them on tours to the starfish pond in between sandwiches.

Having made friends with an attractive young girl during the tennis match, Mike led her around the point. Elena had seen her on the courts before and, as the game progressed, she had been vaguely aware that the two of them were engrossed more in each other than in the match.

Elena and Todd accepted congratulations as each car arrived. Harold filled plastic glasses with Coke or 7-Up as fast as he could and Susan fluttered around making sure everyone was happy.

"Do you have everything you need, Amanda?"

"Now don't worry about me, Susan. I couldn't be happier. I don't know when I've seen so much joy on Todd's face."

"It wasn't just that they won, Amanda, but that they did it together."

"Yes, I'm sure you're right, Susan. They do make a handsome couple, don't they?"

*

Todd and Elena acted like the children. Carrying Elena in his arms, Todd ran out on Sunset Rock and threatened to throw her over the side. He whirled her around as he had at the moment of their victory while she screamed with laughter.

"We'll both fall over. Then Mother won't be able to say she's never lost a child to the rocks. You wouldn't want that to happen, would you?"

"I have no intention of losing you to the rocks or to anyone else," he said. "You're my partner and we're a team, remember?"

"I'll never forget," she said, brushing back the shock of hair that had fallen into his face and touching her forehead to his.

*

The guests had left and Todd and Elena had been excused from clean-up. They wandered into the woods, where Todd climbed up the forbidding granite verticals of the giant rock. From the top he leaned over and extended his hand to Elena. "Come to me."

"How did you do that? I can't make it up there."

"Sure you can. Come around the back. You can work your way up along the crack and I'll pull you the rest of the way. You're always telling me how you used to do it as a kid."

"I was smaller and more supple then." Elena looked up the giant rock as though it was impossible to master, but the thought of being up there with

202

Todd made the risk worth a try, so she set out to accomplish it. Holding on to the tree beside the rock, Elena edged her feet up a break in the stone that climbed diagonally to the top. Todd reached a hand down to her and pulled her up and over the top.

"The woods look great from up here. I haven't tried to climb it for years and years. I've missed something."

"It wouldn't be nearly so nice up here alone. I think you were waiting to come here with me."

"Maybe I was," she agreed, showing him her dimple and sitting down.

"Now that the woods are clean, as you survey your land, do you still think the spot we picked is the place to build your cabin?"

"I think just about any spot here would be fine, but I think God picked that one," Elena pointed up the hill where the storm had cleared the land of trees.

Todd lay down and put his head in her lap. "Tell me," he said, gazing up at her with a serious expression. "Tell me again how your house is going to be, inside and out."

"It will be of wood and stone," she said without a moment's hesitation, "with sleek modern lines, not a flat box like early modern, but with angles jutting skyward. My bedroom will be on the second floor in the tops of the spruce trees. Toward the ocean, it will be all glass with a panoramic view of the bay.

"The downstairs will have a great room with an open kitchen and a huge rock fireplace. The dining room table will be across the front so we can look at the water as we eat, just like we do now. In the back we'll have two small bedrooms, each big enough for two beds, and a bathroom, of course, and behind that, we'll have a big playroom. There will be room for a Ping-Pong table and exercise equipment for rainy days, and it will have large picture windows on the side overlooking the cove. The view will be completely different from the great room but equally beautiful."

Todd chuckled softly. "I'll have to practice my Ping-Pong before I visit you."

Elena turned away from her dreaming and surveyed his face for a hint that he would like to share her dream. The question hung in the air between them, but neither attempted to handle it at the moment.

"Are two bedrooms enough for all your children?" he asked, nudging her safely back to the dream.

"Yes, I used to think I wanted a baseball team of boys, but now I think four will be enough—two of each, just like Mom and Dad."

"Don't you want a career? Most women seem to these days, especially when they're as intelligent as you are."

"Yes, I'd like to do something worthwhile with my life, either before I get married or after the children are grown, or some of each. But when I have young children, I want to be home to raise them. I will even consider homeschooling them.

"Do you know that the orphanages in Russia are full of children whose parents were brought up in week-long daycare centers? Those parents never bonded to their own parents, so they couldn't bond to their children either, and many of them just abandoned them when the going got tough. I can't imagine that. I know I want to give my children the security Mom and Dad gave me. Not many of my friends have experienced that, and they have serious emotional problems because of it. I want to raise really healthy children."

"Do you think I'm messed up emotionally, Elena?"

"Oh, I wasn't thinking of you, Todd."

"But my family fits the description."

"You have deep wounds that need healing, but you're no emotional mess. As a matter of fact, I think you're pretty special, and I wouldn't change a thing, even if I could."

"You're good for me, Elena. When I'm with you, I taste a peace and contentment I've never known before."

"Maybe it's the place, Todd. It affects people that way."

"The woods and the sea and Elena—all strangely intermingled. I don't know where one starts and the other ends. I'll never be able to separate them. I love them all." He searched her eyes.

"Then you don't have to. The woods and the sea are a part of me. They've made me who I am. I belong to them." She caressed the shock of brown hair that lay in her lap.

"I can see reflected in your eyes the place where the water and the blue sky meet, sometimes peacefully, sometimes stormily with lights flashing," he said.

"I'd like to take away the haunted, sad look that's so often reflected in yours." Elena took his cheeks in both her hands.

He cried out, "Elena, Oh, Elena," as he rolled over and buried his face in the flannel shirt that covered her waist.

She held him and rocked back and forth, humming a lullaby her mother had sung to her when she was a child.

*

Elena lay awake in the middle of the night thinking about the afternoon when she had sung lullabies to Todd. It had seemed so natural then for her to comfort him, but in the middle of the night what she now knew about his family haunted her. Remembering the icy feeling she had when he confessed to her that his father was involved with child pornography, she shivered. They had seemed to go on as if nothing had changed. But had it? Was his confession a warning to her that she must stop encouraging him? She tossed and turned on her bed and could not get comfortable.

The dream she had had soon after they met of Todd slipping from her grasp into the icy water passed through her mind. She remembered how frightened she was when he disappeared into the dark water. Was that dream a warning of what was to come?

"Lord, Lord," she cried out in the night. "What You have given us seems so good. Help me know what I should do. Could I love his mother? Could I love his father? Is it enough just to love him?"

33

THE RICHARDS SAT AT THE BREAKFAST TABLE. The sweet smell of blueberry muffins still hung in the air, the plate on the table empty. They lingered over their second cup of hot chocolate until Harold glanced at his watch. "Time for us to get moving. Boys, we should leave soon if you're going to make your tee time at the Club."

Mike had asked his new friend, Kelly, to play golf and Harold had granted Doug permission to play with them. Kelly's parents had offered to drive the boys home. Harold and Susan planned to drive Dar and Harvey to the judge in Ellsworth for Harvey's sentencing. Since the hearing, Dar had been working on an alternative to a juvenile detention home and the Richards had offered to go along for support and relieve Dar of the driving.

Harold turned to his daughter. "Elena, the weather report indicates this will be the last day of good weather for a while. They expect fog to roll in tomorrow with a cold front. You and Todd could spend one more day on the water. It might not clear again before we leave."

"I knew this weather wouldn't last indefinitely. How long do they expect the front to last?"

"The only sunshine predicted in the next four days is today. You know as well as I do, when rain settles in, it can easily last a week."

"Thanks for the suggestion. I'll call Todd." She got up eagerly from the table and left the room.

Returning to the kitchen all smiles, Elena said, "Todd is delighted with the idea, and Mrs. Faraway didn't seem to mind at all. I'll do the dishes, Mom. You go ahead with Dad."

"Thanks, dear, I'd appreciate that," Susan said. "I do hope things go well before the judge today. I'll feel much better if the judge accepts Dar's plan. I'm afraid the wrong place will only harden Harvey and stop all the progress he's been making with Dar."

"We'll be anxious to hear about it when you return. Don't worry so much, Mom. Pastor Dar is very persuasive." Elena cleared the dishes and started washing them even before they left.

By the time she had brought out the sandwich material, Todd burst into the kitchen. "May I help with the lunch?"

"My, you're in a good mood today. To what do we owe your cheery disposition?" With her nighttime doubts dismissed by the sunny day, Elena greeted him in equally good humor and handed him a jar of mayonnaise.

"Memories of winning the tournament yesterday with my best girl and thoughts of spending a day island-hopping with her today."

"As my grandmother never tired of exclaiming," Elena said, 'Aren't we the lucky people?'"

"Lucky, yes, and blessed. Call it whatever you like. It's a perfect day to be on the water. And since it might be our last, I intend to enjoy it to the fullest." Todd put down his knife and picked her up and whirled her around, being careful to hold her with his arms instead of his hands, which were smeared with mayonnaise.

"It's hard to imagine it could be anything but bright and sunny tomorrow," Elena said, "But I'm glad we can go today. I'll finish the lunch. Why don't you take the gas can and the life preservers down to the boat and pull it ashore? I'll meet you there. Better throw in the slickers so we don't get drenched on the way home if it starts to blow."

Todd washed his hands and collected the map, slickers, and boat gear. Elena threw in an extra apple for each of them and a box of Fig Newtons. She sang as she pulled everything together. With such a start, it couldn't help but be a wonderful day.

*

As they pulled out from the shore, Elena unfolded the tattered but trustworthy map that had served her family many years. "Let's go back to our island," she called to Todd over the noise of the engine. "The one that doesn't have a name, where we found all the Neptune pieces."

"Sounds good to me. You point the way, and I'll get us there."

Elena guided them through the Stonington Thoroughfare, past Sheep Island, to the far side of Stonington where clusters of less familiar islands awaited them.

"We're getting close to it now." She pointed between two islands ahead of them. "There it is. An island just for us!"

At half tide a large stretch of accessible sandy beach lay before them. "Anywhere along here would be fine," she called out to Todd, who by now had become skilled in cutting the motor at the right time. As the boat glided smoothly onto the sand, Elena jumped over the bow and pulled it up so Todd could pass her the lunch, the water jug, the seat cushions, and the yellow backpack that always held the slickers, camera, and necessities for island picnics.

The boat secured and the picnic spot selected, Elena combed the island for shells. Todd grabbed the camera and started taking a series of shots of Elena. "Hey, look up and give me a big smile, like this is the happiest day of your life."

She did as he asked. "It very nearly is," she said. "Who could ask for anything more?...well, maybe a whole Neptune." She answered her own question before turning to Todd. "I think you have quite enough pictures of me shelling."

"And I think you've done quite enough shelling for a while. Let's walk around the island."

Putting the bag of shells with their belongings, she took his hand. They walked along the shore close to the tall trees that dotted a bright green meadow of tall but slender grasses. "I bet you can see fairies and elves dancing on the meadow in the early morning when the mist is heavy and the sun shines into it. The spider webs are beaded with water droplets, making it look like a magical place. Can't you see Tinker Bell swinging on one?"

"What an imagination you have, Elena. You make every view more interesting than it already is."

She crossed the little strip of woods in the middle of the island and found a spot on the shore protected from the winds. "Oh, it's deliciously warm here, Todd. Come and join me." She patted the sand beside her.

They both lay back with their faces toward the sky, soaking in the welcome heat of the sun.

Todd reached for her hand. She willingly gave it to him. "I'll remember this day all winter long." He sat up and stared down at her long hair spread over the warm sand. Still holding her hand with one of his, he stroked her hair with the other and gazed at her upturned face. "So fresh, so innocent. You're perfection, Elena."

She searched his eyes, waiting for more. *He acts like we'll be only a memory this winter. How I wish he'd say something about the future, anything at all.* Suddenly feeling uneasy, she jumped up and ran along the shore on the outside of the island. Todd followed her. As suddenly as she had run from him, she stopped and fell to her knees.

"What's this?" she said, loud enough for Todd to hear. Investigating the little point that protruded above the still wet sand, she began digging around it. "Wow." Now she dug in earnest. "Look at this, Todd."

It was the outline of a large Neptune shell.

"Is it really whole?" he asked, sharing her excitement.

Elena tugged at the shell, freeing it from the sand that encased it. She held it up for both of them to inspect. As she turned it over and over in her hand, she exclaimed, "It really is whole! The very first whole one I've ever found. Isn't it beautiful, Todd?"

The soft brown ridges circling the shell were complete. The circles started at the delicate tip, grew larger toward the center where the shell widened, then smaller again, ending in a graceful curve at the top. The design and craftsmanship of the shell were more delicate than many rougher shells of the area, which seemed more in keeping with the character of the rugged coast. Too fine to withstand the battering of the waves against granite rocks, whole Neptune shells were scarce.

"I told you this was going to be our lucky day. I'm glad you found it with me."

Elena continued to stare at the perfect shell, remembering all the years she and her mother had looked for a whole one and never found one. "Mother will be so excited. I can't wait to show her."

*

Susan and Harold arrived in Ellsworth with Dar and Harvey. During the long drive, Harvey had seemed happy, chatting about his new life in Pastor Dar's home. His father had appeared, nosily drunk, the night after Pastor Dar took him in, waving a leather belt around and threatening to give him the licking of his life. Pastor Dar invited him in to see Harvey and to talk to them both, but he refused to step inside, hollering that he had come to fetch his son to take him home where he belonged. When Dar stood firm, continuing to invite him inside but refusing to bring Harvey out to him, he cussed and complained about the preacher interfering with his right to handle his son. Then, slinking off into the night, he left them alone. He had neither been back, nor had he demanded his legal rights to his son in court.

Dar kept a sharp eye on Harvey, but Harvey made no attempt to leave. Instead, he followed Dar around the house, asking endless questions. When he objected to doing the dishes and Mrs. Olsen suggested he could get his own meals, he quickly agreed. Mrs. Olsen was such a good cook, he had never eaten so well.

He played with the four Olsen children, roughly at times, but they seemed to enjoy him. Uncomfortable during family devotions, he nevertheless found it pleasant to be included in the family circle and saved his many questions for later when he helped Pastor Dar with the chores.

Dar spent an hour every day instructing him in Scripture. He gave him daily assignments to work on while he made his church calls. Harvey had to look up passages in the Bible and write out answers to questions about them. Unused to applying himself to such tasks, his sentences were seldom complete and often full of grammatical errors. Dar instructed him in the rudiments of the language as well as the meaning of Scripture. Harvey seemed to sense that Dar meant all this for his good and completed his lessons most of the time.

"Harvey is making so much progress, it's a shame he can't continue to stay with us," Dar told Susan and Harold as they waited for their turn to see the judge. Harvey's face brightened at the possibility. "But the judge said that was out of the question," he added, noting Harvey's expression. "He feels it's essential to put many miles between Harvey and Rhodora so she doesn't feel threatened by his proximity."

Harvey hung his head as he was reminded of the reason he had been enjoying Pastor Dar's hospitality and instruction. "I'll never do anythin' like that again, Pastor Dar. I lost my head. I didn't mean her no harm. In the videos, the girls liked it."

"Yes, Harvey, but you understand the films and magazines fill your head with wrong ideas, don't you?"

"Yes sir, I won't do it again."

"We have to convince the judge of that, don't we?"

Susan and Harold listened to the two of them with avid interest, marveling at the relationship that had developed in one short week.

A sour-faced woman of advanced years appeared before them and said with disdain, "The judge will see you now. Follow me."

"Shall we wait here, Dar?" Susan asked, intimidated by the woman's frown.

"No, come in with us. Harvey will need all the support he can get. You don't have to say anything unless the judge addresses you, but you can lift up the conversation to the Lord and ask Him to bring about what is best for Harvey."

*

Elena and Todd had finished their lunch. Elena held up the Neptune shell, admiring its deep color and graceful lines now that it was washed clean.

"It must be the finest specimen of a Neptune shell that's ever been found," Todd said.

As if waking from a dream, Elena laughed. "You're right. I'm overdoing it. But it's fun. Mom will be green with envy. She's been looking for one like this longer than I've been alive. I'll wrap it in the sandwich paper and put it in the cooler, so nothing will happen to it."

"The tide is slack. Let's go to one of the islands between here and Isle Au Haut," Todd said. "I'd like to stretch my legs and do some exploring. We've about exhausted the possibilities of this island."

"Great idea." Elena started cleaning up the remains of the lunch. "I feel adventurous, too. No telling what we might find."

They gathered their belongings and returned to the boat, reloaded, and climbed aboard. Todd settled in by the motor as Elena pushed the boat off shore.

"Good-bye, our special island," she said. "You've given us wonderful memories and a priceless treasure."

Todd lowered the motor as the boat glided into deeper water. "Before we leave, I want to take one more picture. Can you find the camera, Elena?"

"Sure," she said, reaching for the yellow backpack. "Here it is." She passed it to Todd.

"That's perfect. Our island in the background and Elena in the foreground."

"Another one for long winter evenings?" She sighed.

"Exactly," Todd said, handing the camera back to her.

As the sun began to fade, they choose a large island with a landing beach. "Look way out there," Elena said. "Tomorrow's fog is forming already. It can hang out there all day and not move in, but we'll have to keep an eye on it."

They secured the boat and took off around the outer ledges of the island, running hand in hand over the rocks. When they tired, Elena collapsed on a tiny patch of sand. "Let's rest a minute. I'm almost out of breath."

"Look, Elena, there's a path into the woods." Todd directed her attention to a well-worn path leading from the little beach into a patch of raspberry bushes and into the woods. "Let's take it and see where it leads. Do you suppose there are sheep on this island, too?"

"I don't think so. There aren't any cleared places for them to graze. The tide is beginning to change. We'll have to be careful the wind doesn't pick up," she said as she followed him into the woods.

Unlike most of the islands, which were overgrown with underbrush and nearly impassable in their interiors, these woods had been tended by someone. The path appeared to lead to a particular destination. Green grass and an array of mosses from the brittle blue-green reindeer moss to the brilliant yellow-green pin cushions lined the ground beneath trees that had been thinned and allowed to grow to their full width. Colorful red, yellow, and orange mushrooms added to the charming picture.

"Someone either cleaned up these woods or used up all the small trees and fallen branches for firewood," Elena said.

"It does look like someone's taken care of the place," Todd agreed.

The path led them deep into the interior of the island. "I can't see water anywhere, and I think we've been moving steadily upward," Elena called to Todd as she climbed a series of rocks just off the path to see if she could determine what lay ahead.

When she reached the top, she let out a gasp. "Todd, come here."

A surprising scene lay before them. The hillside fell away sharply. Only giant boulders, piled one on top of the other, held the ground behind her in place. Halfway down, a spout of water trickled out from the rocks, falling to a small pool at the bottom. Wild ferns grew between the cracks, making a garden spot so ideal it could have been the scene of a movie. At the bottom, a wooden platform stood in the middle of a clearing. An old-fashioned stone well sat beside it. "Look, Todd, there's enough water on this island for a well."

"What a beautiful campsite. No one passing the island on the outside would suspect it's here."

"The platform must hold their tent," Elena guessed. "Over there is their table and chairs." She pointed to the far side of the clearing where a rough-hewn table sat beneath a large tree. A tree trunk had been cut into four two-foot sections that served as chairs.

"Do you suppose a family lives here in the summer?" Todd asked, noticing a pile of rocks and shells that had been left behind.

"They haven't been gone long. The grass is still crushed down. Do you suppose they heard of the bad weather coming and left while they could still get out?" Elena looked toward the sky and realized the sun had completely disappeared. Patches of fog clung to the tree tops. Elena shivered as she realized the weather had changed and she hadn't even noticed. "Todd, we need to get back to the boat before we're stuck here ourselves."

This time they ran in earnest, back down the path through the long winding trail to the shore. When they reached the water and looked seaward, they could see nothing. With the change of the tide, the wind had strengthened and pushed the wall of fog in from the sea toward the mainland, covering everything in its path with a thick blanket of gray.

Elena looked toward Stonington. She could still see its houses rising from the shore, but wisps of fog rolled over them, obscuring every familiar landmark. "Quickly, Todd, to the boat."

Running around the shore, they could hear other motors passing by, making their way home.

Without a word, they gathered their belongings and pushed the boat into the water. Elena could still see nearby islands, but Stonington had disappeared. "We'll take it one island at a time. Head for that one," she called to Todd, pointing to the island just ahead.

Even that island disappeared from time to time, but Todd kept it in sight until he reached it. "Now what?" he asked Elena, looking around for another landmark. Fog now enveloped the island from which they had come and everything in front of them. A fisherman's boat came close to them and passed them by.

"Follow that boat," Elena called. "He must be headed for Stonington Harbor."

Todd did as she said, following the boat first by sight, then by sound as it pulled into the grayness that surrounded them.

"Just keep going in that direction," Elena called over the sound of the motor. "How stupid of us not to have brought the compass. It looked like such a beautiful day. I can't believe this is happening."

Todd struggled to keep going in the direction they had headed.

Elena called to him again. "Better slow the boat, Todd. If we come upon rocks, it will give us more time to react."

She strained her eyes in every direction to see something, anything that would give them a clue about where they were. They should be in Stonington Harbor by now. If they were in the Harbor, they would be passing boats moored every few feet, even hearing the motors of other returning boats. She could see nothing but the blanket of gray that had settled around them. The only sounds were their own motor and the slap of the water against the sides of the boat.

Elena looked at her watch. They had been running for nearly three quarters of an hour. She admitted to herself that they were lost. Grateful that they had not run into any rocks, she wondered if they were headed out to sea. She had heard of boats going in circles in the fog. *Have we completely turned around? Will we see land in time to stop if we do come upon it?* She strained to see land somewhere, anywhere. Visibility diminished to a few feet.

She felt as lost as she had one day on the shore when she was little. Instinctively, she turned to the God who had rescued her then. "Please, Lord, direct us to safety. Make an opening in the fog. Show us where we are. And comfort Mrs. Faraway, Mom, and Dad. Don't let them worry unnecessarily."

On the drive home from Ellsworth, Pastor Dar was in good spirits, his plan for Harvey having been accepted by the judge. Harvey had hoped with all his might to be allowed to stay with Pastor Dar, but, at least, he was not being sent to reform school. The judge had listened to Pastor Dar's eloquent plea to send him to a place where his gains of the past week could be built upon and expanded. He agreed that reform school was a place where boys like Harvey became hardened, but he remained determined to send Harvey far away where he could not see Rhodora and be tempted to hurt her again.

Dar had suggested that he be sent to Pennsylvania to a camp whose purpose was salvaging people who had gone astray. For the past three years Dar had been interceding on behalf of island men who found themselves in trouble with the law and facing jail. He had offered them an alternative. Some of them had already returned and, with his continued pastoral care, were becoming upstanding members of the community.

There Harvey would continue his daily study of the Bible, be taught discipline and the joy of doing for other people instead of indulging his baser appetites. Pastor Dar offered to raise the money to send him and to be personally responsible to see that he stayed. If he ran away, he would be returned to the judge for stricter sentencing. Harold offered to make the first contribution.

"The next session doesn't start until September 15, so you'll have three more weeks with me, Harvey." Dar put his arm around Harvey and drew him to his side.

Susan, watching from the front seat, noted the grateful look Harvey gave Dar. If she had any hard feelings left for him, they drained away as she watched the interaction between the two of them. In one short week, Dar had softened the bully in Harvey and given him a taste of what it meant to be loved and cherished. He had responded like a love-starved puppy.

"It sounds awful far away to me," Harvey said, revealing his uncertainty that the sentence was to his advantage.

Harold drew Susan's attention back to the front seat. "Hello, what's this?" he said as they crested a hill and saw thick wisps of fog floating across the dip in the road. "This wasn't supposed to happen until tomorrow."

Concern kicked in. "I hope the children saw it in time to come in," Susan said.

"Elena knows how fast the fog can roll in. I'm sure we'll find them drying out before the fire when we get home."

"It's beginning to drizzle. It looks like we're in for it for a while." She remained uneasy at heart. "Let's pray for the children, wherever they are. Dar, will you lead us?"

"Certainly," he said, bowing his head, his arm remaining firmly around Harvey's shoulders.

*

Elena, not wanting to alarm Todd, prayed for direction with her eyes wide open, still scanning the dense fog for a break in its impenetrable wall. As a feeling of the Lord's presence enveloped her, she felt comforted and peaceful. He would see them through this.

A large shadowy form appeared to her right. "Todd, look. What is it?" A gust of wind thinned the deep mist. "It's a large rock. Cut the motor. I'll get out the oars. Maybe there's an island behind it." The mist filled in again. Todd lifted the motor out of the water and took the oars from Elena.

"I think it was over there," he said, nodding and turning the boat in the direction of his nod. "Tell me if you see anything."

Elena could see nothing but gray. "Thank You, Lord. Please show us again." She willed her eyes to see the rock again, but with such thick fog, nothing showed through. 'Thick as pea soup' is the favorite expression of the natives," she said aloud. "You can see why."

The water became choppy. Surely that meant something. Suddenly they heard the sound of aluminum scraping on rocks. Elena and Todd were both thrown to the floor of the boat as the bow lifted above the water.

"We're grounded," she exclaimed, not yet knowing whether this was good or bad.

"Come back here with me," Todd ordered. "Maybe our weight will lift the bow, and we can slide it back in the water."

"There's land around here somewhere," Elena encouraged him.

The next incoming wave washed the bow off the rock and righted the boat. The fog thinned like an expanding rubber band, and the huge rock reappeared with dark trees shrouded behind it. "There it is again, Todd. This time I see trees behind it. It must be an island."

"I don't imagine you can order up a sand beach to land on, can you?"

"Right now, I'll take anything at all," she said, not quite ready to give a sigh of relief. They were still far from safe.

Amanda stood before the picture window of her cabin, looking into the gray nothingness before her. She remembered times like this from her childhood, but she had forgotten how swiftly the weather changed here. When she lay down for her afternoon nap, the sun brightened her world. She anticipated listening to Todd's accounts of the children's adventures on the water before a cozy fire in the evening.

She remembered the pleasure of curling up by the fire with a good book on foggy days like this. But being out in a small rowboat on the water in the midst of this dense fog could only mean disaster. Her ears strained to hear the familiar motor coming in at the end of the day. Hearing nothing, she dialed the Richards' number.

"Hello."

"Is that you, Mike? It's Mrs. Faraway. Have Todd and Elena come in from the boat?"

"No, ma'am. Doug and I waited down on the shore to help them in, but it doesn't look like they're going to make it."

"What does that mean?" Her heart began to beat rapidly. She sank into a chair, still holding the phone to her ear.

"I guess they'll have to stay on an island until it clears," Mike said in a matter-of-fact manner.

"How long will that be?" She clutched her other hand to her chest.

"It's hard to say. The weather report said it would be bad for the next several days, but the change wasn't expected until tomorrow. I guess nobody knows."

"Can't we send the Coast Guard after them?"

"No, ma'am. They can't see in this weather either, and we don't know where they went. They could be anywhere out there."

"Are your parents back from Ellsworth yet, Mike?"

"No, ma'am."

"Would you have Susan call me when she returns?"

"Yes, I'm sure she'll come right over, Mrs. Faraway. Don't worry. Elena knows not to take chances."

*

"It's starting to drizzle, Todd. We better land somewhere. The tide has pulled us away from those outer rocks. I can almost make out the shoreline now."

"See anything promising?"

"Not really. It's all seaweed and rocks right here. There might be a little inlet over there," she said, gesturing into the fog. "That would give us some protection. Can you make it around the next point?"

"Sure, the wind isn't bad. More of an eerie stillness in the air."

"That goes with fog. A good stiff wind might blow it away."

"Then blow ye winds Hey-Ho." Todd pulled hard on the oars, and the boat glided into the inlet.

"No sand, but it's a fairly flat rock. It will be easy to get out of the boat, and we can pull it up above the tidemark. It's starting to rain in earnest now. If we can't find a ledge or cave, we'll have to turn the boat over for shelter."

"Any idea where we are?"

"Not the slightest. Nothing looks familiar. It took us so long to get here, all I know is it's nowhere close to Stonington. I guess my idea to follow that boat was pretty dumb. It could have been going anywhere." Elena shrugged.

"It made sense at the time. The best option we had," Todd consoled her. "Anyway, we made it to land before we ran out of gas."

They worked fast unloading the boat and pulled it into the woods. "Let's look for an overhang of some sort."

Visibility in the interior of the island was about ten feet, enough to show them the lay of the land. As dense as the fog, the woods were hard to penetrate. "No abandoned cabin or campsite in view. We better look for a cave in the shore rocks."

"Sounds rather cold to me. I guess we'll have to keep each other warm," Todd said, grinning from ear to ear.

"I'm glad to see you haven't lost your sense of humor." She ran back to the shore and poked her head into every overhang, finding none deep enough to keep out the rain. "The boat is looking better all the time."

"A bit cramped for our long legs. Don't give up." Todd ran ahead and started looking in earnest. "How 'bout this, Elena?" he called back to her.

Elena caught up to him and surveyed his find. "It's deeper than the rocks on the shore."

Old roots held up the ground above the cave, which was located where the woods met the shore rocks. It offered just enough room for the two of them and what little gear they had with them.

"We can sit on the life preserver cushions. Leaning against the dry earth will be warmer than leaning against cold rocks, at least until the ground soaks through. I vote yes. Let's camp here."

"Good. We're all set," Todd agreed.

34

As the family car pulled into the parking spot, Doug bolted out the door to greet his parents.

"Did Elena and Todd make it home?" Susan called to him.

"No. No sign of them yet." Doug confirmed her fears. "Mrs. Faraway called. She's very upset."

"Of course she is. Harold, would you drive over and bring her to our cabin? I'll stay with her overnight, if she wants. But for now, invite her to come have supper with us. I'll call Dar and tell him to alert the intercessors." Now that Susan's uneasy feelings had taken form, she became as active as a traffic cop at a major intersection in rush hour. "Doug, call Dean. Ask him when he thinks he can go out to look for them."

"We already did. Did they say which island they would go to?"

"No, they usually go to several."

"He said no use trying to find them until the fog lifts some. It'll be dark soon and with no idea which part of the bay they're in, it would be foolish to go out looking for them. He and Priscilla are praying that they're safe on an island."

"Yes, of course they are. Elena wouldn't go wandering out in a fog like this, but I would have thought she would have seen it coming."

"Probably she was too busy making eyes at Todd. The sun began to dim about 1:30 when we left the Club. By the time we got home, the fog had formed and was hanging out in the bay," Mike explained. "Then before we knew it, it swept in gobbling up everything in sight. I never saw it move so fast."

"Elena must have thought she had more time," Susan said, frowning. She bustled about, putting things away and pulling food from the refrigerator for supper. She heard the car pull into the driveway. "Boys, don't let Mrs. Faraway know how concerned we are. We must comfort her rather than increase her fears."

"Sure, Mom, we understand," Mike answered for them both.

"But I'd sure hate to be out there in weather like this. The fog's so thick, you can cut it with a knife." Doug expressed what they all felt. "I just hope they're on an island and not in the boat."

A shiver ran down Susan's spine as she opened the door to greet Amanda with a smile.

*

The drizzle increased to a steady rain. Elena wondered how long it would take for the water to soak through the ground above them. Relatively dry for now, she appreciated the poncho that covered her layers of clothing. Fortunately, she always dressed for cold weather when she ventured on the water. A sweater and jacket covered her long-sleeved flannel shirt under her poncho. Her warm arms offset the dampness of her jeans, which had become wet when the rain began to fall.

Todd, on the other hand, had only a lightweight jacket over his short-sleeved shirt. They huddled together with their few belongings by their side. If they stretched out their legs, the rain pelted them unmercifully. If they kept them bent, they could remain dry, at least for now.

"Are you sure you're not cold?" she asked Todd.

"No," he said, tightening his arm around her. "Your layers are keeping me warm."

"Are you hungry for dinner?"

"You bet. What do you have in mind?"

"We have two pieces of fruit, a half jar of bread-and-butter pickles, and the extra box of Fig Newton's I threw in at the last minute."

"How long do you think we should make them last?"

Elena sighed. "I wish I knew, but we should probably prepare for three days, at least."

"You're kidding!"

"No, Todd, I'm serious. You heard Dad say this was the last good day, maybe for a week."

"In that case, we better have two Fig Newtons each. How's the water supply?"

"Good. The water jug is three-quarters full."

"Two Fig Newtons and a glass of water. My favorite meal." Todd licked his lips.

"It could be worse." Elena struggled out of his arms to dish out the rations.

Todd asked the Lord's blessing on the meal, which they ate in silence, both wondering how long their ordeal would last. When they finished, Elena settled back into the protection of Todd's arms and let her mind wander over all that had passed between them during the last three and a half weeks.

When he had told her the reason his father was in prison, something inside her recoiled. She thought of all the ways Todd could have been corrupted by what his father had done. She wanted to run from him and not look back. Pornography was such a terrible thing. Look what it had done to Doug, to Harvey, to beautiful, sweet Rhodora. Now it had its tentacles around Todd! He claimed he had not known, had himself been repulsed by what his father had done. Would it make him extra careful to stay away from it? Or had he known and looked at it himself before his father was arrested?

Until then she'd completely trusted Todd, felt safe and secure in his presence. She had herself said that he was only responsible for who he was, not for what his father had done. She wished away those ugly questions that had taken root in her mind. Was she being unfair to Todd? She still felt comfortable in his presence, still longed to hear him tell her they had a future together. *Should I be grateful I found out in time and just let our relationship fade away as most summer romances do? Or can I trust him again?*

She closed her eyes and eventually drifted into a half sleep.

When she opened her eyes, darkness had descended. The rain still fell all around them. Nothing could be seen in the ominous gray, now solid black. The tide had come in. She could hear the sloshing of nearby waves and rain striking the rocks as she shifted in Todd's arms.

"Are you awake, Elena?" he whispered.

"Yes, Todd. I must have fallen asleep."

"I've been thinking. If we never make it back to shore, I won't have any regrets. These weeks with you have been the best of my life."

"Silly, of course, we'll make it back. It just may take awhile." She brushed his remarks aside, not sure if he meant them as a joke. "Do you think we'll be able to sleep through the night?"

"If we could take a good run around the island, maybe. I'm feeling a little cramped. How about you?"

"Your arms must be falling asleep. If we pile up the gear, maybe there'll be enough room for one of us to stretch out. I'll move out to the edge and you can put your head in my lap and stretch out your legs. How's that?"

"Like a bit of heaven," he said. "Who could ask for anything more?"

Elena caressed his hair and sang every lullaby she could remember, "Hush, little baby, now don't you cry. Mama's gonna sing you a lullaby."

Todd sighed deeply now and then but said nothing. Soon his regular breathing told her that he had fallen asleep. She listened to the night sounds until her eyes grew heavy, her head bowed, and sleep overcame her.

*

Susan and Amanda, ready for bed but neither of them sleepy, sat in their bathrobes by the fire in Amanda's living room. Amanda had fretted throughout dinner, refusing to join in the animated conversation, which the Richards kept up for her benefit. Complaining to Susan nonstop and clearly agitated, she had rocked back and forth in front of the fire, decrying the inadequate size of the boat, their negligence in encouraging the children to go out in spite of the prediction of foul weather, and the cruelty of the Maine coast in general.

Susan spoke soothing, encouraging words, assuring her again and again that the children were safe on an island and would be returned to them soon. She appeared calm and confident and gave no expression to the alarm she had experienced when she first saw the fog. She believed what she was telling Amanda, and it strengthened her faith to say it out loud.

"Worry doesn't accomplish anything, Amanda. The Bible says it's a sin. At times like this, we have to release our loved ones to the Lord, recognize that He loves them even more than we do, and trust Him to take care of them. That's all we can do."

"You've done everything possible to comfort me, when you must be worried sick, yourself. I admire your faith, Susan, but I don't believe in your God."

"I'm sorry, Amanda. He's such a comfort at a time like this."

"It's all well and good for you to feel comforted. You have a loving husband and four beautiful children who love you and want to make you happy. I've never had any of that." The bitterness in her voice escalated.

"Tell me about your husband, Amanda."

"He was a good man," she began, "but we had very little in common. Our parents knew each other. Older than I and ready to marry, he wanted a hostess for his business entertaining, but he was more married to his job than to me. After we lost our first baby boy, I was devastated, and he had no idea how to comfort me. He spent more and more time away from home.

"Finally, when Cecilia was born, she had a heart condition. The doctors told us she would live at most ten years. He adored her, a beautiful little girl with a head full of bouncy, blond curls. For a while we were happy together, focusing our attention on her. But we gave her everything she ever wanted and spoiled her terribly.

"When she couldn't have her way, she would have a coughing fit and turn red in the face. We were always fearful of that fatal heart attack, so we gave in and she got her way. As she grew up, her heart became stronger, but so did her temper. She became a very self-centered young woman, a bit on the wild side. She loved being the center of attention at a party. Though not naturally a cheerful child, when she drank at parties, she became very festive and everyone liked her. My husband called her 'our good-time girl.'

"She went to a party almost every night, often staying out far too late. We argued with her about her habits until she moved out and lived with one of her girlfriends. Not long after, she called us from New York and said she had eloped with Todd's father. She broke our hearts. They came home for a visit once, but they both were so drunk, they couldn't stand up. We told them their behavior and lifestyle disgusted us so they stopped coming to Pittsburgh until Todd was born. I allowed them to take advantage of me as a baby-sitter, so we stayed in contact because of Todd, but we never had a good relationship. When Todd was two years old, Henry was struck by a car on a stormy winter's night and killed instantly. He left me well-off, and I was able to help Todd and his brother when he came along. They were the delights of my life, but the rest isn't a pretty story, Susan."

"I'm truly sorry you had such a hard life. But now you have a fine grandson who cares for you deeply and nothing would give him greater joy than to see you make peace with the Lord. Think about that, Amanda, and we'll talk more about it tomorrow. It's late, and you need your rest." Susan arose, turned out the lights, and led Amanda to her bedroom.

She gave Amanda a hug outside her door. "Sleep well, dear Amanda. Remember, worry won't change a thing, and you will need your strength for tomorrow's problems."

*

The day dawned like every other day. Susan had slept fitfully through the night, praying for the children in between each period of sleep. Opening the door of her bedroom, she peered through the front window toward the water, hoping in vain to see some improvement. The rain had slowed to a drizzle, but the fog remained thick and hostile. After making a fresh pot of coffee for Amanda and cooking a small pot of oatmeal, she dressed, scribbled a note, and stepped out into the fog.

Walking up the path to their cabin, she could feel the damp cold the children must have endured all night. *How long until I know what has happened to them?*

222

Harold greeted her in the kitchen. She fell into his welcoming arms. "It's going to be all right, Susan. They're young, and they're strong, and they can take a little weather."

"Yes, of course they can, dear."

She set about making breakfast for the boys, glad she had something to do.

They appeared midmorning rubbing their eyes. "It doesn't look much better. How did it go last night, Mom?" Mike said, giving Susan a hug.

"Amanda is upset, of course, and very bitter toward the Lord and toward her family. We must pray for her to give up her bitterness so she can receive comfort. Harold, will you lead us now and then pray for the children before we have breakfast?"

"Come sit here by the fire, boys."

They all bowed their heads.

*

Todd and Elena had switched positions during the night. Todd had been awake for some time listening to Elena's even breathing, grateful she could sleep. The grayness that had enveloped them still hung on the shore. He could see only a few wet rocks in front of them. The tide had gone out and was on its way in again. Nothing had changed except the gnawing in his stomach had grown stronger. He longed to move his cramped limbs. He shivered, realizing the damp chill had penetrated his thin jacket in spite of his poncho.

A seagull let out a forlorn cry above them. Elena started.

"It's okay, it's just a gull," he said.

She opened her eyes and smiled up at Todd. "What a wonderful sight to wake up to."

He leaned over and kissed her softly on the lips. "Good morning, darling. Welcome to our brave, gray world."

"My kingdom for a toothbrush," she said.

"Don't worry, we're both in the same boat. How about a nice stroll in the drizzle?"

"Seldom have I received such a welcome invitation," she said, pulling her hood over her hair as she struggled to get up and out from under their shelter. "Ooohhh! Does that feel good," she said, stretching in all directions.

They checked the boat, which they had turned over at the edge of the woods. Still well above the high-tide mark, it protected the motor they had stashed beneath it.

"Doesn't look like we'll need it today, does it?"

"Let's circle the island before it starts to rain again and see what we can find." Todd started out over the slippery rocks.

They made their way carefully, feeling privileged to be able to stretch their legs. They found no beaches on the island, nothing that would help them in their plight. Todd picked up two lobster buoys in good condition. "The boys will like these," he said.

"Just what we need at this moment." Elena shook her head.

"What were you hoping for? A cabin floating in from across the bay?"

"Now that we could use." Elena laughed for the first time this morning. "Let's go back to our camp and have breakfast. I think we should eat our apples before they go bad."

"Sounds good to me."

"Hey, look at this," Elena said with excitement. "It's a bit of a clearing."

Todd looked and saw nothing exceptional—trees farther back from the shore, patches of grass with berry bushes growing out of them, but raspberry season had passed.

"Here, Todd, try these." Elena opened his hand and filled it with several plump blackberries.

"They're black," he said.

"Right, try them."

His teeth crunched the soft texture of the berries. "Hey, that tastes like real food. Won't beat raspberries, but it's nectar to a starving man."

"With all the sun this year, they've ripened early. You see, God does provide for our every need." Dropping a handful of berries into her mouth, Elena raised her arms and whirled around in characteristic fashion. "Life is good, Todd."

"Then you and God are of one mind," Todd said.

And they laughed together.

*

Amanda, smelling the aroma of freshly made coffee, made her way to the kitchen where Susan's note on the counter caught her attention. "Hot oatmeal, too. My, she thinks of everything. How fortunate I am to have such a friend at a time like this."

Remembering the children, she looked toward the view. Gray, nothing but gray. It would be a long day. She didn't feel like eating, but since Susan had been thoughtful enough to provide it for her, she thought she should force herself to try some oatmeal. She arranged a place at the table and set out sugar and milk with her coffee and cereal. As she stirred her coffee, her glance fell on Todd's Bible. She opened it to where a piece of paper with Todd's handwriting served as a bookmarker. She unfolded it and began to read:

Dear Lord, You know the desire of my heart is that Grandmother come to know You before we leave this wonderful place. I have done everything I know to bring her to You. I feel so helpless in the face of her bitterness and scorn. Lord, please give her a heart of forgiveness. . . .

Tears filled Amanda's eyes. She could read no more. She sat for some time staring out the window, seeing nothing. She remembered Todd as a little boy, his big, sad eyes looking to her for comfort, for understanding. She was his lifeline, and he had given her selfish life more meaning than she had ever known.

"Todd," she cried out. She could not imagine what she would do without him. *How could you bring me up here and leave me like this?*

Here she was again, reacting selfishly. Suddenly she saw her life pass before her. She had always thought of herself, what she wanted, how she felt. Todd had given up half his summer to bring her here, but she had complained all the way.

Her thoughts became focused. Since she had been here, she had experienced more joy than she had in the last ten years, and here she was feeling sorry for herself because Todd had deserted her. She was indeed fortunate to have a grandson who cared so much for her well-being. And what had she done for him in return but complain and demand? She had helped him materially, she had doted on him and loved him dearly, but she had ordered him about and complained without stopping. He and Susan were both right. She was a bitter and scornful old woman.

Ashamed, she saw herself as self-centered and complaining for the first time. Susan Richards found joy in other people's happiness, in serving others, and thinking of the good of others first. And here she was thinking only of herself when Susan's lovely daughter and her dear Todd were lost in that despair of grayness.

She went to the window and stood staring into the nothingness. "Todd's out there," she said aloud, "isolated on an island and blanketed in fog. And I can't do anything about it." She raised her arm and shook her fist. "God, if You do exist, if You do watch over your children, watch over Todd and Elena and bring them safely home. If You do that for me, I'll know You're real, and I'll try to know You like Todd knows You."

She sat down and felt more peaceful than she had in a long time.

Soon pictures of her life began floating before her. She thought of the happy times she had spent here in Maine with her father. She remembered how faithfully her husband had provided for her. Perhaps she had been so caught up in her disappointment that he did not share her interests and she had never tried to share his. *Did I push him away from me?*

She thought of how she had adored Cecilia, how she had taken the easy way out and denied her nothing. Had she loved her properly, she would have disciplined her more, even though it was difficult. Was Cecilia reaching out to her now in the only way she knew how?

She had thought only of herself when Cecilia called. They had been harsh with each other, but did Cecilia learn that behavior from her mother? She needed to forgive Cecilia. She needed to forgive Frank. He had tried to be a good husband. Had she discouraged him? She needed to forgive Todd's father. And she needed to forgive God for withholding loving relationships from her. Maybe it was not God but Amanda, herself, who had pushed people away from her.

Tears streamed down her face and with them years of bitterness dissolved.

*

Amanda did not respond when Susan knocked. Susan opened the door to find a tear-soaked Amanda sitting in her chair, rocking rapidly back and forth. She rushed over and put her arms around her, "There, there, now, Amanda. The children are going to be all right. You mustn't be so distraught."

"I know they are," she said in between sobs. "I'm crying for myself and all the lost opportunities of my life. I'm an ungrateful, cranky old woman. I have a grandson like Todd and friends like you and Harold and a daughter who needs me and I should be thankful."

"Amanda, what has happened to you?"

Amanda pointed to the open Bible on the table and to the piece of paper that lay on top of it. "Read it."

Susan read it and carefully placed it back in the Bible. "Amanda, do you want to forgive all the people who have hurt you? Do you want me to lead you in the prayer of salvation?"

"Yes, yes, Susan, I do," she said with the eagerness of a young girl approaching a new experience.

Susan could see that Amanda had already shed the stiff pride that held her head erect and caused her to look down her nose as she spoke. Although her eyes were red and her cheeks puffed from crying, her sweet expression revealed an openness and softness Susan had not known existed. She took both Amanda's hands in hers and knelt before her.

"Father, what a privilege it is to bring Amanda before You. You have heard her confession that she desires to forgive all those who have hurt her through the years. You have heard her desire to know You and to turn her life over to You. Lord, I sense that Your Holy Spirit is already at work in her heart. I thank You for giving her a heart of forgiveness, and I pray You will give her a revelation of Yourself. May she receive Your love, may she be assured that You will protect and guide her for the rest of her days.

"Lord, I pray for a new joy that Todd and Amanda can share as they study your Word together. I pray for reconciliation between Cecelia and Amanda. Dear Lord, thank You for taking away all the bitterness of the past and making Amanda into a new creation. May positive thoughts flood her heart. As she turns her life over to You, may she experience a life full of surprises and joys she has never known.

"Now, dear Amanda, I encourage you to tell the Lord what is on your heart right now. Just talk to Him. Tell Him that you love Him and that you want to give Him the rest of your life."

Amanda lifted her head, opened her eyes, and smiled at Susan. Then gazing heavenward, she said, "Dear Lord, thank You for meeting with a cranky old woman. I don't know exactly what is happening, but I suddenly know that my life will never be the same again. There are so many things I need to tell You...."

*

"It's lunch time, Todd. I think we can eat another apple now, and maybe even a Fig Newton. We need something solid."

"I'm ready, I'm ready," he said. "Look, Elena, what's that light circle up there in the sky? Is the sun trying to break through?"

"Yes, Todd, that's exactly what it is. Wouldn't it be wonderful if it would clear so we can go home?"

They ducked out of the rain into the small dry space they called their camp. Elena offered Todd half an apple and one Fig Newton with a large drink of water. Savoring every bite, they watched the sun struggle to break through the blanket of gray, only to disappear as it started to drizzle again. The ground fog held steady.

"Great to know it's still up there," Todd said with good humor. "I guess I don't have to look for an excuse to be close to you in here," he said with a twinkle in his eye. Taking her in both his arms, he lifted back the hood of her poncho and kissed her tenderly at the base of her neck. "As a matter of fact, if I have to be marooned on an island, I'm glad it's with you."

"I guess we're getting to know each other at our worst," she said. "Ouch, you're growing a beard."

"Our dispositions could be much worse considering the overcrowded conditions," he said with an erudite air.

"Oh, the agony of being forced to spend so much time in the arms of a handsome young man," she dramatized. "How will I endure?" Elena stopped their playful mood and became serious. "Todd, what will you do when you return to Pittsburgh?"

"Do you have to remind me that this has to come to an end?" he said, the sadness in his eyes prominent. "What will I do? I guess I'll visit Dad and see if he's changed. At least, he should have stopped drinking while in prison."

"Don't you know how he's thinking? Have you been in touch with him?"

"I wrote him a letter every week. I begged him to go to a Bible study in the prison and to work on his relationship with God, but he never answered. I talked to him last Christmas and the one before that and sent him a present, but he never thanked me. I offered to come see him, but he always said I should stay away from the place."

"How did he sound? Was he bitter?"

"I don't know, Elena. It isn't a happy subject. Can't we talk about something else?"

"I'm sorry, Todd. I won't bring it up again. I was just wondering what your life would be like."

"Very different from yours."

"I'll be with you in spirit."

"I don't deserve you," he said, burying his head in her hair.

*

The Richards spent the day listening to the weather forecast as they stared into the gray world outside their window. Harold kept a fire going, and Susan kept everyone well supplied with food. Amanda held up better than anyone anticipated and insisted she could spend the night alone if Harold would just take her home. She felt Susan needed to be with her family, and Amanda indicated she needed some time alone. Harold took her to her cabin around 8:00 in the evening and built a fire in the fireplace.

"You'll call us if you become the least bit uneasy, won't you, Amanda?"

"Yes, Harold, I will. Now don't worry about me at all," she said as she hurried him out the door and back to his family.

After she had undressed for bed, Amanda went back to the living room and took Todd's Bible to her chair beside the fire. She turned to the book of John, which Susan had said was her favorite Gospel and began to read. "In the beginning was the Word, and the Word was with God, and the Word was God." It had been years since she had read it, but the words came back to her. They were familiar and comforting. She had been reading for twenty minutes when the telephone rang.

She reached for the receiver, hoping for word about the children. "Hello," she said with anticipation.

"Hello, Mother, it's Cecilia. Now don't hang up. I need to talk to you."

"Cecilia," she said, a smile softening her wrinkled face and sounding in her voice. "I'm so glad you called."

"You are?" Cecilia sounded unbelieving.

"Yes, where are you? I didn't know how to reach you."

"I didn't think you wanted to reach me, Mother. I didn't think you ever wanted to hear from me again."

"I'm sorry I was harsh. Your call was unexpected."

"Well, I'm in the West Penn Hospital in Pittsburgh. I'll be here a week for tests, and I don't have anywhere to go when they release me. I've left my belongings at a friend's house, but she doesn't have an extra bedroom for me."

"You must come home and stay with Todd and me. We're both anxious to see you."

"Mother, what's happened to you? Do you understand? This is Cecilia."

"Yes, I understand. I have a great deal to talk to you about. Todd and I will be home next Sunday. We'll come visit you on Monday and make arrangements for you to stay with us awhile."

"I can't believe this is you, Mother."

"Well, it is, and I want you to know I forgive you for everything in the past, and I hope you can forgive me, too. Good-bye, dear." She heard Cecilia's gasp of disbelief just before she hung up the phone. "There now," she said out loud. "I've taken the first step."

A half smile rested on her lips as she stared into the fire. Then, turning again to the book of John, she continued reading. They were right. There was a great deal of comfort in reading the Word.

35

THE NEXT DAY THE FOG HUNG IN THE AIR as it had the day before, dripping big drops of rain. The extended forecast offered little hope. Soon after Susan cleared away the breakfast dishes, Dar arrived at the back door with Harvey.

"Hello, Susan," he said, a note of excitement in his voice. "When we were praying for Elena and Todd this morning, the Lord impressed upon me that I should gather the family together and pray for Him to make a path for them."

"Did He show you where they are?" Susan asked, grateful for the assurance that the Lord was watching over the children.

"No, just that we should gather together and pray. Would you call Mrs. Faraway? I'll go down and pick her up."

"Yes, of course." Susan reached for the phone. Surely this was the answer to all of their prayers.

"Amanda, this is Susan. Are you dressed? Good, Pastor Dar wants you to join us for prayers for the children. He's coming over to drive you here. No, I haven't told him anything. You should tell him the good news yourself." She hung up the phone. "She'll be ready," Susan said to Dar.

Dar turned and went out the door, leaving Harvey standing in the kitchen.

"Doug is in the living room, Harvey. You may go in."

"Thank you, Mrs. Richards."

"Hi, Harv, how's it going?" Doug looked like he was glad to see him.

"Great, Doug. Me and Pastor Dar, I mean Pastor Dar and I are doing great."

"I like your new outfit, Harvey," Harold said. "Come in and sit by the fire."

"Thanks, Mr. Richards. Everything's all arranged for me to go to Pennsylvania. I'm kinda scared about bein' so far away, but Pastor Dar says everyone will be nice to me there, and I'll learn to like it."

"I'm sure you will, Harvey. How are your lessons coming?"

"Good, I study hard every day. Pastor Dar says I'm doing wicked good."

"Have you seen Joey and Eddie?" Doug asked.

"Naw, their parents won't let them see me. I can't go to church neither, 'cause of Rhodora. Have you seen them, Doug?"

"Yes, and they asked about you, Harv. They said to tell you they hope you like where you're going."

"Tell them I said hi."

"Sure, I will."

"My sister came to see me," Harvey said with good cheer. "She brought me some cookies she baked and some of my things. We had a nice talk. She says I'm lucky to be leaving the island, and she wished she could come with me. Pa's been some mean since I left."

"Perhaps I could call on your sister one day, Harvey," Susan offered.

"That'd be awful nice, Mrs. Richards."

Dar had returned in good spirits with Mrs. Faraway, who was all smiles, having just shared with him the dramatic change in her life. He asked everyone to join in a large circle in the living room. Reaching out his hands to those next to him, he looked at each one and said, "You all know the weather report and how it looks outside, not very good. But the Lord this morning has reminded me that nothing is impossible for Him. Anyone doubt that?" He looked around as each person shook his head.

"Now we're all going to release our faith together and ask the Lord to show Elena and Todd the way home. We don't know how He's going to do it, but we all know for certain that He can do it."

Taking their cue from their pastor, they all bowed their heads. "Now, Lord, we know that there's rejoicing in heaven today for the salvation of Sister Faraway. We're thankful that you've already brought good out of the trials that Elena and Todd are experiencing. We thank You for keeping watch over them wherever they are and we ask you now to open a path for them that they may see well enough to reach a place of safety."

Dar continued for some time and indicated that everyone should add a personal prayer to his. When they had gone around the circle, he ended with thanksgiving for God's goodness to them all and asked a special blessing on Harvey as he prepared for his new life in Pennsylvania and on Rhodora as she continued to heal from the wounds she had suffered.

Susan made another pot of hot chocolate. Thirty minutes sped by as they talked about Amanda's conversion and the call from Cecilia. In the midst of their rejoicing, the telephone rang. Susan picked it up and said, "Hello."

"Mother, it's Elena. We're in Stonington!"

"Oh, thank God. Thank You, Lord." Susan cried and laughed all at once.

"What is it, Susan?" Harold bellowed at her in frustration.

"They're safe," she sobbed, turning the phone over to him.

"Elena, is that really you? Where are you?"

"We're at the Fisherman's Co-op in Stonington, Dad."

"How did you get there?"

"It's a long story. Come get us, and we'll tell you."

"We'll be there as fast as we can."

Everyone wanted to go. They piled into two cars and drove past the town of Stonington to the Fisherman's Co-op.

"We've never brought the boat in here," Harold said as they pulled into the Co-op. They had crept along the road since visibility on land was as poor as it was on the water.

They jumped out of the cars, still not seeing anything but fog.

"There they are," Doug screamed as Elena and Todd came out the door of the Co-op.

Susan began to cry again as she caught sight of them. Soon they were all hugging and kissing and laughing.

Mrs. Faraway stood back from the crush and waited until Todd spotted her. He came into her outstretched arms.

"Grandma, I hope you didn't worry too much."

"Praise the Lord, praise the Lord," she repeated.

"Grandma, am I hearing correctly?" Todd asked in astonishment.

"Your grandmother received salvation yesterday," Susan answered for her. "She promised God that if He would watch over you and return you safely, she would know He was real, and she would spend the rest of her life trying to be a blessing to others."

"Forgive me for all those bitter years, Todd."

"Grandma, I'm so happy. It was worth it just for this moment, wasn't it, Elena?" he exclaimed as Elena threw her arms around Mrs. Faraway.

"What a joyous reunion," Dar boomed. "Now, Elena, you must tell us how you came here. Harvey and I must go on our way, but we must know first."

Elena took a deep breath. "This morning we ate the last of the blackberries we found and our last Fig Newton and drank almost all of our water. With still no break in the weather, we decided we better do something. We prayed out loud together, asking the Lord to make a path through the fog for us, so we could see just enough to find Deer Isle.

"When we stopped praying, we saw a pale light in the sky, like we had the day before. It looked like the sun trying to break through the fog, so we turned the boat over, dragged it down to the water, put the motor on it, and loaded it with our belongings, just in case. It was an act of faith.

"We kept watching the bright patch and praying. Soon the fog thinned a little and a pale yellow light beamed down on us, just enough to guide us to the next island. We discussed the wisdom of leaving the safety we had found but decided God had answered our prayers. We should follow the light even though we didn't know what lay ahead. It seemed to stay with us. When we looked behind, the fog had swallowed up the island we had come from, but the light stayed in front of us. Sometimes we could see other islands and sometimes we couldn't, but we followed the light before us. I remember looking at my watch. It was 11:00 o'clock."

"That was when we stopped praying," Dar said with great excitement. "I remember glancing at the clock in your living room. Yes, yes, go on, Elena."

"At that point, the fog closed in again and the light faded away. Out on the water with no visibility, we heard another motor, the first one in all that time. We had no other choice but to follow it. When that motor stopped, we slowed down, and we could hear men's voices. We kept moving toward those voices. Then we saw flashing lights through the fog that guided us to a dock. The men helped us land and told us to leave the boat at their dock until the fog lifted. They wanted to know what we were doing out in weather like this in such a small boat with no instruments, not even a compass. We told them we'd been stranded for two days and the path of light had led us to the sound of their motor. I'm not sure they believed us, but they were very kind. They helped us in with our gear and let us call you. And we're so happy to be back on Deer Isle," Elena concluded.

"So you were all together praying this morning while the light was guiding us?" Todd questioned.

"Yes, we were. The Lord spoke to me early this morning and told me to gather the family together to pray for you. I didn't even know that Mrs. Faraway had become a believer."

"Fantastic!" Todd exclaimed.

"Absolutely awesome," Elena echoed amid another round of hugs and rejoicing.

*

Saturday night came upon them all too quickly. There had been an afternoon of celebration and sharing of tales about Mrs. Faraway's conversion and Todd and Elena's experiences in the fog. A happy time.

Susan's heart burst with joy and thanksgiving as she prepared special treats of hot chocolate, popcorn, and blueberry muffins to sustain them through the long hours of storytelling. The festivities ended with a lobster feast and marshmallows roasted in the fireplace.

The next day Elena and Todd slept most of the day. The fog still had not lifted.

That evening they all attended church together. A murmur of approval went through the church as Mrs. Faraway walked in, holding her head high. News of Elena and Todd's adventures had already spread through the congregation, but Pastor Dar wanted everyone to hear again how the Lord had spoken to him to gather the family for prayer. He called Todd and Elena to the front of the church to tell their story once more. Everyone in the congregation applauded as they concluded by thanking the faithful intercessors for praying for them while they were fogbound.

Finally, he welcomed Mrs. Faraway to the family of believers and asked her if she had anything to say. She rose to her feet and thanked the Lord for His many blessings to her as though she had been doing it every Sunday. Todd squeezed Elena's hand and they smiled, contentment written on their faces.

After the service, Todd approached Pastor Dar and asked if he could stop by the next morning to talk to him. Pastor Dar said he had appointments all morning but suggested they have lunch together.

Friday morning the Richards began preparing their cabins for the winter, the process that marked the end of summer. Todd and Elena drove Mrs. Faraway around the island gift shops as she thought of people she wanted to lavish with gifts. His grandmother surprised Todd with her new generosity, particularly when she bought gifts for his mother in anticipation of their reunion.

*

Todd met Pastor Dar for a late lunch at the Harbor Café, a popular restaurant on the main street of Stonington. Todd would have preferred the privacy of the church office, but they found an isolated booth where he could talk freely.

After ordering from the menu, Pastor Dar said, "Well, young man, you've had quite a summer, haven't you?"

"Yes, one of the happiest of my life."

"Why then do I sense you're deeply troubled?"

"Has Elena told you anything about my family?"

"No, she hasn't. I've only heard from her parents how happy you made her return to the island."

"Pastor Dar, my father is in prison for selling child pornography. He'll be released in a few weeks, and I need help on how to rehabilitate him. I thought during this month I could find some answers, but I still don't know what to do when I see him."

"Well, that is a problem. Do the Richards know about this?"

"Yes, they do."

"Tell me more about your father."

Todd told him the whole story of his parents' marriage, their alcoholism, living beyond their means, and his father trying to pay their debts by selling harder and harder pornography. "He looked at adult pornography himself. That's how he knew people would pay good money for it. He knew child pornography brought an even higher price, but I don't think he had any interest in it himself."

"That's good. It's very difficult for a pedophile to be healed, Todd, but the struggle against adult pornography is extremely common. The magazine *Christianity Today* has said that 70 percent of American men view pornography monthly. It isn't a unique problem."

"Wow. It's hard to believe such a high figure," Todd said. "Once they're hooked, do they ever get over it?"

"Yes, but it can be a long process. Do you think he'll be willing to acknowledge that he has a problem? That's the first step in getting help."

"He can't very well deny it after spending five years in prison."

"Just as important is a belief in God. Perhaps he'll see a difference in your grandmother and come to realize that he can change, too. If you can convince him that God loves him in spite of what he's done, it would be a good start."

"He certainly doesn't seem to know that from his present attitude, but then Grandma didn't know it until just this week. I should pray for him as fervently as I prayed for her."

"Yes, if you can lead him to acknowledge and confess his sin to the Lord and help him realize it isn't a private sin, it affects you and his whole family, the second step would be to turn to someone in your church or community who's trained to deal with sexual addiction. There are very good programs available now and many people have been trained in how to lead a man through them. I have an excellent little book that lists statistics on what happens to men when they view pornography regularly and what the symptoms are. I'll give it to you so you can see for yourself how much it applies to your father."

"Thank you. I appreciate any help you can give me."

"There's also a great book by Dr. Mark Laaser called *Healing the Wounds of Sexual Addiction.* I ordered a copy online to work through it with Harvey. I think you'd find it a great help, especially in understanding the chemicals that are released in the brain by viewing pornography. One chemical brings about tension relief and produces intense pleasure and relaxation. The other, epinephrine, creates arousal, excitation, and the desire to take risks. The combination leads to the addictive affect of pornography. Understanding this will help you both deal with it, but I highly recommend you find your father an experienced counselor. He'll most likely take correction from a stranger better than from his son."

"Pastor Dar, this has been very helpful. I haven't known where to start and now I do. Thank you so much."

"Let's start your prayer journey for helping your father right now," Pastor Dar said, reaching out his hand to Todd.

Having prayed regularly with the Richards the last month, Todd did not hesitate. They bowed their heads as Dar implored the Lord to open his father's heart to receiving help and to lead Todd every step of the way to his father's healing. He asked for reconciliation between Mrs. Faraway and Todd's father as a first step in mending the broken family. Todd added a prayer for his mother and for some kind of truce between his parents. He prayed that the Lord would send the Holy Spirit to reveal Himself to both of his parents and to introduce His life-changing power into their lives.

When they had finished, Todd smiled at Pastor Dar. "What a relief your advice is to me. You've given me real hope that I can help my father. I didn't know where to start, but you've shown me the first steps. It's kind of like the Lord shining that light in front of Elena and me to get us started on the path to safety.

"If the situation doesn't change right away, Todd, don't be discouraged. Remember that men are being delivered from their addiction all the time and many marriages are being saved. There's no telling what God might do if your father is willing to turn the rest of his life over to Him.

"There's another ministry you might want to look up on line. It's called Pure Life Ministries. It's been helping people with sexual sin for over twenty-five years. I've heard that their programs are excellent. You and your father might want to attend one of their conferences together."

"If one comes anywhere close to Pittsburgh, we will," Todd said.

"I'll be praying for you, Todd. Here's my card. Call me any time."

"Thank you. I'd appreciate being able to talk to you when things get tough."

*

Friday evening Todd and his grandmother shared their last dinner in the Richards' cabin, rejoicing when the radio announced that the fog would blow out to sea during the night.

On their final day, they awoke to sun shining through their windows, a welcome sight after the long days of fog. Mike and Doug helped Harold bring the boat home from the Co-op. The rest of the day they packed, made the final trip to the garbage dump, cleaned the refrigerator and stove, and prepared everything for the renters next spring. Harold and the boys took up the mooring, brought the boat ashore, and carried it to the front of the guest cabin. The last job before departure would be to lift it into the boys' room for the winter.

Amanda insisted on taking them all to dinner at the Fisherman's Friend, where their vacation had started. Ignoring Susan's protests, she said, "It's time I repaid you for all of those marvelous dinners, Susan. I don't want you to have to cook on your final night."

"Thank you, Amanda, I know better than to thwart you when you've made up your mind. I'm sure we'll all enjoy it."

As they reminisced over dinner about all that had happened during the past month, Elena remembered their plans to take Mrs. Faraway to Bar Harbor for lunch at Jordan Pond. "Todd, we never drove your grandmother to Jordan Pond or took the mail boat to Isle Au Haut. We didn't even rent a boat to go sailing."

"We'll save those things to look forward to next time, Elena," Mrs. Faraway said. "It's always nice to have a reason to return. Now that we know you're here, I won't have to coax my grandson to come back with me."

Everyone laughed but Todd.

Elena turned to him, hoping for an affirmation that he wanted to return. His creased forehead hinted that he had given in to his dark mood. "Not tonight," Elena's eyes pleaded. He avoided her gaze and said nothing.

Amanda's chatter filled the silence during the drive home. Todd stopped the car at Elena's cabin, walked her to the door, and promised to return for their final good-bye as soon as his grandmother was settled in bed.

*

Elena, bursting with anticipation when he returned, wondered what he would say to her in their parting moments.

"It's such a beautiful night, let's take flashlights to the starfish pond to watch the nighttime activity," she said.

"Great idea," Todd agreed.

Arriving at the pond, they beamed their lights on the water and watched as starfish of many sizes and colors moved freely over the surface of the rocks, their tentacles rippling as they went. "How graceful they are," she said. "But my favorites are the sea anemones. Can you spot them?"

"There's one and there's another," Todd pointed to them, "and I remember there was one down at that end. There it is." The incoming tide had just reached the pool, sucking the water back and then surging it forward with each incoming wave. The open sea anemones danced like graceful ballerinas, swaying back and forth with the ebb and flow of the tide.

Small crayfish, like baby lobsters without claws, darted from place to place and large green crabs foraged for their dinner. Drab little sand crabs climbed out of empty shells and scudded about, bumping into slow moving sea urchins that flexed their sharp, green needles in all directions. Snails moved in armies up and down the sides of the pool. "There's much more activity than you can see in the daytime," Todd said. "Just when I think I've seen it all, you show me something else."

"There's much more to see, Todd. You'll have to come back."

"The very first chance I have, I'll be here. As long as you're here, of course."

"You better not come with anyone else." Elena leaned her head against his shoulder.

Todd put his arm around her as he had in their shelter from the rain and the two of them sat silently for a time, listening to the soothing sound of the waves.

Suddenly rising, Todd held out his hand to Elena. "Come," he said and led her around the pond and up the incline to the point. There he stopped, putting both his arms around her but holding her at arm's length in front of him. "Elena, it's hard for me to tell you just what this month has meant to me. Sharing this wonderful place with you, being accepted as a part of your family. It's the best family life I've ever known." He paused.

She hoped he would say something about wanting to be a permanent member of her family.

"But I want you to have a wonderful senior year at college, dating just like you did before we met."

Elena's mouth dropped open as she stared at Todd through the darkness. Her hand shot up to cover her mouth and stifle the scream that rose within her. She staggered, her hopes dashed and demolished as quickly as the driftwood hurled against the granite during the hurricane. She made a feeble sound as she struggled to regain her voice.

Todd pressed his fingers against her lips. She remained silent, listening for more, anything more that she could hold on to over the long winter months.

"I'll write you every week, and I'll call you often. We'll stay in touch." It sounded limp, but his eyes were tender.

Her crumbled hopes re-ignited. "Maybe you could come to Florida to have Christmas with the family." She longed to bridge their separate worlds.

"I'd love to," he said with little enthusiasm, "but I'll have to be with Grandma and Dad and Mother. Who knows how it will turn out?"

Elena could hear both anguish and quiet resignation in his voice. She realized he had spent a lifetime denying his own desires.

"I feel like I'm going back to an explosion that could ignite at any time. Don't you understand, Elena?" He searched her eyes. "I can't make any commitments—not now with my family in such turmoil. It wouldn't be fair to you."

She felt his agony and reversed their roles. Seizing the initiative, she reached up and pressed her fingers against his lips to stop the flow of unwelcome words. "I love you, Todd," she said a little above a whisper. She had yearned to hear it. Now that she knew he wasn't going to say it, she said it for him.

He sighed, allowing pent-up tension to drain from him. Releasing his hold of her, he turned toward the bay. She thought her heart would break. She had made herself vulnerable, and he had turned away from her.

He took a few steps forward before turning back to her. "I should run away from you," he said. "But not tonight." He lifted her face and kissed her fully on the lips. Clutching her head against his chest, he caressed her hair. "I love you, too, Elena. You know that."

"Yes," she said, "but I needed to hear it."

They held each other near the tree on the point while the light of a thousand stars smiled above them. The moon shone down, illuminating a single silhouette beneath a solitary tree. The scent of bayberry and spruce mingled with salt air and waves lapped gently along long stretches of granite. Aware only of the pounding of their hearts as one, Todd and Elena clung to each other there in their final embrace.

Taking It Deeper
Questions for Individual Reflection
and Group Discussion

1. Which character in *An Island Just for Us* did you identify with the most, and why?

2. The Richards, Todd, and Harvey all have very different types of family life experiences. Which one is closest to your growing-up years, and why? Do you think having a family life like Elena's is realistic in today's culture? Why or why not?

3. Elena's family worked hard to maintain family meals at the dining room table with all present. How does this bring them together, even in times of great stress? How might you and your family benefit from this practice?

4. What was the progression of Elena and Todd's interest in each other? What are elements of "true love" that you see in their relationship?

5. In today's society of free love, do you think it is asking too much of young people to wait until marriage to have sex? What are the pros and cons, both short term and long term?

6. Have you ever felt tempted to view pornography? How do you deal with that temptation?

7. Have you ever had to face the consequences of pornography use with someone you love? What changed in your relationship with that person?

8. As much as Elena cared for Todd, do you think she was wise to reconsider her relationship with him when she learned why his father was in jail? Why or why not? Do you think she made the right decision?

9. How has the easy availability of pornography on the Internet contributed to the breakdown of the family? The way men view women? The way men view a marriage commitment and children?

10. Whenever the Richards family faces problems, they pray. Do you view prayer as a solution to problems? Why or why not?

11. What changed in Amanda, Todd's grandmother, and why? Have you seen this same type of change in anyone you know personally? If so, how? Has that change influenced you to think about God differently in any way? Tell the story.

12. What was your reaction to Pastor Dar taking young Harvey under his wing? Do you believe the statement "Pornography is a victimless crime" is true? Why or why not? Are young boys like Doug and Harvey victims, as well as the girls they approach? How might you help those in younger generations understand the powerful pull, and devastating effects, of pornography?

Note: Some have said it's too late to stop the proliferation of pornography in America. But even one person can make a difference. If you've been moved to speak out against it, I'd love to hear from you at **www.barbarahattemer.com.** Other trustworthy websites I recommend are: **http://moralityinmedia.org/** and **www.purelifeministries.org.**

FIELD of DAISIES

BARBARA HATTEMER

Andrea and Lans Mulder met as young teenagers on Andrea's family farm in Pennsylvania, renewed their romance as young adults during an enchanted week in Paris, and married in a storybook wedding in a field of daisies.

With two growing children, their life has been as close to perfect as you can imagine. But when the destructive degenerative disease of Alzheimer's strikes the third generation of Andrea's family, can even a made-for-each-other couple stand strong—and stay together? Especially when Andrea herself faces the worst news of her life?

"An insightful and redemptive treatment of the repercussions of Alzheimer's disease, including the hurt and challenges that accompany the diagnosis and progression. We commend Barbara Hattemer for her wonderfully sensitive manner in addressing the compelling themes of the story."
FOCUS ON THE FAMILY

A poignant story of hope, faith, and determination
to beat seemingly impossible odds.

www.BarbaraHattemer.com
www.oaktara.com

Acknowledgments

As with my first published novel, I am indebted to two friends, Mary Lee Montgomery and Carol Currie, for reading my first attempts at writing fiction. Their corrections, suggestions, and notes about what they particularly liked, helped me begin to mold this story.

It has been a long time coming. As I labored to write it during my summers in Maine, the ladies of the Deer Isle Morning Writer's Group listened to many of its chapters and offered excellent suggestions and corrections.

When the first version was completed, Ted Baehr, the publisher of *Movieguide* and Chairman of the Christian Film and Television Commission, read it and encouraged me to present it to Christian publishers. Some of them liked the setting and the characters, but they did not like the subject. Four Christian editors told me they would look at it if I would take out every word about pornography. I resisted that for many years. Finally, wanting the love story to be published, I did what they asked, but it was no longer the book I had wanted to write. I set it aside.

The day after my first novel *Field of Daisies* was released, my editor, Ramona Tucker of OakTara, asked me if I had another novel. When I sent her the synopsis of this book, which included the issue of pornography, she was immediately favorable to the idea. I put it all back in and added more. Many thanks to Ramona, for recognizing the importance of pornography's contribution to the moral decline of our country and the need for us to address the issue openly. I rejoice now to have an editor who enjoys my style and appreciates my difficult subjects. I am indebted to her for the publication of *An Island Just for Us*.

It is a far better story as a result of its many rewrites. I am especially indebted to Ann Platter and professional editor Linda Nathan, both of whom gave me valuable suggestions about how to make the story stronger.

About the Author

BARBARA HATTEMER, educated at Smith College and Harvard Business School, worked for a management consulting firm before marrying and raising four children.

For 18 years she fought against pornography, often debating the ACLU, and giving hundreds of Radio and Television interviews. She worked with her sheriff to close adult bookstores in Naples, Florida and to pass an ordinance regulating local sex businesses in the 1980s. She founded and served as president of Morality in Media of Naples and Florida Coalition for Clean Cable, eventually co-chairing the National Decency Forum, a coalition of national organizations that convinced the FCC to crack down on dial-a-porn. She put together a film of the type of pornography shown around the country and presented it to the Attorney General's Commission on Pornography.

Featured in *Christian Herald Magazine* and Focus on the Family's *Citizen;* recipient of *Christian Herald's* first James 1:22 Award, she appeared on the *Today Show* with Bryant Gumbel and on Dr. James Dobson's Radio Program. Dr. D. James Kennedy filmed and presented an hour-long video of her work on his Sunday television program.

Her book ~~Don't~~ *Touch That Dial: The Impact of the Media on Children and the Family* (Huntington House) analyzes social science research on the harms of sexually explicit and violent media. Barbara has written a variety of articles for magazines and books over the years. More recently she has turned to writing inspirational women's fiction. Her first novel *Field of Daisies* (OakTara, 2012) offers hope to families experiencing Alzheimer's disease in successive generations. Like *An Island Just for Us*, she weaves a serious subject into a beautiful setting with an intriguing romance to make reading a pleasure.

"*An Island Just for Us* explores the joys of young, intimate, but innocent romance, the benefits of strong family relationships, and the corruptive influence of counterfeits for love," Barbara says. "Pornography can swiftly take over a young boy's mind, permeate a man's thought, and become a consuming addiction, thus hindering a meaningful love relationship. I'm passionate about encouraging parents to take it seriously when their children bring home a pornographic magazine or watch a porn site on the Internet."

The story takes place on an island in Maine's beautiful Penobscot Bay where Barbara has summered all her life. She is considering writing a sequel.

www.BarbaraHattemer.com
www.oaktara.com